O9-BHI-559

NOWHERE
GIRL

SUSAN STRECKER

Thomas Dunne Books
St. Martin's Press ♒ New York

This is a work of fiction. All of the characters, organizations,
and events portrayed in this novel are either products of the author's
imagination or are used fictitiously.

THOMAS DUNNE BOOKS.
An imprint of St. Martin's Press.

NOWHERE GIRL. Copyright © 2016 by Susan Strecker. All rights reserved.
Printed in the United States of America. For information, address
St. Martin's Press, 175 Fifth Avenue, New York, N.Y. 10010.

The Library of Congress Cataloging-in-Publication Data is available upon request.

ISBN 978-1-250-04285-9 (hardcover)
ISBN 978-1-4668-9149-4 (e-book)

Our books may be purchased in bulk for promotional, educational, or business
use. Please contact your local bookseller or the Macmillan Corporate and
Premium Sales Department at 1-800-221-7945, extension 5442, or
by e-mail at MacmillanSpecialMarkets@macmillan.com.

First Edition: March 2016

10   9   8   7   6   5   4   3   2   1

For Kurt, Cooper, and Ainsley,
the people I love the most

NOWHERE
GIRL

CHAPTER
1

The day Savannah was killed, she was fifteen minutes late to meet me. I was cold, standing in the November wind outside our school. Because she'd told me to wait for her, I'd missed the bus, and now I'd have to walk home in the dark. Mrs. Wilcox's red Honda was the only car in the front parking lot. It was just me and a stone cherub above the entrance, giving me the creeps. Finally, I pushed back through the glass doors and plopped down in a leather recliner, furniture meant to make Kingswood Academy's waiting area feel like a living room rather than a school.

I knew I should have been out looking for Savannah, but I'd been a little pissed at her lately, coming home smelling like the cigarettes she'd smoked behind the carved oak trees out back with the upperclassmen girls. She was the one with the older, cooler friends; the secret boy crushes. She was the one who'd been getting high and having sex since we were fourteen. Somehow, she was also where she was supposed to be all the time. Which is how she fooled our parents, never giving them reason to suspect that their identical twin daughters were only the same on the outside.

Kingswood had been renovated the year before, thanks to a generous and wealthy alum. The skylights above me brought a constant brightness like the manufactured cheerfulness of a hospital's children's ward. Somewhere in the office, I heard Mrs. Wilcox typing on her computer. When I closed my eyes, I felt a vague sensual pleasure, as though someone had his warm hands all over me—a feeling rather than a thought. I'd only kissed one boy, barely touched our lips together, so I understood it was Savannah's experience I was feeling. As different as we were, I knew her the way a newborn knows to nurse and birds know to fly in a V.

That morning while she was flat-ironing her hair, INXS turned up too loud on the CD player in the bathroom, she told me to cover for her at the dance planning meeting after school.

"I'll ride the late bus home with you, and we'll just tell Mom and Dad I went."

I'd stood in the doorway of the bathroom watching her, wondering what had been making her smile so much lately.

"Where are you going?" I'd asked. But our brother, David, called us for breakfast, and she disappeared down the stairs.

She was probably off with Scarlet and Camilla, securing her place in that coveted inner circle of senior girls where no other underclassmen were allowed. Maybe my friend Gabby was right. Savannah was too cool for us; she only wanted to hang out with older girls now. There were so many days she'd asked me to take her backpack home and do her homework. Afterward, she'd come traipsing in the front door as I was setting the table for dinner, making up a lie about being at some school meeting that would look good on the college applications we wouldn't be writing for another two years. As I listened to Mrs. Wilcox type, I thought about something I'd been asking myself lately whenever resentment about Savannah began to creep in: *What if I said no? What if I walked home alone and told my mother I didn't know where she was?*

Of course, I knew from the second she didn't meet me outside the glass doors for the late bus that something was wrong. Still, when that hazy sensuality gave way to anxiety, I fought it. Panic crept into my stomach, my throat. If I'd allowed myself to hear Savannah, to listen to the message she was trying to send me, I would have known that, not more than a thousand yards away, she was dying.

I tried to tell myself that I was having an asthma attack, but it didn't feel like they usually did. It was more of a choking feeling in my throat than a tightness in my chest. When it got so bad I could barely breathe, I fumbled in my backpack for the cell phone my parents had given me for emergencies only. I'd never used it before.

"It's my sister," I told the 911 dispatcher frantically. "She's hurt."

"The nature of her injuries, please," the operator said in a robotic voice.

"I don't know. I think she can't breathe."

"Is the victim with you?"

"No, no. I don't know where she is, but she's hurt."

"Miss." The operator's monotone turned to impatience. "If you don't know where she is, how do you know she's injured? Did she call you?"

"She's my twin." I was sobbing, not from the pain in my throat but because I knew even as I was on the phone with the police that it was too late.

I could tell the dispatcher didn't believe me, but she asked where I was and my name, and then she clicked off.

By the time I hung up, I felt weak, so weak I thought my knees might give if I got up. Somewhere far off, I heard sirens. And then suddenly, something left me. I felt washed out, empty. The wind could have blown right through me. Something ineffable and bright, a ball of light I'd been carrying since birth, exited my body.

All my life, I'd remember that moment. But it was when I was thirty-two that Savannah finally returned to save my life by leading me to her killer.

CHAPTER 2

2015

It was Valentine's Day, and as usual, Greg and I were lying in bed, working. "How can you not like this holiday?" I asked him. He handed me a stack of letters three inches thick bound by a wide green rubber band. "It celebrates love."

"It perpetuates mental illness and loneliness"—Greg pushed his glasses up his nose—"and its only purpose is to sell cheesy cards and chocolate." He put the letters on my lap and then picked up a case file. "Anyhow, if you're going to respond to all your fan mail, like your website says you will, you'd better get going."

I held up the elastic. "Is this from the broccoli?"

He gave me a half smile. "I had to use something. The ones in the junk drawer kept breaking."

I aimed it at his face. "Maybe someone in this stack will ask me to be his Valentine." I swerved at the last minute, and the rubber band headed toward our wedding photo. That picture could turn my mood nostalgic. We'd been so happy.

"Really, Cady." He set his file aside, got out of bed, and retrieved the elastic. "Grow up."

I watched him walk to the bathroom and shut the door. I listened for him to lift the toilet seat. The name on the file he'd been reading, gibberish to anyone else, was clear to me. Greg took his HIPAA laws seriously, but it hadn't taken me long to crack his code. Each letter was the one to the right of the actual letter on the keyboard. I'd spent so many years deciphering his files that I could do it almost instantly now.

I glanced at it while I slid the letter opener across the first envelope. What was this patient's problem? With the metal tip, I flipped open the file and got as far as "PP: Complains . . ." before Greg came back in the room.

"Hey." He grabbed the file.

PP—presenting problem. Complains about what? His wife? Thoughts of doing unspeakable things to children? Not being able to get a hard-on?

"If you need material for the new book, you could just ask. You don't have to snoop." He climbed in bed again.

"I might." I sighed. "My new friends at the pokey aren't cooperating."

"I really wish you wouldn't go there alone."

"Why?" The envelope in my hands was smudged with greasy fingerprints and smelled faintly of hot dogs. This one probably wasn't fan mail, but I opened it, anyway.

"It's not safe," Greg said.

"There are security cameras and guards everywhere."

"Can't you just Google whatever you need to know?"

He held his hand between us, palm up, an offering. And I knew I should take it, but instead, I unfolded the letter.

"No, this novel is set in a prison. I have to go there and feel it out." I pulled out my elastic and ran my hand through my hair. "But I haven't been able to find an inmate to talk to yet, so it could be a no-go."

He said something that I didn't hear because I was reading.

> *Ms. Bernard: You have no imagination. You keep writing about the same thing over and over.*

"My website says I'll read and answer adoring fan mail." I handed him the angry scrawl. "Do I have to respond to this?"

He scanned the bottom of the letter. "Maybe Joe Mama is right. Scrap the prison drama and write something uplifting. You don't always have to be so dark."

"Have you met me?" I snatched the letter back. "Dark is all I know." Joe Mama didn't leave his contact information, so I tossed the letter on the floor. "I don't do cheery. Puppies and rainbows are not interesting. Besides, I must be doing something right. A lot of people love my books."

He opened the file. "Except your mother."

This was true. Every time I sent her a bound galley, she'd call, make small talk about how gorgeous Saint Augustine was, and tell me that the book was beautiful but upsetting.

"Let's leave my mom out of this. I don't blame her for not wanting to read about dead children and murderers."

"It wouldn't kill your family to talk about Savannah every now and again."

I winced at his choice of words. "I see my parents twice a year. I don't think that's what we want to discuss at Christmas dinner." I could feel another fight coming on. "Besides, you know why we don't talk about her."

"I know your reasons. I just don't agree with them."

I reminded myself that I chose to marry a shrink. And that once upon a time, we had loved each other. "I don't talk about my sister because I don't want to. It fucking hurts too much, okay?"

He patted my hand. "I'm sorry. I didn't mean to upset you."

I didn't feel like fighting. "It's fine."

"You are a strong writer, you know."

"But?" There was never a compliment without a *but*.

"But your work is disturbing, hard to read."

"No shit. My life is disturbing."

He slid his hand over and set it on top of mine. Greg's hands were big and boney. "It is not disturbing." He said it in the way you might talk to a child. Or a patient. "You live in a beautiful house." After my first book was published, the same year we got married, Greg found this place. It was much too big for us, but we bought it, anyway. The day we moved in, I stood in the foyer with its echoey, sterile feel and cried. "You're happily married." *To a man who wanted to fix me and hated Valentine's Day*, I thought. "Nothing about your life is disturbing. You're happy." No. I wasn't. He leaned over and gave me a dry peck on the cheek. "Right?" Quick kisses were all I seemed to get anymore. I didn't know if I was disappointed or relieved. I just wanted things to be the way they were before the money fights and miscarriages.

"Yes." I had at least seventy-five letters to read and didn't want to waste time arguing about something we were never going to agree on. "Life is good."

I thought he might kiss me again and then switch off the light, but we hadn't had sex since December after the last miscarriage the month before. I'd been inconsolable for weeks, and there was probably nothing else he could think to do to comfort me. Now, though, he went back to his file, and I sifted through the mail until I found one I wanted to answer.

I woke the next morning with the letters spilling off my chest onto the floor. Greg's side of the bed was neatly made, his reading glasses against his bedside-table light. The weight of my dream pushed against me, and I sat up, careful not to disturb the duvet. I heard the shower shut off. Greg knew about my Savannah dreams, but I hadn't told him how real they were. He didn't know that every time she came to me, I woke with a slight depression on my side of the bed, as if someone had been sitting next to me. It was there now. An indentation where a person might sit if they were watching you sleep. Or trying to wake you. I could feel that warm, melting feeling pouring out of me, leaving me cold in the room. It'd been months since Savannah had been in my dreams, but after New Year's, she'd come back. Usually, she appeared in bright colors, ringing out her singsongy voice, her eyes full of mischief. I'd wake up smelling her honey shampoo. But when she came back a few days into January, it'd been in memory and feeling. I couldn't recall the specifics, just a strange sadness as though she were reluctant to do what she had to do. The only thing I remembered from the initial dream was the prison.

Before those dreams began, I'd been planning to call Deanna and tell her I was quitting, that there would be no fifth book. I was stumped and stuck beyond recovery, but when I'd woken from that first one with that strange sensation in my body—as though I'd not only seen Savannah but I'd actually *been* her walking toward a prison in weak sunlight—I'd gotten up groggily and Googled directions to the South Jersey Penitentiary. I didn't know why she wanted me to go. But I had one small hope: maybe the son of a bitch who killed her had landed there, and I was finally supposed to find him.

Because I hadn't known who to call about an interview and it was only twenty minutes from my house, I'd driven there, hoping to charm someone into talking to me. It was a long shot. Skinny girls with flirty smiles were charming. Awkward, fat girls got sent away. But they hadn't denied me. And now I'd been there three times already under the guise of research and had spoken to the head warden, two psychologists, the continuing education teacher, and a public defender. But when I asked about the prisoners, I got shut down. "Inmates don't give interviews," the warden had told me. "They're convicts, not movie stars."

Now I ran my hand over the depression on the bed. Through the bathroom door, I could hear Greg humming. He turned on the sink. I closed my eyes and entered again the blurred world of razor wire and armed guards. Deep in me, I knew what Savannah was really doing. She was telling me there was a reason to go back to the prison. She'd find someone to help me. Behind the guards, metal detectors, and bulletproof glass, I might come one step closer to finally knowing what happened to her.

It was Thursday, so after I made a cake for my weekly dinner at my brother's house, I got in the car and headed south on the Jersey Turnpike toward the prison. It was a nickel-colored day of spitting snow, and the forecast was for nothing but that and freezing temperatures for the next week. I was in a down parka and a ridiculous hat, and because the Volvo Greg had bought me had heated leather seats, halfway there, I was sweating my ass off.

A blond guy with handcuffs dangling from his utility belt handed me a plastic box from a visitor's locker so I could stick my purse in it. His left eyelid was limp, and it made him look sneaky and a little terrifying. His good eye stared at me as if he'd never before seen a porky girl with a notebook and a voice recorder. "Here to see?"

"Please," I said, glancing behind him at the glassed-in office where other employees were doing paperwork. "I don't actually know any of the inmates. I've been here before and have interviewed some staff members. Everyone has been super helpful, but I'm trying to write a book, and now I really need to speak to a prisoner." I was talking quickly. "Preferably someone with a life sentence, because—"

But the guy put up his hand.

"Please?" I asked him, leaning across the counter. "I only need one inmate."

"No can do, ma'am." His limp eye scanned my body from one end to the other. "Rules are rules."

He staked both hands on the counter, and I tried to focus on his good eye. It was hard and steadfast, and I knew I wasn't getting anywhere. Having no one else to see and feeling foolish, I thanked him and hurried down the metal stairs, pushed the heavy door open, and stepped out into a gray landscape. Savannah, I thought, had steered me wrong.

I was unlocking my car door when someone in a blue DOC jacket came down the front steps. He was rough in a sexy kind of way, strong cheekbones, full lips. And as he got closer, I saw it was Brady Irons, the boy from high school whom I had loved from the moment he'd transferred in as a junior at the end of my and Savannah's freshman year. He was a military kid whose father was stationed at Fort Dix, and I used to watch him as he walked through the halls with his head down, a white T-shirt on, and cigarettes rolled in the sleeve like James Dean, but I could never make myself speak to him. I did, however, talk about him endlessly to Gabby and Savannah. He seemed older, more experienced than all of us; he'd lived all over the country and in Panama and the Philippines, and I was just a stupid freshman. I was pretty sure Brady Irons never even knew I existed, and still I found myself shutting my car door and calling out his name.

"Brady!" I yelled.

He turned toward me, and I walked quickly to him. I could feel my thighs rubbing together as I went.

"Hey." I was out of breath. "Brady, right?" He nodded, and there was no doubt it was him. He still had the same slicked-back hair and slightly uneven gait. Now he stood staring at me, not speaking. I could only imagine what he was thinking. It probably wasn't every day a fat girl charged him in a prison parking lot.

"I'm Cady Martino. Well, Cady Bernard now."

He shifted his keys from hand to hand. I couldn't tell if he was nervous, late, or had no idea who I was.

"David Martino's sister. From Kingswood?" I knew if I'd said something about Savannah, he'd recognize me right away, but I didn't want to talk about her. It had been 5,914 days since she'd been gone, and it was still hard to speak her name.

"That's right." He looked profoundly uncomfortable. "How're you doing?"

He was holding the door handle of a baby-blue antique Ford pickup. "I was just leaving." The prison took up the landscape behind him.

"Yeah," I said, checking the time on my phone. I had forty minutes to get to David's house. "Me too. I don't mean to hold you up, but do you work here?" It was a ridiculous question given his attire, but I was a little desperate to keep the conversation going.

"Sure do." He jiggled his keys. "Everything good?"

How was I supposed to answer that? "Um, sure." And then I got it. What he really wanted to know was who I was visiting in prison. "Oh, I'm here on business."

He let his eyes travel up and down my body, maybe trying to figure out what I might be pedaling.

"I'm a writer, doing research for my next book." I'd forgotten how startlingly blue his eyes were.

He cracked a beautiful white-toothed smile. "I thought you called yourself a novelist." That Brady Irons would know this shocked the hell out of me. The word *writer* made me think of a red-faced, sweaty reporter with a cigar hanging out of his mouth, pounding out stories for *The Post* about why the Jets hadn't had a winning season in forever. But for some reason, I couldn't say *novelist* to him.

"You're on Facebook?" I asked, thinking of the *About* section of my page.

"Nope. I don't need to know when the guy next door buys new underwear. But I've been following your career." He said this shyly, ducking his head as if unsure of himself. "It's not every day a friend from high school becomes famous."

Friend. If only he knew that I'd spent more than a year signing my name in cursive as *Cady Irons.*

"Is your new book set in a prison?"

"It was going to be, which is why I'm here, but I need interviews with guards and inmates. There's only so much information the front desk clerk or the guy who runs the metal detector can give me." I was rambling, but I couldn't stop. Seeing Brady Irons again after all these years made me nervous. It was like the crush had come rushing back in, or the feeling had never gone away. "Are you a guard?" *Please, please, please be a guard.*

"Corrections officer." He said it with the same disdain I did when I corrected people on my job title. *Right, you didn't call them guards.* But at least he wasn't a lunch lady.

"I really need some help." I felt myself stepping toward him. "Can I pick your brain sometime? My agent is going to kill me if I don't get a move on." I was doing it again. Babbling.

He spun his watch around on his wrist but didn't answer.

"Might you have time tonight? I'm going to David's house for dinner. He'd love to see you."

I thought of my brother cooking Indian in the new fat clothes I'd bought him. He'd eaten his way out of his monogrammed oxfords and pleated pants since Emma had left him.

"That sounds great, but I volunteer at Hope's Place on Tuesday nights and sometimes Thursday, too."

"The women's shelter?"

"They have kids there too. But yes."

"Wow. That's so nice of you." Every year in December, I'd donate a couple of thousand dollars to the ASPCA when my accountants told me I needed to make some charitable contributions. I thought of how good that made me feel and imagined it was nothing compared to what Brady Irons did.

He shrugged off the compliment. "They feel safer with me there. I teach them self-defense and give them all my cell number in case their boyfriends and husbands find them."

"Wow," I said again, feeling shallow and stupid. "Can I give you my number?" As if Brady Irons, the do-gooder, were really going to call the chubby novelist from Kingswood, but I told it to him, anyway.

He winked at me. "Okay," he said. "How about next Tuesday? I'm off on Tuesdays."

Twenty minutes later, I parked behind David's side of the garage. Now that Emma had left him, I guessed both sides were his.

"The cake's here." I stepped into the kitchen, and there were the people I loved most in the world: Gabby; David; David's best friend, Chandler; and Chandler's boyfriend, Odion. Chandler was standing at the stove, stirring a pot. Odion was at the sink washing what must have been a month's worth of dishes. It smelled like curry and dirty laundry. Gabby was sitting amid piles of socks and undershirts on David's kitchen table, pouring a thick, orangish drink into five glasses. Emma was a bitch, and I was glad she'd run home to her police chief father and overprotective mother, but she'd kept a clean house. Through the doorway, I could see my brother building one of his model cars.

I set the cake on the counter. "Smells good," I said.

"Hope you like it spicy." Chandler was wearing a half dozen rings and a chunky bracelet Odion had brought back for him from his last import trip to Cameroon.

I picked a piece of chicken out of the hot skillet and popped it in my mouth.

"What's with the stupid grin?" Gabby asked, putting Chandler's glass on the counter. She was wearing a heavy leather jacket with a fur collar, which explained the Harley sitting outside, even though it hadn't been above freezing for weeks. She'd changed her nose ring to a silver star, and it twinkled as she brought me a drink.

"You will never guess who I ran into at the prison." I peeked in the living room, where David's head was bobbing to music on his iPod, all those little Mustang parts spread out in front of him. "Is he still at it?" I asked.

"He's moping," Chandler said, turning off the stove.

"He's heartbroken," Odion told Chandler. "Give the poor boy a break. It was Saint Valentine's Day yesterday, and he was alone."

"Did you see Emma?" Gabby guessed. "Is she an inmate?" She gave Odion his drink, and he sniffed it before taking a sip. "Chief Fisher would have a hell of a time explaining that his perfect daughter got arrested for being a cow."

I laughed. "No, I did not see Emma, and let me get David. He needs to hear this."

We walked into the dining room with our drinks. David had on dorky magnifying glasses, because everything in a model car kit was about an eighth of an inch long. I handed him his drink.

He pulled out an earbud. "Is dinner done already?"

"Guess who I saw at the South Jersey Pen today?"

Even though his eyes were gigantic behind the magnifying lenses, David was handsome in that messy, absentminded professor way that sometimes made me wonder if he knew how to shower. "What the hell were you doing there?"

I waved my hand at him. "Research for the new book, but that's not important now." I couldn't wait to tell them. "Brady Irons." I took a sip of my cocktail—which, from the taste of it, was mostly rum.

David raised his eyebrows. "Brady Irons is in jail?"

I balled up my napkin and threw it at him. "Of course not. He works there. Isn't it amazing that after all these years I found him?"

Odion disappeared into the kitchen and came back with five plates. "Who is this Brady Irons? I missed so much not going to high school with all of you."

Gabby took them from him and set the table as she talked. "Cady loved him in high school."

"You did?" Chandler and David asked at the same time. Jesus, boys were so dense.

Gabby peered up and saw my flushed cheeks. "And apparently she still does."

I picked up the napkins and silver I'd brought in and followed her around the table, setting each place. "I do not." I could feel my face getting even hotter. "It was just really nice to see him again."

David finished his drink in one long gulp and then let out a loud burp. "I don't think a married woman should be this excited about seeing an ex-boyfriend."

"Hardly," I said. "I don't think I ever spoke a word to him in high school."

"Just because you were too shy back then doesn't mean you're too shy now," Gabby said, puckering her lips.

David reached in his pocket and handed me his cell phone. "Call Lover Boy up," he said. "Invite him for dinner next week. We won't tell Greg."

"I'm not inviting him anywhere near here until it gets a little less sty-like." I swept a pile of crumbs off the dining room table into my hand. "You know, sometimes I miss Emma."

"Fuck you," David said pleasantly. "I'll clean . . . eventually."

"We can argue about Cady's crappy marriage later," Chandler told us, bringing the chicken vindaloo in on a platter. "It's time to eat."

"My marriage isn't that crappy," I told them. But the whole way through dinner, I couldn't get Brady Irons out of my mind.

CHAPTER
3

Tucked in a corner booth at the Westin on Village in Princeton, Deanna was sifting through my unnamed fifth book, and she still hadn't replaced her coffee with Grey Goose. That was a good sign. Hell, it was a great one.

Deanna liked nice hotels because she liked money. I liked them because they were potential material. All bars, especially swanky ones, were a breeding ground for fights between lovers, undercover cops pretending to be high-dollar call girls, and drunken fraternity boys acting out their Mrs. Robinson fantasies. But today, the bar was relatively empty since it was before noon on a weekday.

Deanna held her Sharpie aloft while she read. Ten years earlier, she'd called me after reading one of my articles in *Harper's Bazaar* and asked if I had an agent. When I told her I didn't even have a book, she'd sighed into the phone as if she were already exasperated with me, even though we'd never met. "Of course you do," she'd said impatiently. Greg and I had recently moved into a great little cape that belonged in a children's story. It was brown with red scalloped trim and had tall, willowy flowers in the front yard. He was working sixteen-hour days as a psychiatric intern, and I was freelancing for all the Condé Nast and Meredith publications, ignoring what I knew I would someday have to write about: my sister. "If you can

handle a five-thousand-word piece like this one about Mr. Right being a serial rapist, there's a bestseller in your future."

And then Deanna had met me in a frantic sushi restaurant in SoHo and
on the back of drink napkins showed me the architecture and scaffolding of
a novel. She'd ordered sake for the table and then drank it all. And though
I'd known then she was a mean drunk, I also knew she was smart, and she'd
figure out how to sell my books. Still, I hated her for feeling like she was
whoring out my pain to make a buck. And she hated me for not being tougher.

Writing in small chunks, in scenes, made it manageable for me, orderly.
And I liked order, but I wondered what she'd think of this book. It was all
over the place, which is why I needed Brady Irons and why I kept checking
my phone, hoping he was still planning to come over.

"This is good stuff," she finally said, flipping quickly through the pages
like she always did when she was done reading.

"I know I need to develop Susannah more," I said, beating her to the
punch. "This is only the first draft."

"Slow down, Zippy." She laughed nasally. "I was going to say it could be
your best work yet."

She poured seven sugar packets into her third refill of coffee. "So far,
the writing is excellent, the voice compelling. But," she continued, "I'm
not sure where the story is going." She put her pen down and reached for
her drink. She had long nails, painted an ugly sage green. "Have you even
named it yet?"

"Not really."

She glanced at the manuscript, and I saw her mascara was clumpy. It made
her tiny eyes appear even smaller, lost somehow in the lashes. "Hell House
wants a title, Zippy."

Hollerly House was my publisher. Deanna had a derogatory name for
everyone.

She rose from the table and picked up her purse. "I'll be right back."

I watched her teeter on ridiculously high heels to the corner restroom
and disappear. In a way, music had saved my life, so I'd told Deanna when
we first met that all my books would be named after songs. *Alibi*, my first,
was a David Gray song. The main character accidentally killed her brother
and spent the rest of the book trying to cover her crime. *The Rising*, by Bruce
Springsteen, came to me after finishing *Alibi*. Being free of the beautiful

burden of writing my first novel, I'd felt open and inspired, as if something were rising up in me. I liked the name so much I created an entire story around a cult that had named itself the Rising. *Empty Corridors*, about a teacher who'd had an affair with a student and then killed her, was named after a Ben Howard song. He'd contacted me after it debuted on *The Times* bestseller list. Since then, we'd stayed in touch, having dinner whenever we were touring near each other. I came up with *Dark Roads* while on tour for *Empty Corridors*, when I'd gotten lost taking a shortcut from Bank Square Books to my hotel in Mystic. As I drove, the streetlights went out one by one, as though a phantom killer were flipping a switch. *What a perfect place to murder someone*, I'd thought. "Dark Road" was an Annie Lennox song, and I figured that was close enough. But I hadn't been able to think of even a working title for this book. I'd scrolled through all fourteen hundred songs on my iPod, flipped through atlases, and spent hours wandering the stacks at Sarandius Library, where Gabby worked, hoping for inspiration.

When Deanna came out of the restroom, her lips were alarmingly red.

"I thought I'd take a new route this time," I told her when she sat down. "Maybe I'll put a summary of the manuscript on my website and let my readers name it. You know, as long as it's a song."

She set her purse firmly next to her. "Oh, Zippy."

She'd started calling me that after I'd written three bestselling novels in five years. I hated it.

"Sweet Jesus." She reached for her drink, and when she saw it was almost empty, she waved to Sunshine, the waitress, who was standing at the bar, watching us. "You have to have a plot to have a summary."

Sunshine arrived with a new cup of coffee for her. I wondered if there was vodka in it.

"You know the plot," I told Deanna. "It's in the outline. Hopper's kid sister drowns in the skating pond, and he's positive she was murdered."

"Murdered?" she interrupted. "I thought she went skating on a warm day and fell through the ice."

"Yes, that's how it started." I was getting more excited about this book as I was talking. "But it doesn't make sense. Susannah hated skating. She never would have gone out there alone." I had a flash of a red scarf on the ice and Susannah's lifeless body floating under the surface, eyes wide, mouth open as if maybe she'd been screaming. "And Hopper knows that. He's sure something bad happened to his sister—that someone pushed her or lured her out there. So he gives up everything to find the killer and even becomes a prison guard because he thinks the murderer is a serial killer who's already doing time. Then he plans how he's going to kill him."

"Yes, darling, but you need a twist."

"How about he's in love with the person who really killed her?"

"He's gay?"

"No, a girl killed her." I touched the thirty or so pages I'd written. "Isabelle, the best friend."

Deanna set her cup down and peered at me with those dull brown eyes. I waited for a sarcastic remark, but there was none.

"I love it. I goddamn love it. He's planning to kill the wrong person, and he's in love with the murderer."

"Right." I wondered if I could bend the story line to have Isabelle be the one who whacked Susannah. Isabelle was a little odd, with her raven hair and nails, her obsession with wild animals, and her unnatural preoccupation with bizarre ways people died.

"When the dust settles, Chopper will realize his princess is the devil," Deanna said.

Hopper. I didn't bother to correct her. "That's it," I said excitedly. "*Devils and Dust*. That's the name of this book."

"Is that even a song?"

"It's off one of Springsteen's solo albums." Outside, a fountain was streaming over big stones, and now I wanted to leave. I wanted to go home and write.

"Good work, Zippy." She clinked her coffee mug against mine. "I talked to Roger at Hell House. He wants book five when *Dark Roads* is out of production and before you go on tour for it."

"But I'm only thirty-three pages into it." Deanna's news about the deadline startled me, and I fought the urge to ask Sunshine for an entire bottle of Stoli.

Deanna reached across and patted my hand, her ultimate and only act of kindness. "I don't call you Zippy for nothing." She made eye contact with Sunshine. "And, yes, I know you want it to be 333 pages. You only have three hundred to go."

Sunshine arrived and set down a long leather billfold with the tab in it.

Deanna licked her thin lips. "You'd better get cracking." She reached in her purse for her wallet. "You know, word on the literary street is your attachment to the number three is some cult knockoff." She set her credit card on the table. "Three three three, you know, is half of six six six."

Sunshine picked the card up, and I said, "I've heard the jokes. I'm a lightweight and can only handle half the Satanism." I knocked back the rest of my coffee. "You know why I do it. I want to be different. Like that author from Roanoke who publishes one copy of each of his novels longhand."

"If I were you, I'd be careful."

"Careful?" I wanted to be in my car, heading out of Princeton.

"Your readers might start thinking *you're* the murderer if you keep up with these strange habits."

CHAPTER
4

On tour, readers asked me if writing eased my past suffering. But it was more complicated than that. Trauma climbed along the corridors of my mind and wrapped itself around the present so I couldn't really tell the two apart. The day Brady Irons was supposed to come to my house, I woke after Greg. He was already downstairs, listening to a Bach concerto, getting ready for work. I thought about Isabelle, the ice, the strange way in which Hopper both knew and didn't want to know that his sister had been murdered. My books were not physical truths, but they were emotional ones. In order to write from Hopper's perspective, I only had to go back to the front hallway of our high school the day Savannah went missing.

Somewhere far off, I'd heard sirens. I felt weak, so weak I thought my knees might give out. A cop named Patrick Tunney responded to my 911 call, the blue spinning lights of his car warping the glass doors of my school. Mrs. Wilcox stopped typing and had run out of her office. "Honey?" She'd stood over me with her bob and those Bermuda shorts she wore year round. "Did you call the police?" I thought I might vomit.

Officer Tunney had a sweet face. He squatted in front of me, called me Cadence, and asked what had happened to Savannah. No one called me

Cadence. Mrs. Wilcox had stepped back as soon as he knelt next to me, her hand on her mouth as though something might fly out.

"My sister's out there." I was crying and gasping. I wished I could get up. I needed to stand. "Please. You have to help her."

Officer Tunney spoke quickly into the radio on his shoulder, asking dispatch to send another patrol car and to call our parents. There was silence before a staticky voice came through: "Dispatch reached the mother. She says the sister is staying late at school for a meeting."

How could I tell him that Savannah was lying so she could sneak off with a boy and get high with the senior girls? My parents had always accepted that Savannah and I knew things about each other that no one else did. They attributed it to the fact that we were identical. I'd never told them that I felt a psychic connection to most people, especially my family. Sometimes it was a wave of pain minutes before my mother would get a migraine. I'd hand Gramma a tissue the moment before she'd sneeze. My timing was always such that no one ever noticed. I didn't want them to. The things that Savannah and I could do with each other, for each other, made us different enough as it was. As I watched Officer Tunney communicating with dispatch, I saw clearly that he was good. It was a feeling I got. I knew that if anyone could find her, this man could.

"No." My strength was slowly coming back. "She's here. She's here, and she's dying."

Patrick Tunney squinted at me, and I understood he believed me.

Another patrol car arrived, and Chief Fisher, Emma Fisher's father, walked into the school. And right away, as Patrick Tunney went forward to meet him, I heard Fisher say teenagers were never missing; they just don't want to be found. Even while Patrick was refuting this, telling him this was a different case, Fisher was dismissing him. He was a huge man, and he strutted, his hand on his belt as though any minute he might take his gun from its holster and shoot me for wasting his time. Emma had his coppery-brown eyes. She was in David's class—part of the Snobby Six, as I called them—and as he came forward, running his hand over his golden hair to smooth it, I knew where Savannah was. I saw a flash of the crumbling chimney, the overgrown grass. Before he could speak to me, I reached for Patrick.

"She's behind the school, in the Wolfe Mansion," I said.

Chief Fisher's smile revealed a cracked front tooth. "If her sister is truly missing, how would she know where she is?" he said to Tunney while he watched me.

Savannah and I had always been connected. We were conceived from the same egg, slept face-to-face in our crib, spoke our own language, and loved and sometimes hated each other in the same way you love and hate yourself. I knew what was happening the way an arthritic feels a storm coming in the ache of her knee or a junkie feels the twinge of the jones before the drug is completely out of his system. I knew because it was getting harder and harder to breathe.

"Chief," Patrick Tunney had said. "I think she knows."

The cop who'd arrived in Fisher's car joined them. Maybe for lack of knowing what else to do, Captain Fisher and his partner set out toward the abandoned house. Officer Tunney stayed with me. While we waited for my parents, he talked about inane things, his voice filling the silence of my missing sister. I learned that Patrick was twenty-two, fresh out of the academy, a Van Halen fan, and had three greyhounds named David, Lee, and Roth.

They say it took three minutes and forty-four seconds for the ambulance to arrive after they found my sister. In the span of that short time, we lost her.

Instead of letting that memory drown me, I'd write. I'd write to stay alive. I'd write to keep the pain out of reach. Sometimes I didn't even shower. I'd put on a pair of sweats and a hoodie, get my laptop and my car keys, and head out the door to find a place far away from the cold, gray fortress Greg had insisted we buy. I wasn't spewing words on pages as my therapy or capitalizing on a past tragedy like some people thought. I believed that if I wrote enough, did enough research, interviewed enough perps and victims, got inside the minds of murderers, went back again and again to that day, I might actually find Savannah's killer. It didn't matter to me that years of doing this yielded nothing. I would never give up.

When I looked at the clock, it was 9:30 in the morning, and my first thought was that Brady Irons was going to be there at noon. Greg had left hours ago, but Bach was still playing downstairs. After my shower, I wrapped myself in a towel and stood in front of the walk-in closet, trying to decide what to wear. I finally found a cashmere periwinkle turtleneck sweater and a pair of pants that sort of flattened my stomach.

Downstairs, the white walls of our house seemed to vibrate with the Brandenburg Concertos. "In the words of Dylan Thomas's Organ Morgan," Greg had said on one of our first dates, "Bach is the best." That was back when I didn't realize he had a habit of quoting people, as though the ability to regurgitate what others said lent credence to his opinions. I went over to the cabinet, turned off Bach, and instead set my iPod to Mary J. Blige and Bono singing "One." Then I sat down on the couch with my thirty-three pages of *Devils and Dust*. I couldn't concentrate because I kept thinking about Brady Irons. Before I could write a whole page, I closed my laptop and went to the kitchen to make croissants.

He was on time. Actually, he was early. The croissants were still in the oven when I heard his truck coming up the driveway, so I shut the oven off and ran to open the front door.

"Wow, your house is so . . . spacious." Brady followed me through the foyer to the kitchen and draped his jacket on a hard-as-concrete bar stool that I didn't let anyone sit on unless I hated them.

"Yeah, that would be Greg. We used to live in this great little cape down by the train tracks. And now we live"—I turned around in the mammoth house—"here." I felt like I was borrowing it. I would have stayed in that tiny house forever. Greg and I bought it together, we made it ours together, we had loved each other in it.

Brady's boots echoed on the marble floor as he wandered from the kitchen to the great room. "How long have you been married?" He seemed somehow out of place, standing near the grand piano with the sound cabinet on his left and that stark living room in various shades of white and silver to his right. The wall of windows with the view of Stanwich's conservation lands was behind him as he studied the Underwood typewriter on the antique sewing table I'd found at the Golden Nugget Flea Market.

"Seven years." I'd put photographs between the Underwood's keys, old black and whites from childhood and from when Greg and I were first together. Brady picked up one of Greg holding my hand on the Ocean Grove boardwalk, his sun-bleached hair pulled back in one of my elastics. Chandler had taken that picture. I'd been out of college a year, freelancing for $1.50 a word at *Glamour* and *Cosmo*. I felt self-conscious having him in my house studying my photos and asking about my life.

Brady put the picture back between the old keys. Greg hated the typewriter. He thought it didn't go with the modern décor. "It goes with me," I'd told him. He'd answered me with a non sequitur. "You love writing more than humans."

"Coffee?" I asked. "We have some great Kenyan."

"Sounds good." He was studying another photograph—Savannah and me with her horse, Bliss.

I measured the coffee and silently prayed he wouldn't ask about her. "How 'bout you? Are you married?"

He shot me a look before turning back to a picture of David, Chandler, and me smooshed together on a seesaw at Baskin Park.

"Not officially. Colette and I have been together five years." He sounded exhausted. I dumped coffee in the filter and watched him run his hand across the shelf where I kept translations of my books.

"Not everyone needs a piece of paper to prove their love." I wondered if Greg and I would still be together if we weren't married. I poured water in the coffeepot and watched him pull down a book, open it, and then put it back. "Colette's a pretty name. Do you have pictures?" I had no desire to see his girlfriend, but I didn't know what else to say.

"My phone's in my truck; I'll show you next time."

Next time, I thought, realizing how much I wanted to see him again.

"How many languages are here?" he asked.

The machine started whirring. Coffee tasted like ass to me, but if Greg was going to spend two hundred bucks a month on it, I might as well get my money's worth. "Forty-seven, I think. I can't really remember."

He whistled low.

I pulled down two mugs and waited for the heat in my face to fade. I hated talking about my success.

"Colette's a great girl," he said suddenly, putting his hands in his pockets and standing in front of the west-facing windows where the stark February maples lined the Autumn Hill Reservation. He was wearing jeans, tight enough to make me notice. "But she's . . . complicated." His voice trailed off.

I pictured her, a woman with big eyes and very thin with bloodred lips. "Aren't we all?"

He turned quickly, his eyes suddenly confused, almost hurt. "What makes you say that?"

"Greg's a shrink." The coffee was slowing down, and it smelled so good I wished I liked the taste. "He thinks everyone's damaged. Eight years and he's still trying to change"—I swept my hands up and down my sides—"this." I grabbed a carton of half-and-half from the fridge.

Brady walked toward me. "What's there to change?"

"Oh, who knows?" Heat was creeping up my neck again. I didn't want to talk about relationships, especially mine. I poured the half-and-half into a creamer, grabbed a sugar bowl, put it all on one of the trays my grandmother had given me, and then headed to the couch. "I'm so happy you're here. You have no idea. I'm totally up a creek." I set the tray down and tossed a copy of *Biological Psychiatry* on the end table.

Brady sat next to me. "What's the book called?"

"*Devils and Dust.*"

"Great title." He watched me pour the coffee into the cups.

"That's pretty much all I've got. A title and about three dozen pages written. Oh, and a deadline." I answered his next question before he asked. "It usually takes me six to seven months to research and write a first draft. I have 125 days."

"Then we'd better get a move on." He grinned a delicious bad-boy smile and ran his fingers through his hair. "Let's talk prison."

Brady spent the next hour and a half listing average length of time served depending on the crime; the breakdown of how inmates' days were spent, provided they weren't in solitary or maximum; and the pecking order, from the armed robbers, who were kings, to the mass killers, who were exempt from social filing.

While he talked, I could smell him, a mixture of leather and smoke. I was a Princeton girl. The boys I knew held doctorates; they were M.D.s and stockbrokers. Brady was a different species, and there was something unbearably beautiful about sitting next to him, his boots, the hands that had trouble resting anywhere. The same hands that had restrained criminals, arm muscles so taut they made me feel spacey. Brady set his mug on a coaster, and I knew as he continued to chat, his sad eyes scanning the room as though memorizing it, I had no business thinking of him in any way other than as someone who was helping me with research. I was married. And plump. I'd slept with two men and kissed three others.

"And of course, there are the untouchables, the rapists," he was saying, focusing on the middle space between us, "and pedophiles."

An awkward silence hung over the room. It had started raining, and it pinged against the glass. I set my mug down next to his.

"This is great information," I said. "But what I really need is to talk to an inmate and not someone in there for petty crimes. I need a murderer."

Brady glanced at the Chopard clock by the fireplace Greg had gotten for me for Christmas. "Is that clock right?"

"Yep. Do you have to be somewhere?"

"Shit. Yes, I've got to get home before I go to Hope's Place." He got up so fast he almost knocked over his coffee.

I cleared our mugs. I had an odd, insatiable need to know more, to follow him to the prison, to go home with him and keep up our conversation.

"We're at David's every Thursday night," I said as I walked him to the door. "He'd love to see you if you ever wanted to come."

"Every week?" Brady was working his hands into leather gloves.

We'd been going to David's once a week for dinner for as long as I could remember. The origin of the custom had long since escaped my memory, but we were as loyal to our dinners as wolves to their alpha, as bees to the flowers they pollinated.

"It's been a tradition for years. We almost never miss a week," I said.

Over the years, David and I had extended the obligatory invitation to our spouses to join us for homemade beef burgundy or frozen lasagna, but Greg was always playing his bassoon or drinking a hundred-dollar bottle of scotch with his golf buddies, and Emma was busy with her sorority sisters. Eventually, we stopped asking them. I always wondered if David put out the dishes after Emma and her badly done highlights left to sip espresso with some girl named Chippie or Twinkie and discuss the new seasonal colors being introduced at J.Crew.

"That's so nice. Who goes?"

"Other than David and me, it's usually my best friend, Gabby, and sometimes her boyfriend. Also David's best friend, Chandler, and Chandler's boyfriend, Odion." I waited for him to react to Chandler being gay. Chandler'd come out in middle school with the support of his parents and practically the entire student body. When Brady appeared not to care, I continued. "If they can't get a sitter, their daughter, Madelyn, will make a guest appearance. She's the only child any of us has, so we all adore her. You should definitely come. We love visitors."

"I remember Chandler and Gabby from Kingswood."

"Odion and Chandler have been together since college, so he's one of us. And Gabby's been with Duncan for a while. Just two librarians in love. You should come. It's a good time. Sometimes we're at Gabby's or Chandler's, but usually we go to David's."

"Greg doesn't go." It wasn't a question.

"No." I opened our massive front door. The lawn seemed to be bathed in ice. "He doesn't like to go out on work nights. But really, my friends don't like him."

His eyes flickered, but he didn't say anything. "And David married Emma Fisher, right?"

"Yup." I closed the door a little. The wind was making me cold. "And now she's divorcing him."

"She always seemed like a handful." Brady was out the door now, his collar pulled up against the rain. "I'd love to come to one of your dinners. Maybe I can swing it. I don't have a lot of time between the shelter and tutoring at the prison."

"Wow! You're an angel in people clothes. Tutoring? What subject?"

"All of them. I help inmates get their GEDs."

"Well, if you ever have time, you're more than welcome to come to a dinner."

"Thanks, but between my job, volunteering, and Colette, I stay pretty busy."

"Bring her if you want to," I said hurriedly, though I wasn't at all sure I wanted to meet her.

Brady made a sound that seemed like it might have wanted to be a laugh. "Colette doesn't go out very much. She, uh, has trouble with social settings." There was something in his voice that told me not to ask. He put his hand on the door, and I stepped back. "Did they ever catch the guy?" He kept looking out at the ice spitting on the grass.

I knew exactly what he was talking about, and there was something intimate in his never mentioning Savannah's name, never referring to the actual crime. But the question baffled me. I was sure everyone knew they hadn't. "Nope," I said, trying to sound blasé. "The fucker's still out there."

After Brady left, I called Gabby, but she must have been working at the library; her phone went right to voice mail. I didn't really have anyone else to call and tell that not only had I sat next to an insanely beautiful man for the last few hours but I'd also found the key to my next book. Finally, I sat down to write up all the notes Brady had given me about prison life, but I found myself staring out those huge windows in my living room, watching the rain turn to snow and wondering why I felt so lonely, and trying to keep myself from believing Brady Irons could ever solve it.

CHAPTER
5

Sundays, Gabby and I met at Cookies on Prince Street for hot drinks and treats. We called it our church. It had a wraparound porch for summer and an old cast-iron potbellied stove that Victor Jebbings stoked in winter. Victor's wife, Sassafrass, made the cookies, and he made the drinks, and they played swing music and hoarded paperbacks you could trade out if you brought one in.

I was sitting in the corner window with my laptop, trying to piece together a flashback scene, when I saw Gabby pull up on her 1968 Harley-Davidson—no helmet, her dyed-black hair pulled back with a Jolly Roger bandanna, and bright-orange earmuffs. She was probably the only head librarian in the United States who rode an eighty-two horsepower motorcycle. In the dead of winter.

I watched her disappear into Cookies' stairwell and reappear a moment later. She said hello to everyone, including Sassafrass, who was always inconsolably grumpy. Then she ordered and plopped down on the seat across from me with a cookie the size of a steering wheel and a hot chocolate with whipped cream.

"Christ," she said, picking up my chai and taking a sip. "I am so glad February was a short month."

"You're going to die of hypothermia." I took back my tea.

Gabby snapped her gloves together and checked her short fingernails. "If I'm going to do the Hoka Hey, I have to ride all year round." She licked whipped cream off the top of her drink.

"I pitched it to *National Geo Adventure*," I told her. "I thought it'd be a fun feature piece." I had no time to write magazine articles, but for Gabby, I'd do anything.

She quit licking the whipped cream. "No shit. What'd they say?"

"They don't want to run it because, Gab"—I leaned toward her—"people die. D-I-E."

She rolled her eyes. "It's the American dream, Cades. Six hundred Harley-Davidsons riding across thirty-three Indian reservations, a couple dozen forests, eight deserts, and six national parks. And only one or two people bite the dust." She twisted a new ring on her pinkie, a tiny silver cross. "Anyway, I'm riding it. And not for nothing, but Duncan thinks it's the sexiest thing in the world. He can't get enough of me. Speaking of which—"

Victor was whistling to the music and feeding the fire, and everyone else in there was set off in twos, gossiping intimately, a Stanwich hobby that was one of the reasons I had no friends outside of our little circle. "Time to change partners." Gabby sang the Crosby, Stills & Nash tune softly. "You must change partners." She grinned at me. "I want an update." Normally, we serenaded each other at grossly inappropriate times like when I sang "Another One Bites the Dust" at her great-uncle's funeral.

"He came over once," I told her. "That doesn't mean I am supposed to change partners." I took a bite of my cupcake. It was pink with a little white princess face on it. Sassafrass was surprisingly cutesy given how grouchy she was.

Gabby leaned back and crossed her arms. "You'd make a good couple."

I groaned. "He's my research study, Gabs, a freaking prison guard."

"So what's wrong with a guard? They make good money—not as much as psychiatrists, of course." She grinned. Gabby had a beautiful space between her teeth that made her look tough and exotic all at once. "Or bestsellers. But you can make the money, and he can cuddle with you."

Besides babies, money was one of the reasons Greg and I were headed for splitsville. I definitely didn't want to talk about money.

"He's got a serious girlfriend," I said as if someone like Brady would ever be into me even if he didn't. "And, uh, I'm married," I added quickly. I'd actually thought it might be easier if my marriage suffered the quick death of an affair.

"Chandler told me his girl is a loon."

I quit eating my princess. "How does he know?"

"She comes in the store sometimes. He didn't put it together that she was his girlfriend until you mentioned him at dinner. He says she talks about someone named Brady. It must be his girlfriend."

Her phone buzzed, and she madly texted someone. Gabby had a whole city of friends I didn't know. Rather than making me feel left out, she was a safe lifeline to society if I ever needed one.

"Totally and completely nuts," she said while her thumbs went wild. "Every time he sees her, she's goes on and on about her garden." Her phone buzzed again, but she left it alone. "Chandler says he can't get a word in. He just listens to her ramble about her flowers."

I took the last bite of my princess and immediately wanted another. "Why are you always trying to drag me away from Greg?"

She put her phone down, and it buzzed again right away. "You only like him when I rag on him." This was true. "He constantly puts down your career, but has no problem spending all your money. And he's fucking his receptionist."

"Maybe," I said, straining my eyes to see if there were more pink cupcakes in the glass case.

"Anyway," Gabby said. "You are a star, and you deserve to be with someone who loves you completely." She wiped her mouth with her napkin. "And celebrates you."

"Some things you shouldn't get too good at. Like smiling, crying, and celebrity," I sang.

"Bono would be proud."

"Selling a few books hardly makes me a star."

She rolled her eyes. "You're the only author—sorry, novelist—I know who gets followed by paparazzi." Another side effect of a murdered sister. Gabby nibbled on her cookie. "Isn't it weird we haven't seen him?" Her eyes were green and pretty and familiar, and all of a sudden, I felt a wave of gratitude that she was in my life. "Has he been here since graduation, wasting his beautiful self at the clink?"

"I'm not sure. We mostly talked about his job," I told her, as if that explained everything. "But I do know he's renting a place near Kingswood now."

She gestured toward her cookie. "Can you eat some of this? Because I feel like I'm going to throw up if I eat any more."

"You took one bite," I told her. "Pass it over."

"I love a woman who eats," Victor said approvingly, coming by to wipe down the table next to us.

"Feel free to eavesdrop," Gabby told him.

"What's wrong with it?" Victor was so thin I could see all his veins through the skin. It used to scare me when I was a child. "Everyone else does," he said.

When he was gone, Gabby said, "So?" She took a sip of her hot chocolate, and some of the cream stayed on her top lip.

"So what?" The cookie I'd taken from her smelled like sugar-coated chocolate—not as good as a princess, but it would do.

"You said you'd do it before winter was over. And it's almost March, in case you don't remember. I'll come with you. I'll wait in the parking lot."

"How?"

"Bring him lunch," Gabby said. "That's when doctors screw their receptionists. But go early in case he's taking her to the Westin to fuck her in a real bed."

"Nice," I said.

The cookie didn't seem nearly as interesting when I thought about Greg at a hotel with Annika Lee, his receptionist.

Gabby drank her hot chocolate. "At least then you'll know."

On the street below, the people of Stanwich were hurrying from church to their cars to brunch. Sarah Bryson, one of Emma's best friends from Kingswood, was standing next to her car with her husband and two people I didn't know, and she was so pregnant she could have been hiding the moon under her coat. Why could Sarah Bryson keep a baby in her belly and I couldn't? I knew it was mean to think that way, but I'd wanted to be a mother for as long as I could remember.

"I'm not sure I want to," I said.

"That's what they all say." She licked the cream off her lip. "But what we don't know eats us up inside, so you might as well get it over with."

I broke the cookie in half and dipped it in my chai. "I love you," I told her.

She smiled her gap-toothed smile. "I love you too."

"So don't die in the Hoka Hey in July."

"Oh no," she said. "I'm gonna win that bitch."

CHAPTER
6

I sat in the parking lot in front of Greg's office waiting for the last car to pull out. His Mercedes was near the side door next to a Nissan SUV I was pretty sure was Annika's. "He'll be a good provider," my mother had told me. My parents had been up for Thanksgiving, and I'd announced we were getting married. We were in my kitchen cubing sourdough bread for stuffing. She hadn't stopped what she was doing to hug me. She hadn't been emotional at all. And for some reason, I had felt something go dead inside, like you do sometimes the day after Christmas. It hadn't ever occurred to me that Greg would have an affair. He was too straight, too square. Yet maybe he wasn't. The truth was, I wasn't sure I wanted to know, but the brie was melting, and the homemade Caesar dressing I'd attempted was probably going sour, so finally, I opened the door.

His office was locked, like I knew it would be, but I'd snatched the spare key from the hook in the kitchen, and I slid it into the keyhole, turned the knob, and walked into the waiting room. Annika wasn't at the front desk, and Greg's door was closed. The space was completely devoid of artwork or décor. He said it was because he wanted to let his patients project their own ideas onto the walls. He didn't want them to be affected by his style, his influences. But I thought he was cheap. He had a separate bank account for his practice. Expenses, rent, and payroll were all paid out of the account for Gregory Bernard, M.D., Ph.D., LLC. It was easy for him to buy $20,000 persian rugs for our house and bid on Monet paintings for the great room, because those were paid for with our joint account.

While I was standing there thinking mean thoughts, Greg's door opened, and a girl the size of a twirling baton emerged. She quickly shut it behind her and jumped as if I'd walked through a wall like Houdini.

"Hi," I said.

She crossed her arms over her chest. "Dr. Bernard's office is closed for lunch." She was Asian, and her hair was as black as a record album and perfect. "Do you need to make an appointment?" She slipped behind the receptionist's desk, somehow both seductive and prim in a translucent silk blouse buttoned to the top with a champagne cami underneath. Greg had told me she was working on her master's in public health at Rutgers, and that suddenly seemed far more accomplished than a commercial fiction writer.

"I'm Cady, Dr. Bernard's wife." I wanted badly to set the picnic basket down. I'd crammed it with so much food the muscles in the back of my neck had started to ache, but I wasn't sure where to put it.

"Oh." She sized me up. "Annika. Pleased to meet you." She smiled a curt, closed-mouth smile.

Now having seen her, I knew she was exactly the kind of girl Greg would go for. I didn't stand a chance against her. I only had one thing going for me: I was Greg's cash cow. Emphasis on *cash*. And *cow*. Well, cow compared to all ninety pounds of Annika.

"I'll get Greg—I mean, Dr. Bernard."

But before she could slink back to his office, I said, "I'll just go in."

He was sitting at his desk with a sandwich and a coconut water and a stack of files in front of him. "Cady." He wiped his mouth with a cloth napkin. "What are you doing here?" A chair had been pulled up to the other side of the desk, and a salad was sitting in front of it.

"I brought lunch." I held up the picnic basket. "I guess I'm a little late." I could feel Annika in back of me, and I suddenly felt fat and horrible standing there with my stupid homemade dressing that was too garlicky and the underripe strawberries I'd dipped in stove-top chocolate.

Greg stood up. "Have you met Annika?" He gestured toward the open door where she was standing, so poised and slender, like a perfect doll.

"Yes," I said brightly. It was important that Greg see I wasn't jealous, that I wasn't feeling at that moment like I might sit down on his industrial gray carpet and cry. "She showed me in." I tried to smile. "It's good to finally meet you." I stuck out my chubby hand, and we shook. "Greg has such nice things to say about you." I set the massive picnic basket on the floor and pulled Greg in for a stiff hug. Her fruity perfume was not on his skin.

"There's plenty." I faced Annika. "Would you like to join us?"

"No, no, no." She picked up her salad. "You two go ahead. I have some work to do at my desk."

"Nice to meet you," I said, feeling like a dog peeing on a tree in its yard.

Greg sat on the edge of his desk and eyed me as I unpacked sparkling water and the twelve-dollar-a-pound pecans that he liked, crabmeat salad, and asparagus tips I'd picked up at Olives.

"Why are you here, Cady?" It sounded like a reprimand.

"I think she likes you," I said.

"Who?"

"That childlike creature you hired to answer your phones." I set the french bread and brie on the desk.

"Really, Cady, don't be . . . Is that why you're here? To spy on me?"

"Yup." I pulled a few grapes off the vine. "She's pretty."

"So are you."

It unnerved me when he complimented me like that, and I found myself sitting down in front of all the food, startled and a little bit exhausted. "Don't you ever wish you'd married someone more like you?"

"Geeky and a workaholic?" He took off his glasses and placed them lopsidedly on me. He looked younger, softer without them. "I did."

If he'd turned me away at the door or ate lunch in silence, I would have been less suspicious. Greg wasn't sweet or playful. He was a scientist. He studied facts, neurons, and numbers. Emotion was of no use in his world. And yet I saw the way he'd looked at Annika as she'd picked up her salad and left his office. It was exactly the way he'd never looked at me.

CHAPTER
7

I accidentally on purpose ran into Brady at the Market Fair Starbucks. He'd told me he stopped in for coffee almost every day on his way to work. I'd been there to write a few times when I needed dialogue and couldn't stand that stupid house anymore, and now as I went to pick up a vanilla latte I probably wouldn't drink, I wondered if I'd ever stood behind him or if we'd both been in the comfy chairs on opposite sides of the front door at the same time.

Slipping the cardboard sleeve on my cup, I pretended I didn't see him.

"Hey," he said, touching my shoulder. He was wearing his DOC jacket, and his hair was still wet.

"Oh, Brady." His hand felt hot through my sweater. "What are you doing here?" I tried to sound surprised to see him.

"I come here for a double grande something or other on my way to work." He grinned, glancing at the wall clock. "And I'm late, as usual."

The barista, a pretty girl with a pierced nose, handed him a drink, and when he took a sip, foam stuck to his lip. I had a sudden urge to wipe it away. He licked it off and then wiped his mouth with his sleeve.

"How's the book?" he asked.

"Good." I watched the line get longer. "It's fine." In truth, I'd been avoiding it, and Deanna was probably going to be on the next train to Jersey to rip off my head. I needed Brady again, but I didn't know how to ask without feeling like I was hitting on him. "Thanks so much for helping me with it."

He held up his drink as if to toast. "Glad to." He glanced at the clock again, and I realized I was holding him up. "Anything I can do."

"Thanks," I said. "Thanks so much."

He put his hand up in a kind of salute, stepped backward once, his eyes somehow sad again, and turned to leave. But when he got to the door, his hand on the metal bar, a plain gold band on his right ring finger reflecting the sun, I caught up to him. "Actually," I said quickly. "I have a few more questions."

"You free for lunch tomorrow?" It felt like he'd been waiting.

I nodded, relieved.

"There's a great little deli near Marquand Park." He touched my arm as if emphasizing a point. "Their honey mustard is amazing."

I hated mustard, but I knew the deli. It was famous for it. In the summer, I sometimes ate my lunch in the nearby park under the corkscrew branches of a threadleaf Japanese maple.

"Sounds great. What time do you want to meet?"

He lowered his voice as if suddenly aware that people might have noticed us. "I could pick up something there and come to your house so you don't have to interrupt your workday."

The thought of having him in my home again made me ridiculously happy. "Are you sure?"

"I love talking about my job." That deep, calm voice, I could have listened to it all day. "Anything I can do to help."

"That would be fantastic," I said. "Thank you."

It was odd how much I thought about Brady when he wasn't around. I knew I was being unfair to Greg, questioning his loyalty and spying on him and his office sprite while I'd been thinking about another man, but I couldn't stop myself. All through my evenings with Greg, revising scenes and picking up Thai for dinner, I thought about Brady. I owed Deanna a chapter I hadn't written yet, but I was going to have to clean. I shouldn't have cared if Brady saw dishes in the sink and Greg's moccasins on the kitchen floor, but I did.

The next morning, I finished vacuuming, skipped mopping, and stuffed two days' worth of coffee mugs and plates in the dishwasher. I'd been dodging Deanna, and I saw her number flashing on my cell, vibrating wildly on the counter. I didn't pick it up. Time was ticking. I put the vacuum away.

I had the music on high and didn't hear Brady come up the driveway or let himself in the front door. He was ten minutes early again. "Sorry the music is up so loud!" I shouted at him when I saw him watching me dancing across the kitchen.

He picked a pen off the counter and sang, keeping one arm awkwardly behind his back. "Show a little faith, there's magic in the night." It made me like him even more that he was so off-key.

I laughed and clicked the volume on the remote. "You ain't a beauty, but hey, you're all right," I sang back to him. "What was Springsteen thinking? That's not exactly going to win over a girl's heart." I stealthily looked around my house, hoping it was clean enough.

"Will this?" In the second it took him to step forward, I thought he was going to kiss me. It terrified and excited me, but he pulled a bouquet of bright-orange marigolds from behind his back.

"Oh, thank you." I held them to my nose out of habit and smelled their strong, musky scent. "Let me get a vase."

"I know they're a little unconventional," he said as he followed me to the kitchen and set a deli bag on the counter, "but I thought your house could use some color."

Even surrounded by gray and silver, there was something mildly insulting about this, yet he was right. I filled a cut-glass vase with water, added a teaspoon of sugar to help the flowers live longer, and realized with surprise how relieved I was about the kiss. Maybe I wasn't ready. Maybe my marriage deserved a chance. "No one has ever brought me marigolds before." Maybe Brady didn't even want to kiss me. Maybe this connection between us was all in my head.

"Colette turned me on to them." He opened a few drawers until he found a pair of scissors. "She suggested I bring you some after I told her I was helping you with the book." He cut the bottom inch off the stems. "She used to own a flower shop, but now she grows them at our house. She says tending to the garden is calming, almost like meditation." He set the scissors in the sink.

"Please tell her I love them." I put the flowers in the center of the black granite island and tried not to sound jealous. I hated that granite. Our designer had imported it from a riverbed in South America. The cross sections of rock were stupidly expensive and ugly. Impressions from smaller rocks left white rings in the black surface that I was constantly mistaking for water marks and would scrub them until I remembered they were supposed to be like that. The flowers were a shock to the granite, like an unexpected wave on a calm ocean.

"They're so pretty," I said. How cuckoo could Colette be if she told Brady to bring me flowers? And how into me could Brady be if he was talking to his girlfriend about me?

Brady had brought lunch from the deli, and I took a couple of plates, two cans of Diet Coke, and our sandwiches into the sunroom. Surrounded by windows on three sides and a view of nothing but trees, it was the place in the house where I felt most comfortable.

"I hope you like roast beef," Brady said as I unwrapped my sandwich.

There was about half a pound of meat piled between two thick slices of sourdough bread. It was sweet and mildly embarrassing that he knew I wasn't a dainty girl and would eat it all.

I took a bite. "Oh my God, the mustard is delicious." I wasn't lying. It was sweet and sticky and tasted like summer.

Through the sunroom doors, I could see the flowers, a reminder that Brady had someone, and he talked to her about me. Which meant I wasn't a secret or a threat. "You said Colette *used* to own a shop."

He finished chewing before he spoke. "She had Pocketful of Posies in Princeton."

I vaguely remembered it, an expensive shop that had occasionally delivered to Sotto Sopra, my parents' restaurant.

"That didn't work out, so now she tinkers in our garden. She occasionally sells arrangements at the farmers' market in town."

I took another bite of my sandwich and chewed quickly. "I think working with flowers is an art. I'll buy a bunch of different kinds at the grocery store and come home and try to arrange them. They end up looking like a toddler did it. But then I see bouquets at weddings, and they're so beautiful I want to cry. I really wish I had some talent for it."

He spoke quietly. "Sometimes I'll watch Colette in the garden, and I swear to you she's communicating with those flowers. It's almost like poetry."

This sounded so odd coming from someone who probably carried a knife in a sheath and drank his whiskey neat that I almost laughed, but something in him had shifted at the mention of Colette. He took another bite of his sandwich. I noticed a bruise on his neck and had a quick, sickening flash of Savannah. Had someone tried to strangle him too? I wondered about the inmates and what his job held every day. I wrote about horror. Brady lived it.

He ducked his head as if embarrassed and wiped his mouth with his napkin. "Do you write here?" he asked. "Or do you have an office in New York?"

"No, this is it." I crumpled up the plastic wrap my sandwich had come in. "Unless Greg's home."

He cocked his head at me and quit eating.

"He likes to practice his awful bassoon or listen to Bach on high while he's catching up on patients' notes. I mean, I always write with music playing, but not flutes and cellos, and I need to hear myself read out loud without listening to something that makes me want to stick a steak knife in my ear."

Brady smiled. "I'm pretty sure it's big enough for both of us," Greg had said when I complained about the noise, but there was no place to hide in our house; with its cathedral ceilings and marble floors, sound bounced off the walls. I couldn't even talk on the phone in the kitchen without Greg hearing me upstairs.

"So sometimes I write in public," I told Brady. "I get good material people watching. And believe me, I need all the help I can get."

"I don't follow."

"I'm not naturally creative," I told him. "I have to rely on conversations between people standing behind me at the post office or the girl on her cell phone in the bathroom at the library, how she cocks her hip in one direction or the other while she waits in line, how men who are introduced to women rarely offer to shake hands. Coffee shops are great places too. I sit there and write down everything I see and hear."

"I'd say you're pretty creative. I've read all your books," he said quietly. "I especially loved *Alibi*."

This surprised the hell out of me. I almost couldn't speak. Out the window,

I could see a squirrel suspended on a branch. "That was more of a memoir than a novel," I said. "Except I changed the names and made my character forty pounds lighter."

Brady looked at me, not straight at me but sort of sideways, as though giving me space.

"It wrote itself. I couldn't not tell the story. I needed to get the words out of me to stay alive." I'd tried to tell Greg once, but I felt like he was analyzing me. "I didn't write it to get published or because I wanted to be a novelist. I needed to somehow pay . . ." I couldn't think of the word, I wasn't even sure I was talking—I had thought this so often to myself. "Homage to her," I finally said. "I needed to remember my sister."

"I may be being dense here, but the main character in *Alibi* accidentally killed her brother. You didn't have anything to do with your sister's death."

I was grateful that he hadn't spoken her name. "Didn't I, though? She was my identical twin. I should have known what was happening to her."

Silence spread between us like a fog. This was too much to tell him now, yet I couldn't stop myself.

"Anyway, thanks for bringing lunch."

After we ate, he told me about prison slang. I sat next to him on that hideous white couch and wrote down everything he said. Understanding prison talk, he said, was like learning a whole new language. *I'm doin' all day* meant a life sentence. *All day and a night*—life without parole. *Back-door parole* was to die in prison. *Dance on the blacktop* meant to get stabbed. They called their orange jumpsuits *peels*, and psychiatric meds were *brake fluid*. What struck me was how they'd softened everything. An entire life became a day. Dying was only a back door. Stabbing turned into dancing.

"I never thought of it like that," Brady said.

"What do you think of them? Is it just a job? Or do you ever feel any kind of connection or sympathy?"

The clock ticked the seconds by, and he didn't answer. His face had gone still. Finally, he met my gaze, and his blue eyes were serious.

"I feel lucky." He swallowed. "Some of them are in there because they made one stupid mistake."

He watched me in a hard way that made me feel completely naked. I had the odd feeling I would reach over and touch him, his throat, his cheek.

"We all do stupid things," he said. I saw him swallow. "Things we regret, wish we could take back. I guess I feel lucky that something didn't land me in there with them."

I was trying desperately to figure out what to say. I could feel the warm air from the wall vent on my back and outside. Stanwich's church bell rang once.

"I'd better go."

"Do you want something?" I asked. "For the road?"

"No, thanks." He patted his stomach—which, as far as I could tell, was rock hard.

I followed him through the kitchen and into that cavernous foyer. I wanted to say something to keep him there. "Thanks for everything," I said lamely.

Brady turned at the door and touched the handle. He had a way of standing on one hip that was movie-star sexy. As I was about to close the door behind him, he spoke. His tone was different, almost cold.

"I'm not sure I should come here," he said. I felt myself almost step back as though slapped. "I don't know, Cady." He looked at me one more time with those smoky eyes. "I'm a little fucked up inside."

And before I could tell him I needed his help, I enjoyed his company, why didn't he join us for a Thursday dinner, he was halfway to his truck.

Out the door's beveled window, his taillights went on, and then he headed down the driveway and took a right toward the prison. I realized he'd added to that fantasy man I'd made up in my head. Not only was he the tortured bad boy, he'd given me the feeling that I might actually be able to save him.

After being with Brady, I felt different. I wanted to blame Gabby for telling me I should have an affair with him, but even before she'd said it, I'd been drawn to him in a way I couldn't explain, and when he left, I didn't feel like an overweight girl who by some dumb luck was a bestselling author. Running water in the bath after Greg got home that night so I could be alone with the feeling a few minutes longer, I felt beautiful, if that were possible, my cheeks flushed like those pretty pregnant ladies at Stop & Shop I saw on school day mornings, my normally dull hair a bit brighter. Brady seemed to leave me in a humid perspiration.

I never talked to Greg about my books, because he was too clinical with his input, too removed, so there was no reason for me to mention Brady. But also, Brady was a secret I wanted to keep. I let my head sink under the honey bath. If I said his name aloud, especially to Greg, that feeling I got when we were together, that melted feeling from those stupid romance novels I used to read as a kid, would have disappeared.

I was fantasizing, of course. And I didn't blame myself. Brady was the kind of guy girls dreamed about, the tough guy in leather who knew how to fight but could also recite the words to Shakespeare sonnets. The kind of guy that all my life I'd close my eyes and imagine saying my name, except I wasn't me. I was some other skinny, shiny girl with gorgeous eyes and to-die-for skin, the kind of girl Savannah would have been.

I relaxed in the bath for a long time, and when I finally got out, I thought about the flowers Brady had brought and how relieved I was they weren't daisies. The first summer Savannah and I had been allowed to walk to town by ourselves, my mother had given us five dollars each to go to the dollar store. I'd picked out a set of bangles and cherry Lifesavers. Savannah had bought five packets of daisy seeds. When we got home, she threw them like confetti on the lawn. A month later, daisies haphazardly dotted our yard, waving their happy faces in the breeze. From then on, Savannah loved daisies—daisies stuck in the buttonholes of her shirts, in her barrettes, between her toes when she sunbathed, and, little did my parents know, a daisy tattoo on her left hip she'd gotten after she'd bribed one of those senior girls to drive her to Dark Side Tattoo and lend her an ID.

CHAPTER
8

David was away at a model car workshop, and Gabby was in Florida with Duncan for Hoka Hey training, so I tried to work on my novel. I took my laptop into my office and closed the door even though Greg wasn't home. I was so used to him blaring classical music or practicing his bassoon that shutting myself in my brightly lit office was habit now. I sat at my desk and opened my computer. It came on, dim for a second, and then brightened like an old friend smiling at the sight of me. Writing was a solitary thing, not that I minded. For so many years after Savannah was murdered, I craved being alone. What could have been worse than running into an acquaintance on the street, both of us groping for benign and appropriate words? Even now, after I'd had countless offers to join and then lead writing groups, teach workshops, and head the English department at a small community college, I preferred to work alone.

My problem was that with every scene I wrote, I was starting to like the best friend in *Devils and Dust* a little more. Isabelle killed Susannah. And Hopper, Susannah's brother, a CO in a high-security prison, was bugging me because he kept getting the shit kicked out of him by corrupt guards. It was accurate in terms of the reality of prison, but it wasn't really good to have a main character who appeared like a victim.

By the time Thursday-night dinner rolled around again, I was exhausted and worn out from working and wondering about Brady. I knew I should have been more concerned with whether Greg was fucking his receptionist, but I hardly noticed him anymore. I kept thinking about Brady saying he shouldn't come to my house. His prison notes were tucked in my computer bag, and whenever I pulled them out for reference, I got a sort of wavy feeling thinking about him. Even though Gabby would never approve, I texted him. "Going to David's for dinner at 7. You should come." And then I wrote my brother's address. He responded right away with "At Hope's Place now. Will try to make it."

Sometimes on my way to David's, I thought of driving with my mother down High Ridge Road while she frantically dialed her cell phone. It had been getting dark, and I could only vaguely make out the ghostly shapes of the oaks and maples along the side of the road. "Carol," she'd said into the phone. "Tell David to wait outside. I am going to stop the car in front of the house, and he has five seconds to come out. No, everything's not all right." She'd thrown the phone down between us, but it slid off the console and landed on the floor by my clunky sneakers. Savannah wore cute canvas Tretorns on gym day, and she always made fun of my sensible shoes. When she twisted her ankle playing volleyball, she said it didn't matter as long as she looked good doing it. I thought of that and tried not to know what I knew.

My brother was waiting in Chandler's yard when we drove up, jeans belted around the middle of his ass, hat on sideways, backpack slung over his shoulder. "Get in," my mother said. Miraculously, David did. He smelled like pot. On the way to the hospital, he kept asking what happened. No matter how many times my mom told him Savannah had an accident, he kept saying, "But what happened?" until my mother finally said, "I don't know, David. Jesus, don't you think I'd tell you if I knew?" And then he shut up, because she never talked to us like that.

I'd been in the ER at County General one other time when I'd had an asthma attack in seventh grade after someone brought some kind of weird hamster to class. The school nurse dialed 911 while I lay wheezing on the small cot pushed up against the cinder blocks in her office. Three doors down in English class, Savannah was having a coughing fit.

It seemed so different now, disorganized, frantic. The last time, they'd laid me down on a bed behind a blue curtain and given me an albuterol nebu-

lizer. When the doctor came in to recheck my pulse ox, I was at 100 percent, back at school by fourth period. But now, the loudspeaker was paging
doctors to oncology, to labor and delivery. In the waiting room, a man was
holding a towel to his bleeding head, a girl was cradling a crying baby, and
an old woman, oddly slumped in a chair, was completely still.

Officer Tunney and the other cops were in the hall, standing around
our pediatrician, Dr. Bassett, and when we got there, they made a break in
their circle for us. Dr. Bassett touched my mother on the arm. "Come with
me," she'd said. My father had appeared, and the four of us, missing Savannah, left the cops behind and followed Dr. Bassett. I remember wishing Officer Tunney would come with us, but it was a vague thought, as though
something buried deep in my subconscious knew I would be safer with
him there. He was the only one who'd believed me that I knew where Savannah was. David, my parents, and I stood in a small room with suede
furniture and southwestern art on the walls. None of us sat down.

Dr. Bassett pushed up her rimless glasses. "Lyndie, Bob," she said to my
parents. "Savannah was hurt very badly."

My father had a spot of red sauce on his white oxford. It was Thursday,
pasta night at the restaurant. He usually brought home leftover cavatappi, a
chunky bolognese sauce, or vegetable lasagna layered with mushrooms and
broccoli.

"Did she fall and break something?" he was asking. "Did she have an
accident?"

My dad, the youngest of four and the only boy, had thought every little
boy let his sisters dress him in frilly skirts and paint his fingernails a spar-
kly pink. His father traveled a lot, selling leather to companies like Coach
and Gucci, so he'd spent his childhood surrounded by women and girls and
girls becoming women. A self-described mama's boy, he cried at chick flicks
and sappy commercials. He cried when I fell out of our tree house and broke
my arm. But now, as Dr. Bassett's silence told us everything we needed to
know, he stood stoically. I could see his fingertips digging into my mother's
shoulder, but otherwise, he was as still as a soldier at attention.

My mom didn't move. She didn't seem to be blinking. I leaned against the
wall and watched Dr. Bassett take off her glasses. Years later, I would understand she didn't want to see my mother's face when she said what she said
next.

"It appears Savannah was attacked, sexually."

I was having a hard time breathing.

"No, Michelle," my mother said to the doctor. "No. No. No. No."

They called each other by their first names, exchanged Christmas cards, and Dr. Bassett came to the Sotto Sopra holiday parties.

"What happened?" David asked again. Even with the faint smell of pot tangled in the fabric of his sweatshirt, I'd almost forgotten he was there.

"How?" My mother sounded impatient, as though this was a waste of time.

"He strangled her," I said so quietly I almost couldn't hear myself.

Dr. Bassett nodded, nearly imperceptibly.

"He put something around her neck"—my voice sounded programmed— "and he killed her."

My mother covered her mouth. "No. God, no. Oh, my baby."

I knew what she was thinking—that being violated must have been so much the worse for Savannah because she was a virgin. She called us her twin angels, such good girls, never any trouble. She was so careful not to choose between us, but it was clear Savannah was her favorite, the prettier twin, more charismatic. It was hard not to look at Savannah, not to pay attention to her. She drew you in. And as I watched my mother crumble to the floor, my father and Dr. Bassett trying to comfort her, I wanted to run out of that tiny room, through the electric doors, into the parking lot, down Mareside Highway to Mulbury Street, to that tiny one-way, forgotten lane, grass growing out of its cracks, where broken glass lay along its crumbling curb. The lane that led to the Wolfe Mansion. I'd never been inside. I'd heard it was where kids partied because the cops didn't like to go there. You couldn't get a car past the curb; you could only walk single file on the lane. The place was surrounded by tall, knotty pines, I'd heard, and a root system so complicated you had to hold hands not to trip, almost impossible to enter, even on foot. Haunted, they said. I wanted to go there. I wanted to die in that exact spot where my sister had lain, suffocating. We were too late. I'd been too late. I hadn't looked for her.

Dr. Bassett came forward and stood beside me like a sentry. I felt her rubbing my back. She was warm and soft, and smelled like powder. "There's evidence of strangulation, bruising around her neck, and petechial hemorrhaging. We'll have to do an autopsy, but she was only partially clothed, which can be an indicator of—" But my mother put up her hand, and Dr. Bassett didn't finish her sentence.

My father had gone a pale, waxy color I'd never seen before. Someone killed my sister, and he was out there, right now, maybe washing his hands in the bathroom at a turnpike rest stop.

"Cady." My mother was coming across the room, her face wasted, her brown eyes fierce. She squatted in front of me. I felt Dr. Bassett quit rubbing my back. "Tell us," she'd said. "What else do you know?"

I opened David's back door to see Chandler and Odion at the stove. "It smells good," I told Chandler, and he pulled me into a quick hug.

"Lover Boy met someone," he whispered.

I'd brought a bottle of Chilean from Greg's wine cabinet, and I passed it to Chandler. "David?" I asked while he opened the wine. "Where?"

"That dorky workshop he went to last weekend."

"The model car one?"

"That's the one," Chandler said.

A girl who played with toy cars. Perfect. David came in wearing his microscope glasses on his head, his hair messy like he'd just gotten out of bed.

"How was it?" I kissed him on the cheek.

"It was what it was," David told me. His eyes were red as if he hadn't slept. "Where's Gabs? Did she desert us?"

"She's on her way back from Hoka Hey training."

And then there was a knock on the kitchen door, and when it opened, Brady Irons was standing there.

"You're here." My voice was full of holes, breathy, the pudgy girl with her high school crush.

Brady was wearing jeans and boots, and his hair was slicked back. It suddenly embarrassed me, standing in David's kitchen with Brady—Chandler and Odion glancing up blankly.

"Come in," I said.

But as he stepped through the door, he seemed so out of place.

"Look who's here," I said to David, throwing my voice over my shoulder, hoping he'd act hospitable. "Brady Irons from high school."

"Hell," David said. "Great to see you again." His hair stuck up like a jack-knife. "It's been a while." He put out his hand.

Brady shook it, watching him the same way he had me in the parking lot, like he was remembering something and wasn't sure if he should say it or not. I was certain it was Savannah. It was always Savannah.

"Nice place."

"I haven't had time to clean," David said quickly, stacking a pile of magazines on the kitchen table. It occurred to me he was going to kill me when this was over for not telling him Brady was coming, but in fairness to me, Brady hadn't told me for sure.

Brady was holding a bottle of wine, and Chandler took it from him and extended his hand.

"Chandler Morris," he said. "Good to see you again." Then he nodded to the lasagna sitting on the stove. "Hope you like Italian." Odion stepped forward and stood beside Chandler. "This is my boyfriend, Odion Eze."

"Nice to meet you," Brady said, shaking his hand. There was a beat of silence, and then Brady turned to me. "Thanks for the invite," he said quietly. It seemed like he didn't know what to do with his hands, and finally he stuck them in his pockets. "Are you sure it's okay I stay? I don't want to intrude."

"What? Of course. I invited you, didn't I?" Suddenly, I felt feverish with the need to keep him there. "You guys have like sixteen years of catching up to do."

But David was turned away, scrubbing dirty glasses in the sink as if he cleaned all the time.

"I'll open Brady's wine. I think we're going to need two bottles tonight." Chandler winked at me.

Odion took five plates out of the cupboard. "Come," he said to me. "We will set the table."

"Aye aye, Captain." But I was worried; I wanted to stay in the kitchen to make sure David and Chandler were being nice. Brady and I had already spent a few afternoons together talking about prison life, and besides my fascination with him, I was starting to feel like I might have a book, even if the murderer was growing on me.

Chandler brought in the wine, and I tugged on his shirt, leading him to the corner of the dining room.

"What's up with David?" I asked. "He's so grumpy."

He glanced in the kitchen. David was putting on pot holders to pick up the lasagna.

"You really need to ask him, but I'm sure it has something to do with Emma."

David and Brady brought in the lasagna, salad, and bread. But conversation was slow and stilted and mostly focused on Odion's homemade sauce and how good the french bread was even though carbs were supposedly the root of all evil.

"We're usually more fun than this," I said, glaring at David. "I don't know what's wrong with everyone." I felt like I was on a blind date with someone I had nothing in common with.

"Cady-did," Chandler said. "Don't you have any trivia from the book world? Dazzle us with some fun literary facts." His eyes flickered from David back to me.

I couldn't think of anything to say. Brady saved me.

"You know that saying about there being an elephant in the room?" he asked, wiping his mouth with a napkin.

Oh no, not now. David had been quiet all night. I didn't know why he was in such a shitty space, but having Brady point it out wasn't going to help.

"What about it?" I said.

"Do you know where that expression came from?"

"I bet you're going to tell us." Chandler poured more wine for Brady and then lifted the bottle to me.

Brady took his wineglass back and smiled, revealing those deep dimples all the high school girls had loved. "Kings in ancient Thailand gave exotic white elephants as gifts to peasants who couldn't afford to feed them. Instead of telling the king they'd rather be paid with money, they took the gifts without complaint."

We all stared at him.

"Where the hell did you hear that?" David asked.

Brady dug his fork into the lasagna. "I'm a voracious reader." He smiled at me. "Now that I know Cady."

Brady was mixing his metaphors. An elephant in the room was something that no one wanted to talk about. A white elephant was an unwanted gift. But I wasn't about to bring that up. I was happy somebody, anybody, was talking.

"Does anyone know where the phrase *raining cats and dogs* came from?" I asked.

David rolled his eyes. "I can see where this is going."

"Where?" asked Odion.

"I don't know," I said. "But I really want to."

Odion laughed so loud, David had to smile, and Chandler patted my back. Brady lifted his glass to toast us, and I was relieved.

After finishing dinner and the poached pears and candied walnuts I'd brought but not made, we drank the rest of Brady's wine during a great game of Fact or Crap. I watched Brady throughout the night, shy at first and then relaxing a bit. I saw him again as a seventeen-year-old kid coming out of fifth period, when I used to pass him on my way to lunch, his books under his arm. Sometimes he'd seem to recognize me, giving me a two-finger salute as though I weren't a chubby freshman and he wasn't a high school god.

After Brady, Chandler, and Odion left, I lingered behind to clean up the kitchen, hoping David would say something about Brady, maybe tell a story about him in high school so I could tell him all the crazy prison trivia he'd given me and how he'd come over for lunch a few times, but he washed the dishes in silence, the kind of quiet I knew not to disturb. When I went to put the wine bottles in the recycling bin in the mudroom, it was over-flowing with soda cans and beer bottles.

"You need to make some room out here," I called to him.

He pushed past me, and I watched him try to tear the cardboard of an old pizza box, but it wouldn't give. The tendons in his neck stood out until finally I grabbed a pair of scissors from the junk drawer in the kitchen, pulled it out of his hands, and cut it in four squares.

"I could have done it," he said when I was finished.

I faced him. "What's up with you?"

He turned and walked into the kitchen, and I followed him. "Do you know she still hasn't given me a reason?" He threw the scissors on the counter.

Chandler was right. It was always about Emma.

"Does it matter? I don't think she's coming back."

As a kid, David could never let anything go. When he asked why it was raining, he wasn't satisfied with "God is crying" or "Because there's water in the clouds." He needed the whole explanation about how the air had to be saturated with moisture, how dropping temperatures bring water vapors that cling together until they're big enough to form raindrops. He used to take apart our mother's Timex because he needed to know how watches worked. Of course he needed a reason.

"I met someone, okay?" he said, picking up the beer he'd uncapped earlier and taking a long sip. "I took her out to dinner in Minneapolis, and she asked me why my marriage broke up."

Somewhere between dinner and Fact or Crap, David had taken his glasses off his head and now was his sloppily handsome self, and I could imagine some girl sidling up to him, having no idea what a broken-up mess he was.

"And you know," he said, sipping his beer, "I don't even know. Emma won't talk to me. Women never talk when they're done with you."

I watched him take another sip of beer. "Emma is Emma," I told him. "You know how she is. Once she's made up her mind, there's no turning back. You need to be dating. It's good you went out."

I thought he was going to be mad, but he took another sip and then set his beer down on the edge of the sink.

"I fucking hate Thursday nights," he said.

The words surprised me so much, I almost jumped back.

Outside the kitchen window, I could see the lights of a low-flying plane.

"I love it when you're here, but then you all have to leave, and everything feels so lonely," David said. He had green eyes and dark lashes, and I felt sad all of a sudden for my big brother, alone in that house. And then he drew his hand across his face. "Forget it," he said. "Forget I even brought it up."

"No, I won't forget it. I'm going to find out why."

"Jesus, Cady, no. Leave it alone."

Dishes were piled on the counters, and dirty laundry was balled behind the couch.

"I hate what she's done to you," I told him. "If you need a reason why she left, other than she's a tart, I'll get you one."

"Don't do that."

But as soon as I got in the car, I scrolled through my cell to see if I still had Emma's number. I did.

CHAPTER
9

"We should be raiding Greg's stash of Dom Pérignon," Gabby told me as soon as she walked through my front door on Friday.

"It's not even noon yet."

"So?"

"What are we celebrating?" I knew perfectly well what we were celebrating, but I feigned innocence, poured her a coffee, and set it in front of her as she slid onto one of the camel-colored leather chairs Greg had ordered from Dubai.

"Don't be coy. You know." Gabby looked fantastic all the time, bright and eager as a teenager, her black hair sexy messy, her coal eyeliner smeared around her eyes, her Mediterranean complexion flawless.

"*Alibi* is now available in Turkish and Thai?" I guessed.

"Not that," she said. "But don't get me wrong. That's fantastic. Did you know your Facebook post has more than a thousand likes already?"

"I love my readers," I said. "I'd die without them."

It was still hard for me to believe that so many people cared about what I wrote. Outside, the sun had actually come out after an entire winter of sleet and rain, and it threw spots of light through the maples. Gabby smiled at me over her coffee cup.

"What?" I asked.

"Don't you have something to tell me? About dinner last night?"

"It looks like Chandler already did."

Gabby took a sip of coffee and then set it down. "Your brother, actually."

"You've been back from your motorcycle thing for twelve hours. When did you talk to David?"

"He stopped at the library this morning for a book on model car making."

"Did he tell you he met someone?"

For once, Gabby was speechless. "No," she finally said.

I unwrapped the tinfoil on a blueberry cobbler I'd made earlier in the week. "Want some?"

"Who'd he meet?"

"Some car girl, and now he wants to know why Emma left him."

"Emma left because she's a bitch."

As I was getting down plates, Gabby reached over and grabbed a blueberry from the pan.

"You're a little savage," I told her.

She ate the berry and licked her fingers. "Where does Car Girl live?"

"Montana or Minnesota or somewhere way out in the middle of the country."

Gabby contemplated this. "So have you slept with him yet?"

"I'm married, Gab—Jesus, no. It was Thursday dinner, that's all." I stuck a blob of ice cream on the plate next to a slice of cobbler and slid it over to her. "David was so grumpy I'd be surprised if Brady ever calls me again." I put down my fork and sighed loudly. "I have to ask you something," I said tentatively. "And I need you to give me an honest answer."

She rubbed her hands together. "You're going to confess something. I can feel it."

"Would it be the worst thing in the world if I did sleep with Brady?" Saying the words out loud was somehow both relieving and terrifying.

Gabby reached over and held my hand. "Honey, you've been trying for eight years to make Greg love you. If it's someone else's turn now, then so be it." She glanced around at the house we both hated. "This is not what you signed up for. If Greg wanted you to be a housewife and make babies, then he should have mentioned that before you got married."

I had a visceral ache for my old gingerbread house, for the way it used to be with Greg when I was a magazine writer. "Maybe it's not his fault. You know, I never asked him what he thought about my becoming a novelist. And he's not the one who keeps miscarrying."

She waved me off. "Don't make excuses for his poor behavior. If you'd wanted to be a teacher, would you have asked him permission?"

"That's different. They only make like forty grand a year."

Gabby pushed our plates away and swiveled my stool so we were face-to-face. "Do you hear what you're saying? Greg should be happy for you; he should be celebrating your success, not making you feel guilty about it. And sooner or later, he has to stop acting like you lose pregnancies on purpose." She reached for her fork. "So no. If something does happen with Brady, it doesn't make you a bad person."

I wanted to ask about Colette. She was innocent in all this. But Brady hadn't acted interested in me at all, so what was the point? "Thanks, Gabs. You always make me feel better."

"Don't thank me yet," she said seriously. "Now I have to ask you something."

I closed my eyes while she talked.

"Is it okay with you that he's a prison guard?"

I opened my eyes. "What? Why would that matter?"

"Look, girlfriend." Gabby stabbed a blueberry with her fork and nibbled on it. "I don't give a shit. I told you that when you first saw him again. What's in a guy's pants is pretty much the same, Ivy League or not, but you're a bestselling author with a Princeton education, and he's . . . not."

"I hated Princeton," I told her. "In case you forgot." I'd found college exhausting, the buzzing library, a roommate who thought having sex in the kitchen at two in the afternoon was acceptable, all those girls who believed fraternities and football games and getting drowned in keg beer was important.

"True," she said. "But still."

"He's helping me with my book." I smeared a spoonful of ice cream on the cobbler and ate it. "That's it. Anyway, how was the rally?"

Gabby rolled her eyes. "It wasn't a rally; it was training for the race, and it was a bunch of bike geeks who are as crazy as I am and want to ride across the country in the blaring sun as fast as they can." She grinned.

I loved that the braces she'd worn when we were in junior high had never closed the gap between her front teeth.

"It was amazing." She checked her watch, a pink plastic digital with Minnie Mouse on the face. "Holy camels. I'm late for Libby." Her nickname for Sarandius Library. "You know I love ya." And then she was gone.

After the oversized door clicked behind her and the motion sensors went on with her footsteps, a familiar knot traveled from my stomach to my throat. Once I was alone, I remembered again the depression on my side of the bed that morning, the flash of blond I'd seen in my sleep, an exhale as though someone had said my name. I'd woken with a start, and Greg had woken with me. "What was that?" he'd said instantly. But I'd rolled over and feigned sleep. I didn't want to tell him that Savannah had come to me again. I waited until he went into the bathroom to brush his teeth and get changed into his running clothes before I saw what I knew would be there—an imprint next to where I'd slept.

Since Savannah had died, I broke time into before and after. There was before her murder, when we were a perfectly happy family of five. And there were the sixteen years since, when nothing made sense anymore and my family slipped past one another instead of ever really talking. My parents said they'd moved south because the winters were too much, but I secretly thought it was easier to not be around everything that reminded them of their lost daughter.

I was thinking about going to Savannah's grave. It had been a while since I'd been there, but the phone rang. It was a number I didn't recognize, so I almost didn't answer it, but there was something about the dream I'd had the night before that made me pick up.

"Hi, this is Cady," I said, hoping it wasn't Deanna trying to trick me into talking to her.

"Cadence." The voice sounded familiar. "This is Patrick Tunney."

"Shit," I said softly. It couldn't be a coincidence that I'd had another Savannah dream the night before. "Officer Tunney? Is everything okay?"

"Are you busy? I'd like to talk to you in person."

Fifteen minutes later, I watched a black Suburban with tinted windows pull in my driveway. Patrick Tunney got out of his car, bent down by the side-view mirror for a moment, and headed up the walk. I opened the door before he rang the bell.

"Cadence." He put out his hand. "It's so good to see you." He stopped speaking abruptly and stared at the ceiling for a moment, as if thinking. "Sorry. You prefer Cady, right?" I nodded but didn't speak. Had he remembered that from sixteen years ago?

I took it and remembered how comforted I'd felt whenever he was around after Savannah. I led him through the formal living room into the great room. We never used it, and it reminded me of my parents' house. In all the years I lived in that little yellow colonial on Bickford Lane, the only time I ever remember using the living room as anything more than a shortcut to the TV room was at Savannah's funeral. It seemed like every high school student in town was crammed in there during the reception.

We sat down on opposite sides of the white couch, and I watched Patrick as he put a cracked, brown messenger bag on the floor by his feet. It had been fifteen years since we'd been in the same room. The last time I'd seen him was when he'd come by the house when Fisher had put Savannah's case in cold storage. I remembered the bitter December night like it was yesterday, how sorry he'd been. There was no reason for him to be here now, years later. Unless . . . unless they had a new lead.

"Officer Tunney," I said, thinking of Savannah in the dream, her quick flash of white-blond hair, "is there something new?"

"It's actually Detective Tunney," he said, picking at a callus on his palm. "But please call me Patrick." His auburn hair was darker, and his shoulders were broader if that was possible, thicker, but he still had that gentle voice, that presence that made me feel maybe everything would be okay.

"Patrick," I repeated.

"Captain Fisher is retiring." He shifted so he was facing me. "Actually, he's been asked for his resignation, and so have about six other officers on the squad."

Emma's father? "What happened?" I asked.

Patrick sounded apologetic when he spoke. "I'm not at liberty to say. We're going through quite a transition. I wanted to come and tell your family, because—"

"My parents don't live here anymore."

"I know, which is why I called you. But if you don't mind giving me their number, I'd like to talk to them too. And David."

"I'm sorry, but I still don't understand why you're here." I pulled my hair back to put it in a ponytail, but I didn't have an elastic. "Is this about Savannah?" It was weird, saying her name, and as soon as it was out of my mouth, I felt a strange hush. I never talked about her. It was too much.

"Yes," he said quietly. "It is." He stretched his fingers toward me, and for a second, I thought he was going to take my hand. "Fisher was the one who decided to make her case inactive, cold." Patrick watched me with his dark eyes. "And as of next Friday, he's gone. I'm being put in charge of cold cases, along with a detective named Jon Caritano."

I remembered him. He was the cop with Captain Fisher at the school.

"We're going to investigate her case again, because—" He stopped himself. Patrick's hair was short, and he had a muscular build, but there was something soft about his face, and I thought how he might be one of those sweet, tough guys who cried at weddings. "There's a lot I can't say right now. But we're going to go back and look at forensics, evidence, anonymous tips." He stopped talking, and something about his expression made him seem sorry, regretful.

My stomach twisted. I couldn't believe it. Finally, finally, someone was going to do something for my sister. "You're really opening her case again? Why?"

Patrick inched forward. "Because I owe her that much. Your sister deserves justice, and I think now I'm ready to give it to her."

His words stopped me. "Don't you mean *get* it for her?" But he stared at the floor.

Finally, he spoke. "The nature of Savannah's injuries was so disturbing . . ."

But I didn't hear the rest of his sentence. I was remembering how often, in the months after Savannah was murdered, people whispered that her attacker must have been deranged, a sociopath, an escapee from a mental hospital. Normal people would never choke the life out of someone with a belt.

"We were told to view the case as if she were a victim of opportunity." Patrick watched me. "We spent a year building a profile based on a perp—" He stopped and cleared his throat. "Um, a bad guy who was disorganized and erratic. Possibly mentally ill. Maybe schizophrenic." He wasn't fat but husky, and that made me feel more comfortable. Suddenly, I didn't think I could ever handle hearing news about my sister from anyone but him.

"And now?"

Patrick tented his hands and fixed his gaze at the middle space between us as if planning what he was about to say. "And now I want to examine it from all angles. It's been my experience on the job that sometimes when this much time has gone by, perpetrators are ready for confession. They don't want to carry the burden of their crimes any longer. I know I don't."

I'd tried so many times to channel my connection to Savannah and feel who hurt her, but either I didn't have the capability to make myself feel her in that way, or—and I sometimes tried to make sense of this when I couldn't sleep at night—Savannah didn't want me to know. My sister had kept secrets from my parents. She'd gotten stoned in the woods with the upper-classmen girls. She'd had sex with Chapman Sharp and three other boys. She'd sneaked out countless times. It only dawned on me after she died that she could also have been keeping secrets from me.

"Excuse me?" I asked quietly.

He was wearing an upside-down shamrock on his right ring finger. "We all made mistakes back then, but now that Fisher is out, it's time to make things right."

For a minute, I felt like we were the only people left on earth. "Are you going to tell all this to my parents and to David too?"

"Yes," he said. "The more people we can talk to, the more it'll help us understand what happened, what we may have missed the first time around."

There were things I'd never told my parents. The medical examiner had determined the bruising on Savannah's neck was caused by someone chok-ing her with a belt or a strap, probably something leather. Her hymen wasn't intact, and the investigators concluded, based on conversations with my par-ents about Savannah's history, that she'd been raped. I'd never said anything different. I felt sure I never wanted my mother to know Savannah wasn't a virgin. For that reason, I couldn't tell Patrick everything.

"Cady." Patrick leaned in as though confiding in me, his voice as sooth-ing now as it had been years ago. "We think it's worth taking a second look. That's the only reason I'm here."

"Is there anything you need from me?"

He pulled a manila envelope out of his bag. "In here is the original list of contacts, everyone we talked to."

I wondered if Chapman Sharp was on there. He'd cried to me after Savannah died. He'd called me up, and we'd stood on the empty football field one Sunday when my parents were at church, freezing our asses off while he cried so hard I thought he'd collapse. "I loved her," he kept saying. "I should have been there." But Chapman had been at lacrosse practice when it happened, along with almost every boy Savannah had ever kissed.

"What can I do?" I asked.

"We need to reach out to everyone from her past. Well, as many people as we can." He leaned forward, and I saw the skin around those kind eyes had grown crow's-feet from squinting. And smiling. "We checked out all her friends," he said. "No one raised any red flags. What we want to do now is to concentrate on people who knew Savannah but who she may not have been aware of."

"If she wasn't aware of them, how are you going to find them? Especially now?"

He answered as if he'd been waiting for the question. "We'll start with the funeral. Is there any chance your parents might still have the guest book? Do you remember if they packed it when they moved?"

"They didn't take it with them."

He opened the envelope and pulled out a typed list of names. "Oh. That's too bad."

"It's in storage."

His face brightened. "That's great news. Okay, then we'll definitely need your help. A good place to start will be to check every name in it and see if there was anyone present who Savannah didn't know."

"There are 333 names in it," I told him. The reason why all my books were that many pages.

He held the envelope very still. "How do you know that?"

The same way I knew it'd been 5,951 days since Savannah died. I remembered everything about her murder. "Because I went through that book after the funeral," I said.

And now I felt my hopes crashing down. There wasn't anyone suspicious in that guest book. I'd studied it again and again before my parents hired movers to pack up everything of Savannah's and put it in a storage unit on Cranberry Street. I knew as well as anyone that criminals loop back to crime scenes and often show up at funerals and grave sites. And I'd done my homework. I'd been through all this. Now here was Patrick, almost seventeen years later, asking me to do the same thing all over again. This wasn't a lead. It was a recycled approach to the same old thing.

"I'll do whatever I can to help, but I'm telling you right now, there's no one suspicious in that book."

He looked resigned when he stood, but he drew a card out of his wallet. "Please call me," he said, handing his card to me, "when you find the guest book." Navy print on nice card stock. PATRICK TUNNEY, DETECTIVE. Unaffected and strong, like him.

I walked him to the front door and thanked him for not giving up on Savannah. After he left, I stood in my driveway, facing the abandoned house across the street, its dark windows like closed eyes. The daughter of the people who'd lived there had gotten hooked on heroin and run away into the bowels of Hell's Kitchen. The mailbox still had their name on it in fancy script, but they'd moved to LA, because they couldn't stand driving by Rebecca's elementary school or the hotel where her prom had been held, the shelter where she'd adopted a matted dog. Sometimes I wondered what it would be like to cut that cord. I'd gone to college and graduate school at a university twenty minutes from where I grew up and bought two houses less than seven miles from where my sister was attacked.

CHAPTER
10

I called Emma four times before she texted me back, a cryptic and acerbic message that told me how busy she was at work. I scoffed as I read it to Gabby. Emma's idea of work was to ring up overpriced clothes at Sarah Bryson's boutique ten hours a week for the employee discount.

We finally settled on a Monday morning at Witherspoon Bread Company in Princeton, which struck me as odd, since Emma was absolutely a Stanwich girl who loved to show her flawless face in public. But when I came downstairs that morning to find *The Stanwich Star Banner* on the breakfast table, I understood why she was hiding out in Princeton. A simple headline ran across the front page: FISHER FALLS. Once I'd made my coffee and had a muffin in front of me, I sat down and read the entire article.

> *Malcolm Fisher ended his twenty-five-year career Friday as Stanwich's police chief by announcing his retirement, the first jolt in what appears to be a cleaning out of the city's top ranks. He follows in the footsteps of former city manager Stanley Lawson, who resigned in December. The new city manager, Adrian Allay, is planning what some are calling a "clean sweep" of Stanwich's police*

force. Four directors of city departments have announced plans for resignation.

Allay appointed Assistant Chief Gerry Polson as acting chief.

Fisher, 58, didn't respond to messages seeking an explanation for why he stepped down.

The chief's exit comes during two investigations involving him. One relates to a federal complaint filed by Deputy Chief Gillian Maves, who alleges she was denied a promotion because of gender-based discrimination.

Another focuses on an accusation from Detective Patrick Tunney that Fisher tried to force him to resign. Details of that case are under investigation and not yet on public file.

I read the last two sentences again. And then I thought about Patrick sitting in my living room, trying hard not to break some precinct oath not to talk. Was all this related to Savannah? I went on to read more about standard retirement notices, deputy city managers, starting salaries, and votes of confidence, but I wasn't really reading it. I was thinking about the night Savannah's case had landed in the basement of the police station.

Patrick had stopped by the house that night after dinner to tell us the case was being moved to cold storage. It was December then, and he'd brought with him the smell of wood smoke and snow. He was a year older than when we'd met, still boyish in the roundness of his face, still with the ability to make me feel calm when he was around, to make me believe everything might be okay. He sat on our couch with his hat in his hands and told my parents that while he'd never stop searching for Savannah's killer, it was no longer an active case. "I know this is horrible," he'd said. I'd gone completely still. "I know how this feels." But he seemed almost relieved that the case was now inactive. He talked for another thirty minutes, doing his best to convince my parents that Savannah's murder had been a crime of opportunity. That the perpetrator saw a pretty girl crossing the school yard and grabbed her. Her story had been all over the news for months. We became a morbid kind of famous. The restaurant was booked to capacity almost every night for a year. Everyone knew about me, Savannah's twin, and how I'd told the police exactly where to find her. Since her case was never solved and the cops thought someone took her because she was pretty, I was going to make sure that he didn't come after me too. It wasn't that I cared if I died. I really didn't; I already felt dead without Savannah. But I had to stay alive for my parents. They'd already buried one child. I couldn't let them bury another. And if Savannah got killed because she was pretty, then I'd make sure I never was.

I felt numb, somehow removed from myself, and I remember drawing inward as though I were looking out from a long way away. When my parents got up to walk him out, I'd sat alone in the wing chair without being able to move or speak.

That was when it had gotten bad. That was the point I always went to when I thought about Sound View and what led me there. I might have been able to deal with Savannah's murder if I thought her killer would actually be caught. I'd started cutting myself after she died. I'd wake up every morning feeling like I was inhaling water instead of air. Cutting was the only thing that stopped me from feeling like my lungs were being crushed. But even that didn't work as well as it once had. And now knowing the police were giving up on my sister drove me to chat rooms. It wasn't sex I was after. It wasn't online shopping or the weird community of other people whose sisters had been killed. It was necessity. I'd needed to find a way to stop the pain.

I turned the page of the newspaper. "We're hoping for stability," the article quoted the new chief as saying, "and we're certainly headed in that direction."

"Hey," Patrick said when he answered as if he knew it was me, as if he'd already programmed my number into his phone.

"What happened with Fisher?"

I heard him intake a breath. "I can't say. At least right now. If it goes to court—"

"I'll help you."

"What?"

"I'll help with Savannah's case any way I can."

Silence. I thought maybe somehow we'd lost the connection, but then Patrick's voice came through—strong, deep, and somehow so relieved.

"Thanks," he said. "I needed to hear that, today of all days."

"I'm here," I told him. "I don't care what it takes."

CHAPTER
11

My mother hadn't wanted me to see Savannah in the morgue. "Please," I'd said. We were about to leave the hospital. David and my father had already started toward the exit, and Fisher was writing on his pad after asking us if we knew anyone who'd want to hurt Savannah. Did she have any enemies? "She's barely sixteen," I wanted to tell him. "She's beautiful. She's always laughing. Everybody loves her."

We were almost to the glass doors when I'd turned to my mother and whispered that I needed to see my sister. Dr. Bassett and my mom looked at each other, and Tunney, who must have heard, offered to stay with my father and David in the private waiting room until we were ready.

Years later, I'd learned my dad had been asked if he wanted to see Savannah, and he'd said no. When David finally told me, it was late at night in my Princeton apartment, and he'd come to help me pack up for the summer. We'd smoked half a joint. It was May, right after finals, and the air coming in my six-foot windows was balmy and humid. "He couldn't handle it," David had said. And my mild-mannered brother, who never seemed to get terribly angry, suddenly shouted, "If it was my daughter, I'd make sure I saw her!" He turned to me, and his eyes were wet, maybe from the pot or maybe because he was furious. "I'd never leave that fucking building until I laid eyes on her!"

But the day Savannah was murdered, David and my father stayed in the tiny waiting room while Dr. Bassett led my mother and me down two flights of stairs. It was at least ten degrees cooler than Emergency, where we'd been standing shivering when the ambulance came in after blowing through four red lights and still not arriving in time to save her.

We entered a brightly lit room. In the center of the back wall, a large window was covered with a plain white curtain. Next to that was an ominous black CALL button. Dr. Bassett touched my shoulder, and then she stepped forward and pressed the button. I watched her speak into a small metal grate. "We're ready," she said. The other side of the glass buzzed, and the curtain moved. *We're ready. We're ready.* I'd never be ready for this. I closed my eyes, thinking maybe when I opened them, I'd be back at school in that leather chair while Mrs. Wilcox typed away, that this was some horrible nightmare. I couldn't possibly be about to see Savannah's dead body, waiting to begin what was left of my life. My mother took my hand in hers, and I opened my eyes.

Savannah was on a rolling metal table under a sheet. My first thought was that she must have been cold. Standing next to her was a guy with red, curly hair, earbuds snaking out from under his scrubs. I could tell by the way his knee was jiggling he was listening to music. I wanted to kill him. Dr. Bassett tapped the glass, and he stepped forward. She made a twirling gesture with her hand. The kid with the earbuds reached for the top of the sheet. And then he pulled it back.

She was naked. I knew this from her bare shoulders. Her blond hair was spread like a fan, and her face was tilted slightly to one side. She was stark, stripped of color except for the purplish bruises on her neck.

I'd only seen Savannah use makeup once. Cass, a junior she smoked with behind the school, had driven her to Blue Mercury on Palmer Square, and she'd come home with fifty dollars' worth of liquid foundation, lip gloss, liner, and navy mascara to match her eyes. She never told me where she'd gotten the money. She just sat still while I made her up exactly like the article in *Glamour* said. When I was done, she'd paused in front of the mirror and then washed her face with Noxzema, muttering something about clowns and hookers. I'd made her bed and did her laundry for a month in exchange for her leftover makeup. I needed the foundation to cover the pink blotches on my forehead and chin, the blackheads that sprouted like tiny constellations on my nose. So the fact that she looked bare now did not have to do with makeup; rather she was so completely un*done*. And then I knew.

"Where's her necklace?" I turned to my mother.

My mom's eyes were on Savannah, but her body was angled away as though it could not stand to bear witness. "Michelle," she asked Dr. Bassett, her voice shrill, "did they take off Savannah's necklace while they examined her?"

Dr. Bassett hit the button on the wall again. "Andrew," she said loudly. "Did you remove a necklace from Miss Martino?" He startled and then pulled out his earbud and answered her with a nonchalant no.

He took her necklace. "We have to go back." I pulled my mother toward the door. "We have to find it."

Dr. Bassett moved us up the stairs, pushing past nurses and orderlies and hustling us to the same waiting room we'd been in before. She cornered Officer Tunney, and I heard her say the words *missing* and *cataloged*.

Tunney turned to me. "Cady, can you describe Savannah's necklace for me?"

I reached into the neckline of my sweater and pulled out a thin gold chain with a pendant that resembled a slanted, backward *f*. Two together were the Chinese symbol for twins. We'd been wearing them since before I could remember. Our midwife, a kind Vietnamese woman who had delivered most of the babies in town, gave them to my then hippie parents when we were born. "Very powerful, these girls, almost dangerous power," she had told my mother in her thick accent, and then my parents had told us she had laughed, a silky laugh, a merry, happy laugh that defied what she'd said. It had made us feel like superheroes, and each time we grew, we'd gotten bigger chains to match our size. "We've never taken them off." I had a terrible feeling that without her necklace, Savannah wouldn't be able to come back to me, wouldn't know how to find me. And I knew she would try. We were the same, after all. She was me. I was her. One zygote.

Tunney spoke a series of numbers and codes into the radio on his shoulder. When he finished, he put a hand on my back. "CSU is still at the scene," he said over my head to my parents. "If it's there, they'll find it."

They never did. At my dad's insistence, after CSU finished their investigation, the police searched the woods and the Wolfe Mansion with a metal detector, but Patrick had shown up unannounced four days after Savannah's funeral to tell us in person that the necklace hadn't been recovered. I'd been sitting on the ottoman in the living room when I saw it in a flash, a hand holding it, a closed fist. But that's all I could see. And then my mother had sent me to the kitchen to get coffee. I knew from her nervous eyes and the way she pulled at her fingers she was trying to get rid of me. So after I poured the coffee, I pressed myself against the bird-of-paradise wallpaper and listened as hard as I could above the microwave's soft whir.

Patrick Tunney lowered his voice as if he'd known I'd be eavesdropping, but I managed to make out *assailant* and *taken it*.

That night, I took the jewelry box I'd gotten for my fourth birthday off my bureau, white with tiny painted roses and a spinning ballerina that sprang up when I opened it. It played some vague lullaby I'd never been able to name. I pulled out the bottom drawer where I kept my social security card and birth certificate. Swirling the clasp of the necklace around under my chin, I worked on trying to get it unlatched, but I couldn't. And while I struggled with it and my chubby fingers fumbled with its clasp, I realized I'd never take off that necklace.

Before I closed the lid, I had a strange feeling that I wanted to pull the tiny ballerina out, cease her endless dancing to that unknown song so I wouldn't have to see her every time I opened the top, wouldn't have to see her perfect little body, tiny blue eyes, the blond bun and satisfied smile. But I didn't take her out. I left her where she was and closed the lid. When the music stopped, the room I'd shared with Savannah went unbearably still.

It was Emma who had made me get a longer chain for it, so long I could hide the *f* underneath my clothes; it hung almost to my belly. Before that, I'd worn it on my breastbone, like I had when Savannah was alive. It was my senior year in high school, and we'd been at the Sotto Sopra Christmas party.

"What's with this necklace you always wear?" Emma had been in a red lamb's wool sweater, and she tugged at it with her small, perfect fingers. Around us, people were getting drunk on screwdrivers and tequila.

"It's nothing," I'd told her, reaching for it, but Emma had it in her grasp. She'd raised her shaped eyebrows.

"Anytime someone says it's nothing," she'd said, "it means it's something.

What's the *f* mean?" She had fingered the tiny symbol, and because I was drunk, because Emma smelled of mint and perfume, and because she seemed so sorority-sister intimate, I told her. Told her about the midwife and how we'd never taken them off and how when Savannah died, it had disappeared.

Emma had dropped the necklace and then said, as though somehow erasing me, "Cady, I'm sorry, but that's really creepy."

In fact, I think that's why David loved Emma, because she wasn't sentimental. There was no chance in hell you could wallow when you were around her. She was a doer. She took action and moved on.

"He wants an overly efficient mother," Gabby said when David kept dating Emma even after he'd graduated.

"He has a mother," I told her.

"Yeah, I know," Gabby'd said, "and now that he's out of the house, he wants another one."

Off went David, getting stroked by Emma's pretty pink manicured hands. Until one day she stopped stroking.

And now I stood at Witherspoon Bread Company, right when Deanna was breathing down my neck for another chapter, and I should have been home drowning that poor girl under the ice and figuring out about serial killers. Instead, I was waiting to find out from Emma why she left my brother. The lady in front of me was taking forever to order, blowing my plan to have my coffee on the table and my book open to a page I hadn't gotten to yet so I'd appear relaxed. Emma made me nervous. And so did the Witherspoon Bread Company, solely because it was far from home. I was sure not only that Emma did not want to face anyone in Stanwich after her father was all over the papers but also that she was probably a little bit worried one of her pretty sorority sisters would happen upon her while she was with her fat ex-sister-in-law. Emma had gone to William Paterson, so she wouldn't be too far from David, and as a result, her sorority sisters were everywhere.

She was wearing knee-high boots and a black dress, and her silky red hair was tied in a neat ponytail on the nape of her neck. "Hi, Cady," she called, coming up behind me with her black leather Coach bag, smelling like balsam. "Sorry I'm late." She air kissed me, which I hated, and when she drew away, I saw, despite her lovely makeup job, Emma Fisher had dark circles under her eyes.

"Hey," I told her, and then by some invisible force of etiquette, I offered to add her to my order.

"Oh, sure, yes, that would be lovely."

"I'll have a vanilla latte," I told the girl. I wanted to add a lemon cruller to the order, but I didn't want to give Emma the satisfaction.

The girl arched her eyebrows at Emma, waiting for her order.

Emma smiled as though she didn't notice and said, "Oh, I'll take a green tea." Emma was terribly underweight and hadn't eaten a carb since Dr. Atkins said not to. "And, Cady, you don't mind, do you?" She opened her brown eyes wide. "But I'd like to bring something to those homeless men on Lincoln, the ones who make sculptures out of soda cans?"

"Be my guest," I told her. *Leave my brother in the cold, but be my guest.*

"I'll take a dozen everything bagels," Emma said, smiling sweetly at the girl, "and a tub of full-fat cream cheese." She turned to me. "They love bagels," she said in her daydreamy, see-through voice.

"Great," I told her.

And then we waited in complete silence for the Princeton babe to bring Emma's tea and homeless goodies and my latte.

We found two leather chairs in the corner with a square table between them. I'd forgotten a sleeve for my cup, and it was too hot to hold, so I set it down and blew on my hand, which made me feel clumsy and awkward. I always felt that way in front of Emma. I didn't even want my medium (not grande as the lady with the dog in her purse in front of me kept calling it) coffee, anyway, but Gabby said it was one of my best habits, a great diuretic. And because I needed something to get rid of the extra puffiness in my ankles, I thought it might be worth it. As it was, I had cankles, and that morning, I couldn't even zip my low-heeled boots.

"Listen," Emma said. She had perfected speaking without moving her lips. Gabby and I called her the Muppet Master. "Tell *him* that I'll send back his INXS CD as soon as I can. I didn't realize it was in my car when I left." She smiled quickly at me.

I ran my hands up and down my upper arms. "Brr. Is there a draft? It suddenly got chilly in here."

Emma's smile turned to a grimace. "You're exactly like him," she said into her cup. "I hate to say this, Cady, but you really are passive aggressive."

I dumped four packets of Splenda in my mug. When next I spoke, I lowered my voice and tried to sound unsure. It was a trick I'd learned researching. It was called *going one down.* Apparently, if you got all sad and pathetic, people might tell you what you wanted to hear. "Can you tell me why?"

"Why what?" Emma sipped her tea. Her giant bag for the homeless was sitting at her feet.

"You broke his heart." I leaned in closer and said as pleasantly as possible, "Can you pretend you have one and tell me why?"

Her pretty cheekbones went pink, which only highlighted how gaunt her face was. "He hasn't told you?"

"He has no idea."

A group of college students flooded through the door, noisy and happy. I envied them.

"Your family does not deal," she said, "with Savannah."

In the 5,963 days since Savannah had been gone, I'd never really thought about how losing her affected David. Once the FBI pulled out, the story stopped getting played every night on the news, and Patrick Tunney no longer came by once a week to give a progress report, we rarely talked about her. Our parents made sure they never neglected David or me because they were too sad to come to a soccer game or too wary of having to answer the same questions over and over again to go to a school function. They plastered ridiculous smiles on their tired faces, gripped each other's hands, and carried on.

My family prided itself in carrying on. We patted ourselves on the back because we were coping. We all had good jobs. My parents toughed it out and remained in the 20 percent of couples who stayed together after the death of a child. None of us camped out at the cemetery anymore.

"What does that mean?" I asked.

"It means you never deal with your . . . shit."

Maybe Emma was onto something. There was a part of us, a part that we rarely talked about, that wouldn't be right until we found the man who murdered Savannah.

"And you do?" I could feel myself clenching my fists.

Emma put her drink down. "Yes," she said. "I do."

"And are you dealing with your father getting fired by hiding?" I wanted to ask, but instead, I said, "And what does *dealing* mean, exactly?"

"Well," she said, "for one thing, it would mean that David wouldn't have sent his little sister to do his dirty work. He had plenty of time to ask me what was wrong before I left. But no one in your family ever talks to each other."

"We talk plenty," I told her. "For example, we talk about why your father put Savannah's case in the fucking cellar."

A woman and her friend, both in expensive cashmere, turned toward us. Emma gave them a curt smile.

"What my father does is not my problem," she hissed between clenched teeth.

"Well, thank God for that, since he's on the front page of all the papers." It was a low blow, but I couldn't help it.

Emma mashed her lips together. "I've asked your brother time and again to explore his feelings about what happened, to stop burying it in dinners with you people and his model car building, and he just gets mad. I'm done with people who are assholes when I try to help them."

"You started dating him after . . ." I couldn't even finish that sentence. I hated it that Emma was right. "You must have known what he was like."

She rolled her eyes. "We were eighteen years old, and David was a beautiful, laid-back tech geek. And we were crazy about each other. Maybe what happened to Savannah drew us together in some way that's difficult to explain; I don't really know. But the point is, we're not kids anymore, and now I realize that stuffing all his feelings down—"

"Like your father stuffed a very important murder case in cold storage?"

She went on as though I'd never spoken. "That was not healthy, and if you don't mind, I happen to want children and a family and someone"—she appeared to be lurching around her rather empty mind searching for a word—"*normal*." She pushed the table toward me and stood up. "I've put up with your sad, wronged family for way too long." She heaved her pretty Coach bag over her shoulder. "And you know what? I don't want to anymore. You." She stabbed her finger in the air at me. "The whole lot of you is toxic."

Toxic. A therapist's favorite word.

"Why don't you try doing something your family never does?" She clutched her bag of goodwill bagels I'd bought. "Talk to each other, Cady. Ask your own damn brother what his problem is. Our town's so angry at my father for putting your sister in storage? Well, maybe you should be focusing on the truths none of you have ever been willing to see."

The ladies had completely quit talking and were staring at us.

"What?" Emma said to them, and they quickly went back to their conversation.

I felt my cheeks go pink. She wrapped a light scarf around her neck in a fashionable way I never could manage.

"I know you think I'm a bitch for walking out on sad, sweet David, but after years of him shutting me out, I decided not to take it anymore. I couldn't save him," she said. "Maybe you should start focusing on saving yourselves."

"I'd say we're all okay." I'd never told such a big lie. "My parents are happy. David and I have good jobs. We're happy."

She snorted. "You people have no idea how to be happy. Your parents couldn't stand to be here anymore. David never leaves the house. And you." She spit the last word at me. "At least I don't use my family's dirty secrets to bring me fame." Then she twirled around on her pretty leather boots and walked out into the sunshiny day.

Later, I sat in my car and tried to breathe. It was horrible that little red-headed Emma could make me want to cry, but it was as if, out of every single button she could have pushed, she'd chosen the one that made me feel the worst about myself. I called Gabby, and while it rang, I remembered years ago my whole family had been invited to a wedding. The chef at Sotto Sopra was getting married. His older brother was a groomsman, and his younger sister was a bridesmaid. I'd watched the three of them all night with fascination and hope. On the ride home, my eyes heavy with sleep and my dad's tuxedo jacket draped over me, I saw David, Savannah, and me all grown up. We'd live near each other; we'd have cookouts and parties and vacation together in the Outer Banks. Even after we lost Savannah, I'd been determined to keep that dream alive, but I realized now as I listened to Gabby's voice telling me she wasn't available that the dream hadn't ever had a chance in hell of surviving, considering whom David had wound up marrying—never mind my workaholic husband, who was probably fucking the receptionist.

CHAPTER
12

My weekends with Greg were predictable. He came home around eight on Friday nights and liked to go to bed at what he called a "reasonable hour," which meant pajamas on and case files stacked on the bedside table at about nine thirty. Then he got up at some awful dawn hour and ran about fifteen miles. When he got back, he put classical music on the stereo, and I'd hear him in the office with his mini tape recorder, dictating notes on patients.

Saturday nights, we often went into the city if we had tickets to Lincoln Center to see the symphony, the opera, or, once in a while, the ballet. I never knew what to wear, but I had a couple of black dresses that I'd gotten over the years, so I'd put on one of those with stockings that itched and my mother's long string of pearls she'd given me when I graduated from Princeton. We usually met up with another couple at a midtown restaurant, and I'd feel fat because the portions were miniscule and I was always hungry after dinner, and I'd make polite conversation with the wife while the men talked about their work or with the husband if the wife was a psychiatrist, or sometimes they were both psychiatrists. They seemed to marry each other. I liked the opera, I loved it, but I always cried, which no one else in the audience ever appeared to do.

Greg would hold my hand in the car afterward and kiss it, and when we got home, sometimes we'd make very tired love before drifting off to sleep. This is how I got pregnant already three times and had miscarriages every time, so the sex part was somehow both hopeful and scary.

Sundays, Greg went to Gratitude Yoga in Princeton, and he came home flushed, carrying a green drink, and ready to practice his bassoon.

I admired it all very much. I wished I were the kind of person who wanted to jump right up and jog and do yoga, and I wished I liked sophisticated, learned couples and tiny portions, that the symphony didn't bore me and that I didn't get so emotionally involved with opera. But here was my secret: not only did I want to sleep late, I wanted to throw rock-paper-scissors to see which of us would go down and get coffee and crullers at Cookies, and then I wanted to loll around in bed eating pastries and drinking java and reading *The Times*. I wanted to stay in my PJs and cook in the afternoon. I loved finding new recipes and wanted to try every one of them, whether it was fattening or not. And then it would be nice to go on a dusk walk and look in people's windows and tell each other stories about them. I wanted a smaller house with a woodstove, where we could snuggle up and read aloud to each other. I wanted to watch TV shows on Saturday nights, to curl up with a big bowl of popcorn. I wanted someone else's life.

But none of that ever happened, and so on Sundays, after I'd gone to Cookies with Gabby, I'd drive the narrow dirt roads to Ravenswood to see Savannah's little bay gelding, Bliss. Savannah had fallen in love with horses when she was twelve, and by some miracle that defied the economics of our family system, she'd convinced my parents to buy her Bliss and keep him at a barn in town. We couldn't stand selling him after she died, so I'd taken over grooming him and cleaning his stall. Eventually, I started taking lessons on him. When he got too old to ride, I moved him to Ravenswood, a retirement barn in Hunterdon County. Now he was twenty-six, old for a horse, but he was fat and happy, and I secretly believed he'd live forever.

This Sunday, I'd brought carrots with the greens still attached. I went out to the paddock and gave one to Bliss, and then I brought him in to pick his feet and clean him up. When I went to the tack room, I left him on crossties, and I could hear him pawing in the aisle. He nickered when I came around the corner, his forelock covering a Texas-shaped star on his forehead. I took another carrot from the bunch and fed it to him. His whiskers were too long, and tiny bits of flaxseed stuck to them.

"Don't tell anyone, but you know you're my favorite," I told him.

He answered by licking my cheek.

"You mean I've been ousted by a short, hairy man with a girl's name?"

Brady was standing at the barn door in jeans and a leather jacket, his hair messed from the wind.

"Hey," I said. He gave me that half grin, and I wondered for the millionth time what it was like for Colette to slip in bed with him every night. "You're here. What a nice surprise."

"I remember you said you come on Sundays."

He started to walk toward Bliss, but I stopped him.

"Be careful," I said. "He's not much of a people horse."

But Brady was already in midstride, and by the time I got the words out, he was standing in front of him. Bliss took a tentative step forward and lowered his head. I watched as Brady scratched the horse behind his ear.

I stood there, stunned. I'd never seen Bliss act like that with a stranger. Brady must have seen the surprise on my face.

"Animals love me," he said. "I'm the person dogs run to when they get off their leashes. My mom used to tell me I should have been a vet."

"If you say so," I said. "It took me a year of bringing him molasses squares every day before I could catch him in the paddock." I dropped the hoof pick in my grooming bucket. I tried to pet his velvety nose, but he was more interested in Brady.

"He seems pretty happy to me." Brady turned and grinned at me, and I had a vision of him at the park with dogs bringing him their Frisbees.

"He's plenty happy when he's with other horses."

He was the horse we turned out with the babies when they were weaned from their mothers. They'd run around calling frantically for their dams until finally they'd give up and follow Bliss around the paddocks, nipping at his tail and trying to nurse. I'd never once seen him be rough with a youngster, but he could do without people.

"I need to pick his feet and brush him. Do you want to hang out for a minute?"

"Sure. I'll help if you want." He pulled a curry mitt out of the grooming bucket and held it up. "I have no idea what to do with this, but I can make something up."

"It's okay. I'll be done in a minute." I took the mitt from him, unreasonably pissy that the horse who'd chased me out of his paddock for a year was warming up to someone he'd never seen before.

Brady watched me clean the mud and dirt out of Bliss's hooves and then paint the outside of his feet with peanut oil. When I'd told him where the barn was, I didn't think he'd ever drive all the way down here, but I was stupidly happy to see him. This was the most intimate we'd ever been. Far more intimate, even, than sitting in that huge, cold house that was supposed to be mine. I curried Bliss and brushed him, glancing at Brady every now and again. He was still sitting on my trunk like he wanted to say something but hadn't figured out how to spit it out.

I hooked a lead line to Bliss's halter. "You want to walk with us? I was about to graze him."

He got up and followed me outside. "I need to talk to you about something," he told me when we were in the open air.

"Okay."

The grass was starting to turn green. From where Bliss was grazing, I could see the parking lot. A motorcycle was parked next to my car. I hated motorcycles. I hadn't known he had one, and I wondered if he and Gabby had ever talked about their shared interest. It surprised me I hadn't heard him pull in. He spoke as if he could read my thoughts.

"I cut the engine about a quarter mile up the road." He reached up and pulled a willow switch off the branch above him. "I didn't want to scare the horses."

"That was sweet of you." I heard the flirt in my voice and tried to stamp it down.

Bliss dragged me toward the pond, where the spring grass was best, and Brady kept a step behind.

"This is serious," Brady said suddenly.

I felt my neck go warm. "Okay," I said.

But then he didn't say another word until we were down by the water.

"What's up?" I asked quietly.

"I have someone for you to interview."

"Who?" I said it so loudly Bliss quit grazing and raised his head. I walked over and scratched his withers. It had been weeks and finally, finally, Brady had someone. Deanna would have to back off now that I'd scored an interview with a maximum-security inmate. "When can you get me in?"

"Slow down," Brady said. "We need to talk about this first."

"What do you mean?" I took a step toward him, and Brady glanced around as if someone might be hiding in the patch of unbloomed forsythia.

"Have you ever heard of the library murders?"

The air between us went still.

"Those seven girls in Philly?" I watched the wind make ripples on the pond and tried to remember what I knew about Larry Cauchek and the girls he'd murdered one after another in Philadelphia. "Is that who you want me to talk to? Larry Cauchek?"

"He has library privileges. Ironic, eh? The guy who killed seven girls and left each one on the front steps of a different library can check out books like the rest of us." Brady peeled the leaves off his willow switch one by one.

"So you think he'd talk to a writer?"

He raised his eyes to me. They were so blue it was almost unreal. "He's checked out all your books, Cady. Twice."

Suddenly, the sun felt hot, and the smell of hay and spring mud and manure were overpowering, nauseating.

"He's been reading me?"

I saw his Adam's apple move when he swallowed. "Yeah. He leaves sticky notes about your characters, the villains, all over his bunk."

I ran through the plots in my books, the people who had been murdered, committed suicide, or died in terrible accidents, and the characters responsible for the deaths. "Who's his favorite?"

"Thomas Derringer," we said at the same time.

Of course Larry Cauchek would like the murderer from *Empty Corridors*, who killed his first victim in an abandoned house.

"You don't have to do this," he told me quietly.

"Oh, I'm doing it," I said. Bliss pulled me to the paddock. I watched him touch noses with a yearling. "I have the chance to interview one of recent history's most prolific serial killers. If this gets leaked to the media, Hollerly House wouldn't even have to promote *Devils and Dust*. This would be all the press I'd need."

"Since when did you become a fame junkie?" Brady sounded irritated. He was squinting, trying to figure me out.

"That's not why I'm doing it," I told him. And I wished now that I was alone with the horses. That Brady had texted me this news. I felt macabre, sick for my preoccupation with the characters in my books.

"I want you to think about this before I arrange a meeting with Cauchek." Brady's willow was free of leaves now, and he drew it between his fingers. "He's a dangerous guy. The worst." His eyes were so intense it was hard to keep contact.

"Set up the interview."

"Jesus." He dropped the switch on the ground. "You're brave."

I felt that familiar irritation rise in my chest. "It's hard to be afraid," I said quietly, "when I've already survived the worst thing that could ever happen to me." But I knew that night I would have a hard time sleeping, thinking about Larry Cauchek reading my novels. Thinking about him *identifying* with the villains.

When I pulled up to my house, three shiny SUVs were in my driveway, so I had to park on the street. As soon as I walked in the door, Bach flooded the room. A bottle of Boodles and a six-pack of tonic were sitting next to a cut-up lime on the kitchen island.

Greg was rummaging through the crisper drawer. "Where's that cheese?"

Through the archway to the living room, I saw three of his golf buddies sitting on our sofas. The one facing me waved.

"The cacky vacky polo or whatever you call it."

"It's caciocavallo podolico, and you and those three assholes in there melted it and ate it with Fritos last week."

"Would it have killed you to get some more?"

"That hunk of cheese cost as much as my first car."

He closed the refrigerator a little too hard, and I heard the salad dressing bottles on the door rattle. "What's your point?"

His shirt was untucked, and his beeper was attached to his belt loop, which meant he'd probably been at his office. I wondered if Annika had been there and if he was screwing her. I hoped he was. Life with Greg was like swimming in the ocean with no sight of land. But it was too much effort to have *the talk* with him. To break down the breakdown of us.

"Can't you eat Cracker Barrel cheddar like the rest of us?" I asked.

"I *could*. But why would I?"

For a second, my vision went black, and all I could see was freedom, a life without Greg. A peace that didn't include a man who loved my money and a house that made me want to cry every morning. I could feel my pulse beating in my neck.

"Sorry," I muttered. "I'll get some more next week." Suddenly it was too much—pretending this life was okay with me. My parents were right. The shortest distance between two points was the truth. I rehearsed the words in my head. *I'm not happy. I've been thinking about someone else.* Would it matter what I said? The end result would be the same. I'd finally get my wish of being alone.

Greg watched me. The kitchen counter was between us, and I remembered when we were kids how Savannah and David used to chase each other around the island, sparring, trying to figure out which way the other one was going to run. He watched me, waiting for me to say something until one of his golf buddies called his name and he left me alone in the room.

CHAPTER
13

Chandler called Thursday afternoon and said that everyone had bailed on dinner, but if I'd already made it, I should come to his house for lunch on Friday. Odion was overseas on an import expedition, and Gabby had to do inventory at the library, which probably meant she and Duncan were going to have sex amid the periodicals after it closed. But I knew David wasn't busy. He was pissed that I talked to Emma, and now he was avoiding me.

While I drove, the car filled with the smell of bay leaves. Usually, Chandler's mother brought him food when Odion was away, but since his dad had died after a long bout with bone cancer, she was busy with the business. They owned White Glove Linens on Route 571 in Princeton. White Glove supplied and laundered tablecloths and napkins to almost every restaurant in the tristate area. Sotto Sopra hadn't been one of their biggest accounts, but it'd been one of their first. Savannah, David, Chandler, and I used to play hide-and-seek in the kitchen at the restaurant when he'd come with his dad every Monday to deliver a week's worth of clean cloths and pick up the dirty ones. And that's how we'd met Chandler, whom we loved right from the start.

His mother had been like me. She lost one pregnancy after another before Chandler finally came along, and his parents let him do pretty much anything he wanted, including starting his own brewing company in college, which was odd because he really didn't drink, but he liked science. He sold the beer at parties, which made him a kind of demigod and started him on the entrepreneurial track. When he graduated, he opened Chand Brewery in the old, run-down Victorian his parents bought for him in town. He kept it shabby for a while—orange carpets, linoleum flooring, and bad lighting. But when he and Odion got serious, they started a small import business in the garage and began working on the house almost every day. When they were done remodeling, the result was a cozy space I never wanted to leave.

Whenever I walked into the bottom floor, I got sort of happy to be there. Everything felt deliberate, from the wood floors with their worn patina to the gold gilded mirrors to the antique Louis IV couches in the waiting room. The wall was lined with pictures of Chandler, Odion, and Madelyn. The effect left me feeling cared for and loved.

"Cadence," Chandler said, coming around his old mahogany desk. He and Patrick were the only people who ever called me by my real name, and he'd been doing it for so long I didn't mind. It was sweet and old-fashioned, like him.

"Thanks for having me." I kissed him on the cheek. Chandler's bone structure was strong, almost Native American, and he had deep brown eyes that made me feel safe as hell.

He grinned. "Anything for my little sister." He used to call Savannah and me his little sisters and kept right on doing it after she was gone.

"You skipped one." I pointed to his oxford, where he'd missed a button.

"Oh," he said. "Without Odion, I'm a mess." I watched him rebutton. He couldn't match his socks, never mind an entire outfit; he was a horrible slob, and his jawline was rugged. "Do you mind eating here? Upstairs is messy."

"I like it down here. It's comfy." I set the chickpea dish I'd made the day before on his desk and sat in a squishy chair that sucked me in.

He reached into the bottom drawer of his cabinet and pulled out some paper plates, plastic forks, a stack of napkins, and two Dixie cups. A bottle of wine was on his desk.

"Lovely," I said, indicating the bottle. "That's my favorite kind of dessert."

"Italian." Chandler smiled. "David and Gabby are going to wish they hadn't blown us off."

"David's pissed and not talking to me, which is probably why he canceled last night."

"Oh yeah?"

I couldn't tell from this noncommittal answer if David had talked to him about what was bugging him or not. Chandler gave us each a plate and uncorked the wine. I studied a photo of him and Odion with Madelyn on the desk. He poured the wine into our Dixie cups.

"I met Dog Breath—I mean Emma—for coffee last week because David is dying to find out why she left him."

Chandler tilted his head. "And?"

I opened the tinfoil and passed him a piece of naan. I always had the feeling Chandler knew exactly why Emma had bailed. "She said if he wanted to know, he should have asked her." I took a bite of naan, which was still warm from when I'd heated it in the oven before I left.

Chandler watched me. His cell phone rang on his desk, a snippet from a Lumineers song. He didn't answer it. "So," he said, sitting in front of his lunch, "she thinks you shouldn't have done his bidding for him?"

I could tell from the tone of his voice that he agreed with her.

"You know what, Chand? Our lives pretty much went to hell 5,974 days ago when our sister got murdered. David not being able to talk to his wife is the least of our problems."

He dug into his lunch with a plastic fork. "She was your sister too," he said. "And look at you. You're okay."

I rolled my eyes. "I'm thirty-two years old, fifty pounds overweight, and I hate my husband. What about that screams well adjusted?"

He pointed a manicured finger at me, a contradiction to his appearance. "That, right there. You're still funny and happy." He paused. "And, honey, fifty pounds is such a fucking overstatement I'm not even going to touch it." He wiped his mouth with his napkin. "You found a way to live through your pain with your work. David's just living around it."

"He's a guy," I said. "That's what guys do, isn't it?"

"Maybe." Chandler quit eating. "Why don't you ask him?"

"Ask him what?"

He took a sip of wine from his Dixie cup. "Don't you see it would be much easier if you two actually talked?"

"Fuck. Now you sound like Emma." I realized I wasn't really tasting my chickpeas; I was shoveling them in my mouth hoping the conversation would take a turn for the better. "We talk all the time. Why do you think I spent a morning having coffee with Emma?"

"You talked to Emma," Chandler pointed out, "not David. And now instead of asking him about his pain, you show up here and ask me."

"Okay, okay," I said. "I'll ask him." But I was not at all sure I would.

"Speaking of directness," Chandler said. "How about some total honesty?"

That meant he wanted to ask a question, and I had to tell the truth, no matter what.

"What?"

"Is there something going on with you and Brady?"

I tried to think of something to say. A million lies flashed in my mind, but there was no bullshitting Chandler. He always could see through me. Plus, we weren't allowed to lie during total honesty.

"I'm completely crushed out." There. I said it.

"Thought so. Odion owes me ten dollars."

"Oh God. You guys bet on it? Was David in on it?"

"Good lord, no. You know your brother. Dear, sweet boy, but never one to think outside the box."

"Or someone inside my box."

"You naughty girl." He raised his eyebrows at me. "Did you two ever?"

"No, I'm married," I said indignantly. "First Gabby, now you? Am I the only one here with a conscience?"

"Sugar, a conscience only comes into play when you're doing something wrong. And if that man of yours treated you a little better, then we'd have something to talk about. Until then, I think you should do whatever"—he grinned—"or whoever makes you happy."

"It doesn't matter, anyway. He has a girlfriend." I thought about Brady coming home from the prison, still in his uniform, and eating dinner with Colette. For the first time, I wondered how much money he made. "Do you think Brady likes me because of my work?" I asked.

"What do you mean?"

"The money."

Chandler watched me. "No," he said, and it was so definite it surprised me. "It's something else."

"What?" I said. "Tell me. You think a guy like that would never be interested in me?"

Chandler stared at me. "It seems like he's trying too hard to make you like him. It's a little, I don't know, desperate."

I felt heat rise into my neck. "I guess I sort of like it." I wouldn't have admitted this to anyone but Chandler. Except maybe Gabby. I thought of Greg in bed at night, going through patient files, hardly even noticing me lying right next to him. "Sometimes it feels good not to be ignored."

Chandler's eyes got soft. "Aw, honey, why stay?"

"Because you're gay." We laughed. "And I'm fat."

His laugh disappeared. "You're not fat," he said. "You're beautiful."

And for one stinging moment, I thought I might cry. "Thanks, Chand."

He reached over and squeezed my hand.

When we were done eating and he had fed me some fabulous French chocolates and we'd thrown away all our paper products, Chandler walked me to the door.

"Now go talk to your brother." He squeezed my neck. "For once."

"Okay," I told him, and I kissed him on each cheek.

But when I got to the car, I noticed Patrick had called. Twice. "What's up?" I said when he answered.

"Hello." He laughed. "How are you?"

It had started to rain, and as I pulled out of the driveway, I put my wipers on. "Sorry," I said. "My social graces go right out the window when I'm anxious."

"Fisher's out," he said.

"What does that mean?" I passed Cookies and the courthouse and was about three blocks from the precinct.

Patrick drew in a quick, hard breath. "It means your sister's case is officially out of cold storage. Caritano and I want to go over it again with you."

"Does now work? I'm five minutes away." I pulled over at Stanwich Savings and Loan so I could turn back toward the police station.

"How about a week from Monday?"

"As in ten days from now?" I couldn't stand the thought of having to go that long without knowing exactly what was happening.

"I'm sorry, Cady. I don't mean to leave you hanging." I could hear a beeping in the background as if his car door were open. "But I'm actually on my way out of town."

I pictured a tiny blond girl in the passenger seat, bags packed, ready for a vacation in Bermuda or Jamaica. "Oh, sorry. Next Monday is fine."

"Thanks. I've been signed up for this school safety training seminar for months."

"No worries." I caught my smile in the rearview.

Patrick hesitated. "Okay," he said. "But, Cady?"

"Yeah?"

"I don't think you're going to like what we have to say. It's . . ." I heard him searching for a word. "Difficult and—"

"I'm okay," I interrupted. "I'm ready for anything."

But in fact, driving through Stanwich in the pouring rain, I had that strange feeling I used to get in high school, before they sent me to Sound View, that the earth was spinning at an alarmingly fast rate, and everyone seemed to be able to keep their feet on the ground, and I was the only one who was about to get thrown off.

On my way home, I thought of calling someone and talking about the good news—Gabby or Chandler or David or even my parents. But I knew not everybody approved of the silent vigil I held for Savannah. Gabby occasionally quoted some unknown philosopher about the importance of moving on. Chandler had said once while we were up late watching an '80s movies marathon that maybe it was best to let some things go. But *St. Elmo's Fire* had been on, and all I could think of was that finding Savannah's killer was like what Kirby thought of Dale Biberman. It was the meaning of life. My life. And even though my parents had played like they had moved on, right up until they went to Saint Augustine, there had been five place mats set at their dining room table.

CHAPTER
14

My period was late. I lay in bed Wednesday morning feeling achy and wanting to stay there and watch Showtime reruns all day. But because I didn't want to loll around getting my hopes up, I showered. Even if I was pregnant, there wasn't any guarantee it would stay put. "You're perfectly healthy," Dr. Hansen had said. And so had the two specialists I'd been to for second and third opinions. "It must not be the right time," one of them told me. And then she put me on a regimen of vitamins that made my breath smell. When none of the experts had an explanation for why I kept miscarrying, I couldn't help thinking it was because the baby was waiting for us to figure out our marriage.

I was thinking about calling Greg on his cell phone at work so there was no chance I'd have to talk to Annika. Maybe I could tell him I was sorry, even though I wasn't, and we could be done with this teenage bullshit of ignoring each other because of some stupid fight about cheese. But it was so much more than that. Just as I found a good place to take a break from *Devils and Dust*, Deanna called.

"I found a serial killer," I told her.

"Well," she said briskly. "Hallelujah. But *Vanity Fair* has an assignment, which I already told them you'd take. A feature."

"What? But you know I'm on deadline. Why would you do this to me?" I actually liked magazines. I loved the short efficiency of knowing I had only a few thousand words to tell what could be a book-length story. I liked the busyness of fact-checking. But I didn't have time for any of that now.

"Relax, Zippy," she said, dismissing me. "It's a four-thousand-word piece about a hypnotist. You'll be able to bang it out in a day. Besides, it's *Vanity Fair*. It'll be good exposure for *Devils*."

And there it was, the real reason she was dumping this on me.

It never did me any good to argue with her. She always bullied me into taking on extra work.

"A hypnotist?" I sighed.

"World renowned. He's at Princeton this semester." Deanna started talking fast like someone had a gun to her head. "He hypnotized celebrities in Europe in the seventies, but his claim to fame is that he was friends with Altman and Steven Meisel and all the other big names. Mainly, he helped directors get their film actors off drugs, so really he knew them all, and now he's settled down with Anita Pallenberg—or so they say. You'll have to find out. I'll send you the assignment, and you can get started. Good luck with your serial killer," she said. And then she hung up.

I stared at the phone. Hypnosis. I thought about that strange period I had gone through in high school, the razor blades and sharp objects like silent sweet friends that made the pain go away. "What did it feel like?" Dr. Holley at Sound View used to ask me. *Like getting hypnotized*, I'd think, but because I didn't want to sabotage myself with wrong answers, I'd kept my mouth shut.

My e-mail pinged, and there was a message from one of the senior editors at *Vanity Fair*, full of superlatives, how happy they were to have me back, and what a fun assignment this was, and how wonderful this hypnotist was, and as I was scrolling through his pictures with Jane Fonda in the 1970s, I thought how much I never wanted to get hypnotized. I'd rather meet face-to-face with a serial killer than let go of reality in the presence of a stranger.

CHAPTER
15

"I think Emma is right." Gabby's fingernails were painted bright blue. She was smoking a cigarette and trying to maneuver us around town in her tiny MG ragtop she'd bought from a crazy used-parts guy in Trenton.

"Right about what? Jesus, I thought you were going to make me feel better, not take her side." Stanwich passed by with its striped awnings and town circle.

Gabby ashed her cigarette out the crack in the window. "Maybe you should talk a little more. To David. To your parents. Maybe even to Greg." She turned down the radio. "Have you ever thought about therapy?"

"Oh God." I groaned and closed my eyes. "I'm married to a shrink. Doesn't that count?" Greg had tried to get me to go to couples therapy after the miscarriages started. "As far as my brother and parents go, what's there to talk about? We lost someone we loved. And now we're sad. End of story. And you know what Greg's problem is."

A light in front of us turned from yellow to red. Gabby sped through it. When we were past the intersection, I saw Kate and Missy Turkit, sisters who had gone to our high school, outside of Khaki and Black on Main, and I remembered Missy had been one of Emma's best friends. I couldn't get away from her.

"I guess I do, and that's my point. Your husband isn't supposed to be a dick because you started making more money than he does." Gabby ran her fingers through her curls. "Maybe a therapist could help him get his head out of his ass and be thankful for such a great girl."

"Or get his head out of his receptionist's ass." I smirked. "I know I should want to go to counseling, but I had so much therapy at Sound View, I think I'm set for life." I watched Emma's friends get smaller and smaller in the side-view mirror. "Anyway, you hate Greg."

She blew smoke out her nose. "I know, but I love you. And since you won't divorce him, you might as well try to fix him."

I couldn't talk about Greg anymore. "You do know smoking is bad for you, right?"

She held the cigarette out in front of her. "It helps me not eat, and the lighter I am, the more liable I am to win the Hoka Hey."

"Eat," I told her. "Eating keeps you alive. Smoking kills you."

She honked her horn at a Walmart truck. "Is Brady coming tonight?" she asked. When the truck moved over, she smiled at the driver.

"He only came to that one dinner. I'd feel weird asking him to another." I wiped steam from the front window. "But he did find a serial killer for me to interview." I leaned back in my seat. I didn't want to tell her that I'd seen him again, that he'd shown up at Ravenswood and spent an afternoon with Bliss and me. I felt like by keeping it to myself, it made it more intimate, more real.

Gabby mashed her cigarette in the ashtray. "Your job sounds terrifying," she said. "I'm glad I'm a librarian."

We turned onto Chandler and Odion's street, and their proud, blue Victorian came into view.

"If I go to therapy, no one is going to understand about Savannah," I said.

"Then don't talk about her," Gabby said. "There's a lot more to your life than her."

As we turned into the drive, I had the swift knowledge that this wasn't exactly true. There really wasn't anything about my life that didn't in some way connect to my sister, and for that reason, Gabby was probably right. Maybe therapy was in order.

I'd changed my clothes three times before Thursday dinner. I wasn't trying to impress anyone, but I was feeling especially fat. The long, brown skirt and silk top I'd tried on first made me look like one of those root beer barrel candies, all round and shapeless. The denim overalls I'd worn for a night of board games when I was in college would have been perfect if I were painting a house. Finally, I'd pulled on a pair of elastic-waistband khaki capris and a pink sweater. Then I'd filled my travel mug with extra-hot cider and gotten in Gabby's car. And now I realized it didn't matter what I wore; this was one of the only places I felt completely at home.

The bottom floor of their house was their showroom and offices. The top floor was where they lived. They'd blown out walls and renovated with recessed ceiling lights, crown molding, and Carrara marble countertops. They'd thrown down antique rugs and moved in some bleached-white slipcovered couches you could sink into. There was a fire in the fireplace when we got there, and it smelled like they'd been cooking for hours. Rosemary and thyme filled the air.

"Bonjour, my beautiful guests," Odion said, meeting us at the door and giving us down slippers.

We left our shoes by an umbrella stand and put them on.

"You ladies had better love a good Bordeaux, because Odion brought it all the way from France on his last import trip," Chandler called.

"Twist my arm," Gabby said. "I love France."

Suzanne Vega was playing on the radio, and Odion ushered us inside and pulled out a couple of leather stools from the bar. Chandler kissed our cheeks and put goat-cheese-stuffed figs in front of us.

"Where's David?" I asked. Of course, even after my lunch with Chandler, I hadn't called my brother.

Odion turned away to uncork the wine, and Chandler kept his back to me, moving something around in the frying pan. "Not sure if he's going to make it," he said.

I frowned, and Gabby took a sip of wine. "Oooh," she said. "More of this deliciousness for us."

"Should we call him?" I asked. "This is two weeks in a row he's missing."

But I knew why he was staying away. He was still pissed at me about Emma. Chandler was right. It wasn't going to get better until I told David why I saw her even though he didn't want me to.

Chandler slid a few sweet potato slices onto a pretty butter plate in front of me. "Do as you wish, princess."

But for some reason, I had a funny feeling about it, and I didn't.

Instead, I let David recede. I let Emma recede. We didn't talk about Brady or Greg. We sat around the table passing poached asparagus with lemon and candied mandarin Cornish game hens and wine and finally port and truffles. Then we lounged in front of the fire and quizzed Odion on his flash cards for his upcoming citizenship test. Chandler got out his atlas, and we traced Gabby's Hoka Hey route and asked her a million questions. We were nervous for her, overprotective aunties, but Gabby wasn't worried, and July seemed so far away. Plus Chandler had gone to the grocery store and gotten a stack of tabloid magazines, and there were charades to play about three-headed siamese twins and Alec Baldwin's pregnancy.

By the time Gabby and I got out to the MG, it was past midnight, and she said she was too drunk to drive. She crawled into the passenger seat of her cold car and immediately curled up in a ball and went to sleep. I was left to drive the MG through the quiet town of Stanwich, thinking how amazing it was that Gabby still had such a trust in the world, even after her best friend's twin sister was killed so mysteriously when she was sixteen. She still wanted to drive off with hundreds of bikers across Indian territory during the Hoka Hey.

I passed Stanwich's town hall, dark now, save a single lamppost near the flagpole, past the library and the Congregational church and the quaint boutiques and eateries. The quietude and stillness reminded me of those months in the wake of Savannah's murder when Fisher had mandated a curfew in our town. It was as if the grim reaper had arrived and haunted the place at night, clearing the sidewalks after 9:00 P.M. so that walking home from a school game or a friend's house made you suspect.

And then fifteen months after Savannah was killed, Gabby had called me and said to get outside. It was close to ten, and the whole town had been shut down for an hour. I went out to the front porch. A little while later, my parents came out. David was the last to join us. It seemed some kind of informal, unplanned telephone chain had been devised, because all down our block of little colonials, there were people outside, watching.

No matter where you were standing in town, you would have seen the flames shooting up. Stanwich is mostly flat, but the Wolfe Mansion had been built on a hill, and so it seemed the flames were lording over us, sent by some mysterious god to move us all to hushed awe. The house where Savannah had been killed burned to the ground while the town of Stanwich watched. It was too cold to spread, they said later. Too much snow on the ground to move the fire anywhere but up. No one knew who started it.

As I stood on the porch, hugging myself for warmth, I thought about all the afternoons I'd come home and found my mother alone in the kitchen going through her recipe book. She had thousands, recipes she'd created after having a similar dish in a restaurant or dreaming about pork chops with a fig reduction or new ways to serve sugar snap peas.

"Where's Dad?" I used to ask.

With one pencil tucked behind her ear and another between her teeth, she often seemed not to hear me. When I'd opened my mouth to ask again, she'd hold up one long finger to shush me. I'd never seen anyone focus the way she could. She'd redo a recipe a hundred times, first with basil and then thyme, cilantro, and a dozen other spices before she'd switch to different kinds of salt and pepper, white, gray, pink. There'd be twenty glass bowls lining the counter, each with half a cup of gazpacho that tasted the same to me, but she insisted each one embodied its own distinct flavor.

Finally, she'd lift her gaze. The way her lips were mashed into one tight line answered my question. My father was at the house. She'd check her watch and then go back to flipping pages. "He's been gone an hour."

My dad had spent the first year after Savannah's murder at the house where she died. Every day, he filled a thermos with coffee as black and thick as mud and sat by the front door of the creepy, abandoned house in a folding canvas chair. He said it made him feel close to her, to sit where she'd last been alive and read to her or talk, as if she might answer him. Or maybe he thought the murderer would come back. Either way, now the Wolfe Mansion was burned down. And my father would never be able to go there again.

The day after the fire, I'd been trying to focus on an experiment in chemistry when I heard Layton Barnhill, one of the detectives' kids, tell his lab partner that there were no fingerprints now. Nothing to go by. No sign that anything had ever been there. "Not even Savannah Martino," he'd said. And because I couldn't help it, I turned around. A slight boy with a lisp who played Dungeons & Dragons at lunch, he was forever pushing up a pair of square, smudged glasses. He had ducked his head. "Sorry," he said. And I had turned around again. Gabby was absent that day, so I didn't have a lab partner, and no one volunteered. I wasn't sure if I alienated everyone or if

people kept a wide berth. It hardly seemed to matter. I'd touched my necklace with the backwards *f* and wondered if the matching one had burned in
the woods that night or if maybe it was still in someone's closed fist.

Now I turned onto Broad Street, where the huge old colonials of the town's
forefathers still stood. Gabby lived on the top floor of what had once been a
rectory for a now defunct church. I parked in front of her place, and before
reaching over to wake her, I saw how much like a little girl she resembled,
her long lashes making shadows on her tanned cheeks, one curl falling across
her forehead.

"Hey," I said. And she woke up as if the world had been waiting for
only her.

She stretched in her suede coat and kissed me on the cheek, her dark
eyes bright. "We're here," she said happily. "But how will you get home?"

"My car's here." I pointed to the Volvo. "Remember?"

"Oh yeah." She kicked open her door. "The minitank." She laughed, and
I handed her the keys. "I love ya, girl," she told me.

"I love you too," I said, and then I got out of her tiny car, climbed into
my Volvo, and headed home.

CHAPTER
16

I'd been going to David's a couple times a week to do his laundry and clean, but I was still getting static from Deanna to finish my fifth golden cow or cash goose or whatever she called my books. So I met a Merry Maids consultant at David's when he was out, got an estimate for weekly cleanings, and then left a bunch of messages saying I was hiring someone, but I hadn't heard back from him. That and him missing the last two dinners could only mean that my bitchy sorority girl of an ex-sister-in-law told him that I talked to her. And he was pissed. But I knew that already.

My family had a few things in common. We never forgot anything, and we held grudges. Depending on how mad he was, I wouldn't have been surprised if David skipped the next year of Thursday dinners, so I ambushed him at his house in the middle of the afternoon, when I knew he'd be working. I'd already gotten the first invoice from Merry Maids, so at least he'd be home in clean sweats while he wrote code for the video games he was creating. As I was about to push open his door and call out, he swung it open as if he'd known I was coming. His gray eyes had gone dark.

"You shouldn't have talked to her, Cady. Why can't you ever leave anything alone?"

His anger surprised me. "You said you wanted a reason why she left."

Behind him, I saw the TV was off. For once. "I got one." Even while he worked, *Emeril Live* or *Kitchen Nightmares* was usually blaring in the background.

"Why? For your next book? Did you run out of stories about murdered brothers and runaway sisters?" He'd never lashed out at me like this before. He was my early reader, the one person who could tell me what worked and what didn't. He'd loved all my books.

"David." I took a step back. "What is the matter with you?"

"And thanks for the fucking merry pranksters moving all my shit around and making me feel like I'm in an alien invasion." He turned around and headed into the living room, so I took it as an invitation and followed.

I automatically leaned down to clear the couch, but it was clean. A load of gaming magazines was neatly stacked on the bottom shelf of the coffee table. As I sat on the arm, I noticed the olive-green cushions had been cleaned. I didn't know if David's new maid was in fact merry, but she certainly was good.

"Why are you so pissed? I thought I was doing you a favor."

He let out all his breath and sat. "I can't talk to you about it."

"You're joking, right?"

But I thought about what Chandler had said. David did a bang-up job being my confidant on matters of which housemate I should sleep with senior year in college (none of them), whether I should try shooting heroin, just once, so that I could get in the head of a drug-addicted character (too risky), and if I had to tell Gabby when I saw her old boyfriend kissing someone else at a downtown bar when we were in our twenties (absolutely), but there was one thing we never talked about, and I didn't think it was going to happen now. But I heard what Chandler had said at lunch, and I realized I wanted to try.

"Let it go." His voice was cold with warning.

"Whatever happened with Emma or whatever is going on with you, you can tell me."

He put his head in his hands. Tiny white flakes dotted his dark hair. I wondered if I could send the Merry Maid on a shopping trip. Origins sold a great all-natural dandruff shampoo.

"I know more about your sex life than I'm willing to admit," he said. "You've made a strong argument again and again why there should be more plus-size models. I know that you think Cris Collinsworth and Bob Saget are the same person."

"Have you ever seen them in a room together?" That didn't even get a smile out of him.

"But what is the one thing we never talk about?"

"Savannah," I said. "All this is about Savannah. So Emma wasn't bullshitting me the other day? She left you because of our sister?"

David stopped. "Did she actually tell you that? Did she finally admit that our family history was too much to explain to her fucking sorority sisters and that people still hate her because her father, the *chief*, closed the case?"

I was quiet for a moment. "She said we don't deal with anything." And all at once, I saw him as a little boy again, that sort of sorry expression he used to have right after he got in trouble.

He stared out the kitchen window at a bright-red bird on a branch. "I don't know why I love her so much," he said. "I mean, it's Emma, right? I know she's not the greatest. She's sort of a pain in the ass and a princess. So why do I care?" He stuffed his hands in his pockets. "What's wrong with me?"

"You don't shower enough," I said.

That got a half smile out of him.

"And you should wash your sheets and throw away your pizza boxes and start going to the gym and quit rotting your mind on video games. You should probably get a nose job while you're at it and a haircut and brush your teeth."

Then he started laughing, and I laughed with him. And when we were done, David said, "I was so pissed at you for meeting her because, I don't know, I guess I'm ashamed."

I thought again of what Chandler had said. "That I went instead of you?"

"No, that Emma is right. We can barely speak our sister's name aloud, never mind talk about what happened to her. And then to us."

CHAPTER 17

"Cady." Patrick was in jeans and a T-shirt, his face clean shaven, a razor nick on his chin. He reached out his hand and I took it, surprised at how good it felt to touch him, how familiar was his smell of coffee and lemon soap.

"Thanks for coming in," Detective Caritano said.

"No problem," I told him. The week felt like it had dragged by.

He rubbed the stubble on his chin. "Have a seat." He pulled out a chair for me, and I sat at the table where I saw they'd placed a small microphone. "So we don't forget anything." Jon Caritano smiled. "Coffee?"

I held up my hand to indicate I didn't want any.

Patrick sat down next to me and grinned. Out the window, the rain kept on as it had for most of a week, sliding down the pane in gray streaks. "How's the book coming?"

"Slowly. I finally found a key piece to my research, though."

Patrick's eyebrows shot up.

"I needed to talk to a murderer, to really understand how they think. I never thought it would happen, but I finally got one." I smiled despite the fact that I was trying not to. "Added bonus. He's a serial killer."

"Jesus Christ," Caritano said. He adjusted the microphone.

Patrick's voice was intense. "Who is it?"

My neck flushed, and I suddenly wished I hadn't said anything. "Oh, just someone a guard at the South Jersey Pen hooked me up with."

Patrick leaned forward, and he put one of his huge hands on the table. "There's only one serial killer at that prison."

"Yeah. I know." I felt like he was going to yell at me.

"Cady," he said again, his voice urgent. "We need to talk about this."

Jon had started to speak, and I really didn't want Patrick or anyone to try to talk me out of interviewing Larry Cauchek, so I put my hand up to stop him.

"I can't talk about it," I said. "I promised them I wouldn't."

"So . . ." Jon smiled at Patrick, maybe asking permission to get back to why they'd called me. "Patrick told me all about you, and he thinks now that we can bring this case up from the basement, you might be able to help us. I know this is difficult for you, so we'll go slowly."

"You don't think this was some random killing done by a sociopath on his way through town," I said.

They both studied me.

Finally, Jon spoke. "This is what we've come to know. Whoever killed your sister cared about her. I've never said anything before now because I couldn't prove it, and frankly, the politics around this case were hell."

"Politics?" I asked. Patrick and Jon exchanged glances. "What does that mean?"

Caritano sighed and undid the buttons on his cuffs. "Cady, there are things we can talk about here and others that we can't discuss. One of them is Captain Fisher and the way he ran the department."

Patrick drew his eyes up to mine. "We need to focus on your sister," he said quietly. "The mur— The crime scene is not exactly what it seemed."

"It's okay," I said. "You can say *murder*. My sister was murdered. I know that."

"There was something about the murder scene that . . ."

He paused and studied the middle distance between us. I did the same thing when I was writing and couldn't think of the exact right word.

"That didn't quite add up," he finally said.

Was he fucking with me? "What?"

He held up his hand. "I know, and I'm sorry. But there are things that didn't make sense. She'd been bound, but her hair was still in its braid. And her assailant took the time to remove whatever he'd used in the attack. In some ways, it didn't look like she'd struggled." He was talking fast. "It didn't seem as though she'd tried to escape. She was still wearing a sweater and skirt, but her underpants had been removed. Yet there was no sign of penetration." He quit talking. "Shit," he said quietly. "This isn't going to be easy."

"It's hard to fight when you're being choked," I said. "Maybe he used a condom and she thought that if she let him rape her, he'd leave her alone after." I turned to Patrick. His green eyes turned serious. "Savannah was a hundred pounds with all her clothes on. There's no way she could have over-powered anyone." Patrick got up and took three bottles of water out of a minifridge in the corner.

Jon's voice was low, almost apologetic. "Cady, people either run or fight when they're attacked. They freeze, yes, but only after running or fighting fails. It doesn't seem like Savannah tried to do either."

"So you're saying it was her fault? She didn't fight hard enough? She didn't scream loud enough?" I could feel myself losing control, wanting to get up and strike Jon Caritano for blaming my sister for her murder. "Was her skirt too short? Did she have it coming?"

Patrick passed out the waters and sat down.

Caritano spoke. "No, not at all. Of course this wasn't Savannah's fault. It's never the victim's fault. But you have to understand—"

"But I don't understand! I don't understand how someone could murder a sixteen-year-old girl and get away with it." I was trying to stay calm, trying to remind myself that Patrick and Jon were the good guys. The ones who cared enough to open a case that had been all but forgotten more than fif-teen years before.

"Listen," Caritano said. "Oftentimes, the police will make a choice to keep information from the public so they can search without the perpetrator know-ing he's under suspicion. Perps tend to get sloppy when they think we're on the wrong track."

Patrick leaned over and turned off the microphone. "The truth is, Cap-tain Fisher didn't want to focus on this case. He wanted it to die down. He wanted the town to believe it was a frenzied stranger attack, not someone who lived here. Captains get reelected when the town believes they are safe. If it was someone who lives here—"

I got up. I could feel that strange sensation in my veins, as if the blood was jumping, the same one I used to feel in the months after Savannah was murdered, a fiery restlessness.

Caritano watched me pace. "We told the town it was a crime of opportunity. We made them believe everyone was safe. But we continued the search for what we call a friendly perp, and when none turned up"—he showed me his hands—"they closed the case."

A white rage blurred my vision. "Did you know this, Patrick?" He kept his gaze on the table. "Did you?"

Finally, he lifted his head, and his eyes met mine. "Yes," he said.

"And you never told me?"

"You were a kid, Cady, and kids talk."

"I wouldn't have told anyone."

"I know," said Patrick. "But that's what he was worried about."

"That changes the whole fucking profile." I felt caged, empty, as though I'd been carved out.

They exchanged a look I couldn't quite identify. Shame? Regret?

"Yes," Jon said. "It does. And we feel badly about this. We realize you've been barking up the stranger tree for years, and in truth, we should have told you well before this that we thought it was someone Savannah knew. But Fisher was at the helm, and we've never been able to prove our theory, so what was the point? Fisher's opinion was that community is important here. You start pointing fingers, and a town can fall apart."

I sat back in my chair and crossed my arms over my chest. "So you lied," I said.

I was thinking about my dreams. Not the ones where Savannah came to me with a message, a missive, but the ones where I might be seeing her killer. And then, although they said it was impossible, I saw a shadow on the other side of the one-way mirror. Were we being watched? Did they bring in a profiler to gauge my reaction, search my expression for clues? If they were convinced that whoever killed my sister may have loved her, was I now a suspect? All the research I'd ever done said that the person who calls in the crime usually committed it. I even knew where to find her. All this time, I'd thought they'd believed that I shared something with Savannah, an internal GPS, an emotional current that kept us connected. But maybe now they thought I held down my skinnier, prettier twin and choked her.

"I need to ask you both a question. Why are you reopening the case? My parents moved away. David and I aren't pressuring you. I doubt the new chief of police will want the headache of stirring everything up again. So why are you doing it?"

Patrick got up and came around the table. He stood for a moment, towering over me, before he sat down. "Because certain cases are meant to be solved. For some people, the burden of a secret is too much. It's been my experience that perps want to confess. Especially when they're people like you and me."

By the time I got home, the rain had let up, and darkness was falling. One light was on in the living room, and Greg was sitting on the couch. He had his feet up on the coffee table, and he was wearing suede slippers. I stood in the living room doorway.

"Hey," I said.

His hair was messy, as if he'd run his hands through it a bunch of times. "Hey," he told me.

I sat next to him with my back to the windows. For once, he was relaxing. He wasn't standing on his head in a yoga asana, reading a patient's file, ordering wine from some vineyard in Napa, or making plans to go to Lincoln Center.

"Sorry about the cheese," I said. That fight seemed so long ago, I felt stupid apologizing now, weeks later.

He rested his head against the back of the couch. "Long day?"

I thought of Patrick in the interview room, the strange way I felt being back there, how that whole horrible time came flooding back. "Weird day," I said. "Yours?"

"It was all right. Don't be mad, but I found a therapist for us," he said. "Nice guy. I think you'll like him."

I felt something like hope rise in me, and I had a quick, sweet vision of Greg and me before the bestsellers and the miscarriages, when he was still in medical school and I was still writing for Condé Nast glossies. Blueberries in bed and sleeping till ten, watching old movies and giving each other massages before we fell asleep.

"When do we meet him?"

"Wednesday," he said. "At lunch."

That he would schedule therapy during lunch when he might have a chance to be with Annika made the hope bloom harder.

"That sounds good," I told him.

"What was weird about your day?" he asked. I could have told him about meeting with Patrick and Jon Caritano, how the cold case was out of storage and Fisher was officially gone, but instead, I said, "My period is late."

There was only a moment's hesitation before he reached over and took my hand. His felt familiar, that same odd knuckle on the second finger, the calluses in the tips from playing instruments all his life. I kept it on my lap and ran my thumb around the palm. And as twilight moved in, I saw Savannah watching us from the keys of the Underwood across the room, looking so alive it seemed like she might step out of the picture.

CHAPTER
18

I was supposed to be researching the hypnosis article for *Vanity Fair*, but I didn't have time for it, and I'd called Deanna once to try to get out of it. "You're the perfect author for this, honey." Deanna called me *honey* when she was feeling desperate. I'd been silent on the phone. And finally, she said, "Over two million readers, Cady. Do I have to spell it out? What's the problem? You can crank this out in twenty-four hours."

Out the south window, a woodpecker was drilling into an old maple. I admired him, banging his head against something again and again until he got what he wanted. I hadn't been able to work on *Devils* or the article all morning. I was completely stuck. Instead, I studied the photos on the walls of my office. Savannah was in every one, of course. She was the reason I wrote my books; having her around me was essential. Seeing her everywhere somehow made me think about the time she ran away from home when we were eleven. David was thirteen, and our parents had let him go to a PG movie she'd wanted to see. I couldn't remember now what the movie was. But when they told her she was too young, she put four tubes of lip gloss, a hairbrush, her Walkman, and an INXS tape in her backpack, crawled out our window, and headed to Linda Smyth's house. Linda's parents were divorced, and her mother was always out somewhere—sleeping with men, we suspected. It was the perfect place to go if you were dying to be bad.

Savannah's timing had been off. It was already dark and had started to rain hard before she got to the privacy hedges surrounding our yellow colonial. She'd sneaked back in the side door and was halfway up the stairs, cold and wet, before our parents stopped her. I remember how her hair dripped on the carpet, silently listening as my mom told her David had more privileges because he was older and breaking the rules was not going to get her what she wanted. My father cleared his throat. "It's dangerous," he'd motioned to the window, "out in the dark. At your age." I'd been standing in the doorway of our room, watching them, and I'd seen Savannah make the decision to cry. It came over her face like a veil. As soon as the first tear fell, our parents backed off.

Later that night, we lay in bed, listening to the rain on the roof, watching it fall in rivulets down the windowpane. "You awake?" she'd asked.

"Yeah."

She hadn't unpacked her bag, and it was on the floor at the bottom of her bed, a hulking shape that for some reason scared me in the dark. "I hate being pent up in this house. Obeying all their rules." She'd turned her head, and in the glow from the night-light, she appeared featureless, a silhouette. "I'd run away if I could." She turned back to the window. "I'm not afraid."

I'd said nothing, just kept my eyes on that constant rain. But I'd felt stung, knowing she didn't mean to bring me with her. She'd run away by herself. I hated that she would ever think about leaving me like that. When she'd packed her bag, she hadn't asked me to come. She'd known I wouldn't. I was too good.

"Look where it got you, Savannah banana," I said, now holding that picture of us on our first day of high school. "Maybe being good wasn't such a bad idea, after all."

CHAPTER
19

That week, I didn't work on *Devils*. I read everything I could find on Larry Cauchek, because although what I had said to Brady had sounded brave, I was actually terrified to sit face-to-face with a serial killer, and I thought knowing as much as I could about him might help. Patrick called the day after I met him and Jon at the police station and assured me of two things: Savannah's killer's MO didn't fit Cauchek's, and meeting with the notorious murderer was a spectacularly bad idea. Despite Patrick's warning and his almost begging me not to do this, I still insisted to Brady that I needed to meet this man. The time frame and location fit. Patrick couldn't tell me with absolute certainty that Cauchek hadn't killed my sister. So maybe he had.

I met Brady at Starbucks on Wednesday morning so he could brief me. He was wearing his prison guard uniform and looking sleepy and uniquely beautiful.

"You okay?" he asked. He had a gentle, deep voice that made me want to crawl inside of it and take a nap.

"Yeah," I said. "I'm fine."

He watched me. I couldn't meet his eyes, because I was lying. I was not fine. I was shaking inside. I studied his strong hands curled around his coffee cup.

"Don't say anything personal," he said.

"I'll try not to."

"Cady." He touched my hand.

"What?"

"Do *not* reveal anything personal." His hand was warm, and I wanted to hold it forever.

"Okay," I said.

Later, standing outside the door of a basement room with a guard whose name tag read Jacobs, waiting for Brady to lock Larry Cauchek's handcuffs to the table, I felt feverish, sweaty, like I get right before I'm going to throw up. Jacobs was bald with an uneven head and straight teeth, which I thought might be veneers. On our way in, he'd told me he was going to stand right outside the door. I didn't want him. I wanted Brady to be on watch, but there were a bunch of prison protocols I didn't understand. Brady opened the door. "You ready?"

"Yes." My voice sounded small, even to me.

Brady stared at me, and I didn't think I'd ever seen him like that. It was the same as when my father had taken the training wheels off our bikes. Like maybe we were going to flip over the handlebars and smack our faces, and he would have been a major part of making it happen.

"I'm fine," I said. I stepped in and heard the door close behind us.

The first thing I noticed when I walked in the room was that it was entirely one color, gray, and it was surveyed by a video camera in the upper-left corner. The barred window framed a patch of crabgrass and mud. Larry Cauchek was tethered to the far side of a steel table, more like the leader of the Young Republicans than a serial killer.

"Ms. Bernard," Brady said formally, as if we weren't friends. "Larry Cauchek." He put his hand on my shoulder. "Jacobs will be on the other side of the door. If you'd like him to stay inside, please let us know."

That stage fright feeling had arrived, the one I used to get before I cut myself, that feeling I was being strangled, suffocated. I fought it as best I could and said calmly, "I'm okay, thank you."

It occurred to me I'd get more out of Larry if I had him alone. His feet and arms were shackled, and he was far enough away so he couldn't bite me.

Brady backed away, and as I watched him, I could feel Larry's eyes on me. I wasn't ready yet. I needed a few more seconds to steady my breathing.

Brady pointed two fingers at his own eyes and then to Cauchek's face. *I'm watching you.* And I understood now that Jacobs would stand guard at the door, but Brady would view by video. I busied myself opening my notebook to a page with a list of questions and peeked at him: short, clean cut, his dark-blond hair combed neatly and parted on the side. I hated him, purely and thoroughly. Digging my favorite pen out of the bottom of my briefcase, I thought again of how he'd begun killing in Philly in the early '90s and worked his way up the East Coast until he was caught in 2000. He'd been convicted of seven murders, but the police believed there could have been more.

I finally lifted my gaze from the notebook. His black eyes bled like ink into the pupils, and he was staring, with unwavering concentration, at my throat.

"I know why you're here." The intensity of his tone unnerved me.

"Tell me." Patrick had said Cauchek would try to psych me out, pretend to know things about me.

He was sitting very straight, as though some phantom drill sergeant had brought him to attention. He blew air out of his nose the way a horse would. "I've read your books. I understand why you write them. I. Know. Your. Secret."

I put down my pen. My chest felt like there was a terrified bird trapped in it, frantic to get out. "You do?"

The flower tattoo on his wrist had seven petals. In each one was a letter. "First initial of each of his victims," Brady had told me. After I'd said I was set on interviewing Cauchek, he'd called me three times, relaying more information he'd learned from Cauchek's cellmate and two informants.

"You want to find the man who murdered your sister." Larry's voice was level, like a math teacher reciting equations. "Your books, your bestselling 'novels' "—he made quotation marks with his fingers—"they're a front."

I stared at him. I felt naked. We'd been in there two minutes, and he'd seen straight through me to something even my psychiatrist husband couldn't recognize.

"You don't write because you love it." He laid his hands on the table. His nails were perfectly trimmed, filed, buffed. "You do it because it's going to help you find the man who squeezed your sister until the light went out in her eyes." His eyes went to my neck again. "Without your books, you'd just be a grief-stricken sister playing amateur detective."

My breath was rushing out of me, but not in fear. It was exhilaration, some kind of odd freedom. No one had ever known why I really did this. He leaned forward, and I willed myself not to move away. His voice was robotic, a little hypnotizing.

"So what have you learned? In all this time, have you gotten any closer?" This animal whose expression never changed when the judge sentenced him to seven consecutive life sentences had exposed my biggest failure.

"Survivors blame themselves for dressing provocatively or staying out late. And offenders fall into two categories. Those who are sorry—"

He cut me off and lowered his gaze. "And those of us who aren't."

I'd heard of sociopaths, of people who had no conscience, but they'd been only vague shapes in my imagination like the devil, a concept to keep the rest of us on the straight and narrow. I leaned back in my chair. "So here I am, interviewing Lucifer."

He smiled, a welcome and a warning. "Don't be afraid, love. The devil was just a fallen angel. We all started out good, once." His voice was mesmerizing. His milky skin. I understood how those girls trusted him when they answered his ads. He'd been a child model and then acted as an agent of beautiful girls. He could have killed my sister. Larry loved beauty. Savannah had been beautiful.

"Even—"

He tried to put up a hand to stop me, but the metal chains jerked against his skin. "Even the man who delivered Savannah home." He finished my sentence.

"Is that what you did? Delivered those girls *home*?"

"Oh, heavens, no. I sliced them open from shoulder to opposite hip, just to see what was inside."

He showed me the tips of his teeth, and I saw they were slightly yellowed. That must have bothered him, having that imperfection.

"Too bad you got caught by a profiler." I said the last word like it was dirty. "Just when you thought you were going to get away with it."

"You're a live one. I like that." He leaned back, closing his eyes. A smile spread across his face, and I had the sickening feeling he was reliving his kills. "Let's play a game, shall we?" He opened his eyes wide.

"Truth or dare?"

"I was thinking something along the lines of you show me yours and I'll show you mine." He reminded me of Anthony Hopkins's character in *Silence of the Lambs.*

I stiffened my spine. "What do you want to know?"

"Did you see her? While she lay dying?"

I opened my mouth to say how much I hated him, what filth he was, when I realized that's what he wanted. He'd taunted the police, sending them photos of his victims, clues printed out on a label maker. He was baiting me now.

"No. I told the officer where to find her and that she was still alive, but I couldn't make myself see her like that."

"By *officer,* you mean Patrick." It hadn't occurred to me that he'd researched me too.

"My turn. What made you think you were smarter than Agent Walters?"

"Ah, the beautiful Samantha Walters. Profiler extraordinaire. I knew she'd catch me. I just didn't think it'd be till I was done. I never did get to finish." He made a carving motion with an imaginary blade.

"What do you mean, till you were done?"

"Eight is the perfect number. According to the Epistle of Barnabas, on the eighth day, Christ rose from the dead. Eight people were saved from the floods on Noah's ark. There are eighty-eight constellations and eight planets."

"So there was one more. Who was she?"

"Does that matter? They were all the same to me, begging for their lives, promising they wouldn't tell." He tapped the table with his pretty fingers. "The banality of it all kind of took the fun out of it."

For once, I was thankful for Greg and his ridiculous breathing techniques. Inhale through the nose, push it out through the mouth, count to ten. "How banal was it when they tricked you into coming to the police station?"

"Ah yes, the story they planted was pure brilliance. Too bad that reporter didn't live long enough to enjoy his stardom."

I wished they'd let me bring my phone, I would have pulled it out and

Googled the reporter's name. See if Cauchek was bluffing. I hadn't slept since Brady had told me about him reading all my books. I'd been too busy studying every article and interview I could find. I didn't remember seeing anything about Aaron Markson dying.

"You walked right into Agent Walters's trap."

He rolled his eyes. "That was rather amateurish of me, I'm afraid. But to be called mentally ill in the press was an insult. I couldn't have my girls' families believing that some drooling ninny who heard voices took their daughters, their sisters, their nieces from them. I had to set the record straight."

"Fuck the record," I said with confidence I didn't feel. "You had to take credit for your work, the meticulousness of your crimes, the forethought that went into the planning and execution, the exactness of the cleanup, how you never left any physical evidence."

Cauchek had no way of knowing the story had been a plant to draw him out.

"It was a spectacular sight. The entire task force: nine detectives, two undercover officers, another six plainclothes cops, Agent Walters, and three of her assistants were all waiting for me when I opened the glass doors of their precious police station."

"Did you know that she predicted you'd arrive at the precinct between two and three P.M., the time between getting off work and waiting for your kids to get off the bus?"

He lowered his eyes. An admission of defeat. Was he aware that Samantha Walters's uncanny ability to know things about criminals like him must have made it impossible for her to ever get a good night's sleep?

"Did you also know that when the surveillance team alerted the task force that your Dodge minivan, the exact vehicle Agent Walters had surmised the perp would drive, had pulled into the lot, a cheer erupted from within the station?"

"As soon as I stepped into the foyer and realized all the officers had their hands on their weapons, I knew I'd been beat."

"What were you going to do there if they hadn't been waiting for you?"

He drummed his fingers on the metal table, slowly, rhythmically. "What was it like? Touching your dead sister? You did touch her, didn't you?"

There was no question in the tone. Was he guessing that I needed to feel my sister's skin one more time before we buried her, or had he been there?

I had been alone in the morgue and could hear my mother crying outside the door when I'd finally convinced Dr. Bassett to let me in the room with her. Savannah's skin was perfect, like unspoiled cream.

"I wanted to crawl inside her and die." I had to give him what he wanted. An overweight, sad novelist was no match for a sociopath.

He seemed satisfied. Before I could stop myself, I blurted out the one question I told myself not to ask. "Why?" There was no answer he could give that would make me understand how he could take seven lives and destroy so many others, but I asked it, anyway. "Why'd you do it?"

He made a *tsking* noise and wagged his index finger at me. "Try again, love. You know that's the million-dollar question. That's what everyone wants to know, isn't it? Why I dissected those seven lovely lasses. You're going to have to give me something of great magnitude in return."

"Something made you do it." I could hear the desperation in my voice, and I was sure he could too.

"You're missing a very important piece to this puzzle that has confounded you for almost two decades."

I tried not to lean forward in anticipation. I had a quick vision of him confessing to killing my sister.

"But you're going to have to wait." He yelled loudly for Jacobs, and the heavy door swung open.

"What? No! You said you'd talk to me." I glanced at my watch. "You can't do this. You said you'd talk."

Jacobs freed Larry Cauchek's hands from the table. Still cuffed, he stood silently by the door, waiting to be led back to his cell. "I guess you'll have to come back to see me, love."

When he was gone, I waited for Brady to come in the door. As disappointed as I was that Cauchek had sent me away, I was still elated at my secret finally being told. I couldn't wait to talk to Brady about it.

Brady appeared from around the corner. "Let's go," he said to the floor.

"That was amazing," I said. "Thank you."

But he kept walking two steps in front of me. We got all the way to the front desk before he finally spoke.

"Come with me," he said.

"Okay," I told him. I was still shaking inside, as if I'd gotten very cold and couldn't warm up.

I followed him down the prison steps and into a cloudless day. As soon as we got outside, Brady turned around, and I saw his face was red, his eyes furious.

"That's the last time you ever get in a room with Larry Cauchek."

I took an involuntary step back. "Why? What do you mean?"

He pointed to the building. "What the fuck were you doing in there?"

"I thought I was interviewing a serial killer for my book."

Brady put his hand through his hair and started walking. Not knowing what else to do, I followed. I had to rush to keep up.

"What?" I said.

Every single part of his body was tight, pent up. "I told you nothing personal," he said when we reached the first row of cars. He turned around, not so much angry as confused, almost betrayed.

"I know, Brady. I'm sorry. It happened so fast, I—"

"Don't you see?" he interrupted. "Don't you fucking see?" He showed me his little finger. "That's how that son of a bitch got all those girls wrapped around his fucked-up pinkie."

I swallowed. "Okay," I said. "Listen, I'm safe. Nothing is going to happen to me in there. He's in shackles. He can't touch me."

"But, Cady, it's not your body I'm worried about." Behind him, a group of men came out of the prison. "It's your mind."

After Brady went back in, I sat in the driver's seat. It was a warm late-April day, and the sun beating in my window calmed me. Larry Cauchek was not what I had expected. Even though the newspapers stated that he was an articulate, handsome man, I'd expected a monster, someone who barely spoke, and when he did, it'd be in monosyllabic grunts. Someone dirty and unintelligent. But what scared me most of all about Larry Cauchek was that if he'd been in a suit and tie, he would have blended right in with bankers on Wall Street or dads at school conferences.

CHAPTER
20

After we met at the precinct, I didn't hear from Patrick Tunney again for three weeks. The morning he called, I was doing volunteer work at the rec center, packing lunches for Stay & Play, a family-owned indoor playground that sold homemade sandwiches and pudding cups to their patrons. I'd been in the prep kitchen since sunrise, cutting crusts off peanut butter and jelly sandwiches and stuffing juice boxes into brown paper bags when my cell phone rang. I didn't hear it because I had the radio so loud, but the screen lit up with *Det. Tunney* in bright letters across it.

"Detective Tunney." I wiped my sticky hands on the short white apron I'd taken from the linen closet. "Hang on a sec." Picking up the remote, I turned down an Arcade Fire song. "What's up?"

"I'm going to arrest you if you don't start calling me Patrick. You're making me feel old."

No matter how big he was, Patrick Tunney had never outgrown the boyishness he'd had about him the first time we met at the school.

"Okay, *Patrick*," I said. "Since prison stripes aren't flattering, I'll do as you say."

"On you, I bet they are," he said quietly.

I felt myself blush even though I was alone with two hundred snack packs of pretzels and carrot sticks.

His voice turned businesslike right away. "I'm sure you're busy, so I'll get right to it. I wanted to thank you for meeting with Jon and me. I know the stuff we told you is upsetting."

I thought about another Savannah dream I'd had the night before, and although I didn't believe in divine intervention, this seemed like a sign. "I'm glad you called," I blurted before I lost my nerve. "I need to talk to you about something."

I could hear his breath through the phone, slow and steady. "Is everything okay?"

I didn't know how to answer that. "Yes, but I need to see you again."

"It sounds important. Do you have time today?"

I checked my watch. "I'm at the rec center. If you don't mind packing lunches, I could talk to you now."

"I'll be there in a few," Patrick said. And then he signed off.

I ran to the bathroom to take inventory of myself. I hadn't showered that morning, knowing I was going to spend it alone among sticky, messy sandwiches, and I'd dressed in workout shorts, hoping it would motivate me to go for a run later. I'd been wearing gym clothes for years, and not once had it gotten me off my ass. Before I could even pull a comb through my hair, I heard footsteps and went out to see Patrick through the porthole window in the swinging kitchen door. I pushed it open. "How did you—"

His cheeks reddened, and I wondered which of us embarrassed more easily. "I called from the parking lot."

I fixed my hair with a bobby pin that had come loose and tried to smooth my T-shirt. "How did you know I wanted to see you?"

"A boy can hope, can't he?" We both flushed scarlet.

"But how—"

"I'm a detective." My eyes widened, and he quickly added, "I remember you mentioning your volunteer work when channel eight interviewed you."

"Here, come sit with me."

I took off the apron, tossed it on the stainless steel counter, and led him to a small table in the playroom. He sat across from me in his pressed shirt and a blue tie with hunting dogs on it. He was so broad the dogs appeared lost and tiny.

"Are you undercover in the banking world?" I asked.

He frowned in confusion and then followed my gaze to his shirt. "Oh, this?" He held up the tie. "I'm actually off today, just trying to look present-able."

"You passed with flying colors."

He clasped his hands together. They were huge. They could do anything from building a house to strangling a man.

"Patrick, I have to tell you something."

I'd had no intention of ever talking to anyone about my dreams, but after our meeting at the police station, I knew they were another piece to this puzzle. He had a hunch, a feeling about the original profile being wrong. Something that might not mean anything, but maybe it would. It was exactly the same as my dreams.

So I told him about them, how I'd been keeping a journal, how some seemed to mean something, and I was positive Savannah was pointing me toward a clue. "I had another dream last night," I told him. It'd been the clearest and most disturbing one yet. "She was still alive." I couldn't speak my sister's name out loud. Not now. "She was talking to me, but I couldn't hear her. There was too much noise, but she was so desperate for me to understand what she was saying."

"What was the noise?"

I could hear it again as if it was happening right then. "Someone was crying."

"Was it Savannah?"

"It couldn't have been her. She was talking, trying to tell me some-thing."

"Do you recall the voice? Was it male or female?"

"It was definitely a man's voice. And I woke up thinking that judging from the baritone, it was a big man, a broad man." I suddenly realized who it was. For a second, I couldn't breathe. "It was the killer."

Patrick stared at me for a long time, his green eyes lighter than I remem-bered. Gold shot through in prisms.

"Oh God," I finally said. "You must think I'm insane. I'm sorry. You did not come here to listen to my psychotic ramblings."

"I came here *because* of your psychotic ramblings." He put his hands on the table. "That didn't come out right. I'll listen to anything you have to say."

His confirmation felt like a cool shower on a hot day. "Is there anything else about that dream?"

I took a long time to decide if I should tell him. "Even though I can't hear what she's saying, I can see her neck."

"Her neck?" He pulled a small notebook and a pen from his breast pocket and wrote down a few words. "That makes sense, considering how she was . . ." He let his voice trail off.

"She wasn't showing me what was there. She was showing me what wasn't."

"I don't follow."

"Her necklace." I pulled my matching necklace from under my nylon running top. "She was trying to tell me something about this." I held up the slanted, backward *f* so he could study it.

He fingered the pendant. "We never found that necklace," he said. "I thought it meant something back then, when the case was fresh. I tried to get Captain Fisher to let me investigate it in more detail, but he said we didn't have the resources."

I closed my eyes at the mention of Emma's father. I'd always kind of hated him, and now I hated his daughter too.

"That's what I think the dream is trying to tell me. Find the necklace, and you've found the killer."

Patrick let go of the pendant and leaned back against the plastic chair. "We had vehicles on the grounds. It could have gotten crushed or mashed into the earth. And the crime scene was contaminated. It's hard to keep a site clear with that much activity. Anyone could have picked it up." His memory for all things Savannah was as good as mine.

Tears pressed against the backs of my eyes, surprising me. "Why do you sound like you're trying to talk me out of this?" I hadn't realized until that moment how much I cared what Patrick Tunney thought, how much I needed him to believe in this with me. "I have to get those lunches out by ten." My voice was edgier than I'd meant it to be.

Patrick's lips parted in surprise. I thought he was going to say something, but he didn't. I'd seen my father do the same thing a million times, when my mother was trying to pick a fight. He'd sit for a minute and then keep talking as if my mom wasn't about to lose her shit.

"I'm sorry," he said. "I made so many mistakes back then. Giving up before we found the necklace was one of them. I've taken up enough of your time. I'll let you get back to work."

He got up and headed for the door. I followed him, stopping at the window to pull back the white linen curtain. The parking lot was empty save for our cars. A crow on the power line was calling out, a dark, frantic sound, and Patrick stopped, his hand on the doorknob. I heard him take a deep breath before he finally turned to face me.

"We don't have any new evidence or leads," he said. "But now more than ever, I am convinced that Savannah knew her killer."

That was the one thing I'd been sure of after the dream. "I know," I said. "I guess I've always known."

CHAPTER
21

Of course, Greg and I had talked about therapy before. When I got the first book deal and the film option offers started rolling in, the power dynamic had shifted, and one of us, in some argument or another, had suggested it but never followed through. And after the first miscarriage, he'd proposed it again when I couldn't stop crying one Sunday morning, and he couldn't get me out of bed. But therapy was something I associated with things being very bad. Not marriages in tough spots but girls with razor blades who didn't mind the sight of their own blood but rather welcomed the relief it brought.

The first time I cut myself had been an accident. I'd come home from school early, an in-service day for teachers, early March, the frozen puddles along the roadsides starting to thaw and that wet mud smell in the air. The slog of late winter was a cruel reminder of Savannah's light, her blond hair swinging, the excited giggle, the way she'd run into the house breathless, hungry, grabbing snacks and soda so we could team up on the couch to watch those after-school soaps she loved.

I'd done it cutting a bagel in the kitchen, the knife slipping and slicing the soft part of my palm like you might crack a door. Spots of blood on the floor, bright—beautiful, even—and it wasn't until I lunged for the dishrag and had wrapped it tightly around my hand that I realized I wasn't in pain.

The rhythmic pulsing in my palm felt good. With every heartbeat that seemed to pump there, I felt alive, deeply free.

Years later, I would realize it was somehow erotic, the pain sensual. But back then, I only knew it felt comforting. I fumbled through the cabinet in the bathroom, found the clean, raggedy towels my mother used for dusting, and sat at the kitchen table with a *Seventeen* magazine with the intention of waiting it out. But as the shock wore off and the bleeding slowed, I had a hard time focusing. I wanted instead to study the blood seeping into the towel. The more I watched, the better I felt. The weight that had been crushing me for months was gone.

When my mom got home, she freaked out, and the whole way to the hospital, swerving in and out of traffic, she kept asking why I hadn't called her at the restaurant. "You poor thing," she said. "That must have been so *painful*." Once there, the doctor gave me nine stitches, and then like some kind of clockwork synchronicity, we had a school assembly on cutting a week later. The crisis du jour, like drive-by shootings and school massacres.

Dr. Nobleman, Kingswood's shrink, paraded a series of sad girls and one boy into the auditorium. Under the hot stage lights, they sat on folding aluminum chairs and told their stories—locked doors and stolen knives, the sweet relief of tearing their skin. They were all freaks, of course. Black combat boots. Dyed hair. Pale skin and bright-red lipstick. Even the boy was wearing eyeliner. I sat next to Gabby, slouched in my seat, horrified, fascinated. I wasn't one of them. But maybe, I thought as I saw again the bright blood on the towel, those kids on stage with their worried eyes and scarred arms were onto something. As they shifted nervously from one foot to the other, telling four hundred strangers that cutting took away the pain of their parents' divorce or losing a boyfriend, it dawned on me that they had found a portal into painlessness.

If they said that cutting left scars, landed them in psychiatric hospitals, distanced them from friends and family, made them feel like freaks, I didn't hear it. I heard only that it afforded them some relief. And if it worked for them, it could work for me. If only poor, stupid Dr. Nobleman had known that his assembly would encourage me.

That afternoon, with the memory of those kids on stage and their stories of cutting the bottoms of their feet, the tops of their thighs, any place that wouldn't be noticed, I found myself pulling a restaurant-sharp julienning knife from its special drawer. Then I went to the upstairs bathroom, took off all my clothes, and carefully lay in the tub and searched my body for a place that I could keep hidden. My first cut was under my left breast.

After that first time in the bathtub, I got better at it. I could do it quickly and cleanly so there wasn't a lot of blood. And I always did it in a place no one would notice. My parents knew I was uncomfortable with my body, so they didn't question me wearing long sleeves in the summer.

Then, without warning, it wasn't enough anymore. I'd cut and wouldn't feel relief, only the dull ache of the blade. All cutting did was make a mess and give me one more thing to lie about. It got even worse when the chef from the restaurant came by, and while I sat in my room, I overheard him say he'd been going to AA. He knew he was in trouble when eight drinks no longer did what four used to. It made me feel desperate inside. Nothing, absolutely nothing, would be big enough to take away the pain.

I'd never told Greg about all that. I'd told him what had come afterward. I didn't think I could marry him without telling him about Sound View and the time I spent there. But I'd never mentioned the cutting. In the rare moments when I was completely naked, getting out of the shower, or undressing in the closet, he must have seen the scars, but he never said anything, so I couldn't know for sure.

I was afraid that a therapist would have some magic touch that would force me to tell all, and Greg would not only realize I'd held something huge back from him all this time but in some weird way, it would be ammunition, a sure sign that I was who he'd thought I was all along. Some broken animal he could fix.

But for some reason, this time, I decided to risk it, and the following day, I found myself sitting with Greg in front of a short, balding man who could have passed for my fifth-grade teacher, Mr. Lord. The couch was long and made of soft leather. Greg sat next to me with his work shoes flat on the floor and his hands folded in front of him.

Mr. Lord's doppelganger introduced himself, but I was thinking about how it had been sixteen years, four months, and six days since the first time I went to a shrink after Savannah died, and I missed what he said. Now I glanced around the room, searching for a diploma or a business card, anything with his name on it. It sounded like one of those fancy Pepperidge Farm cookies my mother used to put out when her friends came over. Milano or Mirano or something like that.

Pepperidge Farm had one leg crossed over the other and a writing pad on his lap. "Cady." His cheeks were puffy like a squirrel's, but he had soft, kind brown eyes. "Can you tell me why you're here?"

A clock was ticking somewhere. I thought about giving him a semifictional, cookie-cutter response. I'd cry and tell him how I'd fallen out of love with Greg and was lonely. Or that Greg didn't pay me enough attention, and he was sleeping with his receptionist.

But I didn't have the energy for a bent version of the truth, so I didn't say anything. Finally, Greg cleared his throat. "We're not communicating well," he said.

I could feel Pepperidge Farm's eyes on me as I studied a spot on his oriental rug. This was a bad idea. This was almost as bad as sitting across from Larry Cauchek.

"What about when you were first married? Let's start there. Was it difficult to communicate then?"

I was wearing camel-colored boots Gabby had picked out last spring when she made me buy something special for myself after *Empty Corridors* fell off the bestseller list. And I thought about our wedding night. I'd been flattered when Greg asked me to marry him, but also suspicious. That night, I'd come out of the bathroom wearing a short, gauzy bathrobe. I hadn't tied it tightly like I normally did, and my breasts spilled out. With all the lights on, I stood at the foot of the california king bed and let it fall to the floor. It was the first time Greg had seen me naked with all the lights on. I'd known he'd been engaged before. It was something he blew right by in conversation, something, I noticed, he never mentioned in front of his parents. But when I got into bed that night, prepared to make love to him, he'd closed his eyes and put his head back on the pillows.

"Cady, I know this is horrible, but I'm not sure I can do this." And then he told me she'd left him a month before the wedding.

We'd been married seven hours, and he chose then to explain that the pretty girl, the size 2 doll, left her engagement ring on his nightstand with a note. And then I knew. I'd been happy but wary of Greg's attention up until that moment, and that's when I got it.

"Cady?" Pepperidge Farm asked. "What brought you and Greg together?"

Years of unspoken rage colored my cheeks. And suddenly, I was glad we were there. Finally, finally, I could tell Greg that I'd known all along why he'd chosen me. "Greg married me because I'm not some Brooklyn Decker beauty who's going to leave him." It almost burst out of my mouth. "Men don't set their drinks down to watch me when I enter a room. Girls don't love to hate me. My friends' boyfriends high-five me instead of kissing me when we get together. I can't tell you if we used to communicate better than we do now, but I can tell you the whole reason he married me is because I am completely safe."

Dr. Cookie's eyes narrowed, and I could feel Greg staring at me.

He actually sputtered when he spoke. "Don't act like you're some wounded bird in all this." Greg never raised his voice at me. It was one of the things that made me crazy. A fight without yelling wasn't a fight. It was a discussion. And I was so tired of the discussions that had ruled our marriage, but now he was yelling. "I know why you married me too! And you're no better than I am!"

"What are you talking about?"

"You did it for your parents." His words stopped me cold. "You thought that if you had someone to take care of you, they would stop worrying you'd try to kill yourself again. And you know what? I was okay with that. So what if we weren't the kind of couple who tore each other's clothes off? Is it so bad to want to take care of someone?"

"Then why haven't you?" I was trying to catch my breath. That Greg would blurt out that suicide line left me choked with fury I was afraid would turn to tears. "All you've done since I started making money is treat me like a servant. Like my job doesn't count for anything except to buy you toys."

"Cady." His voice was quiet again. "Try to see it from my point of view. I'm supposed to be the breadwinner. I'm—"

I cut him off. "Breadwinner? Is it nineteen fifty?" *And how dare you talk about suicide in here? How dare you bring that up?*

"Don't be snide. I want you to understand how hard it is for me to have gone to school for eleven years, only to be outdone by—"

"Your wife?"

Greg closed his eyes and threw up his hands.

I offered my own hands toward Dr. Cookie as if serving Greg up on a platter. "And there it is. Do you understand now why we are irretrievably wrecked?"

Pepperidge Farm had been silently watching us from his chair. "Those are strong words, Cady. Is that truly how you feel?"

"Is it?" Greg asked. His eyes had gone glassy.

What the fuck was going on here? Greg didn't cry. Especially not over me.

"We don't even like each other anymore." I let myself flop back into the buttery leather. "And we say horrible things when we try to talk about it, so what's the point?"

Greg's arms were crossed over his chest. Mine were down at my sides, like a rag doll. And Dr. Soft Baked Sausalito was motionless with the pad on his lap. We sat there for a little while. Greg finally put his hands on his legs and smoothed out his pants.

"I'm sorry I lost my temper," he said.

I cast my eyes at the rug. "Me too."

And it was true. Tempers were terrible things. Once you said what you really thought, you got hurt, and now the worst thing about me was out. But Pepperidge Farm did an odd thing. He gave me a soft half smile, and I had the distinct feeling that he didn't judge me.

"You want to try telling me what drew you together?" Dr. Brussels asked. What the hell was his name?

Greg leaned forward, his elbows on his knees. "Cady's smart," he said. "Her mind works in fascinating ways." He swallowed. "I like listening to her talk."

When we first met and Greg had a loft in Princeton, we used to roll around in bed and talk for hours. Maybe the sex wasn't perfect, but the conversation was. "How do you think up those things?" he used to ask. And I'd giggle, and for maybe the first time in my whole life, I actually felt interesting.

"Greg's a good listener," I said. "I can always tell he's thinking about things after I say them. And he builds on them rather than dismissing them." I stopped. "And he's a really hard worker. But so am I, and maybe that's part of our problem."

Pepperidge Farm shifted in his seat. "Why do you work so hard?" he asked. He was watching me.

My tongue felt dry in my mouth.

"Cady is a very big name in publishing," Greg tried to explain when I didn't speak up. "They want her to turn books out every ten to twelve months."

This somehow sounded lame. Double Chocolate Milano wasn't watching me anymore; his eyes were cast somewhere in the space between us.

"And"—Greg leaned back and smiled at me—"Cady loves her readers, and she never disappoints them." Somehow, therapy had turned into a love fest.

"Yes." Pepperidge Farm's eyes drooped as if he were sad or sick. "So I've heard."

Outside in the parking lot, the sun had come out, and it was almost muggy. I fished around in my bag for my sunglasses.

"Well, that was sort of horrible," I said.

Greg stopped walking. "What was horrible about it?" he asked.

I put my sunglasses on. "Um, yelling at each other in front of a stranger?"

Greg kept walking, and I fell into step beside him. "I thought it was a relief," he said. He pointed his key fob at the Mercedes, and it lit up.

I stopped at the Volvo. "What was a relief?" I watched him walk toward his car.

He reached for the handle and stood for a minute before he spoke. "To finally talk. To finally tell the truth." He opened the door, got in the car, and sat there. "I hope it's not too late."

"Me too," I called after him, but he'd already closed his door, and I watched his car get smaller as he drove away.

CHAPTER 22

"I couldn't stop talking," I told Gabby.

We were sitting on a bench at Baskin Park putting on Rollerblades. Around us, people were jogging with baby strollers and walking along merrily listening to iPods, not realizing that in a few moments I was about to mow them down. I didn't even know they still made Rollerblades. "When I got in Pepperidge Farm's office," I said, "it was like my mouth was a motor."

"That's good, right?" Gabby said while she was strapping those killers on my feet.

It was Saturday, and when she called, I thought it was to go to Cookies a day early and drink chai and eat sweets with the twentysomething crowd, but she'd insisted I go out Rollerblading with her since it used the same muscles as she would need to hold up her bike during the Hoka Hey. I'd reluctantly agreed to a pair of rented ones that terrified me.

"It makes me feel totally out of control," I said.

Gabby snapped my last binding down. "Good." She stood up, completely relaxed, balanced on a row of tiny wheels that were about to bring me to an early grave. "You should feel out of control."

"What?" I re-Velcroed my kneepad, killing time before I made a complete fool of myself. "No, I shouldn't. Being out of control doesn't suit me. Did you bring helmets?"

"I hate helmets. They make me feel like a dork." She had a pea head; I couldn't imagine any helmet would even fit her. "Therapy is all about being out of control." Gabby twirled her hair around her finger while I struggled to my feet. "You have to sort of pretend no one's in the room and say every single thing you think in your head, and then you have a breakthrough." She held out her hand.

"Or a breakdown." I bore down against her and tried to stand, but it felt like my knees were going to buckle from the pressure of holding it all together.

"No time to stress about therapy. We have skating to do."

I pushed off against the pavement and stuttered forward.

"Great job. It's a gliding motion, like skiing."

"I don't ski," I reminded her.

She ignored me. "Put your legs together and then push out. Like this."

I watched her pushing one foot out behind her like a ballerina. I had a feeling I would never be able to do anything on Rollerblades but keep my feet awkwardly hip-width apart and stumble along after her while she went twirling off like Dorothy Hamill.

"I wish you'd brought helmets," I told her. I was about an arm's length behind her. "And if we keep holding hands like this, people will think we're lesbians."

Gabby turned her head and rolled her eyes. "So?" she said. "It's not like we didn't make out at David's wedding."

I laughed. "I loved horrifying Emma and her parents."

"You are an excellent kisser," she said, puckering her lips. "But now back to business. Squat. Not that much. Perfect. Now push off from the side like this." I tried to mimic her movements. "How was the serial killer?"

"He's a lunatic," I said. I was getting a feel for the squatting-gliding motion, and although I had no intention of telling Gabby, it was kind of fun. "And fascinating."

"You're brave," she said. She hadn't even looked back to see how I was doing. "I mean the guy's a fucking maniac. Were you terrified?"

"I was at first. But he was"—I lost my balance but righted myself—"kind of mesmerizing."

"What's going on with Brady?"

"He's mad at me."

Gabby slowed, but since I didn't know how to stop, she had to keep going. "That's good," she said. "Guys only bother to get mad at you if they like you. What's his beef?"

"He thinks I said too much to Larry Cauchek. He hasn't called me since, and I don't really know if I can call him. It's so weird."

"Call him," Gabby told me.

I opened my mouth to tell her I had no reason to call Brady, but instead I said, "That cop who worked Savannah's case called me a few weeks ago."

Gabby dragged her toe and stopped. I crashed into her, but she grabbed my arms and steadied us both. "Officer Tenney? What did he want?"

"Tunney," I told her. "And he's a detective now. They're reopening the case."

She took my hand and pulled me to a bench. "Holy shit. Why are you just telling me this now?"

I had no answer. "I don't know. It's been so much to take in; I think I've been avoiding it a little. I mean, this is all I've ever wanted. I've spent my whole adult life trying to piece together who could have choked my sister to death. And now this cop shows up out of nowhere and says that's what he's going to do."

Gabby pulled me into a hard hug. "Cady! That's great. You must be so excited."

All I felt was a stone in my stomach. "What if nothing happens? What if it's like last time and they spend a year asking questions and scaring the shit out of everyone, and then they give up again?"

Gabby patted my leg. "No, honey, it's different now. That asshole Fisher is gone, and Officer Tunney is involved. They'll catch him."

I hadn't thought I'd tell Gabby about Patrick reopening the case. But now that I had, I felt something like relief. Even if he didn't solve it, at least I knew someone still cared. Gabby and I sat on the bench, not talking. After a few minutes, she got up and offered me her hand. We took off gliding around Baskin Park. The breeze was sweet on my face. I liked how my muscles pushed and then relaxed. I could smell the mud loosening from the winter months and saw tiny crocuses coming up. After a while, I felt secure enough to let go of Gabby's hand. This great gliding sensation arrived, like I might actually launch. And then fly.

"This is fun!" I called to her. "I think this is the only exercise I've ever really liked."

Gabby laughed. She was a little wonky herself, and I liked that, two wobbly friends, gliding along as best we could, trying to move forward around a really pretty park.

CHAPTER
23

What Patrick and Jon Caritano had told me kept popping up in my mind. I'd be driving to pick up Greg's suits at the dry cleaner, and I'd think of what Patrick had said. I could feel myself looking for Fisher everywhere, and I had a fantasy of getting out of my car and screaming at him in public, but I knew I never would.

Saturday night, I dreamed that Savannah stood the boys who used to be in love with her—Chapman Sharp, Dylan Freeman, Jeff Kilbourn, and Eddie Zygmont—in a row and then paced back and forth in front of them in her jean cutoffs and a bathing suit top. "Eeny meeny miney moe." She was pointing at each of them in turn. "Catch a tiger by the toe—" I woke up with the space beside me already empty. Greg had run off to yoga. Savannah's voice was still clear in my mind, and the mattress was indented as if she'd watched me while I slept.

Boys. Savannah had found them early. They had exhilarated her much the same way getting model cars at Christmas had excited David. She was unafraid of them. She had a sort of playful power that when I was an adult I recognized in only very beautiful, often famous women. I'd been terrified for her, though I couldn't have said why then, but now I wondered if it was a premonition. "Tell Mom and Dad whatever," she'd said on that fateful night when I finally realized Savannah's childhood was over and mine was still in full swing. "Just cover for me until midnight."

But my parents hadn't even come into our room after she'd slid off the shingled roof onto the back porch and gone running to Chapman Sharp's waiting car. I'd pretended to be asleep when she crept into our room at midnight. I lay there, listening as her clothes dropped to the floor. I heard her open the pajama drawer, put her earrings on the dresser, and then walk over to my bed and pull back the covers. I rolled toward the wall, but she crawled in with me and put her mouth next to my ear. "I did it," she whispered. I sighed as if dreaming. She'd never let me be, but I tried anyway because I didn't want to hear that a girl who looked exactly like me except for twenty pounds had kissed boy number six and let him lift up her skirt and bear into her.

I knew what french-kissing was, but I couldn't figure out why you'd want someone else's tongue in your mouth, how you kissed if you had a cold, if people with braces like Lita Edelton and Michael Pritchet got stuck together. And, most of all, why anyone would want a boy's penis jammed in where it didn't belong. I had a hard enough time using a tampon. I'd walked in on David a few months before as he was about to shower, and I saw him, all of him. His penis had been sticking straight up, and I couldn't imagine how it could fit inside a girl.

But that night, alone in my bed while Savannah was out and knowing what she was going to do, I'd wanted to feel what it was like, so I'd put my fingers inside me. It would be years before I'd learn that it only felt good when I rubbed the top part with my index and middle fingers, but that night, having no experience at all, I put one finger up there, my nail cutting the thick part of the labia. It hurt so badly, I yelped. There was no pleasure. None at all.

"Did you hear me?" she whispered again. She sounded giddy, like she had when our father gave her that cell phone she used all the time even though it was for emergencies only or when she finally got her braces off. Mine were still on, one more reason I'd never kissed a boy.

"I did it. Can you believe it?" Her feet were freezing against my calves, and she smelled of cigarettes.

"Wow." I rubbed my eyes and feigned excitement. "Congratulations, I think. I mean, am I supposed to congratulate you on something like this?" I wasn't going to get any sleep until I let her tell me every gross detail.

She kissed me on the cheek, her lips soft, as though they'd been rubbed raw of anything but tenderness. "Yes!"

"Did it feel good?" In the pale light of the streetlamp, I could see her messy hair, the smudged eye makeup.

"Of course it did." She crawled deeper under my sheets. But I knew it hadn't. I'd felt a stinging pain down there when I was drifting off to sleep.

"Did you . . ." I whispered.

"Did I what?"

"Have one?"

But Savannah said she didn't know if she'd had an orgasm. We had no idea what one felt like, so how could she know? The year before, Mrs. Davenport, our gym and health teacher, had told all sixty-seven girls in the eighth grade that orgasms were like sneezes. "You feel the tingling coming, and then it's like a miniature explosion." After a smattering of questions about what an explosion in your privates feels like, the red-faced teacher told us that we'd know it when it happened.

"Well, are you going to do it again?" I asked her.

In the light from the streetlamp outside, her eyes sparkled as though someone had thrown glitter at them. "Every chance I get," she told me, and then she closed her eyes and snuggled up beside me like she used to.

But I knew what was happening. I knew it more than ever that night. After losing her virginity to Chapman Sharp, the cutest boy in school, in the backseat of his dark-blue Jetta, I knew I was losing Savannah forever.

Then the phone rang, and I reached across the bed to grab it. The caller ID said it was my mother.

"Hi, Mom," I said. "Everything okay?"

"Sweetheart."

She sounded surprised I answered. We didn't call each other often, and when we did speak, I got the feeling my mother was walking on balloons around me, wearing an imaginary pair of stilettos.

"Honey, your father and I have something we need to discuss with you." Patrick must have called them. "He's on another extension, and we have your brother on call-waiting." Perfect. A long-distance family reunion.

I sat up in bed. My mother never wanted to talk about anything. She was famous for stuffing everything under a rug and walking all over it.

"Hi, honey," my dad said. His voice was faint, as if on speakerphone. "Hold on a minute while we get David on the line. If we hang up on you, we'll call you right back."

Then the phone squealed in my ear as if he were pressing buttons, and I heard him say David's name a few times. Finally, it was quiet, and then everyone was talking at once.

I leaned back into the pillow and closed my eyes. "Is everything okay?" I asked again.

My mother sighed. "How's the new book coming?" She was so good at ignoring me I almost believed I hadn't asked the question.

"It's getting there." I got out of bed and took the phone downstairs. I grabbed a yogurt out of the fridge, even though I wanted a Pop-Tart. I went to sit on the front steps. I started eating the bitter plain yogurt to get to the prize of sugary strawberries on the bottom, and my mom began talking quickly, like she did when she was nervous.

"So," she said. "Do you have any idea why we called you both?"

I was sure it was about Patrick reopening the case, but I didn't want to say anything if I was wrong. "Are you moving back?" I asked and heard David gasp. It was so easy to rattle him.

"Of course not," my father said too quickly.

"Hang on a second," David said, and then I heard water running and metal banging against metal.

"Good heavens." My mother sounded irritated. "David, what are you doing?"

"Sorry," he said. "I have to water Willow."

David had planted one lonely weeping willow tree smack in the center of his lawn the year he bought his house. Our parents had had one in their front yard that David had wanted to uproot when they moved to Florida, but the buyers wouldn't let him, even though it was an ugly little tree, a runt that never grew properly. My dad had put stakes in the ground with wires attached to the trunk in order to hold it up, and every time there was a big storm, he worried the wind would rip it up. So David had gone to Madden's Greenhouse in Princeton and asked them for the smallest, frailest weeping willow sapling they had. He'd never told us why he wanted such a sad tree, but I was sure it was because Savannah had loved that little weakling. She always was for the underdog.

"This call is probably costing us a fortune," my dad piped in. "Are we ready to talk?"

"Sorry," David and I said at the same time, even though we hadn't done anything wrong.

"Well." I could almost hear my mother rubbing her hands together. "We wanted to talk to you kids about . . ." *Kids?* "Well, you probably both know that Detective Tunney has reopened the case."

I had no idea if David knew. God, I hated it that Emma was so right about us.

"We think it's important to talk about what this means to us as a family."

This was awkward, because our glue was missing. Savannah had been the light that wound us all together. Without her, we were fragmented pieces, uncomfortable as a whole.

My mom was tall but small boned and birdlike. Yet there was something fierce about her, something tightly gathered that ran the risk of letting loose. Even on the phone, I could sense it.

"What *does* this mean to us as a family?" I asked.

"Well." My mom's voice was too bright. "It can be stressful. It can bring up memories. People in town will be reminded again if word gets out and—"

"Mom," David interrupted her. "Do you think people *forgot*?"

"All I'm saying," she continued, "is that you two are fragile right now, and I think it's better if we don't get too involved."

"That's easy for you," I said. "You're a thousand miles away."

She kept right on talking. "We know this will be stressful, especially for you two, and we're not sure that's what you need right now."

"Shouldn't we be thankful Patrick is doing something?" I couldn't listen to her anymore. "Why do I get the feeling you'd rather leave this alone?"

"Honey," she said. "All I'm suggesting is that we let the police do their jobs; there's no reason to get involved. Your father and I have been talking about this since Detective Tunney called us, and this is what we've decided, what we feel is best for all of us."

My father cleared his throat and finally spoke. "And it's better not to talk about it too much. I'm sure Patrick told you both it's best if this is kept quiet.

One thing that stopped the investigation last time was that the town was upset, and they don't want to disturb people's sense of safety again. We've asked them not to let the reopening of the case be in the news."

It was only with my family and occasionally with Greg that I could let myself feel that boiling rage that was so often barely below the surface, and it was rising now. I wanted to hang up the phone and flee. I had that claustrophobic feeling I used to get in high school after Savannah died, even though I was alone. "Do you think you could do that, try not to get too involved with all this?"

Savannah had been killed. And Malcolm Fisher put her in cold storage because he didn't want to ruffle any more feathers in this snooty town, where everyone wanted to believe in the lie of safety in suburbia. And now, after all these years, Patrick Tunney had the good graces to get her out of the basement, where she never belonged. And my parents were telling us not to get involved?

No one spoke. The tension was like an electromagnetic field that seemed to stretch taut and timeless through space from one of us to the next. "I don't want to forget about Savannah," I wanted to tell them. "I can't, and there's no way in hell I'm going to." I finished my yogurt instead.

"Oh, sweetie, I can tell you're mad." My mother knew me better than I thought. "Please." She sounded desperate. "Will you two please trust us on this?" I'd almost forgotten David was on the line.

"Fine," I said, but I was furious. I wondered vaguely what I had agreed to by not saying what I really felt. How odd it was that we could talk about such meaningless things during our weekly phone calls, and yet we couldn't discuss the one thing that was sitting among us: Savannah, and the possibility that maybe we were going to finally find out who stole her from us.

CHAPTER
24

I had never been on Gabby's motorcycle. When we were teenagers, she begged her mother for a scooter. I think it was Savannah being gone that finally convinced her mom. The two of us had been so miserable. But the second day she had it, we'd gone downtown to Dairy Queen and crashed it into the side of the brick building. We'd been wearing helmets, so our worst injuries were scrapes on our knees, but it was enough to make me never want to be on two wheels again. There was something about that moment of surprise, the brick coming straight at me and not being able to do anything about it, that was too terrifying. I didn't even like to ride bicycles now. I stuck to horses. I could communicate with horses, read them. They weren't inanimate objects whose brakes could fail like Gabby's scooter's had.

I revealed this in articles. I also told the interviewers other things, like I hated sleeping alone when I was on tour, was afraid of the dark, thought milk tasted the way Band-Aids smell, and had almost a million frequent-flier miles. I thought if I gave fans some inside scoop on my life, they'd be satisfied enough, and I wouldn't have to talk about Savannah. I'd given so many interviews over the years, both in print and on TV, that I assumed anyone who followed my work or knew me personally understood certain things about me.

So when Brady knocked on my front door on a Wednesday morning, carrying two helmets, I thought maybe he'd lost his mind. I was trying to research everything I could on hypnotism. I should have told Deanna that writing while on deadline was off limits, but she would have said, "Publish or perish," and it would have given me one more reason to hate her.

"You're coming with me." Brady set the helmets on the counter.

So he wasn't mad at me for talking about personal things with Larry Cauchek. "Where are we going?" I tried not to be embarrassed that my hair was a mess, I was wearing an ancient torn Columbia T-shirt of Greg's, and my yoga pants came from the dirty laundry pile.

"How about the shore?" he asked.

Normally, I would have been thrilled at the idea of being alone with him for that long. I hadn't seen him since the prison, even though I'd texted him twice asking when I could interview Larry again. Both times he'd written back, "Never." And now that I finally had a chance to hang out with him, the helmets were ruining it all.

"What's with the helmets?"

He picked up the purple one and passed it to me. "We're not seventeen, and this isn't a scooter." So he *had* read my interviews. "You're going to love my Triumph. I've never crashed, and it's a beautiful day. Plus, you need to stop writing. You need a break. It's important to have some fun."

I felt like someone was trying to choke me and offer me candy at the same time. "Sorry. I have to write a magazine article."

"You're afraid." Brady watched me. He was wearing all leather, and he looked so hot it made me feel sort of faint.

"Not really afraid . . ." I started lamely.

"You'll have the time of your life, I promise." He set the purple helmet on my head. "I'll have you back by dinner."

His eyes were so bright and his smile so big it was hard to say no. In a weird way, I felt like I owed him for the Larry interview. Or maybe I was just crushed out.

I took the helmet off and held it in my hands, glancing at the clock. It wasn't even noon. I couldn't imagine spending seven hours on something that terrified me. But then I thought about the feature I was supposed to write, and I envisioned my hands around Brady's waist.

"Oh, what the hell," I said. "I'm in. Let me get changed first."

In my room, I frantically riffled through my closet for something to wear and finally decided on a pair of jeans, a suede pullover Gabby had given me when she got back from her trip to Utah, and a pair of boots I'd bought for a book tour out west that I'd never worn. On the way back to Brady, I thought about how afraid some of my students had been of riding horses back when I used to give riding lessons in the summertime. Everyone was afraid of something. Maybe it was okay to push past that once in a while.

Brady was waiting for me outside, holding the purple helmet like an offering. I tied my hair back in a ponytail and put it on. It was too tight, and I wondered if Colette usually wore it.

"It'll be easier if I get on first, and then you slip on behind me," Brady told me.

I did as he said and tried to relax into the hot, black leather seat. When he started the engine, it sounded like a jet taking off. Not being able to talk to him for two hours disappointed me, and as I was considering changing my mind, I heard his voice. It took me a moment to realize there were speakers inside the helmets.

"Ready?" he asked, his voice clear and crisp.

"Yes," I yelled over the roar of the motor.

He ducked away. "Use your regular voice. I can hear you fine."

"Sorry." I felt awkward. "I think I'm ready."

The motorcycle was a lot wider than I remembered Gabby's scooter being, and I didn't feel unbalanced at all. The wind was warm, and the sun was bright and high in the sky.

"When I lean," Brady told me, "lean with me, okay?"

"Okay," I said.

"You'll want to lean away from me, but you have to keep your body in rhythm with mine. Can you do that?"

"Yeah," I said. "I can do that."

When he wasn't talking, asking questions about how work was going, and what I thought of the weather turning nice so quickly, a mix of classic rock and alternative music came through the speakers. Despite the fact that we must have been going close to seventy, I found the warmth and the music and the vibration of the engine hypnotic. Gabby and I went to Massage Envy in Princeton once a month, but hot stones on my back weren't nearly as relaxing as this. And after a while, I did something I never in a million years thought I would: I let my head rest against Brady's back.

It was easier, too, to ask him things when we rode. Not seeing his face gave me some kind of license I wasn't sure I could explain. I asked him about his family. His father, he told me, was a fourth-generation military guy. Captain in the army. He missed Vietnam by a few years, so he hadn't seen combat but wanted to. And his mother did custom embroidery for high-end boutiques out in California, and that's where they'd moved after his dad retired.

"Why did you stay?" I asked.

"I didn't," he said. "After graduation, I traveled."

"Where?"

"Everywhere," he said. "I got a dirt bike and went up the Trans-America Trail, through Canada, down the center of the country to Mexico and Guatemala."

So that's where Brady Irons had been. "Why did you come back?"

"Because of all the places I've lived, this is the only one that ever felt like home."

Then he was quiet for a long time. I wanted to ask him more. I wondered why, with four generations of military men in front of him, he hadn't joined too. But something stopped me, and I let myself listen to the murmur of the road and feel the bike's vibration.

I didn't know how much time had passed when Brady pulled up to Bliss Ice Cream on the boardwalk in Cape May. Savannah's horse, Bliss, was named after this place. We got off the bike and put our helmets on the seat.

As I started to walk, a wave of vertigo hit. He grabbed me around the waist, which was so embarrassing I felt myself flush deep red.

"Stay still for a minute. It's like when you're on a boat for a long time. The world will feel like it's rocking," he said.

I quit worrying about my extra pudge and let him hold me up. He smelled different from when I'd met him on his lunch hour. Today, he smelled like grass and wind and sun. When I had my sea legs back, we went in the shop and ordered ice cream cones. I got pistachio mint, and Brady ordered vanilla.

"Vanilla?" I said to him. "But this place is famous for its crazy flavors." The menu was written in bright colors on a chalkboard. Dandelion, cocoa with whipped cream, bubble gum.

"I like vanilla." It came out like an apology.

Outside, we found a bench by the marsh.

"I love this place," I said. "But I only ever come in high summer. It's usually so crowded the line is out the door."

"Ha," Brady said, sounding a little disappointed. "I thought this was my secret. Sometimes I just get on my bike and ride. You wouldn't believe how many funky shops and obscure stores I've discovered."

Marshes played out before us, the ocean glittering on the horizon.

"Sorry to burst your bubble, but everyone knows Bliss. Best ice cream on the East Coast. We used to vacation here in the summers," I said, catching a drip with my tongue. "Savannah, David, and I would walk down here every night from the cottage my parents rented and get these huge, three-scoop cones. At least one always ended up on the ground." What was wrong with me? First, I got on a motorcycle, and now I was talking about my sister. I couldn't stop thinking about her, the dreams, the fact of her getting pulled up from the basement. "Savannah used to order the cinnamon bun flavor."

Brady watched me. A line of vanilla was dripping down his cone onto his hand. I had the craziest urge to lick it off his skin.

"And now?" he asked. "Did you quit coming?"

"David, Chandler, and I come around the Fourth of July every year. Usually, Odion comes with us. Sometimes Gabby and Duncan too." Maybe, I thought, Brady would come this year.

"What about Greg?"

"He's always on call. Fourth of July brings out all the crazies, and he has to talk them off the ledge."

"And Emma, did she come?"

I laughed at the insane thought of Emma on this boardwalk in July with screaming kids and bikini moms eating hot dogs. "We always invited her, but she never came. Suntans and sand in her bathing suit on a public beach are not her idea of fun. Come to think of it, fun wasn't her idea of fun. She was more of the work-out-at-the-gym-and-get-more-Botox kind of girl."

We finished our ice cream and then walked around town. We meandered, something Greg never did. We went into stores that sold hats and jewelry and summer souvenirs. We walked along the boardwalk and then took off our shoes and picked up shells. There was something about being with Brady that was familiar. The easy feeling kept catching me off guard. Like I would remember every once in a while that I shouldn't feel that comfortable with him. And yet I did.

Finally, we found a wooden swing and watched the sun set. A woman jogging by with her dog stopped a few feet from us to tie her shoe. She stepped on the leash while she tied, but the dog saw a squirrel and took off. She jumped up and called his name, but the dog made a beeline for Brady. It trotted right up to us on the bench and stabbed his nose against Brady's leg. Brady laughed and gathered the leash. By that time, the woman had gotten to us, and he handed the leash to her. She thanked him and continued jogging. When she was gone, he sat back down next to me.

"I guess you weren't kidding. Animals really do love you," I said.

He cocked his head as if he didn't understand.

"You told me at the barn that you're some kind of animal whisperer. Apparently, you are."

The sun was almost gone, and goose bumps were coming out on my arms, but I didn't want to go home yet. Brady must have seen that I was cold, because he slipped his arm around me and rubbed his palms against my skin, the way my dad used to when I was little.

"Is that better?" he asked.

Suddenly drowsy, I let myself lean into him. We stayed like that until a street sweeper came by, blaring rap music from inside the cab.

"Hey," Brady said when the noise died down.

"Is it time to go?"

A star had come out, and I was trying not to wish on it. But then I felt Brady stiffen, and instinctively I took my head off his shoulder. He was watching the water as though he were bracing himself against something.

"Cady," he said, still studying the ocean. "I feel like you came into my life for a reason." My belly turned to water; I didn't move. "That first day I saw you at the prison." He swallowed. "It was like no time had passed. Like we were supposed to meet again on those steps."

"I know." I could feel my heart beating faster. "I can't believe how lucky I got running into you like that." I'd never told anyone that I'd gone there because of a Savannah dream.

"Maybe it was meant to be."

I didn't believe anything was meant to be. If I did, then I guess my sister was meant to be murdered. "There's no such thing as divine intervention," I said quietly.

"Fair enough. I can understand why you feel that way. But I think we were both supposed to be in that parking lot that day."

I wanted to ask him why, but I felt a clenching in my abdomen, an ache in my lower back and a wetness in my underwear. *Jesus, not now.* "Brady," I said, "I hate to do this, but I have to go inside for a second."

He startled as if shaken out of a trance. "Okay, yeah," he said. "No problem."

Stores were closed for the day, but there was a port-a-potty next to the ice cream shop. I ducked in it. There was sand on the floor from last season, and the tiny mirror was smudged from too much salt air and grimy fingers. I pulled down my jeans. And there it was, right when Brady Irons was about to tell me he secretly loved me: my period.

By the time I got back outside with a ton of tissue paper in my panties, Brady was standing near the bikes with his helmet on. "You going to be okay with what you have on?" he asked. His tone had changed from when we'd been on the beach. Now it was distant, formal.

"Yeah." But I was cold, and he seemed to know it.

He opened a compartment over the back wheel and pulled out a leather jacket lined with sheepskin. It was snug on me, but it felt good. I got on the back of the bike.

"There's a seat heater," he told me through my helmet.

He started the bike. "And you can lean into me for warmth," he said when we were on the highway.

When we got to my driveway, the house was dark. "Thanks for a great day." I handed him the helmet and jacket.

"My pleasure." He folded the jacket and put it in the back storage bin.

I wanted to linger, but he checked his watch. "It was amazing," I said. "I got over a fear."

Then he smiled. "Next time, we'll sit in a dark room together."

"Maybe next time we should do something that scares you."

He watched me. "Like what?"

"Like coming to my brother's for dinner again."

"I'll try," he said. "But the end of the academic year is coming up, so I've been doing a lot of tutoring." He put the key back in the ignition. "Have a good night, Cady."

Before he could drive away, I stepped forward, and when I tried to kiss him on the cheek, he turned, and my lips landed on his mouth. He startled, his eyes widened, and something changed, subtly, sublimely, without my consent or wanting. It happened. When my lips brushed against his and I breathed in his clean laundry smell, there was something different, the feel of his mouth, the way I lingered against him a second too long, how my heart felt like it stopped beating for a moment.

Then I quickly started up the front walk. I heard the motorcycle move down the driveway. I didn't turn around. I didn't watch him make a left toward home. I knew as I got to the door and took out my key that I wouldn't stop thinking about standing in my driveway, pretending I was kissing him good-bye the same way I'd done for the last few months. The way his stubble burned my cheek. How he smelled faintly of lavender, as if he had used Colette's body wash that morning.

CHAPTER
25

"You got your period?" Gabby almost shouted it, and since I knew she was at the library, this seemed slightly inappropriate. I was on Route 571 heading to a lecture by the hypnotist.

"I didn't try to get it," I whispered even though I was alone in the car. "I thought I was pregnant. I was excited even if it'd mean staying with Greg."

"Hell," she said. She had decided getting a pair of sneakers with tiny wheels on the heels would make her more productive at work, and I imagined her happily swearing while gliding past patrons. "What horrible timing. What do you think he was about to tell you? He must be in love with you; why else would he say, 'You came into my life for a reason'?"

"But I'm fat," I told her.

Gabby groaned. "You are not fat. You have that peach-perfect skin and that soft hair and those doe eyes that make you look like you're about sixteen."

I couldn't listen to Gabby's compliments right now. I was too anxious about meeting some freak show fraud who I was certain was going to try to make me do something embarrassing. "I gotta go. I'm at the lecture hall."

"Don't let him hypnotize you," Gabby said. "I heard those people do really creepy things to women."

"Now you sound like me," I told her, but she'd already hung up.

Every time I got off the phone with Gabby, I wanted to call her up again to tell her what Patrick and Jon Caritano had said, but something kept me from it. And I realized now, parking on Washington Street and making sure I had my mini tape recorder, I was thinking like Fisher. I didn't want to suspect anyone I knew.

It was weird to be on Washington Street again, heading toward Green Hall. I'd had more friends at Princeton than I'd had in high school. There'd been a feeling of being free, of releasing myself from the hold of the Wolfe Mansion and what happened there. In college, people hadn't known my sister, the beautiful, shimmery twin who had been murdered by a stranger when we'd just turned sixteen. And it had been easier to make friends. Back then, I pretended I'd never pressed sharp edges against my most tender parts to feel relief, I pretended that I hadn't been the girl who had done the only thing she knew how to stop the pain and wound up in Sound View Psychiatric Hospital at seventeen. That girl, I left far behind.

I'd pretended I was just a girl who got good grades, edited *The Daily Princetonian,* and loved to attend extra-credit lectures. I was good at moving through syllabi, and I knew how to ace papers, tests, and devour books. Academics, I knew, wouldn't fail me. Sometimes I stayed up all night on the third floor of the library, where they kept the periodicals and where I could buy coffee and snacks from the vending machine, the floor that smelled like ink and parchment and made me feel safe.

Thanks to a street vendor selling hot, soft pretzels, I was a few minutes late, and I opened the door of Green Hall, ready to sit through an interminable hour, listening to some blowhard drone on about Jung's theory of the collective unconscious. At least I'd leave with some fodder for *Vanity Fair.*

As soon as I took a seat in the last row, I knew something strange was going on. The guest lecturer was old, but he was handsome, his hair was silver, and he was wearing a black T-shirt and dark jeans. There were about a hundred kids there, and not one was talking. As I dropped my backpack on the carpeted floor next to me, I noticed that no one was taking notes, either. The entire class seemed to be hypnotized.

Despite my psychic abilities with my sister, I thought hypnosis was a bunch of hooey. There was no way someone could talk me into clucking like a chicken or quitting my two favorite foods—fat and sugar—but I was in-trigued by the rapt attention of everyone around me.

Something happened while I sat there and listened to Dr. Corcores talk about centered breathing, clearing the mind, and letting go of tension. As my body got more and more relaxed, I felt an acute fluttering inside. It was vaguely familiar, like the smell of Play-Doh, something you should be able to recognize, but it's so out of context you can't. At the end of the fifty-four min-utes, no one strutted half-dressed to the front of the room. None of us were barking like dogs, and I certainly didn't toss my stash of Twix in the trash.

But all the way home, riding the dark roads of Princeton, I kept thinking about the class. I wasn't sure why, but I couldn't get it out of my mind. How had he managed to quiet the entire auditorium? What had happened before my tardy entrance to make so many students still their minds? And what was that strange familiar feeling I had while I sat there?

Greg was sitting up in bed reading when I got back. "Hey," he said.

I'd told him the night before that I had my period, and he'd said, "Cady, what did you expect?" So I'd been mad at him all day. But now I felt relaxed. In a weird way, what Greg said hardly mattered. I didn't even have that strange pang when I thought of another missed chance at pregnancy. I unbuckled my belt and shimmied out of my jean skirt. I could feel him watching me.

"You seem different," he said.

"I do?" I asked on my way to the bathroom. Inside, I brushed my teeth and washed my face.

When I walked out, Greg seemed to be studying me. "Happy, relaxed," he said when I drew back the covers to get in bed.

"Aren't I usually?" I climbed in.

"Actually, no," he said. "But I never really realized it until this evening."

I don't remember answering. When I woke up, the sun was rising. Greg was still asleep, and out the window, the violet dawn of morning was spread across the sky. I understood what I'd been feeling in Dr. Corcores's class. It was the same feeling I got when Savannah visited me in my dreams. I pad-ded downstairs in my nightgown, sat at the counter with my iPad, and e-mailed Dr. Corcores, introducing myself and asking when we could meet.

As I was brewing coffee, my iPad dinged, and he said I could come back to campus that day.

His office was bare and colorless. "Colored walls and paintings may plant foreign thoughts in the minds of people who come to see me," he said when I walked in.

"Okay," I said tentatively.

"Have a seat." A beige wing chair was pushed up against the wall across from his desk.

He picked up a pair of thick glasses and cleaned them on his shirt but didn't put them on. "So you're writing an article," he said. He wasn't as old as I'd thought the day before. Save a few lines around his mouth and eyes, his skin was smooth, almost perfect.

"I am." I leaned forward and drew my pen and notebook out of my purse.

He gave the pad an amused smile. "But really you want to know something far greater than you will ever put in a *Vanity Fair* article."

I stopped trying to find a blank page. "I do?"

He had a slow way of blinking, somnolent, not sleepy, not bored, but sort of somewhere in between. "Yes, you do," he said.

I couldn't remember exactly what I'd written in my e-mail, but I was certain I didn't tell him the reason I wanted to see him. "And what would that be?" I asked.

"You want to know how to access the unconscious. How to see the unseen. How to understand the messages from the realm outside our minds' perceptions."

I felt heat in my cheeks. "Am I that obvious?"

He laughed, and I felt more at ease. "I'm that good."

"You're a genius."

"Well, now you're just flattering me."

"Can I ask a stupid question?" I shifted in my seat, suddenly aware it was warm in the windowless, square room.

"There are no stupid questions."

"That's very kind of you."

"Ha," he said. "I was going to say there are no stupid questions, only stupid people." Then he winked at me.

I laughed and felt an instant rapport. "I'm curious. Do you think people who have died are part of that vast unconscious you were talking about during the lecture?"

Dr. Corcores watched me. "Yes," he said finally. "It's not scientifically proven, and that bothers people in my field. But yes."

He didn't ask me any questions about who this dead person might be, at least not at first. Instead, he talked conversationally about his work with people who were stuck. In bad relationships, unhealthy habits, the monotony of their own lives. "You see, Cady, a person cannot take a suggestion to which he or she is not already open. So the smoker who claims she wants to quit but won't admit to the pack of emergency cigarettes in the glove compartment of her car won't get anything out of hypnosis. Or the man who arrives for his appointment with a Yodel in his front pocket won't lose any weight."

I clutched my bag, hoping he couldn't sense that I had a Ho Ho stuffed in it.

"Close your eyes," he said suddenly.

And because I liked him, because I believed Dr. Corcores could help me, I did.

When he started talking, I didn't hear the words exactly. I knew he was giving me instructions about breathing and the conscious mind, but something else took over I couldn't later explain. I went back in time to the night Savannah died, the night my mother mashed up a sleeping pill and mixed it into my cup of hot chocolate.

I lay in the double bed in David's room. He was still in the basement with his girlfriend, but it made me feel safer, sleeping there. I listened to people in the living room downstairs, my parents' best friends, my grandparents, my mother's brother, and Todd Spencer, the chef from Sotto Sopra.

In real time, Dr. Corcores was saying words about my unconscious giving my conscious permission, but all I felt was that strange humming from the night before. It was as if I were really there, waiting in the dark in David's room, my eyes heavy. Finally, I must have fallen asleep. I woke with a start, a gnawing feeling in my chest. The fact of Savannah dying hit me slowly, in increments. First, I knew something was terribly wrong, and then I remembered waiting in the school lobby, and then it all came back—the blue turning lights on the walls, Patrick Tunney, Captain Fisher, the ambulance. I touched the necklace at my throat.

The house had felt very still. David was in a beanbag across from me, his arm slung over his head. I'd gotten out of bed and gone back to my room. Still half-asleep maybe, I tried to assure myself that it hadn't really happened, it had been a bad dream, and Savannah was still in her bed, sleeping with her socks on. But it was empty, the covers thrown back like they had been that morning. A half-moon shone in the bedroom, and I'd gone over to the window.

The street was quiet, and the lights made bright cones on the pavement. Otherwise, everything was dark. Across from our house, the land sloped up and was filled with hardwood saplings and dead leaves. The Kampsens lived on top of that hill, a sweet elderly couple with a pool that the neighborhood kids liked to frequent during summer. And in that wood, I saw something.

We had strict leash laws in our neighborhood. Still, the Australian shepherd that lived in the cul-de-sac was a master escape artist, and I thought it was Oxer stealing through the darkness. But when the shadow passed through the trees, I saw it was a figure, moving stealthily, hunched. A man with a hood. I didn't take my eyes off him. I didn't move. The seconds that passed were broad. Time seemed to slow. He stopped behind an ancient stone wall we used to climb as kids. When he got to the road, he looked both ways but didn't cross. The hood was deep, and it hid his face. He pulled at his sleeves, shifted from foot to foot as if cold. It was too dark. He was too far away, but it felt in one instant that he lifted his head and put his hands together as if praying. Then he jogged away unevenly, as if something were caught in his shoe.

I stood too long, watching the empty street, as if he'd been an apparition I was not sure I'd seen. I was frozen. It felt like hours I stayed there, and then I hadn't gone to my parents' room. At sixteen, I didn't think they could fix anything. I believed somewhere in my almost-grown-up world that they were impotent, that it was Savannah and me who really had the knowledge.

"What?" David asked when I sat next to him, still in the beanbag, and shook him. He put his forearm up as if to keep out the light, though I hadn't turned the switch.

"I saw someone," I said.

"Where?"

"Out there, on the street."

David sat up. He was wearing a holed T-shirt that read "You Turn My Floppy Disk into a Hard Drive" that my parents forbade him to wear in public. Without a word, he padded down to my room beside me. When we got to the window, the street was empty. He asked all the right questions. Where was he? What did he look like? How long was he there? And even though I felt like an idiot for not calling him sooner, there was some gratification in knowing he didn't doubt me. David, I realized in the dark room where I would not sleep again for a month, was my ally. Even so, I never did tell him the whole truth, that the hooded man came back again and again in my dreams, and I never brought him up. I never said a word to my parents or the police.

"What the hell was that?" I asked Dr. Corcores when I opened my eyes.

"Since you're a Princeton girl, I know you're familiar with the id, the ego, and the superego," he said.

I blinked, wondering where he could possibly be going with this.

"The ego balances out the narcissism of the id and the cautiousness of the superego. The unconscious mind is like a gatekeeper to things it deems too scary or disturbing for us to deal with."

"Someone I love was murdered." I stared at the place on the wall where there should have been a window. "And I see a man in my dreams."

"Who is he?"

I thought about the voice and how I associated it with a big, burly man. "I don't know."

Dr. Corcores crossed his legs. "Consciously, you think you don't know him, but your inability to see his face suggests otherwise."

I studied his handsome features. "You think I know him?"

"No," he said quietly. "*You* think you know him."

As soon as I got in my car, I called Patrick.

"Hey," he said. "I've been thinking about you. We finally got clearance. I've been reviewing the case, and I want to tell you something."

"What?" I asked.

"I need to do it in person," he said. He sounded close by; it seemed like he was right next to me. "Terhune Orchards is open this time of year, but no one goes until the fruit ripens. Can you meet me there on Saturday?"

Around me, college kids were heading to classes, laughing, their backpacks slung over their shoulders, and I remembered being here and wondering where Savannah would have gone to school, if she would have been less wild by then, whether she would have been at Princeton with me. We could have shared a dorm room. I sometimes imagined what it would have been like to be heading across the quad after class and seeing Savannah coming toward me, her blond hair flying, her laugh ringing out, a bunch of books balanced in the crook of her arm.

"Yes," I said. "I can be there."

CHAPTER
26

I'd called Gabby that morning in a panic. "What if Brady comes tonight?" I'd asked her. I already had all my jeans out on my bed and was trying to figure out what I should wear.

"So?" she asked. "Isn't that what you want? So you can stop going to therapy and start sleeping with a hunk?"

"Gabby!" I'd stood in my underwear, examining my options even though dinner wasn't for another nine hours. "I'm totally humiliated. I kissed him."

"You kiss Chandler hello and good-bye all the time," she'd told me.

"But he's gay," I'd replied, even though we both wished he wasn't. Especially Gabby.

"Whatever. You're fine. And the only reason it was weird is because you haven't kissed anyone for so long, you don't even know what it's like to be turned on."

"That is not true, Gabby. I can't have a baby, but I am having sex. Sometimes."

"I have to go," she said. "I haven't cleaned my house since the last time you guys came, and I need to get a steam shovel."

I told myself Brady probably didn't even notice the kiss was anything out of the ordinary. I'd been thanking him for a fun day at the shore. There was no tongue like Gabby pointed out, no second kiss. I was just Cady, someone he barely remembered from high school, a chubby writer who'd had a crush on him. Who didn't?

But still, I felt jittery when I got in my car. I'd deliberated every day about whether to text him to tell him the dinner was at Gabby's. But then I'd tell myself I should wait until he texted to say he was coming. But then what if he showed up at David's and no one was there? Finally, Brady had texted me five days after the motorcycle ride, saying he'd try to come to David's, and I had written back that it was at Gabby's, given him the address, and then stupidly (I wanted to slap myself) said that he could bring Colette. Even though I'd rather lick an electrical outlet than meet his girlfriend.

It was still light as I made my way across town to Gabby's. It had been an unusually warm spring, and when I passed the shops in town, I saw that most of them had already put out their window boxes, and the daffodils and crocuses were blooming. Moving along the streets were the attorneys, shopkeepers, bankers, and café owners who worked downtown. They were all the same, square and clean and if not wealthy then on the verge of wealth. This was the kind of town that did not want to admit people like my sister, a sixteen-year-old girl, could get murdered in an abandoned mansion.

Now that I'd talked to Patrick and the case was getting reopened, Stanwich looked different. And I liked it. The year Savannah died and the curfew was established, kids would complain about it in fierce whispers as I passed by, as if it was my fault she'd been killed.

And yet in my weird way, I loved Stanwich. I was an overweight girl whose sister had been murdered and who made a ton of money writing dark mystery novels, and for that reason, Stanwich left me alone. That made me love my town. I also loved the old-growth trees and church steeples. The town was a true snap of New England in the middle of New Jersey. I also loved how it was laid out around a green, how quickly I could get to the beach and to the city. And, of course, I thought while I parked beside Gabby's motorcycle and in back of Chandler's ancient Volkswagen, the people I loved best were here.

I walked into the kitchen, my hands filled with grocery bags of fresh kale and salmon. Gabby, Chandler, and my brother were standing at the island, chopping vegetables and peeling potatoes. Odion was uncorking a bottle of wine, and Brady, who I secretly hoped would be there, wasn't in sight.

Gabby came over and kissed me on the cheek. She smelled of lemon and peppermint and gave me the knife in her hand. "Chop," she said, taking the salmon from the bag. "I'll start on the fish."

It was her turn to cook. She was using a recipe from the first cookbook my parents had published. I knew most of them by heart. This one was all about plum tomatoes and red peppers and garlic.

Chandler kissed both my cheeks, and Odion passed me a glass of wine. I pulled the kale out of the bag and handed it to Gabby. "I know my brother won't touch the stuff, but it is perfect with this recipe. Odion, how was your trip?"

"Honey, it was fabulous," Odion said.

"Cork," Chandler said, tossing plum tomatoes and olive oil in a bowl and wiping his hands on a dishrag. "It's the new mahogany."

"Cork furniture?" Gabby was laying the salmon out in a glass cooking pan. "That sounds ugly," she said.

Her house smelled like garlic and wine and musty perfume. It was thoroughly bohemian with beaded lampshades and carpets from Turkey and richly colored pillows thrown everywhere and a hookah pipe in the corner that once in a while she brought out after dinner, though lately she wasn't smoking because she said she heard pot slowly eroded the libido.

"No!" Odion said. "Is lovely!"

And he and Chandler told us all about how Cameroonians managed to make cork beautiful, and I chopped the same pepper until it was almost pulverized, wondering if Brady would show up. I remembered how, when we were in high school, Brady was never at the cafeteria. We both had second-period lunch, except he'd disappear somewhere. I followed him one day and watched as he ended up in his old yellow Mazda, sitting behind the wheel and eating.

"What's he doing out there?" I'd asked Gabby the fall of our sophomore year. We'd been in school two weeks, and I was already so gone on Brady, Gabby said I'd been lobotomized. "Let's find out," she'd said. And so we'd sneaked out to the parking lot and hung around the bike rack, pretending we were trying to unlock one and whispering to each other about him. "He's reading," Gabby had told me.

"He's not reading," I said back.

"Yes"—Gabby had perfect vision—"he's reading." We fought back and forth until finally Gabby, in her curly bob and her retro kneesocks, had, against all my fiercely whispered protests, left me alone and knocked on his window.

From my perch at the bike rack, I saw him roll down his window, and then he looked at me briefly, and my skin went hot. They'd talked for a while. I could hear their voices but not the words. Finally, Gabby came strutting back to me. And I started walking away from her, so she had to run to catch up. After I'd told her how crazy and embarrassing and downright horrible she was, she told me he had been reading.

"Reading what?" I asked her.

"A biography of Kierkegaard," she'd said. "And listening to head-banging music that made my ears hurt." This had made me love Brady even more. It was amazing to me that now I actually could text Brady Irons. That Brady Irons might be about to walk into my best friend's house, where every single candle was lit as if we were about to have a séance. Or an orgy.

The paring knife was so dull the peppers took twice the time to cut, and I wondered vaguely whether Gabby kept it dull for my sake. But probably, I thought as I scooped the peppers into a pile, it was dull because she didn't give a damn. Chandler and Gabby were testing Odion on his citizenship exam, and David was in the living room, trying to find the game on Gabby's ancient TV. I tried to remember all the words to "Sundown" as I chopped so I wouldn't think about Brady. I did not want to think about him like that. I'd end up feeling stupid and totally heartbroken. A guy like that didn't go for girls like me.

I'd finished cutting the peppers and was working on opening the wine when I heard the doorbell ring.

"Guess who decided to show up," Chandler said.

I saw him through the kitchen door, peeking out the window.

"Cady, your dreamboat's here!" Gabby yelled in to me.

"Fuck off," I called back.

"Leave Cady alone," Odion told her. "A writer has a very sensitive spirit."

Chandler headed for the front hall, but Gabby cut him off. "He brought wine!" she yelled over her shoulder when she opened the door. "And calla lilies. Holy shit, you're a good guest."

Brady was wearing a worn blue T-shirt the same color as his eyes. "Hey," he said.

David muted the TV. "Hey," he said.

"Welcome," Gabby told him.

Odion gave him a glass of wine and took the flowers.

"We'll open yours later," Chandler said, pumping Brady's hand.

"Pretty, right?" Odion said, holding the flowers. "Now we need a vase."

Brady looked like a boy at his first high school dance, standing there, and I didn't know how to make him feel better. In the kitchen, Odion started searching through the cabinets. Gabby came up behind him.

"To the left," she told him. "Near the fridge."

"Ah yes, here." Odion brought down an intricately cut vase. "So lovely." His huge black hands wrapped around the crystal. "This man Brady has nice taste," he whispered.

Gabby giggled. "I particularly like his taste in women."

I glared at her. "Yes," I said, my voice a warning, "I bet Colette is very pretty." Grabbing the vase from Odion, I filled it with water.

In the other room, I heard Chandler ask Brady, "And why exactly do you work at a prison?"

"I can't believe he asked him that," I whispered.

And Gabby, who had taken the salmon out to check it, laughed.

"You know Chandler. Very nervous for his little Cady." Odion smiled. His dark eyes had laughter in them, and it made me feel calmer somehow.

"Nervous? Why?" I set the vase on the counter, and he stuck the lilies in.

"No reason. But we see how you look at him."

"Told you." Gabby bumped her shoulder against mine. "I'm not the only one who's noticed."

I put my hands on my hips. "You two are hallucinating."

Odion picked up the vase and held it at arm's length, admiring his arrangement. "No," he said. "We are not."

"Odion?" I drew his name out. "Tell me."

He gave me his beautiful white smile and reached down to kiss my forehead. "You need warmth, Cady; that's what I tell Chandler. I say, 'Honey, Cady needs some sunshine after this man who plays with brains all day.' We not so love him, you know, he okay, but this man"—he turned to the living room—"I think he gets Cady. I watch the two of you. You have something. I not know what, but something."

"I've been telling her that for months," Gabby said, and then she slipped into the living room with the rest of the boys.

I felt myself flush. "I don't know," I said.

"We never know," Odion said solemnly. "We just wish. That's all. We wish and we wish." And then he was out the kitchen before I could say another word.

We ate dinner in front of the TV, watching a Yankees doubleheader. I noticed David was wearing clean clothes, a sign that I took to mean he was getting over Emma. Or maybe it was that Merry Maids had left his sweats in the washer, so he had to wear something else. Now he was dressed in jeans and a plain green T-shirt. Untucked, it hid the fleshy part of his middle.

"I can't believe how well the Yanks are playing," he said.

"I smell victory," Chandler said. We were all amazed that they'd won any games since A-Rod had been suspended the entire previous season and Derek Jeter had retired. But they were off to a hell of a start, and I had secret plans to get us all tickets to the World Series if they made it this year. Beside him, Odion read a magazine. Odion didn't give a shit about baseball. And Gabby was busy texting Duncan, asking if he'd get there in time to play Cranium. "Maybe the Mets will experience a miracle, and it'll be a Subway Series." Brady rested his hand next to mine, so we were barely touching. He leaned across me for the bottle of B&B, and I could smell his cologne, earthy and subtle. I'd been trying to get Greg to wear cologne since we'd moved in together the year before we got married. One year before Christmas, he said he'd try it. He picked out Clive Christian No. 1. The bottle was the size of my thumb and cost $2,350. Brady leaned forward in his chair to fill my glass.

A commercial for Coke came on, and David muted it. "How's that sweet daughter of yours?" he asked Chandler. "You need to bring her by one afternoon. I can't remember the last time I saw her."

Chandler grinned, like he always did when he talked about Madelyn. "She dropped the f-bomb in preschool yesterday," he said.

"Yes, we almost piss ourselves," Odion said, happy to be talking about Mads instead of the game, "when this teacher, she called to tell us."

"Yeah," Chandler said. "Margaret Donnell is as scary now as she was in high school." Margaret Donnell had been their class president, a blond, perky girl with a competitive edge and a controlling streak that bordered on Nazi-esque. That she'd wound up as a preschool teacher seemed almost dictatorial. "She said Mads was trying to get her sweatshirt off when she blurted out, 'I can't get this fucking thing over my head.'"

"Oh my God, that's hysterical." I had to put my beer down to keep from spitting it out. "Did she get in trouble?"

"Well, seeing as she learned it from us . . ." Chandler said.

"Us?" Odion raised his eyebrows.

"Okay," Chandler conceded. "It might have been me. But anyway, we gave her a stern talking-to about how we don't use bad words in public. Then we high-fived each other, because her context was perfect."

"You know," Brady said, his voice serious, "there's a correlation between when kids start using curse words and how likely they are to get in trouble with the law."

Odion played with the clasp on a silver bracelet on his wrist. "This is true?" he asked.

I could see Brady trying hard not to smile. It amazed me how well I'd come to know him after only a few months. "Bullshit." I balled up my napkin and threw it at him.

He held up his hands in a *you got me* gesture. "I had you going there for a minute."

Odion let out a sigh of relief. "Mads is good girl," he said.

"All right, in Mads's honor, fuck this," David said. "Let's go play us a criminal game of Cranium."

"I call Gabby until Duncan gets here," I said, tugging on her sleeve.

We gathered around the wooden farm table and squished ourselves on one side so we could see the TV. Brady grabbed the bottle of B&B from the kitchen, wedged his chair next to mine, and knocked over the brandy when he reached for a game piece. It didn't break, but the top hadn't been on, and it spilled across the table.

"Fuck," Chandler said.

"You see?" Odion pointed to him. "Madelyn learned it from him."

Brady got up and grabbed a dish towel off the counter. "Jesus, I'm sorry."

"No problem," Gabby said, reaching for the mop behind the door and passing it to Brady. "I do it all the time."

"I guess we need more B&B," I said. I found my gray-and-black Puma sneakers under the table. "I'll be back in fifteen."

Brady stopped mopping the floor. "I'm blocking you in," he said. "Do you want me to drive?"

Chandler took the mop from him. "Fine," he said. "I'll finish cleaning."

Odion tapped the floor. "Sweetheart, it's mostly all gone now."

"Yeah," David said. "It's good enough."

Brady and I headed for the door, and before it shut behind us, I heard Chandler say, "Do they both need to go to the store?" He sounded exasperated.

"Why not have a little company?" Odion asked back.

David, I was pretty sure, was clueless.

Brady opened the passenger door for me. His truck smelled like the flowers he'd brought and like him, leathery and earthy, and I felt dizzy and nervous as he went around to get in. "Wine Cask is closest," he said.

We didn't speak on the way there. One Eskimo was on the radio. *Why, why, why did you need him? Where was I?* When I leaned over to turn it up, my arm brushed his, and I felt my face flush.

In less than five minutes, we were in the parking lot of the Wine Cask, and in that amount of time, I became convinced that Brady didn't give a shit about me, it was all in my mind, and that kiss was nothing more than a friend with a friend. He turned off the ignition but didn't move. Across the street, a pizza place's OPEN sign blinked in its window.

"Last week . . ." he started. He'd parked in front of the liquor store, and a red neon BUDWEISER sign was flashing on his face. "The kiss." He almost sighed it out.

"I'm sorry about that." I began to babble; it was something I sometimes did at readings when I didn't want to answer a question. "I don't know what I was thinking. I know what it seemed like, but I was giddy from our ride, and I apologize."

I went for the door handle, but Brady touched my arm. "Hey," he said. "Not so fast."

I turned back, my heart doing flips in my chest, and leaned back in my seat. I could feel Brady watching me. I hated my profile; it showed the soft, fleshy part of my neck. He leaned toward me, and I thought he was going to kiss me, but instead, he put his finger under my chin and turned my face toward him. And then he drew away. When he did, I felt a wash of relief and horrible disappointment. But in that same second, he doubled back and kissed me. Gently at first, barely parting my lips. When I didn't pull away, I felt his tongue on mine, tasted the oaky flavor of wine. I leaned into him and felt the seat belt dig into my sternum, before the tightness of the nylon gave way to other sensations, his fingertips on my face, his wet lips, the stubble against my chin. I couldn't breathe. I didn't want to. And Brady seemed hungry. It seemed he was searching for something, his breath coming quickly, as though he were ravenous, starved, and I waited for that same desire to take me, to whisk me away. Here was a boy I had loved terribly, obsessively in high school. This was the boy I'd imagined kissing me, holding me, touching me since the minute he walked into Kingswood, and yet as we sat locked together in front of the Wine Cask, in a sexy tête-à-tête for anyone to see, I felt absolutely nothing, completely flatlined. It was like kissing my brother, as gross as that analogy was. Finally, I pulled away. I saw him swallow and catch his breath.

"Jesus," he said, shaking his head like he was waking up. "I don't know what that was."

"Brady," I said. "Listen—"

He cut me off. "Cady, I don't want to fuck you up. Fuck up your life." He was facing the front again, and the neon reddened his face, pulled back, and then reddened it again. He was beautiful, gorgeous as ever.

Why had I felt nothing? What was wrong with me?

"Cady." Brady closed his eyes.

I thought maybe if I tried it again, maybe if we weren't in front of the Wine Cask, I would feel something.

He took a deep breath. "I'm sorry." He opened his eyes. "I'm not going to do that again," he said. "That was fucked."

Because I did not say anything, because nothing this dramatic had happened in my life with a boy, ever, I sat there, dumbly holding my hands in my lap.

"We should get going," I said as lightly as I could. "They're going to send a search party."

"Yeah," he said. "Okay." I watched him reach for the door handle.

After we'd gotten the B&B, we rode back to Gabby's house in silence. I counted the streetlights to keep my mind busy. Thirteen. Fourteen, including the one that only flickered occasionally. When we pulled into Gabby's driveway, I noticed that, despite all my wishing, the clock had betrayed us. We'd been gone twenty-seven minutes for a trip to a liquor store a half mile away.

"We're not going to mention this," Brady said. "Right?"

For some reason, this was insulting, as though he were ashamed or thought I was a blabbermouth. All the windows were lit up. Inside, I knew they were wondering where the hell we were.

"Under one condition," I said. I felt Brady take a little energetic step back.

"There's a condition?" He cocked his head. "What?"

In the half light, I saw those fine cheekbones we used to speculate about. Gabby said he was Native American. I said he was perfect.

"Promise?" I asked.

"All right," he said.

"I get to interview Larry again."

Brady's jaw flexed. "No fucking way," he finally said.

An orange tabby cat was sitting on the railing on the second-floor porch of the old Victorian where Gabby lived. I had a feeling that I'd never finish the book if I didn't get back in that room with Larry Cauchek, if I couldn't get a sense for the way a serial killer really thought.

"The whole police force knows my name. I am protected up and down. All I need is to get in there one or two more times and talk to a person who is shackled at the feet and arms." Even though I'd felt flatlined during the kiss, I still wanted Brady Irons to have felt what I thought he was feeling during it, but now, with Gabby's house bright in the darkness, I wasn't so sure, and it made me feel a little pissed off. "You promised," I said. "So deal?"

"All right," he said. "Deal."

They were all sitting around the table, still, with the Cranium game laid out before them, waiting. Duncan had arrived, but he wasn't sitting next to Gabby; David was sitting next to her, and Duncan was the odd man out.

Chandler watched me set down the B&B. "That took a while," he said.

I tried to scrunch my face in annoyance. "You wouldn't believe the line in that store. Can anybody count change correctly?" I did my best indignant I-can't-believe-people-can-be-so-stupid spiel and hoped that that was good enough.

Chandler raised his eyebrows at us. "If you want to play, you're going to have to grab chairs from the kitchen," he said.

"Fine," I said. I got a chair and shimmied in next to Duncan.

In truth, I didn't think I could handle sitting with Brady again. Kissing him felt as though I'd been doing it all my life. But not in the sparks-and-fireworks way, in a different way I couldn't quite explain, as though we were family, kids playing pretend, trying to find some semblance of reality in the other's touch.

Gabby and David won Cranium. Duncan and I lost. And Brady, Odion, and Chandler came in second. I kept glancing at Brady during the game, and about seventeen times, I caught his eye, but he'd turn away, and so would I.

It was a quiet game. It was as if our awkwardness spread itself over the table, and I felt at once like I wanted to make everything right again and that I had no idea how. Finally, everyone left. Only Duncan remained, emptying wineglasses and scraping cake into the trash.

"Shoo," Gabby told him, taking a pack of cigarettes out of the drawer next to her stove.

Duncan hunched his shoulders, deflated. He was wearing a nice linen shirt and pleated pants. "You want me to leave?" he asked sheepishly.

Gabby winked at him. "I love you, but it's girl time." She got his jacket from the chair in the living room. It was a Paddington Bear coat with the same wooden buttons. "I'll see you at the library," she told him, patting him on the butt as he went out into the night.

Gabby closed the door. "I much prefer fucking him in the library," she said, grabbing the rest of the bottle of wine Brady had brought. "Screw the dishes," she said. "Let's talk."

"What do you think that was about?" she asked after I told her about the kiss, even though I'd told Brady I wouldn't tell anyone.

"I don't know." I slumped against the couch while Gabby drank wine from the bottle and smoked her cigarette. "Maybe he's not the same person he was in high school. Maybe I'm not."

"You've been in love with him since we were toddlers."

"No," I said. "I've been in love with him since second semester freshman year."

"Yeah." She blew smoke out her nose. "Since we were infants. I think you're stressed. The guy is fucking gorgeous."

I reached for the wine and drank it. "Chandler hates him," I said.

Gabby leaned back next to me and put her feet up. "I know." There was no surprise in her tone.

"I wish I hated him," I told her.

"That would be no fun," she said, taking the wine back and pulling a long swig from it. "No fun at all." She smiled at me in the candlelight. Her little nose ring glinted, and her mouth was the color of blackberries and looked exotic from the wine.

"Why do you like him so much?" I asked her.

"I don't know." She let out a stream of smoke. "I think it's nice to have a guy look at you the way he does. Like he's curious about you."

"Greg doesn't do that," I admitted. "I'm not sure he ever did."

She dropped the cigarette in a glass of wine someone had left behind. "Oh, honey," she said. "Do me a favor."

"What?" I asked, getting up.

She got up with me holding the wine and gave me a little hug, careful not to bonk me in the head with the bottle. "Try again with him."

When I got in my car and headed home, I realized I wasn't sure whom Gabby meant. Brady or Greg.

CHAPTER
27

Terhune Orchards at nine on a Saturday morning in the beginning of May was deserted. The two hundred acres were shaded by apple and peach trees. "We could walk and talk," Patrick had said, "and no one would overhear us." I got there seventeen minutes early so I could think about what I was going to say and get comfortable with the surroundings. Ever since Savannah, I needed extra time to get familiar with new places.

The air smelled of cinnamon, and I felt instantly at ease. The family who ran the orchard had set up a farm stand north of the parking lot, and I thought I'd have enough time to pick up some cheese and cardamom before Patrick got there. But as soon as I started toward it, I heard him call my name.

I wouldn't have known it was Patrick if I wasn't expecting him. He'd tied a black bandanna around his head, tucked a pack of cigarettes into the back pocket of his torn jeans, and was wearing a dirty wifebeater.

"Day off?" I called, using my hand like a visor against the sun.

He laughed, his white teeth incongruous with his attire. When he got close enough to touch me, he said, "Undercover. I'm supposed to be a dirtbag. Do I pass?"

"With flying colors." He smelled like strawberries. "Almost," I told him. "Almost?"

"Um, you smell a little fruity. Have you been wearing your wife's perfume?"

He laughed. "I'm not married." There was something in his voice that sounded apologetic. "My son loves to give the dogs baths with his strawberry-scented shampoo."

"Do you still have greyhounds?"

"Good memory." He smiled. "Want to walk in the shade?"

We headed toward the orchard. "I didn't know you had a son," I told him.

They'd set up a table at the edge with baskets. A sign told us to pick our own, but in early May, there was really nothing to pick. Patrick grabbed a basket anyway and hooked the handles on his elbow.

"Yeah," he said. "Darlene got pregnant before we split up. She didn't really want a baby, but luckily for me, mistakes happen."

I felt bad for this big teddy bear of a guy. "What's his name?"

"Aiden Patrick."

"That's a nice strong name," I told him. And Patrick grinned. The orchard smelled of fresh mud and bark, and I wanted to lie in the grass and take a nap in the sun.

Apple trees were planted in neat rows lining the path, and I told Patrick about my dreams and the hypnotist. "I don't want to believe it's someone I know," I told him. "It's like ever since I met you and Jon at the station, I've been trying not to think everyone I know is a possible killer."

We'd reached the top of the hill. Terhune's had put a little bench beneath one of the apple trees, and a split-rail fence separated us from the acres of blueberry bushes stretching out below.

Patrick went over to it. "It's like one of your books," he said.

I sat down beside him. "Yeah, but in the books, I get to decide who did it."

He didn't answer. It was unusually warm, and I could feel sweat trickling between my breasts, and my breath was coming quickly. Patrick was sturdy, standing there like one of those big trees out on the land in back of our house that I wanted to hug because they were so solid.

It took a while for him to speak again, and then finally he said, "People get obsessed with girls, Cady. And let's face it, girls get obsessed with people—a teacher or someone at your parents' restaurant. I don't know. We interviewed everyone we thought Savannah knew and came up empty. But we've got to try again."

I watched him in that wifebeater, the way he had of moving one foot forward when he stood, as if stepping into life. I got up from the bench and stood at the fence by the blueberry bushes, haphazard and happy. In a couple of months, they'd be bursting with fruit, and Chandler and I would come pick them and then make pies. Beyond the orchard, I could see our town laid out like a little stage setting, the square and the churches and, even though I couldn't see them, all the people, moving about with a possible murderer in their midst. And what had felt sure and right a few moments ago, that steady solidity in Patrick's voice about trying again, rose up like an overwhelming wave, and I felt suddenly like I was drowning. "Do you think he's still here?"

"That's a good question. I want to find out if anyone who knew Savannah left town within a few months of her murder. If we're right and the perpetrator cared about her, the guilt may have driven him away." He got quiet and toed a rock with his boot. "Believe me, I know what it's like to have guilt wrap itself so tightly around you that all you want to do is run."

"Shouldn't the police have investigated things like that sixteen years ago?"

"Yes, of course, but the original theory was that a stranger had done this, not someone who knew her. We thought she had been lured away and accosted, so we concentrated on that vein."

"This is so fucked up." I turned my back to the fence. "One minute it's a stranger, the next it's someone who knew her and was obsessed with her, maybe a teacher or someone from the restaurant." I felt like I might cry. "Maybe the killer left. Unless he couldn't leave. It could be somebody one town over or a mailman or maybe someone from the high school." I could feel something rise in me, something I had been trying to stamp down every minute of every day. "Or you know what? Maybe my parents are right. Maybe we might as well keep the case closed." And because tears were blurring my vision, I left the fence and started walking down the hill, not sure really where I was going. My car sat in the parking lot, waiting for me.

Patrick ran to catch up with me. "Stop, Cady." He pulled at my elbow. "Please stop."

So I did. I expected him to tell me all the reasons we had to keep going, but he did something I'll never forget: he put the basket on the ground and pulled me into a hug.

"I know," he said. "I know how frustrating this is. It's fucking horrible."

And then I cried. Standing there leaning against his big chest, I sobbed. I felt sick I cried so hard. I cried and cried in the heat with that empty basket next to us.

Afterward, we ate lunch in Terhune's café. No one was in there. And they had a nice full salad bar as a result, but they also had a whole table of desserts. Patrick and I decided to eat peach pie with ice cream and skip all the rest. I actually felt happy after my cry. I couldn't explain it. I felt hopeful and relaxed.

"Pie is so good when you're hungover," I said while we ate.

"Yeah. It's the best. Why are you hungover?" He had a spot of vanilla ice cream on his chin, but I didn't say anything.

"David and I closed The Ivy Inn last night playing One in a Hundred."

"What's that?" He scratched at the scruff on his chin, but the ice cream still didn't come off.

"You watch everyone who walks by and have to decide if you'd sleep with them." The game seemed so stupid when I said it out loud, but it'd been keeping us entertained in restaurants and airports for years. "Last night, my brother, the horndog, made it to twenty-five."

"And you?"

"Oh God, I can't tell you that. It's way too embarrassing."

"C'mon, how many hotties?" It sounded strange to hear this giant of a man use a word like that.

"Um." I let a peach slip around my mouth before swallowing it. "In a bar full of guys, I couldn't find one I wanted to sleep with."

"No one?" He smiled. "No hotties at all?"

This was not how I'd thought my meeting with Detective Tunney would go. "That's not really how it works for me. I have to feel like I'd want to wake up with them without chewing off my arm. Or better yet, without them thinking that sneaking out the window naked would be a better option than facing me in the morning."

"Stop it," he said. "You're adorable."

I scooped up the last of my ice cream. "That's nice-person speak for *chunky.*"

I waited to endure a clumsy silence, but Patrick set his fork down on his plate with some peach pie still on it. "Actually," he said, his green eyes sparkling, "*adorable* means *adorable.*"

I felt my face burning. "Does Aiden look like you?" I asked to change the subject.

"Ah, Aiden." Patrick pulled out his cell phone and scrolled through it. "You tell me." He turned it toward me, and I saw the cutest little red-haired boy smiling over a piece of half-eaten watermelon.

He was a carbon copy of Patrick but chubbier and smaller. "Now *that's* adorable," I said. And right when I was about to take the cell to enlarge the picture, it rang. Patrick stood and went to talk over by the window. I could tell from the relaxed tone of his voice that the caller was a girl, and I imagined him waking up with a beautiful, skinny girlfriend with silky hair.

"That was my researcher," he said when he put the phone back in his pocket. "She has a list of who left town in the months after Savannah was killed."

"What can I do?"

"Go through the funeral guest list and the yearbooks again." He put up his hand when I started to say I'd already done that about nine hundred times. "It's been a while," he said. "Do it one more time, please."

"Whatever you say, boss. So," I said, not really wanting the answer to my next question, "who were the main suspects way back when?"

"We had to investigate everyone."

"Everyone? Even my family?"

"Come on. You know this from your books. It's Detectivology 101. First thing you do is rule out loved ones."

"Detectivology?" I thought about all the words I made up for my books. "Is that a real word?"

"It is now," he said, laughing.

"Does that mean at one point I was a suspect?"

"You were only sixteen."

"So what? Children do horrible things to each other all the time."

He was chewing on his lip. "Everyone was on the list . . . including you."

"So what made you take me off . . . the *list*?"

"Cady." He held out his hand, and when I put mine in it, I felt instantly comforted. "No one in your family was responsible for Savannah's death. Plenty of witnesses saw your parents at the restaurant, getting ready for dinner."

"Squeezing melons and not their daughter's neck?" I'd meant it to be funny, but I had a quick, gruesome image of my parents choking the life out of my sister.

Patrick ignored me and kept talking. "I can't remember the name of the kid whose house your brother was at, but his mom was home and gave us a sworn affidavit that he was there playing video games. And you were on the phone with 911, calling it in."

"Yeah, but isn't there some rule in detective land like *whoever smelt it dealt it?*"

"You watch too many cop shows." He tapped the Irish band on his right ring finger on the table. "But yes, because you called it in, we had to look at you."

"What did you see?"

"A terrified girl who somehow knew something awful had happened to her sister." He held his breath for several seconds. "Plus, we subpoenaed your cell phone records."

"And? My parents gave me that phone for emergencies. I made exactly one call on it."

"I know. But it was the time that you made the call. The medical examiner determined there was no way you would have had enough time to get from the Wolfe Mansion back to Kingswood."

"So you really did check me out."

"I never wanted you on that list," he said. "I knew you weren't responsible the first time I laid eyes on you."

I watched a man trimming forsythia on the orchard lawn. "That's where you're wrong. If I hadn't been such a coward, I could have saved her. I knew the minute she was late something was wrong, and I did nothing. I was wholly, singularly responsible. If I'd gone out there instead of—"

"If you'd gone out there, you might have gotten yourself killed too." He squeezed my fingers. A cop's skin shouldn't have been that soft. "If you hadn't made that call and went searching for Savannah instead, this could have ended much worse for you. And your parents."

"Sometimes I wish he'd killed me too." I felt the pressure of tears behind my eyes.

"Stop," Patrick said. He leaned so far over the table I thought he was going to kiss me. I felt my breath stop. "Don't ever say that." He watched me but didn't smile. "I'm going to do everything I can to catch him, Cady. You know that, right?"

I put my fork on my plate, the ice cream scraped clean, no bits of peach left anywhere on it. "Me too," I said. "I'll die before I stop."

CHAPTER
28

Before I left for Sound View, I'd gone to Savannah's grave site every day no matter what—in sleet, when it was so hot even air-conditioning didn't keep me cool, in two feet of snow. On my last day at the hospital, my parents and I sat in soft leather chairs in Dr. Holley's office, reviewing the list of shit I had to do to stay off the crazy train.

CADENCE MARTINO CONTRACTS TO:

1.   Alert an adult if she feels she might harm herself in any way.
2.   Share her "feelings journal" with her parents every Sunday.
3.   Visit her sister's grave no more than once a week.

The list went on. I had to promise to continue outpatient sessions with Dr. Holley. And exercise daily. Holley had told me that exercise set endorphins free in my system, and a gym membership had been part of the release agreement, but my eyes stopped at number three. I heard my mother shift on the couch across from me. It was warm in Sound View that day; the radiators were still clanking, and I'd seen a thin sheen of sweat on my father's upper lip. Holley explained that if I was at Savannah's grave, I wouldn't be out forging new relationships. *Forging?* I'd wanted to spit the word back at that dumb hippie. *Who under the age of ninety uses the word "forging"?* Inside, I'd felt a kind of panic, as though a tightly woven net that kept me together was unraveling at a speed I couldn't keep up with. Holley raised his eyebrows.

"Okay?" he asked.

I held the list tightly in my hands. I felt chilled in the strange way that scary movies made me cold as though I were ultimately unprotected in the world. I either did this or I stayed at Sound View. The difference was, I realized, running my finger over the white space between the words, the rules had loopholes; these things could be ducked, avoided. My mother had worn a belted yellow dress, too summery for the day, and my father was in a suit, one he'd only worn to church, as though this were a ceremony, a rite of passage in every girl's life, and they were leaning forward; it seemed like they were holding a collective breath. I suddenly felt sorry for them.

"Okay," I said.

Dr. Holley smiled a *gotcha* smile and handed me a pen. I scribbled my initials next to all seventeen items and signed the bottom of the page.

On the way home, I sat in the backseat, watching the world pass. It was a gorgeous Sunday; everything was thawing and warming up, the maple trees were sprouting buds, and I saw dandelions on the edges of the byways. I felt unleashed, let loose, the landscape seemed so spacious. There were things on the list I would obey. Seeing Savannah's grave once a week wasn't one of them. How would I hear her? Besides the dreams, that was when Savannah talked to me, on those afternoons I sat under the red maples. Not words, exactly—it was as though she occupied my thoughts, turning them into a Savannah way of thinking. I could hear her spilling laughter, the mischievous way she seemed to take an idea and run with it. The idea didn't have a chance of escaping. And I didn't, either.

Savannah had stayed away from Sound View; that wasn't a place for her. She wouldn't have come anywhere near those wasted girls, the whitewashed corridors, and the terrifying nurses. And now, driving home, panicking about how I would get to the graveyard without my parents knowing, I felt her. She seemed to occupy me as I sat in the car. And I realized with relief she wasn't going to wait for sleep or cemeteries. She'd disregard all boundaries and come to me anytime she liked. The cemetery, I knew as we turned into our driveway, wasn't as important as I thought it had been.

Still, there was something beckoning about a cemetery. And even now, almost seventeen years later, I felt myself drawn there. Two days after my meeting with Patrick, I'd woken in a sloggy, half-dreaming state and had the insistent feeling that I should go to Savannah. It had been raining since that unnaturally warm day at the orchard, and now the morning bloomed sunny and clear. After Greg left for work, I drove under that canopy of old maple trees past the field where the same chestnut horse had been grazing for more than a decade.

A well-meaning but annoying counselor at Sound View had told me that grief doesn't go away, it just gets different, and going to the cemetery was a kind of barometer for that. Sixteen years of living without my sister and grief felt exactly the same, a quicksand that sucked me down day after day, but never deep enough to kill me. That would have been far too kind. I would have taken different, even if it had meant worse. This much sadness was too much sorrow, a headache that wouldn't go away no matter how much aspirin I swallowed. An itch that wouldn't be tempered no matter how much I scratched. An arrhythmia that kept my heart racing and my breath short but wouldn't give me the respite of death. As I drove between the stone pillars, I remembered how, before I could drive, I used to walk the three miles to the cemetery.

I parked underneath that same maple. Savannah's gravestone was surrounded by regulation-length grass so green it could have been Astroturf. My dad's parents had bought fifteen plots when they got married, wanting to keep the Martinos together after death. My sister was there alone.

I closed my eyes and asked her silently why I kept having the same dream about her. Was she really trying to tell me something? A clue about who killed her? That she missed me? Or was it the random firing of synapses that invaded my sleep every night? "Come back to me," I said aloud, opening my eyes. "What are you trying to say?" But there was no answer. The skies didn't open. No divine thought entered my head. There was no sign, great or small, from Savannah. The sun was strong, too strong for the beginning of May, and I felt suddenly exhausted. And then I heard the twig crack behind me. When I turned, I caught sight of a black hoodie weaving between the graves. I could tell by the build it was a big man, and he wasn't so much running as speed walking, like he was trying to get out of there without seeming like he was

in a hurry. It was such an odd sight, a man scurrying away from a row of head-
stones. "Hey!" I yelled after him, but he slipped between a group of graves
that I knew from wandering the grounds belonged to an extended family of
fourteen who had all died in a house fire on Christmas in the early 1950s. I
chased the guy in the hoodie, but he had seemed to disappear into the ether.
It was as if the trees that lined the cemetery were in collusion, hiding him, and
he was gone. I half believed he was an odd figment of my imagination brought
on by grief.

I walked by the embarrassingly large granite memorial for Mathew and
Steven Harris, teenage brothers who'd died in a drunk-driving accident a
few years before Savannah. A thin layer of pollen tinted Savannah's headstone a golden yellow, and I brushed it away with my sleeve and flicked away
a spot of bird poop. Other than that, her stone and the area around it were
pristine. My parents had been paying Stony Lane Cemetery $40.95 a month
to keep the grave clean. I'd found the invoice years before when I'd gone
through my mother's desk, looking for something sharp enough to cut myself. I'd needed a small fix—a pen, an earring, anything that would puncture
my skin enough to release the pain I could feel bubbling under the surface,
and I remembered the strange, almost floating sensation I had when I'd seen
Savannah's name in the subject line, as though for one odd moment she were
alive, incurring expenses on bills in my mother's desk.

The caretakers tended to the flowers my mother had planted in front of
the grave, but I saw now that someone had left a bushel of purple flowers
with yellow centers behind it, as though hiding them. Up front, depending
on the time of year, were tulips and daffodils, gladiolas, lilies, bright, cheery
flowers that seemed to sing silently when you walked by. And, of course, daisies. But the little bushel, which was still in an earthenware container, appeared untamed, like the wild roses that grew along the seaside paths Savannah
and I used to see when we took bike rides in the summer. Once upon a time,
Savannah's headstone had been adorned with photographs, trinkets, statues,
and daisies, loads and loads of daisies, because everyone knew they were
her favorite. After her death, classmates kept up a steady stream of memo-
rabilia. But all that had stopped by the time I went to college. Teenagers have
short memories.

I walked to the flowers and touched their petals. There was no card attached and nothing to give away who'd left them. I pulled one from the bunch

and held it to my nose. It smelled like earth and leaves. And it had the springy middle of a buttercup. I went searching for the caretaker, Mr. Wiley, an old, half-deaf man who took unnatural pride in the graves. While I walked, I heard a woodpecker somewhere to the north and the whir of a motor. When I found Mr. Wiley, he was sweeping out the little shack where he kept the watering cans and gardening tools. I had to shout to ask about the flowers, and in the end, he simply came with me down the dirt road so I could show them to him. "Nope," he said, rubbing his chin and talking too loudly. "Can't say as I know a thing about these, my dear."

Sitting in my car in the sun and searching for flowers on my phone, I finally found a thumbnail picture similar to the wilting flower on my dashboard. Clicking on it, a photo of the *Anemone thalictrum* flower filled my screen, the common name for it, rue flower. Wikipedia told me it's closely related to the buttercup, and the purple variety is really pink. A pretty flower with a melancholic title, it had been named after Shakespeare's *Hamlet*. Ophelia clutched the flower after she went mad because she could not marry her love. Unable to shake the spooky feeling I got from reading about the rue flower, I started my car and drove west on Mareside Highway.

When I got to David's house, I found him in the kitchen with three computers open and a pencil tucked behind his ear. "Hey there, big brother."

He had on an oxford shirt and nice pants. Deep wrinkles around his eyes were making him look more and more like our father. He hugged me quickly and kissed my cheek. "What a nice surprise."

The screens were all filled with letters and numbers that meant nothing to me. "Whatcha working on?"

He tossed the pencil on the table. "A billionaire in New York wants me to create an app to track his daughter's school bus."

"That's brilliant. Think how many hours it could have saved Mom from waiting at the end of the driveway."

"Everything all right?" he asked, saving documents on each computer one by one.

"Yeah. Can't complain." I went to his fridge, hoping he'd stopped by Sotto Sopra for some of Chef Todd's homemade chocolate puddings. All these years later, he kept on making them for us. "I was just at Stony Lane." We never called the cemetery by its name or referred to Savannah when we were talk-ing about it. "Have you been there recently?"

"Not for a while." A shadow crossed his face, and I knew I'd upset him.

"There were some flowers at her grave I'd never seen before."

"Maybe Mom had them delivered. Have you called her?"

My mother and I hadn't talked much in the years since she and my father had moved. We'd grown so far apart, it was like we were shadows passing for mother and daughter. We shared almost nothing, so busy in our respective lives that even when we talked every week, I had nothing to say. "I thought I'd ask you first." Shit. Chandler and Emma weren't kidding. We re-ally had no idea how to talk to each other. I opened the crisper drawer and grabbed a bunch of grapes. "Who do you think put them there?"

David took the grapes out of my hand and rinsed them off in the sink. "Who the hell knows? Everyone loved her."

"You don't think it's weird that some random person is leaving flowers there?"

"Not really." He was maddeningly unconcerned. "We don't know for a fact that it's random."

"Don't you think we should tell Patrick? Or . . . someone? I mean, that's weird. Who is leaving creepy flowers for her?"

David grabbed two bottles of Stella out of the fridge and handed one to me. Apprehension swept over his face. I knew he was trying to hide it, but it crept up anyway, unbidden, letting me know what he really thought of me: that I was a crazy girl who couldn't let go of her sister's death. "It's no big deal. People leave flowers in cemeteries; it's what they do. It is *not* creepy." David clearly wasn't worried, and I wasn't going to get anything out of him.

"Really? You don't think it's strange that when I Googled it, I found that it means regret and remorse? And its name is the *rue* flower."

David closed all three computers. "Of course not, because you're prob-ably the only person who knows that. I'm sure whoever left them just thought they were pretty."

I drank my beer and chatted David up about the app he was creating, but I really wanted to know who would put flowers that symbolized regret and remorse on a dead girl's grave. And why?

CHAPTER
29

Devils and Dust was coming along, but I was stuck on Hopper and why he became a prison guard. I understood he wanted to get close to the person he thought had harmed his sister, but there had to be more to his motivation. As I was creating a riff for him, I realized in the months that Brady had been helping me with research, I'd never asked him what drove him to what seemed like such a hopeless career.

The night before we met, I'd dreamed he wanted to talk in the cooler—what the inmates called solitary—but when I got there, they were on lockdown, and we couldn't leave. As I got out of bed, still bleary from a poor night's sleep, I thought about what he'd been telling me, how there was no rehabilitation in prison. The recidivism rates were consistent, and the more violent the crime, the greater the chance of reoffending within three months of release. Even those who were never getting out or weren't eligible for parole for many years managed to reoffend while incarcerated. There was always a new inmate, a weaker one.

I arrived at Battlefield State Park with my iced tea and settled in the shade of the Mercer Oak offspring that had been planted over a decade ago when the original three-hundred-year-old tree finally went down in a storm.

Brady came from the northwest corner of the park. He was dressed for work—dark-blue pants, gray short-sleeved polo shirt, and his DOC jacket. It was too hot for long sleeves, but I knew he wouldn't take it off. I thought maybe he liked the authority it gave him. Firearms weren't allowed inside the wire, but between the nightstick, his large frame, and his intimidating expression, he was clearly in charge. He sat on the grass next to me.

"Sorry I'm late," he said. "My parents moved into a retirement community and sent me a bunch of stuff that I left in their house after I graduated and started traveling. I started unpacking and lost track of time."

"No problem," I told him. "Thanks for coming."

"Everything okay? You sounded a little stressed on the phone." Despite the distance between us, I could smell him. Pine cologne and hand sanitizer.

"Why'd you become a prison guard?"

"Corrections officer," he said at the same time I realized my mistake. I wondered if there were union meetings where people sat around thinking up better-sounding names. *Sanitation workers. Administrative assistants. Landscaping engineers.* I never called myself a nutrition provider for the four years I waitressed at the EQuad Café on campus at Princeton. I kept my head down and my ponytail tight and brought skinny girls chef salads with no cheese and fat-free dressing on the side.

"Sorry," I told him. I felt bad. He always made sure to call me a novelist. I knew it bothered him to be called a guard.

"Why do you ask?" I opened my mouth, but he held up his hand to stop me. "And don't tell me it's for your book. I've told you everything you could ever want to know about being in prison."

A Y-shaped vein in his forehead was started to pulse. I knew that meant something was bothering him. "You've done a fantastic job telling me what it's like to be a prisoner, but what's it like for you? Is it tough going to work every day knowing there's no way out for most of the people there? I need to get inside Hopper's head a little more." The breeze was warm, and it made me sleepy. It'd been such a cold winter, but it felt like a perfect spring was our reward. "But you're right. There's more to it than that. I guess I'm curious. What made you want to work with people who are caged like animals?"

He was quiet for a long time. Finally, he said, "Imagine making one mistake that changes your whole life and takes your freedom."

I hadn't expected a man who'd been spit on, worked Thanksgiving and

Christmas, and risked his life every day to have so much empathy for a population who had all broken the law. "I know a thing or two about how quickly life can get turned upside down," I said. "Is everyone on your block a lifer?" I couldn't imagine anything more depressing than going to work every day with a bunch of men whose only way out of the South Jersey Penitentiary was in a cheap pine box.

"Does it really matter? A year, five years, the rest of your life. What's the difference?" I started to speak, but he kept talking. "Once you lose control over everything in your life—when you sleep, what you eat, what hours of the day you're allowed outside—you're never the same."

"Jeez, you should be a motivational speaker for at-risk kids. When you put it that way, I think I'd do anything to avoid going to jail. It makes me wonder why the recidivism rate is so high. You'd think knowing what it's like on the inside would make people do what they had to in order to stay on the outside." I'd never heard the word *recidivism* before meeting Brady.

"Look at it from the flip side," Brady said.

I caught his eye, and neither he nor I turned away. After that one night at the Wine Cask, we hadn't kissed again. I couldn't get past how unfun it'd been.

"There's a certain safety to prison. You always know where your next meal is coming from, and you never have to worry about a warm place to sleep."

"That's so sad," I said more to myself than him. "How crappy must your life be to want to go back to jail?"

"Exactly. And that's why I do what I do. It reminds me of how good I have it."

"What would you have done if you weren't a *corrections officer*?"

"I'd wax surfboards on one of the smaller islands in Hawaii."

I laughed. "You hate the ocean."

"I didn't say I'd surf."

"Touché."

"As long as we're playing twenty questions, what would you do if you weren't a novelist?"

I answered without having to think about it. "I'd be an FBI profiler." There was a time in college when I'd researched it as a career, but when I got to the part about having to have less than 23 percent body fat, I closed my laptop and signed up for another creative writing course.

"Sounds like the same thing, if you ask me." I cocked my head, and he kept talking. "When you write, you get inside the heads of your characters. The profilers on *Criminal Minds* spend all their time analyzing people too."

"I've never thought of it like that, but I guess I do have to know my characters inside and out to be able to write about them."

"So profiling doesn't count as a second career choice. It's too similar to what you do now. What would you be if not an author? Pastry chef? Teacher?"

It wasn't lost on me that he didn't ask me why I chose to be a novelist. He knew it was the only way I could keep my grief at bay. Every time I wrote about a slain sister or a lost parent, the gripping panic I'd felt since Savannah died loosened its hold just a bit. I tapped my finger on my nose as I thought.

"An accountant," I said. Before he could laugh, I added, "I like order. I find it comforting knowing what to expect. Numbers don't change. They don't lie. You can break them down and add them up, and they're always the same. Going through life without having to look over my shoulder, wondering what's going to happen next would be my idea of nirvana."

We lapsed into a comfortable silence. "Do you think you'll be able to make it to David's again?" I asked when I could no longer stand the quiet. I pulled a blade of grass and sucked on the thin, white end.

He tucked a loose strand of hair behind my ear. His touch sent goose bumps down my arms. Why couldn't his kiss do that? "I'm not sure. Colette hasn't been . . . um, feeling well lately. When I'm not working or volunteering, I feel like it's best for me to be home with her."

Colette. Something was going on with her, but every time I tried to ask Brady about it, I lost my nerve. "Then you should bring her." That was the third time I'd invited his girlfriend to eat dinner with us, but this time, I was sincere. If Brady wasn't going to be my soul mate, like I'd thought in high school, he was certainly turning out to be a great friend. And how much he cared for Colette was one more thing I admired about him.

He smiled, but it was sad, not joyful. "I don't think that would end well. Everyday things can be hard for her."

CHAPTER
30

The key to the storage unit was hidden in a drawer underneath the silverware separator. It wasn't so much that I thought someone would steal it; I just didn't want it on my key ring, where I'd have to see it every day and be reminded of what it unlocked. I was in my car with my seat belt on before I decided I couldn't face riffling through Savannah's stuff alone. I called Gabby and asked her to meet me there. She put the phone down, and I could hear her fake sneezing as she told the director of Sarandius that she wasn't feeling well.

Fifteen minutes later, we were both standing in front of the metal overhead door at Cranberry Street Storage Units. She grabbed my hand. "Are you ready for this?" As soon as I nodded, she slipped the key from my fingers and opened the padlock.

She hoisted the door open, and it roared as she pushed it above our heads. We stepped in, and she patted at the wall until she found the light. The fluorescents blinked a few times before they came to life and brightened the room. I was wrong. I wasn't ready. Almost everything Savannah had left behind was in here. The Butet saddle that she bought with the babysitting money she earned after an entire summer of watching the Sanford girls across the street. The stuffed rocking horse she'd gotten for our fourth Christmas that she rode so much almost all the fur on its back was gone. And boxes and boxes of her books. Some of them were marked. The entire Nancy Drew series and all of Judy Blume's young adult novels were in one box. Her textbooks were in another. But there were at least a dozen other boxes, most of them recycled produce cartons from Sotto Sopra, that had no markings on them.

"I don't think I can do this," I said quietly. I started to back out of the cold space. "What made me think this was a good idea?"

Gabby stepped behind me and put her hand on my back. "I'm here. We'll do it together. Where do you want to start?"

I sat on a small area rug that had been in our nursery. Two buckskin ponies were grazing on it, nose to nose. "I guess we should each grab a box and start digging. I called my mom last week, and she said the guest book must be in here somewhere. But really, how would she know? I still can't believe my parents had strangers pack up all of their dead daughter's things."

Gabby put one box on top of another and brought them to the carpet. She plopped down next to me and handed me one.

"Thanks," I said. I took a deep breath, closed my eyes for a second, and pulled at the top of the box. It smelled musty, like clothes that had been in the washer too long. I peered in and saw a stack of magazines. "I can't believe my parents kept these," I said, pulling out a *Cosmo Girl*. I flipped through it and saw articles on how to properly french-kiss, what shade of lip gloss to wear if you were a redhead, and which were better—tampons or pads. I flipped the box over, and about two dozen magazines spilled out.

"Check out what's in my box," Gabby said. She held up about fifteen mismatching socks. "Did Savannah have a sock fetish?"

I laughed at the memory of her trying to start a new trend at school of wearing socks that didn't match. She wanted everyone to bring in their single socks, and then she'd sell them in pairs, giving the proceeds to an animal shelter. "Don't you remember that company she wanted to start, selling random pairs of socks?"

"Oh yeah," Gabby said. "What was it called? Match Maker?" She held up two pink socks, each with different colored polka dots, and then smirked.

"What is it?" I asked.

"Match Maker. That's kind of ironic, isn't it?" Her voice was wistful.

I scooped up the magazines and put them back in the box. "I don't follow."

"This is going to sound a little harsh, and I'm sorry, but Savannah wasn't the best at picking out boyfriends."

"She didn't really have any boyfriends." I could hear the defensiveness in my voice.

"That's my point. She slept with all these boys, but none of them ever seemed that interested in her. And it doesn't make sense. She was pretty and nice and outgoing. Why didn't they like her? I mean *like her* like her, like want to be her boyfriend?"

My first instinct was to tell Gabby to fuck off, that Savannah was perfect and everyone loved her. But she was right. Every time Savannah would have sex with a new boy, she'd come home and tell me he was the one. That this was it. But then she'd never mention him again. Instead, I said, "Chapman Sharp loved her."

Gabby laughed. "Yes, he did. I think he still does." She was quiet for a moment, and then she said, "Hey, maybe he was the guy you saw at the cemetery."

"Nah." I got up and lugged over two more boxes. "Chapman was too short. This guy was big. Tall and broad and kind of built like a house."

"You mean like Patrick Tunney?" Gabby had seen him in the parking lot of the rec center a few weeks before.

My stomach twisted. "Yes, actually. Exactly like Patrick." I tried to make myself see the man in the woods more clearly. Was he as big as Patrick? Had I seen wisps of red hair? "Here," I said, sliding a box to her. "We'll be here for a week if we don't get a move on."

We went through another twenty boxes filled with fashion magazines, Cabbage Patch dolls, cassette tapes, and Play-Doh. How had I forgotten there was so much stuff here? Finally, exhausted, we were about to give up and go home, but Gabby suggested we have a pizza delivered and keep going. Not wanting to ever come back again, I agreed. There were still another ten or so boxes left to go through, but we took a break and ate an entire hawaiian pizza. "Good idea," I told Gabby when we were done. "Now let's find that stupid book and get out of here."

I went to pick up another box, but it was too heavy to lift, so I planted myself on the cold floor. "I think there are rocks in this one," I said. But when I opened it, it was filled with notebooks. "Crap." I groaned. "More school stuff." I opened the first notebook to find it was filled with Savannah's handwriting. I thought maybe it was a journal for an English class or something, but after reading a few lines, I realized it was a diary. "Holy fuck," I whispered.

Gabby dropped a stuffed rabbit on the floor and came over. "What is it?"

"Savannah kept a diary disguised as homework." I held up the notebook for her to see. It was a standard-issue CVS notebook that we all used for school. "I can't believe I never knew."

Gabby's eyes got big. "Are you going to read it?"

I put it on the floor beside me. "I don't know. Do you think I should?"

"Maybe there are clues in it."

I picked up the notebook and held it to my chest, hoping to get something from it. Nothing. "Don't be ridiculous. It's not like she knew she was going to get killed."

"I have an idea," she said. "Hand it over and tell me when."

I reluctantly gave it to her, and she started flipping quickly through the pages. She was about halfway through when I said, "When."

She stopped. "I'm going to read what's on this page. If it seems useful, we'll keep going. Otherwise, we'll put it away. Deal?"

"I guess," I said, not sure if I wanted to do this.

Gabby cleared her throat and started reading. "July 14, 1998. I can't believe we've been together for three months. Every day is like the day we met all over again. He brings me daisies and Cherry 7UP." I smiled at how much Savannah had loved that drink. "He's the greatest guy ever." Gabby looked up. "Shit," she said. "Savannah had a secret boyfriend."

I sprang up. "Give me that." I grabbed the notebook, flipped a few pages forward, and continued to read to myself.

He likes it that I have experience. He says it makes me a woman. And he's mine. All mine. I wish I could share him with the world.

I skipped a few pages and read another entry.

I'm dying to try it. He says he won't do it with me, but it's supposed to be amazing.

What in the world was she talking about? I kept reading, even though I could hear Gabby breathing noisily, annoyed that I wasn't reading aloud.

I told him I'd be careful.

"Why didn't she tell me?" I could feel tears coming. "I thought we knew everything about each other. Why wouldn't she tell me she had a boyfriend? What did I do wrong?" Suddenly, a lifetime of being as connected to my sister as I was to myself felt like nothing more than a lie. "I can't believe this."

Gabby stood up too and pulled me into a hug. "You did not do anything wrong. Savannah wasn't an angel." Her face was hard. "Remember how she stopped eating lunch with us to hang out with the seniors? And how when she got invited to parties, she wouldn't bring us?" Gabby's voice was tight. "I'm sorry, Cades, but Savannah was kind of all about Savannah."

"What?" I backed away from her. "She was my sister, Gabby. And someone killed her." I squatted down and pulled a few more notebooks out. Two of them appeared to be more diaries, and the third one had the words *Slam Jam* written across it in green Magic Marker.

Gabby saw the books in my arms. "I'm sorry. I didn't mean to upset you. Savannah was an amazing girl and a great friend. But she was human, like the rest of us." She reached for the notebooks in my arms. "Why don't you give those to me, and I'll go through them for you?"

I shook away the notion that Gabby had had mean thoughts about my sister. "Remember this?" I asked. "Our slam book. We used to keep tabs on people in this one, especially the mean girls. I bet you Emma's mentioned in here a million times."

Gabby laughed, a forced sound. "Here, let me take that." When I wouldn't let go, she tried to tug it out of my hands.

"It's okay," I said. "I'd rather go through these."

She sighed loudly. "Okay, but we should remember that high school was a long time ago, and we all said things we didn't mean."

There were only four boxes left, so we packed them in my car, and I told Gabby I'd go through them later. We locked up the storage unit, and I hugged her good-bye, just wanting to go home and take a shower.

CHAPTER
31

I came home to a dark house and the darker thoughts that my sister had a secret boyfriend and my best friend kind of hated her. For once, I would have liked it if Greg had been home. We couldn't talk about the pregnancies that I'd lost, one after the other, or that there was a distance between us that was like trying to reach through glass, but he was always good at analyzing other people.

I poured myself an inch of Grey Goose, which I almost never drank, and moved the boxes one by one into my office. I'd found one of the crocheted baby blankets that Gramma Martino had made Savannah and me before we were born. Mine was light yellow, and hers was a minty green. Mine had gone to college with me and made the move from the gingerbread house to this one. It was dry-cleaned and folded in the antique trunk at the foot of my bed.

I settled on the love seat with Savannah's blanket on my lap and began reading. I finished the vodka, poured myself another, and read page after page of sentences that were all the same.

I've never felt this way about anyone. He makes me feel so loved. I can tell him anything.

As I sat for hours reading, I found myself jealous of a boy I'd never met. Yet, somehow, I was also comforted by him. Whoever he'd been, he clearly loved my sister. There were entries about the silver toe ring he'd bought her. And how their secret code was $1 + 1 = 1$ because they felt like the two of them together equaled one whole person.

The night wore on, and I got a text from Greg saying he was stuck at the hospital with an emergency placement. I'd been sleeping with the third notebook on my chest when the ding of my cell phone woke me. It was after two in the morning, but I wanted to make a pot of coffee and keep reading. Savannah had had a love in her life by the time she was sixteen years old that I still hadn't experienced. All at once, it made me sad for myself, but I was somehow so comforted to know that she had someone who loved her before somebody else took her away.

I got up to make coffee, but I was so tired I lay back down on the couch, pulled up the worn blanket that still faintly smelled of my sister, and closed my eyes. I woke up to Greg sitting beside me quietly saying my name.

"What's all this?" he asked when I startled awake.

I bolted up, panicked with the thought that I hadn't found the guest book. "What time is it?" I took the notebook and threw it on the floor as if it were nothing.

"Ten after seven. Did you sleep in here last night?"

"Yeah, I was doing research, and I must have dozed off." He glanced at the boxes, and I was terrified he was going to ask me what was in them, where they came from. I was having a hard enough time processing what I'd learned about Savannah and that Gabby had seemed so angry the night before. Now that I'd spent the night alone reading, I wasn't ready to talk about it yet.

Greg kissed my forehead and said, "I made a pot of coffee. I need to take a quick shower and get back to the hospital. Last night was a cluster."

I waited until I heard his footsteps on the stairs before I unpacked the rest of the boxes. Most of the contents were stuff my parents could have thrown out—torn-up jeans, old sneakers, makeup bags. But I understood why they'd kept everything. Stashed between two yearbooks, I found the guest book from Savannah's funeral.

The gold letters on the cover had faded, but the ink inside was not smudged and was as bright as it had been on that cloudless November day when we'd lowered my sister into the ground. I sat on the floor and flipped through the pages. Anyone in that book could be Savannah's murderer. Any of those students, administrators, janitors, the teachers with their black-and-white headshots and bad haircuts. And maybe one of them had been her boyfriend.

"I want to take you to dinner tonight," Greg said from the doorway.

"Holy shit." I dropped the book. "I didn't hear you come down the stairs." He was dressed in a suit and tie. Ever since we'd started therapy, he'd been grinning at me in this forced, sort of scary way that was meant, I guessed, to show me he really cared.

"You up for it?"

I came out into the hall, closing the office door behind me. "You know I have dinner at David's tonight." I thought of Brady and me sitting in front of the liquor store, trying again.

"I know," he said, smiling. "And this time, I'm going to go."

"Oh!" I tried to sound bright, happy. I had too much to think about to deal with Greg right then.

He followed me down the hall to the kitchen. "Is that okay?"

"Yes, yes, of course. Everyone will be thrilled to see you." Even as the words were coming out of my mouth, we both must have known that was a lie.

Greg stopped short of the kitchen, and I went around the island and started washing my hands. I had no idea why I was doing this other than to get away from him.

He was handsome standing there in his suit without a patient file or a yoga mat under his arm, and I felt suddenly horrible about myself. There was my husband, his curly hair so neatly combed and his tie a little crooked and those cuff links he worked on every day slightly askew.

"You don't want me to go, do you?" he asked.

"What?" I dried my hands on the dish towel beside me. "Of course I do. It's just that, you know, we've been doing this dinner for a hundred years, and I'm surprised, that's all." I came around the island, and Greg did something really weird: he grabbed me around the middle and kissed me, open mouthed and soft. And the world rested for a minute, like a carnival ride that stops right before it throws you around again.

"I'm going to try, Cady," he said when we both came up for air. "I really want this to work."

I felt kind of stunned, and for some reason, I thought of Patrick in the orchard, showing me a picture of his son. "So do I," I told him. "I really want it to work too." My voice sounded unnatural in that big echoey space, because what really took my breath away was that I'd felt way more kissing Greg than I'd felt kissing Brady, the hot crush of my high school years.

After Greg left for work, I went back into my office to get my cell phone, and I noticed the slam book on the floor next to the couch. I knew I should get in the shower and work on *Devils*, but I picked it up and brought it into the kitchen with me. I poured a cup of coffee I was still trying to convince myself I liked and opened it to a random page.

"She thinks she's better than us," someone had written in pink ink.

Now that she's the new It Girl with the seniors, she barely even talks to us. It makes me want to kill her.

The word *kill* was underlined three times. I knew that handwriting. It'd been on my birthday cards and notes left on my car for almost my entire life. It was Gabby's.

Of course, no one minded that Greg was coming to a Thursday dinner. Chandler made more risotto, David said he'd thawed too many steaks anyway, and Gabby's salads were always big enough to feed a fraternity. But the night was awkward. David had finished his model Mustang, and we all stood around asking questions like how long did it take and how many pieces there were. And at dinner, Gabby kept sending Duncan snarky texts, trying to pick a fight because she was thinking about breaking up with him. She said he'd gotten clingy and needy. But poor, dopey Duncan kept responding that he loved her. Odion and Chandler brought Madelyn, who refused to eat the steak or the risotto and then spilled her chocolate milk across the table while her parents fought about how little Odion was studying for his citizenship test. I was hoping no one would say anything about last time when Brady had come and we'd stayed away at the liquor store too long. We couldn't discuss the things we usually talked about—mainly my marriage and whether it was working out. And Brady. Of course Brady.

Finally, Gabby said we were going outside for a smoke, even though I never smoked, and I sat on the front porch next to her while she filled the air with lopsided circles.

"Thanks for going with me yesterday," I said. I wanted to ask her if she hated Savannah or if she was mad at her right before she died, but I didn't know how.

"No problem. Did you find the funeral book?"

I picked up the pack of cigarettes and smelled them. I crinkled my nose and put them in between us. I didn't understand their appeal. "I did. This morning. And how about our old rag book? I'd forgotten all about that thing."

"Did you read it?" She ground out her cigarette while she spoke. "You did."

"Gabs," I said tentatively. "I thought you and Savannah were friends."

"Fuck," she said loudly. "Fuck. I was hoping you didn't read that part." Her voice got high and tight. I'd almost never seen her upset. "We were friends. I loved your sister, but I love you more. And I hated the way she treated you. It was so obvious to everyone how much you loved her. I mean, it was like you practically thought you two were the same person. And then that stupid group of seniors took her in, and all of a sudden, she was too good for us. For you. I saw how much it hurt you, and I kind of hated her for it." *Hated her enough to kill her?* I wondered. But I didn't say anything. I didn't answer her. I couldn't think of anything to say. "Can we forget about it?" she asked. "It was so long ago."

"Sure," I said, rubbing my arms like I was cold. But really, I needed to get away from her. "No problem."

We played Cranium, each of us paired up, and Mads finally sacked out on the living room couch. Greg and I lost, and I got slowly drunk. Whenever I drank too much, I also got strangely quiet, so that everyone around me got louder and louder, and I could tell Greg was psychoanalyzing it all, when what I really wanted him to do was loosen up and have fun.

On the way home, I watched the sleeping houses of Stanwich sail by. "Well," Greg said. "So *that's* what you do every Thursday night."

The car was spinning a little bit. "It's usually more fun than that."

He turned up the heat. "I should hope so." He shifted gears, and my stomach felt like it was in my throat. "Are things okay with you and Gabby?"

I supposed I should have known he'd pick up on that. He was a shrink, after all. "Sure. Why?"

"I don't know. It felt like you were avoiding each other a little. I thought maybe you'd gotten into an argument on the porch."

"Maybe we need a break," I blurted before I could think about it.

"But she's been your best friend since you were seven. You've never needed a break."

I turned away from him in my seat, feeling like I might cry. "Well, now we do."

"Does that mean you're not going to Cookies on Sunday? I'd love it if you would come to yoga with me."

Did he say *yoga*? "Why would you want me to do that?" I asked. "To torture me?" I laughed, but he stared straight ahead, his hands gripping the steering wheel.

"It's very relaxing."

"Oh," I said, and then I tried to stop thinking, because I felt so thoroughly confused.

Being drunk always made me feel slightly dirty, especially if it was martinis—which it had been—and when we got home, I stood in the hot shower until I thought I might fall asleep. When I got out, Greg was sitting up in bed, reading files, his rectangular glasses perched studiously at the end of his nose.

"Hi," I said, still feeling mildly drunk and sort of glad he was still up.

He took off his glasses and set them on his lap next to the files. "Cady," he said while I was pulling my nightgown out of the drawer.

"What?" I turned around.

"I want to see Dr. Mirando again." *Mirando.* I never had been able to think of his name. I pressed the nightgown against my chest. It was flannel with roses across it, and I loved how soft it was.

"Oh." I could hear the surprise in my voice. "Weren't we just there?"

Greg closed his eyes briefly, and then with a lot of patience, he said, "We said we'd look at our calendars and get back to him. Do you have some resistance to going on a regular basis?"

"Yes," I wanted to say. I hated sitting in that cramped office with him and pretending I was actually telling the truth. "No," I said, shaking out the nightgown. "I guess I've been busy."

Greg put his glasses back on his nose and picked up his file again. "With serial killers," he said.

"That's research," I told him defensively.

He raised his eyes to me and then settled them back on the page. "Okay, Cady. So you've said."

"What's that supposed to mean?" I quickly pulled the nightgown over my head.

"Nothing." He pinched the bridge of his nose with two fingers. "I think it's important to see Dr. Mirando as soon as we can. I'll make an appointment tomorrow."

"Any day but Tuesday," I said in hopes that maybe Brady would want to spend his day off with me.

"I know, Cady, Tuesday, Tuesday, Tuesday." I slid into bed. I felt myself reaching for his hand under the sheet, thinking I could make amends—for what, I wasn't sure—but before Greg could turn to me, I was already slipping into dreamland.

CHAPTER
32

I woke up the next morning with a headache that made me want to bash myself in the face with a hammer. While I was downstairs making coffee, my phone beeped. I picked it up. There were two missed calls and five texts from Hazel, who owned the barn where Bliss was stabled, saying something was wrong with him. "I'll be right there," I wrote. I ran upstairs, threw my pajamas on the bed, slid into a pair of jeans and a T-shirt, and was out the door in less than five minutes. I sped through yellow lights and got to the intersection of Rattling Valley and Burnt Mill faster than I ever had before. I was almost out of cell range when Brady called. "You coming?" he asked when I answered. I'd forgotten I was supposed to meet him this morning for breakfast to talk more about my book.

"Bliss is sick." I almost couldn't get the words out. "I'm on my way to the barn."

There was a pause, during which I thought I lost him driving those winding dirt roads to the farm, but then Brady's voice came on again. "Are you avoiding me?"

Jesus Christ. "No, Brady. Bliss, Savannah's horse, is sick. I have to go to him. I'm sorry I forgot to call; I'm hungover and—" but I heard the background noise go quiet, and the screen went black.

When I got there, Dr. Stewart's old Denali was in the parking lot, and Hazel's Subaru was parked at an angle to the door. Bliss was almost twenty-seven now, one of my last connections to my sister, and I didn't know what I'd do if I lost him. I'd hardly put the car in park when I jumped out, and Hazel came to meet me.

"He's colicking," she said, which she'd already told me in the texts. "We're having a hard time keeping him up." This she had not told me.

"Shit." I could feel the kick of my heart. Hazel was wearing denim overalls and a pair of ancient muck boots. Her hair was in one long braid down her back, even longer than the last time I'd seen her. "For how long?"

"When I got here this morning, he didn't eat breakfast and kept looking at his stomach. I listened for bowel sounds, and when I didn't hear any, I gave him a shot of Banamine. I finished feeding the other horses and threw hay out to the yearlings in the field. When I came back to check on him, he was down and rolling pretty violently. I called Dr. Stewart, texted you, and have been walking him ever since."

I felt that panic again, the sky closing in on me like I might pass out.

I rushed into the barn and to Bliss's stall. Dr. Stewart had his stethoscope on and was listening to Bliss's belly. He held up a finger, indicating I should wait. After a few seconds, he took the hard plastic ends out of his ears and wrapped it around his neck.

"He has good gut sounds." Dr. Stewart's eyes were rimmed in red, and his hair hadn't been brushed.

"Thank God," I said. "Are you okay?"

Dr. Stewart yawned. "I was up all night with a horse at Market Street. Left that call to come here."

"Was it one of Anne's?"

"Customer's," he said. "That new girl who has the bright-pink coat and matching stirrups."

Riding was a proper sport, immersed in tradition. "Oh God. I know who you're talking about. She's hard to miss. Is the horse okay?"

"Yes, he's stable." He came out of the stall and put on a plastic glove that came to his bicep. "I'm going to do an internal exam now. Does he need ace?"

"No," I said, taking Bliss's muzzle in my hands. "He's perfect. He'll stand like a rock."

Hazel stood in the aisle while I petted Bliss and talked to him about which of the three yearlings was his favorite. Dr. Stewart pulled a few nuggets of hard manure from him. I kept thinking of Savannah the day she'd gotten Bliss. We'd waited on a tack trunk until past midnight when a Brookledge truck finally lumbered down the narrow drive of the barn. She took his temperature to make sure he hadn't gotten shipping fever, made him a warm bran mash, and stayed with him through the night. From that first moment, she was the only person Bliss trusted. Every day, she'd lean her face down near his muzzle and whisper to him. Then she'd swing a leg over his back, her gold hair flying, her face so relaxed and happy it was as if she were lit from the inside out. Hazel kept touching my arm and giving me little sounds of encouragement, and then, about twenty minutes into it, we heard a motor in the drive, and she went out to see who it was.

I talked to Bliss in a low voice, telling him it was okay and to hang in there, and though he rested his muzzle in my hands a few times, for the most part, he concentrated on Dr. Stewart. When the door opened, I turned, and there was Brady standing in the light of the barn. I went to him, and Hazel took my place at the stall. Even though I didn't want to leave Bliss, I walked into the lot with him. The sun was hot overhead, and I saw Brady's bike next to my car.

"I tried to call back," he said. "But I couldn't get you."

"Yeah," I told him. "The cell reception here sucks." I heard Bliss whinny, a sad, troubled sound. "Listen, I have to get back to my sister's horse."

Brady looked helpless; it seemed like he didn't know what to do with his hands. "Do you want me to wait?"

I still had a splitting headache, and I felt both flattered and slightly guilty that Brady had driven all the way out here. "If you want."

"Okay," he said. He put up a hand and backed away. "I'll stay as long as I can."

"As far as I can tell, it's an impaction," Dr. Stewart said when I went back in. "Pretty good-sized one. More Banamine and mineral oil should do the trick. Do you have some paste on hand?"

"Plenty," Hazel told him. "He's already had one dose."

"That's okay. He can have more now and then again in four hours. I have a nasogastric tube in the truck. I'm going to pump him full of mineral oil and electrolytes to rehydrate him. Let's keep him hand walking until he passes manure."

While I walked Bliss around the ring on a lead line, I talked to him. I told him I loved him and that he was all I had left of Savannah and please, I knew he couldn't live forever, and I didn't want him to be in pain, but he'd given me the scare of my life. I walked him slowly and tried not to cry, tried to tell myself he was going to be fine, tried not to see Savannah the first time we went out into the woods and she'd looked for fallen logs, for places to jump Bliss, who seemed light as air with her on his back. It had been a sight like you might see in a film, the light filtering between the leaves and Bliss moving like liquid through the trees. And I remembered feeling unafraid. Nothing could happen to Savannah when she was with Bliss; he was part of her good luck.

It was after noon when Bliss finally stabilized. He passed a pile of hard, pebbly manure. I made him a warm mash, put a cooler on him, and watched him in his stall. He immediately lay down, but this time it wasn't to try to roll the pain out of his gut. He stretched flat out on his side, and a minute later, he was snoring. I walked Dr. Stewart out to his truck, and Brady's bike was gone. After the vet drove away, I noticed a notepad right where the motorcycle had been. In Brady's scrawl, I saw a work schedule for the week. I picked it up and brought it into the tack room and tried his cell. I called later that day, after Bliss and I had been walking again. Still no answer.

When Bliss finally passed a mound of softer, normal-looking manure, I made him another soupy bran mash to help rehydrate him and tried Brady one more time before I left, but he didn't answer. It was almost three, and I decided to drive to his house and drop the pad in his mailbox. He'd told me once where he lived, a little rental on Cove Road, a cul-de-sac near the high school. Gabby and I had ridden by it a few times on spy missions, a compact white cape with sea grass and perennials planted around the perimeter that I imagined were courtesy of Colette.

A smattering rain spit down even while the sun was shining, and I drove with the windshield wipers squeaking intermittently. The driveway was empty, and I parked in the street and walked across the yard to drop the pad in the old-fashioned mailbox by his front door, where I saw other mail, mostly catalogs. And then I went back to my car. That's when I heard it: a sort of singing sound coming from the back. It was so melodious, high pitched and lovely, that I stopped to listen. The voice carried on the slight breeze, and when the raindrops fell, it was as though they were somehow in time with the song.

I crept along the side of the house, past a bunch of kindling, following the song. When I was about to turn the corner, I saw a slight wisp of a woman standing in the midst of a huge garden of daisies. Her black hair was loose around her, and her long, thin arms appeared pale, like a child's in winter. She was the one singing, her tone pitch-perfect. Like her voice, she was beautiful. And the oddest thing was that she was wearing nothing from the waist up. Her breasts were heavy and turned up at the end. Tied around her waist was a gauzy sarong. I stood there watching her as she rhythmically, patiently pulled at weeds.

The song was French, I knew that much, but I didn't know the words. I stood there listening to her singing and wondering if she was cold. Maybe it was the hangover or how emotionally wasted I felt from Bliss, but I had the comforting thought we might actually become friends. Save Gabby, I didn't have many friends. My friends were the characters who populated my books, heroes who found ways to circumvent and catch perpetrators. My confidants were the black letters on the page I strung together to make sentences, paragraphs, scenes, chapters, books. They never seemed to fail me. Now I wondered if this woman might be a kind of kindred spirit. The way Brady had described Colette, with so much to give but so little desire to live, was seductive. She seemed childlike, perhaps a little crazy or maybe free-spirited, but harmless.

She stopped the beautiful singing and started talking. She spoke quickly, hurriedly, as though trying to convince someone of something, as though defending herself. Again, the words were French, but I saw she was working something out, talking animatedly to the willowy flowers in her yard. Watching Colette alone in her garden, unburdening herself of her grief to the flowers, dirt on her knees, I suddenly felt terrible for trespassing, and I tried to steal away. Except I had forgotten about the kindling, and when I backed up, I snapped a few twigs. With nowhere to go, I stood stock-still, willing myself to become invisible. Colette stopped talking, but she didn't turn her head toward me. After a few seconds, she picked up a trowel and went back to work digging in the dirt in silence.

"Oh my God," I texted Gabby out of habit. "Went to Brady's house and saw Colette standing in her garden naked talking to herself. It was sort of creepy. She's really beautiful."

It took her about fifteen minutes to return the text, and by that time, I was already home, unlocking the door. She wrote: "Let's go to Cookies so you can tell me about her."

I stood in my kitchen with my phone in my hand, feeling like I might cry and wanting to confront her again about everything she'd written in that notebook. "Sorry," I wrote, "going to yoga with Greg on Sunday." I thought of Chandler telling me that day at lunch how my family wasn't direct with anyone. But really, I realized, going into my bedroom and dropping my dirty clothes on the floor, I didn't know how else to be.

CHAPTER
33

"Thanks for dropping off the notebook," Brady said the next day on the phone. I was in my office working on *Devils* when he called.

"No problem," I told him. I didn't know if I should mention Colette or not, so I didn't.

"How's Bliss?"

"Good. I checked on him twice in the night and went back when I got up today. He seems fine this morning. I've never been so happy to muck a dirty stall."

"That's great, Cady." It really sounded like he was relieved, and I was touched that he cared enough to ask. "How about tomorrow to prep for and see Larry?"

"Um, I can't. I promised Greg I'd twist myself into a pretzel."

"Oh-kay." Brady drew it out like it was two words.

"Yoga," I told him.

"You're hard to get lately," he said.

We sat there on the line. And I had the urge to burst out that I'd seen Colette in his garden half-naked and she was talking to herself. "What about Monday?"

"Monday it is," he said. "Breakfast first?"

"Yeah," I said. "And unless a horse is sick, I won't cancel."

"Deal," Brady said.

And I felt that flutter again in my belly. I wondered again why it hadn't happened when we'd kissed.

When I went downstairs Sunday morning, there were two folded towels on the counter and two water bottles, already filled. Greg came in from outside, where he'd been pulling weeds since sunrise.

"Is this okay to wear?" I pulled up my yoga pants.

He straightened the straps on my tank top. "Perfect," he said, and it surprised the hell out of me.

"It's called hatha yoga," he told me on the drive over. "And it's not about exertion; it's about letting your body really wind down and relax. It's about coming back to your breath, that sort of thing. You don't have to do anything that feels uncomfortable."

I didn't believe any of this, but I went along with it. With his hair slightly disheveled and his sweats on, he didn't resemble at all the type A guy who worked every waking hour and spent all our money on fancy cheese, wine, and the symphony.

The yoga room was light filled. Windows took up the whole south side, but they were above the view line, so all I could see was sky, and no one—thank God—could peek in. A plump woman slightly bigger than I with black shiny hair cut into a bowl shape was showing people where to put their shoes and giving out mats, and Greg took my hand and walked up to her.

"Tanta, this is Cady, my wife."

Tanta opened her chubby arms and wrapped me into a warm hug. "I'm so glad you came," she said. "I've been telling Greg to bring his sweetheart."

"We're probably going to be in back," Greg told her. "Since it's her first time."

"Sure, sure." The woman gave me a big smile, and her dangling silver earrings caught the light. "Sit anywhere you like, and, honey"—she touched my chin—"have fun!"

"Is that the teacher?" I whispered to Greg when we had our mats on the floor.

He nodded.

"The heavy one," I said to clarify. "Tanta?"

He eyed me. "She's not that heavy, Cady."

I watched her. Tanta carried it well. She wore a tight, plum-colored leotard and leggings, but it didn't matter that she had some extra weight; she was voluptuous, running her hands up and down her sides like she loved her body. I had expected the rest of the class to be slight, model-pretty girls in Lululemon garb, but most were middle-aged, some wearing worn shorts and kneesocks. When Tanta told us to close our eyes, I felt a kind of buoyancy to be there in that light, warm, quiet room.

In grade school, Savannah and I had been invited to someone's birthday party at a dance school, but my mother had gotten the time wrong. When we got there, soft music was playing, some German composer, on low. The instructor, who was doing paperwork out back, told us we could move around the studio if we liked. Savannah had stood at the bar, pretending she was a ballerina. I remembered how I'd closed my eyes and drifted across the wide space, twirling as if my body had no restrictions. When I opened my eyes, the instructor, an older man with a beard in tights and jazz shoes, was watching me. "So free," he'd said to my mother. And then he'd taken off his glasses as if he'd been crying and wiped them on his top.

That was how I felt in the yoga class; one posture led to another, and my body felt fluid in the movement, light. At the end of it, we lay in what Tanta called corpse pose, and she led us through a guided meditation. I felt Greg reach over and touch my fingers. I squeezed them back. And for one brief moment, I saw how our lives might be if we let go of all the preconceived notions we carried around, all the defenses and the fears and the ways we learned to see each other that we'd never let go of, and I wondered if Emma had a point. Maybe we were all living in the past, unable to move forward. We were all damaged. Savannah's death had left us shredded, unable to talk to each other about what it was like to live without her.

CHAPTER
34

Brady was dressed like a movie star from the '50s in a tight white T-shirt and jeans. He had a double latte on the table waiting for me when I sat down. "How's it going?" he asked, tousling my hair like I was his kid sister.

"Hey," I told him. "Thanks for the coffee."

He took a sip of his own. "Are you ready to interview your favorite psychopath again?" he asked, his lips drawn in a tight line.

"*Favorite* isn't the right word."

He watched me. "Cady, it's dangerous."

"But he's chained to the table."

"You know what I mean." He squinted into the sun and then back at me. "Greg must hate me for this."

"He doesn't know."

I saw the surprise in his eyes.

"I mean, he knew the first time, but it was too hard to convince him I needed to go back again. Except for my agent, no one is really thrilled with me interviewing a serial killer."

Brady ran his finger around the rim of his cup. "Least of all me," he said.

"I have a character in my book," I told him, "who thinks a serial killer murdered his sister, but really it was her best friend."

Brady watched me. When he spoke again, his voice was husky. "That's fucked up."

I couldn't get that notebook out of my mind. "But I have to get into my characters' heads. That's how I write."

Brady gripped his coffee.

"I know you think I'm nuts," I said.

"If you tell me what questions you want Cauchek to answer, I'll talk to him myself."

"Thanks." The sun had shifted, and the slanted rays were hitting my knees in a way that made me feel hot and lazy. "But I need to do it."

"Then let me go in with you."

I turned sideways so I could look at him. "Don't take this the wrong way, but I've kind of built a rapport with him. I'm not sure he'd be so open if you were there. Besides, he's vile."

Brady checked his watch. "I'm familiar with vile," he said, gathering his jacket and his backpack, which I assumed contained his prison garb. "I'll watch from the other room. Everything gets recorded, you know, as long as you're not a lawyer."

At the front desk, Brady watched me throw my cell and car keys into a plastic bucket. "Jewelry," the guard said, and I reached around and undid the necklace that I never, ever took off. I'd kept it on once, and it had dinged, so I knew to leave it behind before I went in.

"I can't get it," I told the meaty guard.

"Turn around," Brady said, and I lifted my hair so he could reach the clasp. His hands were warm, and I could feel him fumbling, a little clumsy. Then he drew it over my head. And when I turned around, his face was bright red as if I'd seen him naked. It was so familiar by now, Brady's guilt when we got physically close, that it didn't surprise me. I had to soak my hand in ice water to get my wedding band off, so I'd done that at home.

Prison was about steel doors. There were so many doors that by the time I got to the interior, I felt I was in some kind of high-security bank vault, and if there was a fire, I'd be totally screwed. Brady left me on a plastic chair in a tiny staff room with the requisite vending machines while he went into the locker room to change, and I watched the video camera above my head that switched from the empty yard with its basketball hoops and razor wire to various cell blocks.

When we got downstairs, Larry was already in the room, his back to the glass window, chained up. A guy with a burn mark down the left side of his face was standing outside.

"Butch." Brady shook his hand, and then said to me, "You ready?" He took me into the room, sighed, and then left.

I sat down across from Larry, whose posture was as straight as that of a proper schoolboy.

"Cadence," he said, smiling, showing me his teeth. "How kind of you to come again."

"Cut the shit, Larry. You know why I'm here." I'd done my homework on sociopaths and knew they felt superior.

The corners of his mouth turned up in a grotesque smile, making the metal table that separated us seem flimsy. "Indeed, I shall . . . cut the shit. Cutting the shit. Cutting the shit."

I decided to play Dr. Holley's game from Sound View and be silent until he spoke first, not fidgeting, not breaking his gaze. It was a weak attempt to exert control over someone who was far more calculating than I. Sitting there made me want to scratch my body unnecessarily, pull my hair, pick my nails, anything. As we stared at each other, I remembered something I'd read: profilers often feigned yawning to see if their subject would yawn in return. Sociopaths did not engage in reciprocal yawns, because they lacked empathy. Wanting to know if he really was a sociopath, if there was a bit of empathy left in there somewhere, as casually as I could, I yawned. He continued to stare at me. Pretending to yawn made me have to yawn for real. I yawned again, and my eyes watered. I swiped at them quickly for fear he'd think I was crying.

"Love," he said, his voice pleasant. "Move on. I'm not going to yawn."

I felt my cheeks get hot, but I took him speaking first as a win.

"Indeed I shall," I said, doing my best to imitate him. "Moving on. Moving on."

"And the spunky girl is back." He tried to reach his hand toward me, but he was, of course, shackled to the table. He closed his eyes, took a breath in, and spoke. "Not all murders are intentional. They don't all begin with a plan and end with a death."

I scribbled those exact words in my notebook. The police's original pro-file of Savannah's killer was that he was disorganized. A transient killer. Patrick and Jon Caritano had gone through the twenty-seven boxes of notes and evidence and had decided that Savannah's killing was not really frantic but fervent. Even passionate.

"They might not begin with a plan to kill, but by definition, all murders have to end with a death," I said.

He flicked his fingers at me. "Don't bore me trying to be coy."

"I wasn't. How could a *murder* not end with a death?"

"Let me ask you"—Larry leaned back—"how many people have you duped into doing your investigative dirty work under the guise of research?"

I immediately regretted not preparing notes. I had thought an unscripted, fly-by-my-intuition session might garner more information, but I felt untethered, shaky. "I don't know." The truth was, I kept a running tally of the people I'd interviewed for my books. But this felt too personal, even more intimate than admitting I tried to lie next to my dead sister in the morgue.

"Of course you know." The way he stared at me without blinking made me think he either wanted to fuck me or kill me. Or both. And not necessarily in that order.

I realized Larry knew everything about me. "One hundred and forty-four. Most were offenders, followed by law enforcement and then victims."

"How many victims?"

I spent the least amount of time with victims. In the end, it was very personal for them, and they never really knew why it had happened. "Not very many."

"How many offenders?"

"Eighty-two *felons*." I emphasized the word.

"You are very persistent," he said evenly, watching me, "to put yourself in so much danger." There was something hypnotizing about his mouth; was a deep burgundy and full, and it made me sick to think where it had been.

"I'm quite safe," I said.

"I heard there were a whole team of guards in the room when you interviewed the chap who bludgeoned his teenage daughter's best friend." How could he possibly have known that? Was there some underground secret society of criminals? Honor among murderers?

"Ah yes," I said, trying to keep my voice as even as his. "That chap was even more dangerous than you. So while you get chained to the table like a farm animal"—I nodded to his handcuffs—"that offender managed to kill three other inmates before he was executed."

"Having so little self-control does not impress me. Tell me again his name?"

I didn't want to say a perpetrator's name. My job was to honor victims, not sensationalize murderers. "What's your point?"

He shifted sideways in his seat and crossed his legs. I watched the fluid, almost graceful movements of a body that hadn't seen sunlight in more than a decade. "I'm surprised your loved ones allowed you to take such an unnecessary risk. I would have thought your shrink hubby would have nixed that interview."

I felt pierced, but I also knew naming Greg's profession was his way of letting me know he had access to personal information. His nails were buffed as if he'd had a manicure.

"If you didn't sneak in here against the advice of your friends, how would you know that I kept something from each girl that reminded me of my mom? I took my first lovely lass's earrings. With her ears still attached, of course. And another sweet thing had on the most delicious shade of lipstick. I couldn't part with, well, you know." He said this as if every human being did such revolting things. "Her lips. They were so delicate."

I wanted to vomit, but I sat there and watched that disgusting, beautiful mouth, the dark eyes rimmed with long black lashes girls would have killed for. I made myself keep eye contact with him.

"Kudos to you for not flinching. Even one of the shrinks here, a Dr. Robert somebody or other, poor slob, had to leave when I told him how I cut off my fifth girl's labia because it was so full and round like dear old Mom's."

Robert Shaffer, Greg's friend, had told him not to let me near Cauchek when he'd come for dinner with his wife, Daisy, a few months ago. Greg had told him—braggingly, I felt—that I was doing research in a high-security prison. It seemed that all the psychiatrists within a fifty-mile radius knew Larry Cauchek.

We sat there for a few minutes. Me staring at his shackled hands, waiting for him to tell me what I wanted to know, him staring at my neck, waiting for me to break. The joke was on him. I broke 6,021 days ago.

Finally, I shut my notebook. "I'm bored," I told him.

And for one instant that perhaps no one but me would ever notice, alarm or maybe even panic crossed Larry Cauchek's face. He wanted me to stay. He needed me to. If I left, I got the upper hand.

"Ah," Larry said. "Our girl is not as tough as she lets the world believe."

I stood up. "Fuck you, Larry," I said without emotion. "Guard." I hated calling Brady that, but I never wanted Larry to know about our friendship. I heard Brady outside the door.

"Why don't you stay for tea?" Larry tented his hands in his shackles. "I tell wonderful stories over tea."

"No." I stepped away from my chair. "It's a beautiful day. I'd much rather be in the sunlight."

And where there was once panic on Larry's face, I saw now pure hatred, and then it was gone. Back to a poker face.

Brady walked past me, and I followed him. I made myself not turn back to Larry.

"See you later, love," Larry called to me.

"Maybe," I said back, but I didn't turn around.

"I did it," I told Brady when we were safely upstairs in that little waiting room. "I sat with that animal, and I didn't let him get the best of me." I threw my arms around him, and I actually kissed him. I kissed him. And he kissed me back in that tiny room. And I felt . . . nothing.

"Whoa." Brady broke first, holding me at arm's length, but he was smiling.

"I got him where it hurts," I said, trying to pretend I hadn't kissed him again and wondering why I got as much of a thrill out of kissing him as I would have if I'd kissed a stone wall. "He needs me; I'm the only entertainment he gets from outside. When I come back, he'll tell me everything."

Brady went from smiling to deadpan. "Don't do that, Cady."

"Do what?"

"Start thinking of him as a regular guy. This isn't someone who made a mistake when he was a kid. He's a methodical fucking serial killer."

"I know," I said while he led me out to the main hall. "That's what I wanted—a serial killer. That's the whole reason I'm here."

"You're a hard girl to take care of," he said, almost to himself. "I have to stay on my shift. You going to be okay?"

His face was red again, and he looked hot—I mean not only handsome hot but hot as in boiling up. "Yes," I said. We were standing in one of those vestibules with the metal doors on either side of us, and we could kiss again. No one would see us, but neither he nor I moved to do it; if anything, Brady seemed in a hurry, ready to get the hell out of there or maybe just late to get back to work. I couldn't tell.

"And, Brady," I said, not wanting to forget my manners, "thank you. You can't imagine what this means to me. This will help me so much with my novel."

Brady watched me for a minute and then blinked. "You bet," he said, and he opened the metal door behind me so I could get my things.

Out in the sunshine, I pulled my phone from my purse and wrote to Gabby. Things with her were still entirely weird, but I was trying to pretend they weren't. "I kissed him again. No spark." I waited for her to respond, and when she didn't, I sat in my car thinking about why kissing Brady had been so easy. Since that first day I saw him in the parking lot, I'd been telling myself that I still had a crush on him, that my marriage wasn't working. But now, after kissing him three times and feeling nothing since the first time, I understood that whatever I'd felt in high school was long gone. If my marriage ended, it certainly wouldn't be because of Brady.

Finally, my phone beeped with a text from Gabby. "Come to the library. You'll never believe what I found." I thought about telling her I was busy, but I couldn't avoid her forever.

CHAPTER
35

Gabby and I had rarely ever been in a fight, and in truth, this couldn't be considered one, because she didn't know I was mad. I owed it to her to talk about what she'd written about Savannah. But I was being ridiculous. There was no way she could have hurt my sister. Besides, she was my best friend. I didn't know what I'd do without her. Her friendship for the last twenty-something years was like being given oxygen as I was about to suffocate. It was amazing in a small town how quickly a lone wolf can get kicked out of a herd, how much people wanted to turn their faces away from what hurts. But Gabby had stuck by me, and I realized, driving from the prison to the library, I counted on that more than I liked to admit.

We were an odd couple. Gabby was tiny with slight features, and I was wide open and heavy. She was dark with crazy-beautiful curls. I was blond with straight hair. We'd always been tight and had a little circle of friends we ran around with, not the fast, popular girls that accepted Savannah but smart girls who did well in school. Even these friends petered out when Savannah died, calling less. But Gabby was always there.

My family had lived through a lot of firsts after Savannah was killed. Thanksgiving and Christmas, the first day of my junior year and our birthday, and Gabby had been with me for every one. When we stared down the barrel of the first anniversary of Savannah's death, instinct told me my parents were going to try to keep me home. But I wanted to go to school, to the safety of people who probably weren't thinking about Savannah, the smell of old gym clothes and lockers lined with pictures of boy crushes. Even the monotony of geometry would be a relief. But mostly, I wanted to be with Gabby, who I knew would understand.

My parents had appeared at my bedroom door, all smiles and stiff backs, holding a breakfast tray of french toast, a glass of pomegranate juice, a clementine, and a vase of daisies. They were smiling tight, uneven smiles. Good intentions seemed to be stamped on their foreheads, their bright souls shining through.

I'd been up since four, steeling myself for exactly this scene, making a list of reasons why I needed to get the hell out of the house. I was ready for their tentative knock, the tender offer of my favorite breakfast. But the daisies on the tray knocked me to the ground, and I found myself fighting tears.

Someone had sent an obscenely large bouquet of them to the funeral, and I'd clutched one during the service. Instead of *He loves me; he loves me not*, I chanted in my head, *They'll find him; they'll find him not. They'll find him; they'll find him not. They'll find him.* I stopped before I knew the answer. As they lowered Savannah's casket into the earth, my mother had slipped through the wall of black suit coats and skirts and placed the bouquet gingerly on the casket as if she were trying not to wake it. On the way home from the cemetery, I'd rolled down the window in the limousine and let the flower I'd been holding float to the black pavement.

Now as my parents put the breakfast tray on my new canopied bed, those daisies seemed to be taunting, pointing their petals at me. "Thanks," I told them. "But I've got to get going." I tossed back the covers.

"This is cause for celebration," I wanted to say. The first day of no more firsts. We'd made it through everything. Or . . . almost. There was one first I didn't think I'd ever get to: the first time I could stand in line for pizza at school or mill around outside the movie theater with Gabby without feeling like everyone was looking at me. There she is. There's *that girl*. The one whose sister was murdered. I felt like they all blamed me for not being able to walk home after school anymore, for having to lock their doors and live in a town that shut down at dusk with a nine o'clock curfew. Someone they knew got killed, and it wasn't because she'd skipped town on a Greyhound to Trenton or New York City or was shooting up with the dropouts who hung out at Finley's in Kingston.

Always supportive, my parents cleared the tray and put me on the bus.

School was the same. That was the strangest part about this new world—time kept ticking, the sun kept rising, people kept working, the person who murdered my sister kept breathing. My English teacher made an example of me for screwing up the possessive form of *it*. Ms. Tonzola tossed a pop quiz at us the last fifteen minutes of calculus. Only Gabby seemed to know that it was the anniversary, and she showed her support simply by hugging me hard and fiercely when she spotted me by my locker during morning announcements.

During study hall, the long-term history sub chose Gabby and me to empty the recycling bins in the east wing. We were heading through the language arts wing when the lecherous bio teacher came out of his classroom and flashed his crooked smile. Gabby lowered her voice. "Cleaning his beaker," she said as he continued down the brightly lit corridor. When he was out of view, she sang in perfect pitch, "After ten long years, they let him out of the home. Excitable boy, they all said." I grinned for the first time that day. "How you doing?" Gabby asked in her interested, never pushy voice.

"I'm not toes up yet, so I guess I'm hanging in." I loved that I could be macabre and sad around her, and she didn't try to fix me.

"Do you ever think about *him*?" she asked, emptying the first recycle bin.

"All the time."

"Is it weird to know he's still out there?"

The bell rang, and we leaned against the cream-colored wall to let a mass of students get to their lockers. "Sometimes I wake up in the middle of the night," I told her, loudly enough that she could hear me above the din, "after having one of my crazy dreams—"

"Like the one where Ozzy Osbourne helped you with your French homework?"

"Exactly." I watched the floor. "I'll turn on the light to tell Savannah about it, and it hits me all over again that she was murdered."

A trio of girls pushed past us, and their conversation had quieted at the sight of us. They stopped at lockers a few feet away. Emma Fisher was one of them, and that's when I heard my name. Gabby must have too, because we were about to resume our path back to study hall when we both stopped. "Ever notice how many times she says *murdered*?" I recognized the one talking, a tall girl with jet-black hair who was as prissy and sure of herself as Emma. "We get it. Her sister was killed. Why can't she be like Matt? He just says that his mom died." Matt Flaherty was a junior whose mother had fallen asleep at the wheel the summer before.

"*Murdered, murdered, murdered*," Sarah Bryson chimed in. "We know."

Emma tossed her hair over her shoulder, and the three of them stopped in front of Emma's locker. It was Emma's father who would, in a few days, drop my sister into the basement with the other cold cases.

I wriggled my arm out of Gabby's grip and walked over. "Do you know how to conjugate a verb?" I asked with false courage.

The tall one tucked her hair behind her ear, and something like hatred crossed her face.

"Let me help you out," I said. "To eat. I eat. You eat. He, she, it eats. We eat. You eat. They eat."

Sarah shifted her weight and gave a quick bark of a laugh. "What's your point?"

I felt Gabby's hand on my back. "Verbs are action words. They mean you're actively doing something." I backed up an inch so I could feel Gabby there. "If I said my sister *died*, it would mean she did something. She ate. She ran. She died." I felt myself growing taller. "But somebody did something to her. Someone murdered her." My voice had reached a pitch I didn't recognize. "Savannah was murdered." I couldn't stop myself. "Someone attacked her, choked her, and killed her. She didn't do it. Somebody did it to her!" I was yelling at Emma. She had started this, and she'd never let us forget our inability to erase this tragedy.

A crowd had gathered to witness my meltdown. I might have kept going except Gabby pulled me away. Everyone stepped back for us, backpacks slung over their shoulders, mouths open, and then, as we were about to turn the corner, someone called my name like a cheer. I looked back to see one of those fake gangsta kids who probably hated girls like Emma start clapping, and then everyone was clapping, an ovation of sorts, and after all that time feeling like our town hated me because of curfews and canceled games, I finally knew, on the anniversary of Savannah's death, that they were on my side.

———

Before I met Gabby at the library, I stopped by the house to grab something to eat, and Greg was there. He sometimes came home on his on-call days to play his bassoon, and it echoed off the walls. The acoustics in the barren house were horrible. I grabbed my laptop off my desk, stuck it in its sleeve, and popped my head in his study. "I'm going to the library to see Gabby," I told him. "And I'll probably stay since I can't really work with that kind of noise."

Greg lifted the mouthpiece from his lips, and I saw spittle on it. "Sorry," he said. "But I really don't have anywhere else to practice."

"It's fine," I told him. "I'm happy to go to the library." That sweet feeling I'd gotten at yoga had been steadily fading when Greg played his bassoon even while I was trying to write, when he scoffed every time I stopped to look at a baby, and definitely when he refused to even talk about trying to get pregnant again.

On my way out, Greg half waved, or maybe he flipped me off. And this, I thought, backing the Volvo out the driveway, was what made my marriage so hard. The hope and then the taking back of the hope, like an odd tide I kept trying to count on to be the same.

Gabby was in her roller sneakers when I got there. With her curly hair pulled back in a chignon and rectangular glasses on a chain around her neck, no one would have guessed she'd had sex on the book return box. I knew this because there'd been plenty of times in the past when she'd texted me a selfie of her and Duncan's bare asses.

I told her about the bassoon, trying to make it the same as it ever was, even though I felt weird around her now. "I might have to reserve a quiet study," I told her. "I need to get my first draft to Deanna before she jams one of her stilettos in my forehead."

Gabby laughed, and I started to feel at ease again. "Have any of them you want," she said. "I don't think they're being used until the weekend." I walked quickly beside her as she rolled to her office. I loved the library. There was a hush to all those books that seemed pleasantly cozy and alive. "You know I have a lot of free time here, right?" she asked after she'd closed her office door. It was completely soundproof, and I lay down on the antique chaise longue next to her desk, which reminded me of an analyst's office.

"Ah yes," I said. "Which is why I can't believe you let Duncan go. Is the deed officially done, or are you still deciding?"

"It all comes down to the words. It's over; I just need to set the poor thing free."

"That's too bad," I said. "I liked him."

"You'll like the next one too," she said, and I didn't know if she meant that I usually liked her boyfriends or if she had the next one picked out already.

"Anyway, back to why I called you here. Besides sex, what's my favorite thing to do when I'm bored?"

"Stalk," I said without hesitation. After more than twenty years of friendship, there wasn't much I didn't know about her. "Oh no. Have you been reading the sex offender registry again? Did you find any of our old teachers? I swear to God that bio teacher with the beaker is going to show up on that website one of these days."

"There's something you need to see," Gabby said. Her voice was too serious for this to be something silly. Maybe the physics teacher I'd had a mad crush on had finally gotten caught sleeping with a student.

She booted up her computer and typed something into Google. Gabby would have made one hell of a secretary or a transcriptionist. I'd never seen anyone type that fast. She scrolled through a police blotter, highlighted a paragraph, and turned the screen toward me. It took a second before I understood what I was reading.

"How did you find this?" It was dated five years before.

"I knew something was going on, so I kept digging till I found it."

I turned away. "We shouldn't be reading this. It's private."

Gabby waved her hand dismissively at me. "Clearly it's not if it's out there on the World Wide Web."

"You know what I mean. If Brady had wanted us to know about Colette's . . . struggles, he would have told us."

"Schizophrenia and multiple arrests constitute a little more than struggles," she said.

I thought of Colette in the garden, half-dressed, talking to herself, and I felt like I was reading her diary, peeking through a door, watching her cry. "There's a lot of stuff on the Internet that the world doesn't need to know."

I was getting a little pissed at Gabby, and I didn't know why. It wasn't like she'd made fun of Colette or announced this find at a Thursday dinner.

"Come on, Cades. You can't tell me you haven't been wondering what Brady's story is. He disappears for half our lives, and now he's back and all secretive about his girlfriend and shows up at dinner, kissing you, and then backing off and what the fuck . . ."

Gabby was right. And if Colette were truly mentally ill, that would explain why he seemed so guarded. He was sad in a way that was more than sad; he was almost apologetic, remorseful.

"Yeah," I said. "It was weird when he came out to Ravenswood last week, like he was desperate for company or something."

Gabby stopped chewing the gum she always had in her mouth. "You took him to the barn?" She knew that was my haven, my alone place.

"No." I tried to make my voice light. "He stopped by. I didn't know he was coming. Bliss was sick and—" I already said too much. There was no way I was going to tell her he'd been there twice.

She straightened her chair so we were facing each other. "Then how the hell did he find it? I can't even get there with my GPS."

I really didn't want to get into it right then. "So how about me kissing Brady again?" I said to change the subject. "It was so . . . blah." I couldn't think of a better word.

I was glad her office was soundproof. I lay back down on the lounge and tried to conjure up that feeling I'd gotten in Tanta's class, the corpse pose feeling.

Gabby rolled her eyes. "I know you've been in love with him since you were fourteen, but maybe he's not the right guy anymore. None of us are the same as we were when we were kids. What about Greg? Did you feel something for him after yoga?"

"Actually, yes."

"Why are you so dressed up?" Gabby touched my silk top.

"I went to see Larry, remember?"

"You dressed up to see a serial killer?"

"Well, I'm not going to dress like a slouch," I told her, and we both laughed that laugh we'd shared since we were girls, running around in the world holding on to each other when life sucked the worst.

CHAPTER
36

The phone rang, and in my strange predream state, I thought it was Colette calling to ask for help, but when I got into the hall so I wouldn't wake Greg, I saw that it was past midnight and it was Patrick.

"Hello?"

"Hey."

"What's wrong?" I asked immediately.

"Cady, I have to talk to you, and it's not about Savannah."

"It's not?" It was May, and the nights were still somewhat cold, so I stood in my nightgown in the vast hallway, chilly and uncomfortable.

"Well, it's indirectly about Savannah. But really it's about me."

"Okay." I dragged the word out, waiting.

Patrick said, "I'm outside."

"What? Where?"

"In the street."

Out the window, I saw his Suburban parked on the other side of the road. "Patrick, that's weird," I told him.

He laughed a little. "I know. I was coming home from work, and, well, you can go back to bed if you want," he said amicably.

"No." I was trying to stage whisper. "I'm coming out. And I'll bring cookies."

I'd made the cookies earlier that night when I'd gotten back from the library and Greg had still been hard at it on the bassoon. I held the cookies in one hand as I struggled to pull on the boots I'd worn when I'd gone riding with Brady that time. I thought about that day a lot, and I hoped, with the weather warming, it might happen again.

Patrick's truck was clean, but on the floor of the passenger side was a Nerf football that must have been Aiden's.

"Hey," I said. It was warm in the truck, and Patrick had Ray LaMontagne on low. He was clean shaven now and had on a dark suit.

"Hey." He smiled at me and turned down the radio. I passed him the cookies. Greg wouldn't eat them anyway; he was into the gluten-free craze and had never gone near butter or sugar. "Thanks."

"Take two," I told him. "Hell, take the plate." He took three, and then I put the plate on my lap. I had pulled on Greg's overcoat, and underneath, I could feel my nightgown, soft against my skin.

Patrick bit into one of the cookies.

I tried to be patient while he chewed, but finally I said, "Patrick, tell me."

He lowered his cookie. "I fucked up."

I could feel my heart go fluttery in my chest. "Okay." I waited.

He took a deep breath in, stared out at the empty street, and said, "I knew, Cady."

The cookies felt heavy suddenly on my lap. My heart beat wildly like I might go into cardiac arrest. "Knew what?" My voice sounded see-through.

He spoke levelly, and I could tell he was trying to keep calm. "I knew something wasn't adding up with Savannah's case. I kept trying to tell Fisher, but he didn't want to hear it. He wanted this case to go away as fast as possible." He held on to his half-eaten cookie, and the streetlight across his face made the green of his eyes stand out. "And I was new to the squad—a fucking rookie, really—lowest one on the totem pole. And everyone was afraid of Fisher; I mean, he did some fucked-up things. I knew that, and I also knew I wasn't supposed to tell; no one told. It was like I went in as this really hopeful kid, and all my ideals were getting tromped on." He brought the cookie to his mouth but didn't take a bite. "And so I was trying to balance, you know, what to say and how to keep my job, because I'd al-ways wanted to be a cop."

I felt frozen, a little sick. Finally, I said, "Why'd he want it to go away?"

"The mayor, the city council, all those people that wanted this to be a stranger case didn't want it to be someone any of us knew. The perfect town of Stanwich." He said this with derision. And when he turned toward me again, his face was red. "I've always wanted to be a cop. I don't know if you always wanted to be a writer, but I always wanted to be the guy who people admire. I wanted to be at the scene of an accident, pulling children out of burning cars. I wanted to save people like your sister."

I saw close up that Patrick had small creases on the sides of his eyes and very full lips like kids have, and I felt something like tenderness wash over me when he spoke, even as I was holding my breath, even as I didn't want to know this secret he was revealing.

"And when I came up against city hall, literally city hall, when they were all talking about cold casing it, putting it in the basement, and I was stand-ing in that fucking conference room trying to fight it and they kept raising their voices at me, they kept telling me why I was wrong, I kept on trying to tell them, 'No, we've missed something; there are things we could still ex-plore,' but they'd taken me off the case, and they said it wasn't my business anymore." He swallowed. "And then they threatened me." Patrick sat there staring out the windshield at our dark neighborhood for so long I thought he was done. When he spoke again, his voice was low. "I had a new wife at home. That was before Darlene got into drinking so bad, and I thought we were going to make a family, and my dad was dying of melanoma, and I didn't know he had that life insurance plan that has set my mom up so well. I was picturing having to take care of my mother, and you know Darlene didn't have a job; she'd gotten kicked out of nursing school for stealing pills. And I needed to keep it together." He looked down at the cookie as if asking it for answers. "Anyway, that's a lot of shit-poor excuses. The fact is, I didn't buck the system." I saw that though he presented himself as a tough guy, Patrick was a teddy bear inside. "I caved." He swiped at his eyes. "It's always our business. I know that now. When we know something isn't going down the way it's supposed to, it's our job to not stop until we make it right." I had the strange urge to hold him. "But the only excuse I have is that I was young, and I didn't know what to do." His green eyes went dark. "I didn't feel like I had a choice. One mistake left everything so fucked up."

I thought about that day in the park with Brady. *One mistake that changes your whole life.*

"Did you have a choice?" Patrick watched me as I spoke. "Wouldn't they have just gotten rid of you? And then it would have been almost impossible to get a job somewhere else." I couldn't quite believe I was seeing it that way. But I was. Somewhere deep in me in that place where empathy lived, I understood.

"I guess they would have canned me," he admitted. "But if I had it to do over," he continued so low I almost couldn't hear, "I wouldn't do it like that again. Especially now with Aiden. I'd show him what it was like to stand up for what you believed in. Because if someone did to Aiden what happened to Savannah . . ."

I felt myself reach down and open my window. I needed fresh air. Outside, it smelled of wet spring leaves. Our house was dark, save that light I'd left on in the kitchen when I went to get the cookies. It looked sort of forlorn, massive, and dark, like a ship no one wants to sail. "You know what I think it's about?" I turned to Patrick, and he raised his head. "I think it's about second chances and moving forward." I thought of how books needed to move forward. Too many flashbacks and novels got stuck in the past rather than continuing with the real-time story. "We've got a second chance now," I said. "And we need to focus on that."

I'd never seen anyone look at me quite like Patrick was. I imagined it was what doctors feel like sometimes when they give the right remedy, when the person who was once ill comes back feeling well again.

"You're an incredible woman," he finally said.

"No," I told him. "I'm human. And I'm a really good baker, so eat the cookies before I start feeling bad about myself."

He grinned. "Jesus Christ," he said, lifting a cookie as if in a toast. "Are you sure you can forgive the mistakes I've made?"

I took a cookie off the plate, and we sat there eating together. "I always wondered what Atlas would look like," I said, thinking about going to see the statue of the titan at Rockefeller Center every year when my parents took us ice-skating before Christmas, "if he let go of the globe and stood up straight. After all, the earth floats; he doesn't need to carry it."

Patrick smiled while he chewed. "Actually," he said, "he was carrying the celestial spheres."

I quit eating my cookie. "What?"

He took another bite. "You don't think I read Greek mythology? The titans are my kind of dudes."

I laughed. "They are your kind of dudes," I said. "Come to think of it."

"But it's true," he said, wiping his mouth of crumbs. "Those celestial spheres have been fixed in place for so long, old Atlas is putting his back out for no reason."

"Yeah," I agreed with him. And then I reached over and patted his leg, and Patrick did a funny thing: he squeezed my hand. We sat there, two old friends who shared a horrible memory, holding hands in front of my big lonely house.

It was after two when I let myself in the front door, and I knew I wouldn't sleep. In my office, I pulled out the yearbooks and guest book and started cross-referencing.

Going through Savannah's funeral book was like wading through thick mud. I counted forty-four girls from our sophomore class. Only three either hadn't signed in or weren't there. All the sophomore boys had signed in, as had most of the junior class. I wasn't surprised. Everyone knew Savannah. Everyone loved her. Our school had 360 kids, and I counted 333 names that I either knew or recognized from the yearbook.

There were four names I didn't know, all boys. I scribbled them on the back of a receipt I'd found in my desk drawer and said each one aloud, as if hearing them would tell me if they were the one. Anderson Rider. McPherson Michele. Thomas Small. Sam Bennington. I looked the names up in the yearbook and found that three were in the AV Club with David. When I didn't see Sam Bennington listed on any of the sports teams or in any clubs, I immediately began to create an image of him. A loner with greasy hair who loved my sister and was so angry he couldn't have her he'd done something horrible to her one November day. I rechecked the yearbook. Savannah had a thing for lacrosse players, so I went back to the boys' lacrosse photo and noticed the girls' lacrosse team picture underneath it.

Listed below Alice Adamson was Sam Bennington. She wasn't an animal-abusing, angry teenage boy but a beautiful senior with red hair and dark eyes. Jesus. No wonder it was hard for cops to find killers. I flipped through the yearbook one more time and found the boys who'd been crushed out on Savannah and the girls she'd hung out with. In one shot, I saw her with one of those upperclassmen girls she used to hang out with, Brittain Wylde, out on the café lawn, their arms around each other. Savannah had her eye on someone to the left. The person's head had been cut off in the picture, but I could tell by the build and the giant silver belt buckle that it was a boy.

Going through the yearbook still took my breath away. To see my sister so easily standing with Brittain, the upperclassman queen bee, reminded me of how cool she was and how none of her older friends even knew my name. I made myself turn the page, but the most acutely unpleasant thing about going back through the guest book and the yearbook was that, besides re-membering the shock of losing Savannah, I had to feel again what it was like to be that awkward, chubby, sixteen-year-old girl who was always being eclipsed by her twin.

As the sun rose, I finally slept in my office and dreamed I was in the ceme-tery. My limbs felt thick as if they were made of clay, and someone was say-ing, "Quit playing. You're making me nervous." It was a boy's voice, and I knew my sister was with him. His voice was gentle, kind. Suddenly, though, it changed to high pitched and panicky. "Oh shit. Jesus Christ. Come on—no, really, come *on*." And the sheer panic of it, the fact that I couldn't open my eyes, that I couldn't move, created such terror that I was pulled into con-sciousness. I woke to Greg coming through the doorway, coffee in hand.

"What the hell?" he asked. "What happened?"

I wiped spit off my chin. "What do you mean?"

"You were screaming," he said. "You were saying Savannah's name."

Greg's skin was nicked, and blood came through a tiny piece of toilet paper. "I had a bad dream," I said, flopping back down. I was so utterly exhausted I didn't think I could ever get up again. My eyelids felt like lead.

Greg was still watching me when I opened my eyes again.

"What?" I said.

"Nothing. I need to get ready for work."

I lay there under the ceiling fan, trying to remember the voice in the dream, trying to replay it and see who was there.

Finally, Greg came back in dressed in a sport coat. "Why'd you sleep down here?"

"I was working and got tired."

He stood in front of me in his psychiatrist's garb, so square and intellectual it hurt my eyes that early in the morning. "So you're not going to tell me?" he asked.

"Tell you what?"

"Where you were half the night. I heard you turn the house alarm off at midnight and not come back in until two."

I widened my eyes in surprise, trying to think what to say. I wasn't going to tell him now that we were opening Savannah's case; it was too late. If I hadn't told him when it happened, how could I tell him now? "I needed air," I said. "Sometimes I do that. And then I was working in my office."

"You were out in the dark at midnight?" he asked. "Somehow that really doesn't seem like you."

"Well," I said. "I'm full of surprises."

Greg shook his arms to get the sleeves straight. "Really?"

"Really." And then, to try to show how in the game I still was, I said, "We have Pepperidge Farm today at six."

"His name is Dr. Mirando," Greg said. "And I'm perfectly aware of that."

"Good," I told him as he picked up his briefcase. "I thought I'd remind you so you didn't decide to come home instead and rock out with that bassoon."

"Good-bye, Cady." Greg walked away.

"Bye," I told him. "Have a fantastic day."

CHAPTER
37

After I tried to kill myself, my parents sent me to Sound View Psychiatric Hospital, a stone gothic atrocity that used to be a convent and was now a loony bin for kids. There I spent four glorious months signing contracts for safety and taking personality tests like the MMPI. Some of the questions made perfect sense. *I am often possessed by evil spirits* (true or false). *I see things or people or animals that others around me do not see* (true or false). But others completely baffled me. *I am troubled by constipation every few days* (true or false). *I like mechanics magazines* (true or false). *I have a cough most of the time* (true or false). I'd lie awake some nights, listening to my bandaged, restrained roommate crying, wondering what the correct answers were to the litany of questions Dr. Holley swore had no right or wrong answers.

After my roommate kept holding her breath until she'd pass out in an attempt to suffocate herself, she got shipped to the floor above and replaced with a girl whose real name was Trafton but called herself Stevie because she only spoke in Steve Miller lyrics. It was quite impressive. When I asked how long she'd been there, Trafton replied, "Time keeps on slipping, slipping, slipping into the future." When I'd sleep through our alarm, she'd lean over my bed, her sour breath waking me before her words, and sing,

"Wake up, wake up, wake up and look around you. We're lost in space, and the time is our own." My favorite Trafton/Stevie-ism happened one night when we were in the troubled teen group. Some stand-in was subbing for Dr. Holley, who was out with the flu. Every time the bird-nosed therapist asked anyone a question, Stevie would sing, "Shu ba da du ma ma ma ma." For some reason that night, we all joined in. Finally, the woman left the room in tears, and the other fuckups and I gave Stevie a standing ovation.

Stevie's parents came once a week, and she sat in the visitors' room still as glass and stared out the window, turned away from them, not singing and not smiling and, it seemed, all her cells waiting until they finally left. Her parents dressed like they had a lot of money. Her mother was blond and fat and wore big chunky gold jewelry and too much makeup. Her father was thin and tall, and he wore expensive suits as if this were Wall Street.

My parents didn't visit the first month I was there. Dr. Holley said it was because they were very anxious to have me home, and that kind of agenda could "influence a patient." I'd been sitting in his office when he said this, a bitter February day that made me cold just looking out his plate-glass window. Dr. Holley was a pudgy, pink man who wore suits that were a little too tight, as though he hadn't gotten used to his size. He had a comb-over he smoothed down a lot and wire-rimmed glasses he pushed up his nose even when they weren't slipping. I liked Dr. Holley. I didn't think he had a chance in hell of truly understanding me, but he was nice, and I felt relaxed in his office at three o'clock every afternoon. But maybe that was a trick. Maybe they were trying to get us to feel comfortable with him so we'd tell him things.

While he asked me inane questions and I answered them, I wondered why, if he didn't want me influenced by my parents wanting me home, he had told me their agenda. I flat out asked him if it was a trick, if he was try-ing to make me tell him something. He replied that I only thought that because everyone in my family was trying to fool the world into believing they were done grieving. No one, he said, was ever done grieving.

I felt oddly safe at Sound View. Even though everyone was truly wacky and no one seemed like they'd ever get better, there were no pictures of Sa-vannah. No room we had shared. I didn't have to worry about running into one of her friends or a boy she'd gotten high with and kissed. I felt free there, far away from my mother who wrung her hands and chatted too much and too quickly, my sad father who was always down in the basement with his projects, and David slouching around playing video games while he was so high he drooled on himself.

The first time my parents tried to spring me from Sound View, I'd been there thirty-seven days. Valentine's Day had been the week before, and a garland made of tattered construction paper hearts hung above the doorways. From the fourth-story window of the rec room, I watched my mom and dad get out of the car. They'd left their coats on the seats and were wearing matching khakis and sweaters tied around their shoulders. David was with them, walking a few steps behind looking up as if he could see me, but I knew he couldn't. We could see out, but no one could see in.

My mother surveyed the parking lot furtively before she came in the visitors' entrance. She'd been raised old school. Big girls didn't cry. Families never aired their dirty laundry. And people in her family didn't end up at the funny farm. God forbid someone she knew was pulling in the parking lot to ask directions or use the toilet.

They sat at the visitors' table, their chairs pulled up close with eagerness, while my mother proceeded to name every person who'd asked for me. She sounded like Carole from *The Magic Garden*, the show with two perky girls and a pink squirrel named Sherlock that Savannah and I used to watch re-runs of while waiting for afternoon kindergarten to begin. With a big smile and her long, dark pigtails, Carole would stare right into the camera and name all the kids she could see sitting on their living room floors watching her. "I see Mary and Andrew and Sally and John and Jessica and Stephen." Then she'd glance back at her sidekick, Paula, who'd nod encouragingly and continue with her hand salute style as if shielding her eyes from the sun. "And there's Richie and Anne and Michael and little Samantha!" I always waited, holding my breath, for her to say Cady. Even if she'd said *Katie*, I could have pretended she'd seen me, but she never did. I'd sit morosely wondering why she could see half of my kindergarten class but not me. Savannah didn't seem to notice. It wasn't until they'd start telling jokes from the chuckle patch that I'd resolve to stick it out for one more day.

"Mom," I interrupted, "I get it. Everyone says hi." I felt bad immediately after I said it.

She ducked her head in embarrassment. She always did that when she was trying too hard. "Dr. Holley says you're doing well and we"—she grabbed my dad's hand, her expression shiny and overzealous—"we think it's time for you to come home."

I caught David's eye. His expression said it all. *And then there was one.* I could tell by the way he hadn't taken his eyes off me that he wanted me to come home. Or maybe he wanted to join me. He was in the local community college's computer and information science program, and since there were no dorms, he hadn't moved out. Being the only Martino child at home must have been overwhelming.

"No," I said without thinking about it. "Dr. Honey said I didn't have to go yet." Stevie and I had been on such good behavior that we'd earned a TV in our room. *E.R.* was on that night. I had to know if Carter and Lucy were going to survive being attacked by a schizophrenic patient.

"Oh, Cady, I wish you wouldn't call him Dr. Honey. It's not polite."

"But, Mom, he can't tell any of us apart, so he calls us all *honey*." Did severely depressed, suicidal teen girls possess some common trait that made us look alike to our shrink?

She rolled her eyes, but I could tell she was trying not to smile.

"Dr. Holley says you *are* ready," my father said. His voice was so strong I wondered if he'd been practicing in front of the mirror. Clearly, my mother had been kicking him in the ass to man up and convince me to come home.

"I'm too much trouble," I told them. It was true. At least if I bought the farm on Dr. Honey's watch like the girl two rooms down did when she'd soaked a roll of toilet paper in the sink and eaten it, they couldn't possibly feel like it was their fault.

"Cadence." My mother twisted her rings. "You're our daughter. You're never any trouble. We find strength in each other."

The noise that came out of me was something between a snort and a laugh. "I've been nothing but. Really, Mom, don't you want to keep sleeping through the night?" In the few weeks between me trying to off myself and landing here, they'd been sneaking into my room every night to make sure I was still breathing.

Crimson crept up her neck and spread through her face like it did when she'd had too much wine. "We're up, anyway. Really, it's no trouble to check on you." My mother had always outwardly supported me and done so with a fierce protectiveness, but she had a script she thought we should all follow.

Even before Savannah, she gave me one less cookie for dessert, and she'd pushed David to study, to reach his potential. No child of hers was going to go to community college. The joke was definitely on her when I never got any skinnier, David never tried any harder, and Savannah got herself killed.

"Oh, Mom, don't you get it?" I said. "That's the thing. I hate it that I'm the reason you can't sleep. Just a little while longer, and I promise I'll come back good as new."

They came every week after that. Sundays at noon. At first, they brought boxes of my and Savannah's stuffed animals from when we were little and photos of the two of us together. I'm sure they thought I'd find some comfort in these things, but I quietly slid them under my bed. After two months of visiting and noticing that there were no pictures on my desk or tattered stuffed rabbits on my bed, they gave up and stopped bringing me things that only made me want to kill myself all over again.

Still, they didn't stop asking me to come home. My parents were as confounded by my wanting to stay as Dr. Honey and Stevie were. All the other kids in my ward were counting the days till their release. They borrowed foundation from each other to cover up self-inflicted bruises. They made up elaborate stories about how their wrists got cut. They didn't report that they were still so depressed they couldn't get out of bed without psyching themselves up for group or a visit from their parents.

It was the food that finally drove me home. Meals sucked at Sound View. My parents were both great cooks; they had to be, owning a restaurant. And so the crappy food made me want to leave. The canned vegetables and frozen pizzas were so awful I'd stopped eating. I could tell by how my jeans slid down my hips that I was losing weight. I didn't want to. That'd been the only way anyone could tell Savannah and me apart. She had always been lean, athletic; I got called *solid* and *big boned*. And even though I had wanted to look like her when we were younger, since she'd gotten killed, I didn't want to be beautiful. Not after what happened to her.

I stayed with Dr. Honey and Stevie at Sound View until our insurance benefits ran out. My parents told me they'd have to mortgage the restaurant if I wanted to stay. They'd already lost a child; I couldn't let them lose Sotto Sopra too. So after another round of personality testing and answering questions like *Do you close the bathroom door when you pee even if no one is home?*,

I met one last time with my group, smiled as we ate surprisingly good red velvet cake, gave Stevie a Steve Miller CD, and pulled all of Savannah's stuff from under my bed.

I was hoping I wouldn't have to go back to school. The tutors at Sound View were really good and had told my parents I was the equivalent of a college freshman. The way I saw it, I could slack off in the safety of my house for another year. "Really, Mom?" I asked on the way home when she said David could drive me on his way to his classes the next day. "Are you seriously going to make me go back to that place? Why can't I have a tutor like I did at Sound View?"

I saw her straighten her back when I said the words *Sound View*. "It's time things got back to normal, Cady." And I knew from the grim way she'd set her mouth that if I wanted to get out of this, I'd have to appeal to my father, but it was almost as if he wasn't there. He was still as ghostlike as he'd been before I'd left, almost nonexistent.

It was, of course, Gabby who saved me. She came over that night for lobster, and afterward, we lay on my bed painting our toenails black while she told me how terrible it had been without me. She had to sit with the pretty girls at lunch (she didn't mean it the way it sounded), her lab partner farted all the time, and I wasn't there to make fun of the ridiculous teachers who tried to get the kids to like them by saying, "Yo, dog, what's up?" and "Keepin' it real." She also told me I needed to meet the new history teacher who'd transferred in after Mrs. Jepps had her baby two months early. His name was Mr. Sweetee (Gabby had to show me the newly updated school directory before I believed her). He was skinnier than the cheerleaders who existed on Diet Coke and cigarettes, had more hair than Hannah Delane, who hadn't cut her hair in three years, and every day at the start of fourth period, he'd arrive in the classroom a few seconds after the bell rang, set his Starbucks cup on his desk, and rattle off stupid coffee jokes. "What do you buy coffee with? Starbucks. If you spend too much time in the coffee shop, you'll be latte for work. When my wife spilled coffee on my shirt, I got hot under the collar." Gabby had memorized so many of Mr. Sweetee's terrible jokes that I suspected she had a crush on him. After she left, I went downstairs, where my mother was making desserts for Sotto Sopra. I sat on the stool and ate sugared berries and told her I'd go back to school after all. And sometimes, walking the hall, feeling unprotected as my new skinnier self, I remembered Dr. Holley's office those afternoons at Sound View, how the radiator clanked and the way the sleet or snow came down in the dying light and that feeling of being totally relaxed because finally I didn't have to pretend. He was someone who was actually asking me to be myself.

That might be why when it came to going to Pepperidge Farm again, I got there early. He was with another client, and I sat there listening to the sound machine outside his door, waiting for Greg.

About five minutes before the hour, a woman came out of his office in a flowered dress, a tight bun, and gigantic sunglasses. She kept her head down, but I suspected by how red her nose was that she'd been crying. A few minutes later, Pepperidge Farm stood in the doorway of the waiting room.

"Greg's not here yet," I said, taking my seat on the soft leather couch.

He pushed his glasses up his nose. "So I see," he said.

I crossed my legs, and I felt my foot moving back and forth. I willed it to stop. I was trying to remember when Odion's citizenship test was when Pepperidge Farm said, "So you went to Princeton."

Dr. Mirando—I needed to start thinking of him as Dr. Mirando, because I was terrified I'd call him Pepperidge Farm to his face—was wearing a pair of khakis and a sweater and beneath the sweater a tie. I imagined him knotting the tie in front of the mirror and checking with his wife to make sure it was straight. "Yes," I said.

"I did too." He smiled warmly at me. "Graduated quite a few years before you." He seemed like a nice man, a man who was a good father and probably had a couple of nice kids. "It wasn't as difficult to get in when I went." He sounded like he was contemplating something. "You must be smart," he said.

"I'm not really that smart," I told him. I wondered where Greg was; he was so set on going to therapy again, and now he was blowing it off.

He gave a little laugh. "You did go to Princeton."

"Everyone always says that," I told him, thinking of the raised eyebrows I got whenever I got interviewed and they asked where I went to college. "But I went to Princeton because I studied obsessively as a child. Some girls escape with television or drugs. I escaped by studying. I like learning, but I'm not one of those freaky smart people with a really high IQ." Now I remembered why I had not wanted to come back here. Pepperidge Farm had the unique ability to make me babble about useless, possibly incriminating information.

"But your test scores must have been very high," he said.

"We test well, my family. But also I took the Princeton Review. Twice." My nails were chewed up. I didn't really have that many friends; I had nothing better to do than study, I wanted to tell him. But that sounded sort of victimized and weird.

"What were you escaping from?" he asked.

"What?"

"You said some girls escaped with television or drugs. What were you escaping from by studying?"

My mouth felt dry. "I think you know," I said. There was no turning back now. "The thing I do the most is count."

"Count?"

"Yeah," I said. "You know, standing in the grocery store, I'll count the number of items in people's carts and do the square root of them, or I add the numbers on license plates together and divide them by the number of people in the car." Jesus, would I please shut up? But I had to keep going. "Or for instance, I know how many days—"

And then the door opened, and Greg came in, and for some reason, we both stood up. Greg's hair was messy and his shirt untucked. He shook Dr. Mirando's hand, and I was worried the doctor might tell Greg what had flown out of my mouth about counting, but we settled back in our seats, and Greg said, "Sorry I was late; a client got admitted, and I had to be there." Greg crossed and uncrossed his legs and spent the next thirty minutes telling Dr. Mirando about the last few weeks, how I'd gone to yoga with him and he'd gone to a Thursday dinner with me.

When we were done discussing the time Greg and I had spent together lately, our therapist pushed up his glasses and said to me, "Cady, is there anything specific that you want to discuss?"

"I hate our house," I said.

I felt Greg staring at me. "What did you say?"

"Um, I don't really like our house."

"Okay," Dr. Mirando said. "Tell me what you don't like about it."

"Our house is lovely," Greg said defensively.

"It's sterile," I said. My hands burned; they were chapped from going to the barn every day and taking care of Bliss. "And too big. And the acoustics make me wish I were deaf." I paused for a moment but then started speaking again. "And the whole thing is a gross display of wealth." I patted Greg's leg. "Greg likes money."

He threw up his hands. "What the hell is that supposed to mean?"

Dr. Mirando seemed to be studying me.

"I mean that's one of the things I was attracted to, initially. You have really great taste." I touched the Rolex on his wrist. "High culture, upscale. I grew up in a small colonial, very middle-class, and it was exciting to be with someone who knew about architectural design and the symphony." Here I was again, talking like someone had wound me up. I turned to Dr. Mirando and spoke directly to him. "His parents live on the Upper West Side, and they are both so lovely, and they know Paris inside and out; in fact, they are there now on sabbatical, and they go to places like Tangiers and wander the medinas, and I mean that's the kind of person I wish I could be, but I'm really not."

Greg started to say something, but to my surprise, Dr. Mirando put up his hand like judges sometimes do in court when they want a witness to keep talking. He leaned forward. "What kind of person are you, Cady?"

Greg was watching me, his eyes piercing.

A flash of heat was crawling up my back. I felt like I might break out in hives. "I don't know. I mean, I write mysteries—" All of a sudden, the motor cut out, and not one more word wanted to pop out of my mouth.

Dr. Mirando seemed to know I was done talking, and he sat back in his seat. One of his almost nonexistent eyebrows was up, it seemed, permanently. No one spoke. I smoothed my skirt. I hated my legs. I hated how they spread out so wide, the thighs, it reminded me of the day so long ago when Mrs. Wilcox was typing away while I was waiting for Savannah.

Finally, and I'm not sure where this came from, I said, "I don't like the wall of windows in the living room. I can't get away from them."

"Why would you want to get away from them?" Pepperidge Farm asked quietly.

The therapist's perfectly knotted tie had flip-flops on it. I wondered what his wife did for a living. I imagined she stayed home during the day and cleaned and cooked dinner and ironed the sheets. "They look out over the reservoir," I said. "And I mean, what's out there?" I made a sound like a laugh but not quite. "In the winter when it gets dark early and before Greg gets home, I sometimes can't move. It's like I stand at the windows, and I'm stuck."

I was talking quickly. I felt chilled suddenly. "It goes on for miles and miles that land. I mean, anything could be out there, and I stand in the living room and can't move."

"Can't move?" Pepperidge Farm leaned toward me again. "But what do you see there?"

"I don't see anything. Just my own reflection."

Dr. Mirando leaned back. He tented his hands and watched me. "If you see your own reflection, then you are seeing something."

I kept my eyes on the carpet between us. I felt blank inside.

"Cady," he said softly. "If you're seeing your reflection, you are seeing yourself. And you *are* something."

And then our time was up, and Dr. Mirando said we'd talk more about it the next time.

Gabby had dropped me off at Mirando's office, so I rode home with Greg in the Mercedes and watched Stanwich pass in a blur. For some reason, the non-sense words Savannah and I had spoken since we were toddlers came back to me. *Cryptophasia*, the books called it. A secret lexicon we'd invented that no one else could decipher. I had a sharp ache in the quiet of Greg's car to be able to speak that language with someone again.

"So," Greg said. "You hate our house."

"It's okay," I said. Without Dr. Mirando, it seemed somehow risky to talk about it.

Greg drummed his fingers on the steering wheel. "Well, I guess we should sell it," he said, his jaw muscle flexing.

"Seriously?" I asked him.

"If you hate it, let's not live there." He turned onto State Street, and I felt a soaring lift inside. "One reason we work so hard is to have options. If we have options, we should take them."

"Where?" I asked. "Where should we move?"

Greg took a breath in. "Anywhere," he said. "We can start looking at the MLS, hit some open houses, anything you want."

I thought for a moment he would reach over and squeeze my fingers, but he kept his hands on the steering wheel.

CHAPTER
38

"If she knocked down two poles, how come she only had four faults?" Chandler and I were at the Princeton Horse Show and I'd been explaining to him for an hour how jumper classes get scored.

"It's faults per jump, not each individual part of it. They're called rails, by the way, not poles. Unless they're on the ground; then they're cavalettis."

"That's stupid," Chandler said. "Why can't—"

But my favorite rider ever trotted in the ring on a stallion the color of dark chocolate. "Quiet," I scolded. "You know you're not allowed to talk when Peter's in the ring."

He rolled his eyes and pantomimed zipping his mouth. We watched while the Olympian galloped around without touching a jump. After the duo crossed the finish timers, Peter patted the horse on the neck and noticed us standing by the in gate. He tipped his hat to me, and I thought I would pee in my pants from sheer joy.

Chandler checked the notebook he'd been using to record everyone's scores. "Okay, he went not dirty—"

I playfully punched his shoulder. "Clean."

"He went *clean* and had the fastest time. Does he win?"

"Good lord, Chandler. How many years have I been dragging you to this horse show? Now he goes to the jump-off."

"Face it, sweetheart. I'm not going to pay attention until you start racing again."

"Showing," I corrected. "And that's never going to happen." Riding was Savannah's sport. Not mine.

"Whatever. I just came to be your arm candy." A famous grand prix rider from Europe who was married for the second time with two kids was very blatantly checking out Chandler.

"And beautiful arm candy you are," I said as his phone rang.

He pulled it out of his back pocket. "What the hell?" he muttered.

"Who is it?"

"Brady."

My heart jumped. "Well, answer it."

He did and then walked away as the announcer's voice blared through the loudspeakers. I walked up a small hill to the VIP tent, hoping to eavesdrop on some of the riders. About two minutes later, Chandler came back.

"We have to go. Right now." He was gripping his car keys like they might fly away.

"Is everything okay? What'd he want?" I was shocked that Brady had called Chandler. He was the only member of our group who hadn't clicked right away with Brady. He thought it was weird that he liked such an awful job so much. In the moments when I thought I might want to be with Brady, it was hard for me not to shove it in Chandler's face that not all of us had daddies who'd handed us cushy jobs with padded leather chairs and big paychecks.

"It's Colette," he said, his voice serious. "She's decompensating, and he needs help."

"Decompensating? What does that mean?"

We hustled to his car as quickly as we could without scaring any horses or cutting through the two huge schooling areas. I thought about watching Colette in her garden and what Gabby had found on the Internet.

"Why didn't he call 911? Or me?" I asked when we were speeding down the four lanes of Route 1 in Princeton.

"I don't know, Cady. He was half-hysterical and said he needed help."

Chandler was the calm one of us. He remembered RICE (rest, ice, compression, elevation) when a young horse stepped on my foot, crushing three bones. He had the presence of mind to feel the door of his office when there was a fire years before. Afterward, the firefighters said if he'd opened his door instead of waiting for help, the back draft would have killed him. But now, he seemed like he couldn't sit still in his seat and was laying on the horn, flying through red lights. I stayed quiet until we got to Brady's house.

Brady met us in the driveway. He was wearing jeans and an undershirt. His face was badly scratched. "Cady?" he said. "Thank God you're here. I tried calling you, but it kept going right to voice mail."

I pulled my phone out of my pocket and pressed the TALK button. It was dead.

"And David didn't pick up." He stepped forward and shook Chandler's hand. "Thank you for coming." His voice was breaking. "I'm sorry I called you, but I didn't know what else to do."

"I know you told me to come alone," Chandler told him. "But we were at a horse thing, and I didn't have time to bring her home."

"It's fine. I'm glad she's here," Brady said, heading back to the house. I peered in the front door. A vase was overturned on the floor. Clear marbles and flowers littered the entryway.

"Should I call 911?" I asked in a quiet voice I didn't recognize. From up the stairs, I could hear Colette screaming.

"I'm sorry I never told you more about her," Brady said. I didn't know which one of us he was talking to. "Colette is . . ." He paused, and I wanted to tell him that I knew. He didn't have to speak the words. His girlfriend was schizophrenic. "She's really sick. And sirens are part of her, uh, delusions. They mean that the gravediggers are coming for her." He kicked the flowers out of the way. "So it's better if we drive her to the hospital." I opened my mouth to ask a question, but he cut me off. "Even if the ambulance and cops came with their sirens turned off, the uniforms would upset her. Believe me," he said, his voice stern, "this is the only way."

We followed Brady up a set of dingy, carpeted stairs. He stopped outside a closed door.

"Even though you've never met Colette, I talk about both of you all the time, so your names will be familiar to her. The trick is to keep talking. Use soothing words, do not raise your voice, and no matter what"—he looked between us—"do not tell her we're taking her to the hospital."

My stomach tightened. I didn't think I could do this. What if I said something wrong? What if I upset her and she hurt herself? My mind flashed back to the day I'd tried to kill myself, and I had the crazy thought that Colette was doing herself in as we were standing in the hall.

Brady opened the door, and I didn't recognize Colette as the same girl I'd seen in the garden. Now, her hair was matted, her face was covered in snot, and she was on the floor by the bedside table.

"Hey, sweetheart," he sang to her. "I invited a couple of friends over." He motioned to us, but she stayed on the floor with her hair covering her eyes.

"Colette," I said, slipping past Brady and Chandler. "I'm Cady." I reached out for her, but she recoiled. I sat next to her, but not too close. "My parents are having a party at their restaurant, and I don't know what kind of flowers we should use for the centerpieces. Do you have any suggestions?" I waited for her to answer, but she didn't. "I really like orchids, but I don't know what else they go with."

"Star . . ." Her voice trailed off, and I couldn't understand what she was saying.

"Star what?" I'd read while researching one of my books that eye contact can sometimes be construed as threatening to schizophrenics. I made sure I kept my gaze on my paddock boots.

"Stargazer lilies go really well with alstroemeria," she whispered.

I glanced up at Brady, and he gave me the thumbs-up. "Alstro-whats? I don't think I know them. Would you mind taking me to your garden and showing them to me?"

She grabbed the duvet cover on their bed but didn't get up. I continued talking to her about flowers, asking any question I could think of until she finally tried to pull herself up. I let her hold on to me, and I slowly helped her. As if a scared child clinging to her mother, she wrapped both arms around my waist and leaned all her weight against me. She was as light as air. Once we got her downstairs, Brady murmured meaningless and soothing sounds to her until he was able to ease her into the backseat of Chandler's car. Again, like a child, as soon as the engine turned on and we began driving, she was asleep.

"I will never be able to repay you two," Brady told us in a hoarse, scratchy voice.

"That's what friends do," Chandler said, surprising me somewhat. Chandler was the kindest of all of us, but he was still wary of Brady. But this wasn't Brady. This was his girlfriend. His very sick girlfriend.

I glanced in the rearview. Colette was sleeping on Brady's shoulder.

"Has this happened before?" I asked tentatively.

"Yes," Brady answered sadly. "But it's never been this bad. This episode, before you got here, was downright terrifying. And heartbreaking." He stopped talking to kiss her hair. "I love her, but she's a very ill girl. And now she's a very gone girl."

CHAPTER
39

Every year in June, Greg went to a two-week-long psychiatric conference in the middle of Indiana—or maybe it was Iowa or Ohio; I could never keep it straight—and left me alone in our huge house that maybe wasn't going to be ours anymore. This year, he was also going to Notre Dame to visit his best college buddy, who taught neuroscience there.

I began to write like crazy. That was how I'd always done it. I'd spend months researching and writing down plot ideas, possible twists, and first, second, and third drafts. But, when I finally set to the finished, final, polished novel, the writing came out all at once. The scenes were fully formed, the characters showed up with complexities and quirks and neuroses and pathologies. The plot formed itself into an arc, and the climax happened at the end in a *kabooom* where the killer was revealed, and all of a sudden, it was done.

Of course, this binge happened after months and months of interviewing people, some wretched like Larry Cauchek and others lovely like Molly Kline, the Stanwich postmaster, whom I shadowed for a month when my killer was a mail carrier. The binge happened after months of jotting down notes about my characters and their idiosyncrasies, including what music they liked and their spiritual beliefs and if they waxed or shaved. The binge happened after staring at a blank computer screen hour after hour, feeling more and more panicked that this time the words wouldn't show up. They'd abandon me, and I'd have a deadline looming and an advance Greg had already spent, and I wouldn't be able to produce so much as a character sketch. To make matters worse, the binge usually arrived so close to the due date that I felt like I was falling, and the only thing to grab on to, to steady myself, was a live wire.

I could feel the binge coming. It woke me up at five in the morning the day Greg was leaving. He had a car coming for him that would take him to Newark at six, and for some insane reason, he'd gone for a run, and I'd been listening to him shower in the bathroom when I felt the binge coming for me. The music arrived first. I had a soundtrack for every book I'd ever written, and I would wake up with one of the songs playing in my head. That morning, it was "Scar Tissue," by the Red Hot Chili Peppers. "I'll make it to the moon if I have to crawl." That line reminded me so much of Savannah. Then again, what didn't? Then the characters came in a film reel playing in my mind, so real I felt like I could reach out and touch them with my hands. I could see the rooms they inhabited, the color of their socks, and how they liked their coffee.

"Greg," I called through the closed bathroom door.

The shower turned off. "What?" he answered. He was always grumpy before traveling. Greg was orderly; he liked to control his surroundings. Standing in the terminal hoping the plane would be on time and that he wouldn't have a seat next to some gigantic man with halitosis and the swine flu was not his idea of fun.

"I'm going to the store," I said.

He opened the door. He had a towel around his waist, and his chest was still wet. "Now?"

"Yeah," I said. "The novel is coming."

He grinned. He loved the binge because, I think, he was always a little worried I wouldn't deliver. Sometimes I'd be watching TV or peeling a banana, and he would say something like, "Shouldn't you get to the writing?" It made me want to take out a hatchet and do something to his face that one of my characters might do.

"Well, great," he said, bending down and giving me a quick peck on the lips. "Perfect timing."

"Yeah," I said. "No bassoon."

He grinned sheepishly. "There's that."

The bathroom felt hot and steamy, and if Greg and I had been a different couple, I might have gone in and given him a going-away quickie before his flight. "Have a good time," I said.

"I'll call you."

"Okay, but you know how I get. If it's an emergency, you should probably call Gabby or David to come get me."

"Right. The phone is evil during the binge."

"You got it," I said. "Good luck with the TSA guys."

No one was at the Stop & Shop that early in the morning, and with the place to myself, I stocked up. Today would be a cooking day. While my characters showed me scene after scene and the energy was building in my hands to sit down and transcribe every word of dialogue and description they gave me, I would be making meals I could easily slide out of the fridge, stick in the microwave, and then eat at my desk, reviewing the last chapter before plunging into the next. Roasted chicken, pesto lasagna, sandwiches, and gnocchi.

And then I was home, in the quiet house. By noon, I was done cooking and at my desk, and the fury began. Circadian rhythms be damned; this was a time when I slept in short bursts, I turned off the phone, never checked e-mail, and as far as the outside world was concerned, I'd died. I didn't even go out to get the mail.

That first night, I was up until 4:00 A.M., slept for three hours, and was typing again at seven with another scene knocking in my head. Most of what I had planned to write went right out the window, and what came in was a sort of symphony of characters all winding around each other's lives and telling me their deepest secrets and letting me know the exact trajectory the novel needed to follow.

By the third day, I had a problem. I loved Isabelle. She was the murderer, of course; I'd known that from the beginning. My first female killer. A jealous, young girl, the victim's best friend—none of the readers would have any clue until the end. She was sharp and witty and fun. She wasn't beautiful, but I usually didn't create beautiful people, and she seemed to whisper in my ear whenever I was writing one of her scenes. But it worked. She was a likable character, and readers would love her. Then it'd be even more sur-prising that she was the one who'd killed Susannah. It was Isabelle's love for Susannah that stumped me. I wasn't sure I could throw her in jail for the rest of her life. Maybe an icicle would fall on her head while she stood at the bus stop or she'd discover she was about to be caught and run away. While I pulled a portobello sandwich out of the fridge, I tried to figure that out, but nothing came to me.

After the fourth day and night of writing almost nonstop, I sat straight up in bed. Someone, I thought maybe it was Isabelle or Savannah, told me to go see Larry Cauchek. It was 8:00 A.M., I'd slept four hours, and I called Brady. It went straight to voice mail, which usually meant he was working.

"Hey," I said to his recording. "Can you get me one more sit-down with Cauchek? Call me back, please." Then I went to the kitchen and made a smoothie. At nine o'clock, I texted him.

By noon, I hadn't heard from him, so I called Patrick. When he answered, I said, "I need to see Cauchek."

"Well, hello, Cady," Patrick said. "How are you?"

"I'm totally insane," I told him. "Can you please get me in with him? It's important."

He laughed. "The answer is no."

"Because you can't or won't?"

"What happened to your guard buddy? Did he finally realize how dan-gerous it was?"

"I haven't been able to get a hold of him." I was standing in my kitchen trying to cut a piece of lasagna, which I'd abandon in a heartbeat if Patrick said yes.

"And you need a sociopathic killer why?" I heard a car honk, the sounds of traffic.

"Please, Patrick, my book is due soon, and I need to see Larry."

"You can't write it without the most loathsome serial killer in the country?"

"No, actually. I can't."

I thought he might keep fighting me, but instead, he said, "I'll meet you there at three."

I hung up and saw that I had a message from Brady. "Hey, Cady." His voice sounded bright. "Sorry I missed your call. I was in the attic finally unpacking boxes. You won't believe some of the stuff I found. The nineties was a bad time for fashion." Then he laughed and told me to call him later.

On the way to the prison, I thought about Savannah having a secret boyfriend. I hadn't told anyone, and I felt like I was lying to Patrick by not telling him. I decided I'd fill him in right after I was done with Larry Cauchek.

"I knew you wouldn't be able to stay away, love," Larry said to me.

Patrick sat at the head of the table; he didn't leave the room like Brady had. He leaned back in his chair and then let its front legs fall heavily on the floor. The noise echoed in the barren room. Larry pretended Patrick didn't exist.

"We both knew I'd be back." There was no point in trying to bullshit someone like Cauchek. "But I'm tired of this charade, Larry, and I know you're probably tired of it too, given that you're properly shackled to the table and can't do unspeakable things to me. So why don't we get on with it?" I wasn't sure what I was going to say, really, or even why I was here. I was trying to channel Isabelle or Hopper or even Susannah in hopes one of them would tell me what needed to be done.

"You've got nerve, love. I'll give you that." Larry Cauchek had very few facial expressions, but now he looked at me under his lids as if he might tear me apart with his incisors.

I blurted out, "Is he sorry for what he did?"

"Oh, love, you had to start with a toughie, didn't you?" He shifted in his chair and leaned back, relaxed, two friends chatting. "Does it matter?"

"You can't be serious." I'd done an admirable job not letting him fluster me the last two times I was here, but now I could feel myself unraveling. "I want to know if Savannah's life meant anything to him." Until I asked the question, I hadn't known which would be worse—if her killer felt remorse for what he'd done or if he was incapable of the most basic human emotion.

"Oh, love, they all mean something to us. Every. Single. One."

I flashed Patrick a warning so he wouldn't throttle the guy. I understood Larry Cauchek. In his own taunting way, he was trying to give me the answers I needed.

"Was Savannah targeted, or was she in the wrong place at the wrong time?" I asked.

"Neither," he said. "I've read the case report."

"What?" Patrick startled. "Don't listen to him. He's fucking with you."

Larry opened his hands on the table, palms up. An offering. "Believe what you will, Cady. But I have seen the report, and I do know that your sister meant something to him."

"How could you possibly—"

"There's a whole big world out there. And even I'm allowed visitors."

Larry Cauchek had a following. People on the outside, fans, groupies, people who researched, studied, and discovered the things that kept him going. With no possibility of parole, he'd never be able to kill again, but maybe he had followers on the outside who did it for him.

"Fine," I said flatly. "I get it. The serial killer guru gets some sick fuck to do his dirty work. Tell me something to make me believe he cared about my sister."

"No sign of a struggle?" Larry's eyes went wide. "My girls always struggled."

"Okay," I said. Suddenly, I was so tired. I wanted to go home and sleep, but I knew this was my last chance with Cauchek. Something told me I would never come back to talk to him again. "So he's not a sociopath?"

Cauchek eyed me. "You're hoping he is."

I stared back. He'd hit something. What did I hope for? That she had died knowing no amount of begging or crying would have saved her? That he, whoever he was, crushed her throat as easily as the rest of us swat a fly? Would it have been less terrible if the killer was capable of empathy and regret? Someone who actually could have been stopped if only she had begged enough?

"Here's the truth." Larry made a steeple with his fingers, a weak gesture because of the restraints. "Killing without remorse is a rare, coveted gift I have. The man you are seeking does not possess such an ability."

"What else do you know?" I stared at him.

"You think maybe your sister's killer cared about her."

I waited for him to say more. "Yes," I finally prompted. "We now think he did."

Larry stared down his nose at me. "Oh, love, don't be daft."

I was so frustrated I wanted to cry. "What are you saying?" I could hear the desperation in my voice.

His tone had the patience of a schoolteacher. "Go on. You're almost there."

The notebook. The secret boyfriend. How content she had seemed in the months before she died. How she often held her breath like she had something to say but then would change her mind at the last second. "What?" My insides were frozen. "No." I had trouble speaking; I was afraid of the words. "No one she loved would do something like this to her." I was shaking so badly I couldn't hold my pen.

Larry reached forward as if to comfort me, but the shackles held him back. "Oh, love, you're so close."

Patrick caught my eye and mouthed, "You okay?" But I didn't know how to answer.

"Remember," Cauchek said, his voice amicable, "nothing is ever as it seems."

I stood up and took one last look at the bleached-out room. "Thank you," I said. Then the guard opened the door and let me out. I didn't know what Larry was trying to get me to understand, but if I moved the pieces around enough like a jigsaw with no picture on the box, I'd figure it out.

"Good-bye, my love," Larry called after me. "I'll meet you in your books."

CHAPTER
40

"What was that about?" Patrick asked when we were in the parking lot.

My stomach growled. "That was my brilliant decision to talk to that psychopath one more time."

We stood by his Suburban. "Not that. I don't mean this the way it sounds, but you two seemed to have . . . shared a moment."

I shoved my hands in my pockets, and my stomach growled again. "I know Cauchek is a despicable person, but I really think he was trying to help me. You guys keep saying Savannah's attacker may have loved her. What if she loved him too?"

"Why don't we talk about it over lunch? Can I take you to Iano's? We'll grab a slice?"

I was starving and a little lonely from sitting in my house by myself writing. "Sounds good. But Patrick?" He glanced up at me with those kind eyes. "I have to tell you something, and you have to promise not to be mad."

"Okay," he said, holding up his little finger. "I pinkie promise." I hooked my finger through his. His skin was warm and soft.

So on the way to Iano's, I told him about finding Savannah's diaries while I was looking for the funeral guest book. I apologized for not bringing the book to him sooner and for not telling him that it seemed like

Savannah had a secret boyfriend. We were half a block from the pizza place when I finished talking. "Do you think her having a boyfriend changes anything?"

"Do you?" he asked.

"That's the thing." I could see up ahead that the parking lot was full, and I was glad. I didn't want to get out yet. "Whoever this guy was, I think he really loved her. And I've been kind of happy lately, thinking that she wasn't alone, that she may have had that one crazy true love that I'm still looking for." He raised his eyebrows but didn't say anything. "I just wish I knew who it was and why she never told me about him."

"Do you have any guesses?" The parking lot was crowded, so Patrick kept driving around the block.

"Savannah was, um, how should I put this?" I tapped my knuckles against the window. "She was a little more advanced than the rest of us. A little more adventurous. So the only thing I can think of is that maybe it was someone she shouldn't have been with—like a teacher or someone married, and that's why she never told me."

After circling the block, Patrick gave up and dropped me off and turned right on Washington to find a place to park. I stepped in the crowded restaurant and stood behind a woman who was snapping at the kid behind the counter, trying to get his attention. It took me a second to realize it was Emma. When she turned, her perfect cheerleader smile melted away.

"Hello, Emma," I said. "How are you?" I didn't care how she was, but I thought I should be polite. For David's sake.

Emma flicked her hair over her shoulder. "I'm fine, Cady. I was just picking up my order. A salad, of course; I don't eat pizza."

A bored teenager behind the counter called Emma's number, and she paid for her salad and picked up the bag it was in. She came at me like she might strike me.

"I know you've been spending time with that redheaded cop who worked for my father." I didn't move, so she had to edge past me, toward the door. "The truth is, Cady," she said—and I saw now that her perfect face was drawn, as though someone were pulling the skin down by invisible strings—"it doesn't matter what he's telling you. We all know your secret."

I took a step toward her. "What secret?"

"Savannah."

I got too close to her. "God, Emma, are you on something? What are you talking about?"

She leveled her gaze directly at me. "Cut the crap, *Cady*." She said my name like a bad word. "My father knew it, I know it, and everyone in town knows it: Savannah was no Virgin Mary. She brought it on herself. Did you ever think that maybe what happened to her was her fault?" And then Emma, in her yellow gingham dress, left the restaurant.

I stood there, stunned while the hostess told me it was a twenty-minute wait. I went to find Patrick and tell him we had to eat somewhere else and I could see Emma digging through her bag. I'd stocked my house with so much food for my writing binge that we could have gone there to eat. Patrick was walking toward me, and I met him in the middle of the parking lot.

Emma had opened her car door. "Cady," she called, "wait." Then she approached us.

In what felt like an act of protection, Patrick put his arm around me. "What do you need, Emma?" I asked her.

"Don't you think it's time to stop bullshitting the world? One day, sooner or later, one of you is going to crack and spill the beans."

I had no idea what she was talking about, but she didn't give me a chance to ask. She spun on her pretty spiked heels and trotted away.

"What beans?" I yelled to her back. "What secret?"

I didn't think she'd heard me, but she suddenly stopped. A few seconds passed before she turned to face me. "You people are excellent actors."

"What are you talking about?"

"Tell your parents and your sad brother that it's not working anymore."

"For fuck's sake, Emma, what are you saying?"

Her voice got low. "Everyone knows your family knows who killed Savannah."

CHAPTER 41

After my run-in with Emma at the pizza place, I told Patrick that I wasn't hungry anymore and I needed to get back to work. He dropped me off at the prison so I could get my car and told me to call him if I wanted to talk about what Emma had said or about Savannah and her mysterious boyfriend. I thanked him, but I wanted to be alone.

Every time I got to a scene about Isabelle, I couldn't make my fingers press on the keys of my computer. I was conflicted about her, because I knew how much she'd loved Susannah. Maybe Emma was right. Maybe someone knew something.

I wanted to ask my parents about it. Was there something they weren't telling me? Could they know who killed Savannah? And if they did, why wouldn't they come forward? The only possible answer I could come up with was that if they knew and hadn't said anything for almost twenty years, they were protecting whoever did it. That could only mean one thing. Someone they loved had murdered their daughter.

From that moment, everyone I knew became a suspect, even my parents. Had one of them murdered my sister, confessed to the other, and then they vowed each other to silence? Was it David? Is that why Emma had left him?

Could I have possibly done something so unforgivable that I didn't remember it? I needed to talk to someone. I needed answers, but everyone terrified me. What if I confided in the wrong person?

Then there was Gabby and the horrible things she'd written about Savannah in the slam book. I couldn't make myself believe that she could harm another person, but still, I'd been weird around her. She'd invited me over to watch movies, out for coffee, and to the park to make fun of people. But until I figured out what the hell Emma was talking about, I didn't want to see anyone. I used my book binge as an excuse to avoid Gabby and skip Thursday dinners. I was writing nonstop, my own twisted therapy, trying to make sense of what was happening and what had happened.

I knew Gabby couldn't have been the one. She was just protective of me and sided with me all the times Savannah had ditched us for her new friends. Gabby and I were best friends. We always had been. But Savannah and I were inseparable—or we had been until those older girls took her away. Was it possible that my motorcycle-riding, book-loving substitute sister had been so jealous of Savannah that she'd killed her? I tried to remember where we all were when Savannah was attacked. Gabby had piano practice Thursday afternoons, but no one had ever thought to ask Mr. Hartnet if she was actually there. My parents were at the restaurant prepping for dinner. David was at Chandler's house. Would he have had time to kill our sister and then get to Chandler's? A friend who would not only alibi him but who was willing to lie for half their lives?

I couldn't make sense of what Emma had said, and short of asking her what she meant, I'd never know. I was running out of time before my deadline and before Greg came home, so I tried to ignore what I knew and went back to writing. But every time I'd get a sentence out, Emma's words came back to me. *Everyone knows your family knows who did it. Everyone knows. Everyone knows.* Emma was planted firmly in my head, and I couldn't get her out.

My cell rang, and I didn't bother to check the caller ID before I answered. "I can't talk now," I barked into the phone. "I'll call you later."

As I went to press the END CALL button, I heard Patrick's voice. "Are you okay?" he asked. "You sound frazzled."

"Where does that bitch get off saying that we know who killed Savannah, that we've known all along?"

He let out a low whistle. "I was wondering when this was going to come back."

"Do you think she knows? I mean, what if my brother told her something a year ago or ten years ago? What if my entire family knows, and they're not telling me?"

"Come on, Cady. Think about what you're saying. What reason would your parents or your brother or Gabby have to hide this from you?" I started to talk, but he cut me off. "I've known your family for a long time, and one thing is certain: you all want to know who killed your sister."

"But that's the thing," I said flatly. "What if they know and they're not telling me because it was one of them?"

"Jesus." His tone was both angry and incredulous.

I expected him to give me a speech about me knowing my family could never do anything like this and how everyone loved Savannah. I hadn't expected him to be mad.

"Don't you think we know how to do our jobs?"

For some stupid reason, I held up my phone as if I'd be able to see him through it. "That's not what I meant."

"Then what did you mean?"

"I don't know. I guess I'm just trying to figure out what she was talking about. Why would she say those things?"

"I'm not a psychologist, but it seems pretty obvious that Emma feels guilty because of what her father did. I mean, think about it. This town was so angry at her father for closing Savannah's case, and now he's been forced to resign. She's just lashing out at you."

I thought about the article I'd read a few months before and how it seemed to imply that half of the Stanwich police force was corrupt. "Do you really think that's all it is?"

"Yes," he said simply. "I do. Besides, didn't you say that Emma was a mean girl in high school?"

"She wasn't so much mean as she thought she ruled the world."

"Same thing, really. So would you really put it past her to screw with you just because she can?"

He had a good point. Emma spent more than a decade manipulating my brother, but still, the damage was done. She had me questioning everything

I knew to be true. "Thanks for saying that, but I have to go. I need to call my parents."

"Honey," my mother said into the phone. "What a nice surprise. Your father and I have been thinking about you. We've been talking about coming up for your launch party. Do you have a—"

"Do you know who killed Savannah?"

My mother made a gurgling noise into the phone. "Cady!" Her tone was sharp. "How can you ask such a thing?"

I was expecting that question. "What would you do for me?"

My father had picked up another extension. "Anything. You know that. We'd do anything for you and your brother."

"Would you lie for me?"

My mother spoke. "To protect you, yes, we would."

"Would you lie for David?"

She answered again. "Why are you asking such questions? Have we done something to make you doubt our loyalty, our love?"

I hated it when she got all martyr on me. "On the contrary. I think you'd do anything for us, and I want to know if that includes covering up a murder."

There. I said it. I said what I couldn't help thinking since that bitch Emma had cornered me at Iano's. Too many pieces were adding up to a nonsensical picture of someone killing their daughter, sister, niece, godchild, friend.

"How dare you!" she roared through the phone. "You can call us back when you're ready to apologize."

I sat there, my stomach leaden. I felt as stunned as if she had slapped me. "You can't be serious," I said calmly. "Don't you even want to know why I'd ask such a ludicrous question?"

"There's not one good reason you could ever insinuate that someone who loved Savannah would end her life. The fact that you'd even ask such a question is—" She stopped speaking. "I don't even know what it is," she finally said, and then she hung up.

CHAPTER
42

"Zippy," Deanna said when I finally, finally answered the house phone after it had been ringing for days. "Just giving you a time check. You have three days to deliver the manuscript."

"It's done."

"What?"

"It's done."

Greg was coming home in a few days, and I'd done nothing but write since he was gone. I looked like hell, my eyes had deep circles underneath them, and I was still wearing pajamas even though it was six in the evening.

"Well," Deanna said, "my God, that's wonderful. It's not due till Monday. Do you want to hang on to it in case there are any last-minute changes?"

"No," I said. By now, I was so tired of it. I never wanted to hear about any of the characters or that poor murdered girl under the ice again. I especially did not want to have anything to do with Isabelle, whom I still loved but who had betrayed me, committing the murder "by accident" and then at the end running away. I'd found on the Internet that there existed an underground system of people falsely accused of murder who helped each other disappear. "I'll send it today. I hope the powers that be don't hate it." I was already pressing SEND. "Let me know as soon as you get any news."

I heard her assistant calling her name, and then something dinged in the background. "Hallelujah," she said. "It's already here. Ta-ta."

"Toodle-doo," I said.

I had seventeen texts. Eight of them were from Brady; five were from Gabby; three were a group message from Chandler to me, David, and Gabby, saying that Odion's citizenship test scores had arrived; and one was from Greg. I was sitting up in bed when I read them, and the next thing I knew, it was ten in the morning, and the sun was streaming through my window. I'd slept for fifteen hours straight, and the landline was ringing.

"Are you coming?" Chandler said.

"Yeah," I said, not quite awake. "I mean where?"

"What happened to you? Did you get abducted by aliens?"

"I was on a writing binge."

"Oh, well, we're all at Cookies. Odion got the results of his citizenship test, and he's waiting for all of us to be here before he opens them."

The conversation I'd had with my parents lingered like a bad dream I couldn't shake. I didn't really think anyone who loved Savannah could have hurt her. Larry Cauchek was a master manipulator. I was sure he was trying to fuck with my head. He'd done a spectacular job.

I had no idea what day it was, but I jumped in the shower, then pulled on a pair of jeans and an old Sotto Sopra T-shirt, put my hair in an elastic, and drove into town while dialing Greg on speakerphone. "It's delivered," I told him when it went to voice mail. "Hope you're having fun." I didn't call Brady. His first four texts said I should call him when my binge was over, but I didn't know what to say to any of my friends. I'd only agreed to go to Cookies because Odion hadn't even lived in New Jersey when Savannah died.

"It's here," Gabby told me when I came through the door. "It's finally here." Chandler, David, Odion, Madelyn, and Gabby had commandeered the big corner table, and spread before them was a feast of Cookies' pastries.

Odion was grinning wide, his straight, beautiful teeth shining. I went to him and hugged him hard.

"Well, open it," I told him. "What do you think it says? Did you pass?" I picked up a croissant and sat down next to Chandler.

Madelyn had Odion's flash cards on her lap, and she held them up so I could see them. She was missing a tooth, and she looked so adorable I had the mad thought I'd pick her up and run away with her. I'd come to believe the only way I'd have a baby was if it came from another woman's womb. "Who was the president during World War I?" she asked me.

"Wilson?"

Her face broke into a big grin. "Cady can be a citizenship too," she said to Odion. The next card read, "What's the longest river in the US?" But I didn't know that one.

"Where you been, little sister?" David asked me. He and Gabby were on the other side of the table with a plate of brownies between them.

"I finished the book."

"What?" Gabby's eyes got round. "Have you been writing since you called me? The day Greg left? But that was weeks ago."

Chandler lifted his hand for a high five. "Holy crap, that's fabulous! If it wasn't breakfast time, I'd order champagne."

Gabby popped up from her seat and came around to hug me, plying my face with kisses, and David grinned, his hair like a tumbleweed, and it seemed like he might have crawled out of bed, but he was handsome in his messy, discombobulated way. I could feel myself relaxing, cursing Emma for making me doubt the people I loved most.

The croissant I'd bitten into was still warm, and I felt like I'd woken up in heaven. "Would you please forget about me? Odion, open the damn"—I saw Mads cover her ears—"I mean *darn*. Open the darn envelope."

"In a minute," Odion told me. "Too many nerves right now."

I took another bite of the croissant, and I felt all happy again, my friends around me, relishing in my accomplishment like it was theirs too, and I guess it was. I made myself push out my suspicions. I couldn't let Larry Cauchek and Emma control me like this. Patrick was right. The police knew how to do their jobs, and they must have ruled all of us out. "Gabby," I said when she was done mauling me, "how's training going for Hoka Hey?"

"Oh," she said lightly. "I decided not to do it."

"What?"

The table got quiet. I felt my heart lift; I was so relieved I could hardly breathe.

"I don't know," she said. She was smiling so grandly I thought she was going to tell me she had won the lottery. "I feel like, you know, it's danger-ous." She took a piece of brownie from the plate she was sharing with

David. "And there are other things I want to be doing with my time." She glanced at my brother, who was chewing as if he'd never tasted anything that delicious before in his life.

"Well, that's great," I said. "I mean, as long as you're happy."

Odion and Chandler were busying themselves with Madelyn, offering her juice in a sippy cup.

"It's still sort of surprising," I said. But no one except me seemed shocked.

"Now." Odion stood. "Now I am ready."

Chandler handed him the envelope, and he opened it with his eyes closed. He pulled out the letter and opened his eyes, and as he read, his face went blank.

"Shit," Chandler whispered. Then louder, "Hon, what does it say?"

Odion began saying the Pledge of Allegiance. We all tried to clap when he was done, but then, before we could get the applause out, he put his hand on his heart and started singing "My Country, 'Tis of Thee," his tenor voice so gorgeous the whole restaurant went silent. Even Sassafrass quit clinking dishes in back. I felt myself starting to cry, and when I looked over at Gabby, she had tears running down her face. So did Chandler, and so, to my astonishment, did David. Only Madelyn was smiling happily as if she'd made the song up herself. By the time he finished, our whole table got up and clapped and hugged him, and then I saw that everyone else was clapping too.

CHAPTER
43

After I left Cookies, with the book done and Greg still away, I had nothing to do and nowhere to be. I thought about going to the prison to get one more sit-down with Larry Cauchek, but I knew that wasn't going to happen. I got in my car and started to head home, but I decided I had to talk to my friends and family one by one. I knew none of them had killed Savannah. Now I needed each of them to tell me. I stopped at a convenience store and grabbed a few things I'd run out of over the weeks, mainly toilet paper and toothpaste.

I called Gabby on my way to her house. "I'm coming over," I told her answering machine. I was shaking with nerves. "There are a couple of things I need to talk to you about."

There was only one, but I thought it sounded less ominous. When I turned onto her street, I saw her motorcycle and little MG parked side by side in the driveway behind David's Honda. He was probably changing a lightbulb or the AC filter. Gabby was not handy when it came to her house, which struck me as odd since she was normally so self-sufficient. I took the stairs two at a time and knocked quickly before bursting into her place. She wasn't in the living room, but I heard her laugh down the hallway and I half ran there, calling her name.

She said something back, or I thought she did, but I couldn't hear what, and when I saw her bedroom door ajar, I went right in. And there she was, stark naked, lying beside my brother, her head on his chest like this was the most normal thing in the world, and he had his arm around her. Milky Chance was playing on the radio, and there were panties and boxers on the floor. As soon as she saw me, she bolted up.

"Cady!"

David was frantically trying to cover himself up.

"What the fuck." I looked from him to her and back again. "You two are sleeping together?"

"Well," David started, "it's a lot more than that."

"We've been wanting to tell you," Gabby said, bringing the sheet up to her chin as if I hadn't seen her naked a million times before. "But you've been on the binge, and we want you to be happy for us, because we love you so much—"

"And we love each other," David added, still trying to get the sheet from the bottom of the bed around him without showing me his ass.

"You guys are together?" I ran my hand through my hair. I couldn't quite believe it. I thought I was having one of those weird, delirious dreams I had while I was binge writing. "What happened to the Minnesota girl?"

"That was one dinner months ago," David said. "I've been in love with Gabby forever. Even while I was with Emma."

"We couldn't stop thinking about each other," Gabby said. "And when we wanted to tell you, you holed yourself up finishing your book."

I started backing out the door.

"Don't go!" Gabby jumped up with the sheet over her. "We adore you, Cady. We want it to be a good thing. We can all be together, you know, like a family."

"I'm happy for you," I told them. "I really am, but I have a lot of shit going on in my head, and I'd really rather not work it out while you two are naked."

Gabby jumped off the bed and tried to stop me.

"Please," I said. I didn't want to say that I couldn't let go of what she'd written in a notebook almost twenty years before. "I'll be back later, okay? I'll call you guys tomorrow." I started out the doorway and then turned to them. "I'm thrilled for you two. I really am. Love you both so much." And then I was backing out of the bedroom, running down the hall and out the door. And I realized that I was jealous, not because they were together and seemed so happy but now they had true love like Savannah had had, and where was mine?

CHAPTER
44

When I got home from Gabby's, I called Brady and told him I'd been held hostage by my book but that I wanted to see him. Maybe he could help me understand what Gabby had written and all the terrible things Emma had said to me. I slipped in that Greg was away, so anytime the next day was fine. I waited while I ate dinner and watched the news and took a shower, and then he called. He said he could meet me at my house at one thirty. I thought I should ask how Colette was doing, but I didn't want to bring it up if he wasn't ready to talk about it, so I hung up without saying a thing.

I was reading in bed when I heard a noise. Putting down my book, I listened. I heard it again, and I felt myself go completely stiff. When it happened a third time, my heart started beating hard. I kicked off the covers and went through the halls with a gigantic cop flashlight I kept under the bed.

Our house was alarmed. The man who installed it said it could never be tripped, because it was on a complicated sensor system that ran underground. It cost a fortune to dig, but it was the only way I agreed to buy the house. I knew I shouldn't be afraid since it was the kind of alarm places like the White House used. In the living room, I found the culprit. A maple branch had lost one of its limbs; it had broken but never dropped, and it was brushing against one of the windows in the wind. As I stood about to draw the blinds, I caught sight of myself in the black reflection of the glass. What surprised me most was that for one quick instant, I thought I saw Savannah. It didn't look porky enough to be me. Or maybe the fat me was a product of my imagination. I found myself suddenly not able to stand, and I sat down in front of the window, hardly able to breathe. It scared me to think I didn't have my weight around me, my scar tissue, Greg had once called it. It was what had kept me safe and insulated all these years after Savannah's murder.

And then, I can't say why, I picked up the phone and scrolled through the numbers until I found Dr. Mirando's. He picked up on the second ring.

"Dr. Mirando?" I said.

"How are you, Cady?"

"I count," I told him as if we'd never finished our conversation. I wondered what he was doing in the office or if his patient calls were wired to his home and if I had woken his wife. Or maybe my fantasy about him was wrong. Maybe there was no wife. "I count the days since she was murdered." Dr. Mirando didn't ask me who I was talking about, and it occurred to me he was well aware of my story. "I count, and I write about what I know. I've sold a boatload of books, but I never wanted it. It was just a way to get through the days without her. Like the counting." I was running at the mouth, like I always did with him, and I realized maybe that's what made him a good therapist. "But I made a good living off the books, and I feel so guilty about it. I had no interest in writing anything after *Alibi*, but Greg encouraged me to. He called it my therapy. That's what he does; he tells me things are good for me because they're really good for him." I could hear Greg as if he were in the room using that same soothing shrink tone he probably used with patients. "I mean, it's not his fault, I know that. It's—" I could feel the tightening in my chest, and it was getting harder to breathe. "Every single thing I've done since she was killed is because of her. Living in Stanwich, marrying Greg, staying fat . . . I don't really know what's me, and I need to find out," I said. "I really have to get on with my life."

Dr. Mirando was quiet for a moment, and then he said, "What would that mean, Cady, getting on with your life?"

"I don't know. That's the point. I don't know what I am without counting the days and writing about all these innocent people getting killed."

He didn't answer, but I could hear him breathing. "Okay," he said. "Let's go with it a moment. Let's say you are here on earth to do Savannah's bidding, even in her death. What do you think she'd want you to do?"

I stared at myself in the strange mirror of that black window. "I think she'd want me to let go," I said, and I felt a sob in my throat. "I don't think she'd want me to hang on anymore." And then I cried and cried. It was a different cry from the one with Patrick at the orchard. It was a cry for help, it was a cry for forgiveness, it was a cry to my sister to please help me find a way out of this murderous labyrinth.

CHAPTER
45

I spent the morning cleaning and going through the mail, doing all the things I'd ignored while the binge had taken over my life. By the time I was done, I needed some dark chocolate and mindless TV. And then I remembered Brady was coming. I felt a little sick to my stomach from fatigue, but I also had that high school crush butterfly feeling, and I made a salad in case he hadn't had lunch yet. I'd taken a pair of shears and had gone out to the garden to cut flowers so I could make an arrangement for the dining room, and the house smelled sweet, like roses and peonies.

Brady got there as I was dozing off on the couch. He was carrying a bunch of daylillies wrapped in wet tissue paper, which was amazing since he'd roared up on his motorcycle. I took the flowers from him and gave him a quick hug.

"Shit," I said, "it feels like a million years since I've seen you."

He followed me into the house and waited in the kitchen while I got a vase from the pantry. "Have you gone on the lam? Where've you been?"

I sighed loudly. "You wouldn't believe me if I told you."

"Try me." He went to the refrigerator and took out two beers. He flipped the tops off and handed me one. "Let's sit down, and you can tell me your troubles."

"Thanks." I kicked off my flip-flops, and we sat on opposite ends of the ugly white couch. "I don't even know where to start." As I was thinking about everything that had happened in the last couple of weeks, I realized I hadn't told Brady about Patrick reopening the case or what Gabby and I had found in the storage locker.

"How about at the beginning," he said.

I barked a laugh. "On a cold November day in 1998, my sister was murdered."

"What?" He sounded more panicked than confused.

"You said start at the beginning. There it is."

He put the back of his hand to my forehead. "Are you feeling okay? I'm having a hard time following you."

I shook my head as if to clear it. "I'm sorry. I know I'm not making sense, but nothing makes sense right now. One of the cops who investigated Savannah's murder showed up at my house a couple of months ago to tell me he's reopening her case. And he asked to borrow the guest book from her funeral so he can start reinterviewing people. So while Gabby and I were at my parents' storage unit looking for it, we found Savannah's old diaries." I stopped long enough to take a long sip of my beer. "Diaries, mind you, she never even told me she kept. And guess what we found?" But I didn't wait for him to answer. "She had a boyfriend. My sister was madly in love, apparently, with the greatest guy in the world and never even told me. What the fuck is that about?"

He stopped with the bottle almost to his lips. "Really?" he asked. "She loved him?"

"Seriously? I tell you that my dead sister's case is getting reopened and that she had a secret boyfriend who was probably married, and the only thing you find odd is that she loved the guy? I bet you it was Mr. Fitz."

He set his beer on the table without a coaster. I was sure Greg, wherever he was, could feel it. "The physics teacher? What makes you say that?"

"Two things: she never named him by name, and more importantly, she never told me about him. He must have been someone off limits. Like a teacher or an old married guy."

He reached over and squeezed my shoulder. "Wow. No wonder you've gone underground. That's a lot to deal with."

"Oh, that's not even the half of it. While Gabby and I were looking for the guest book, I found an old slam book that she and I kept. I read it when I got home and found all these entries about how much Gabby hated Savannah. Called her stuck-up and bitchy and a slut." Brady winced. "And then, to top it all off, I went back to see that lunatic Cauchek even though you wouldn't return my calls, and he told me that nothing is ever as it seems." I had a flash of one of my meetings with the hypnotist, Dr. Corcores, and how he told me we have to push past what is easy to see the truth. "I don't even know what that means."

"Don't listen to anything that monster has to say. He was screwing with you, getting inside your head."

I finished my beer and deliberately set the bottle on the table next to the coaster. Fuck Greg. "No, no. I think he may have been onto something, because after I saw him, I ran into Emma and—"

"Jesus, the universe is conspiring against you."

I smiled. "No shit, but it gets worse. Emma all but told me my family knows who did it and we're covering it up." I stopped talking long enough to take a breath. "What the fuck is going on here?"

Brady turned toward me and took both my hands in his. I didn't get that swishy feeling in my stomach like I used to when he touched me. It was like my body knew that if we kissed again, I wouldn't feel anything.

"Okay, let's take one thing at a time," he said. "How do you feel about Savannah having a boyfriend?"

A warmth came over me. "You know what? It makes me happy. Savannah was always in such a hurry to grow up. She started having sex before we were in high school, and she kissed every boy she could. She smoked pot and only wanted to hang out with the senior girls. It was like she was trying to be an adult. And it just made me sad. I know she didn't care about any of those boys, and I wonder if she even liked Scarlet and Camilla and all those other bitchy girls. But knowing she had someone she really loved, even if it was Mr. Fitz . . ."

"Why did girls like that guy so much?"

"Because he was so cute." I giggled, and it felt good. "But anyway, I read all three of her diaries four times. Her boyfriend made her happy."

"Did you find anything else in the storage unit? Pictures or notes or anything?"

I let out my breath slowly. "Nope. I went through every box in there and didn't find anything. Except," I said, thinking of that one odd picture, "for a photo in our sophomore yearbook."

"Was she making out with Mr. Fitz?"

I made a face. "Ick. No. She was with that pretty senior girl Brittain, and she was watching someone. I can't explain it, but she looked so happy. Savannah was restless, always ready to try the next thing, experience something new. But in that photograph, she seemed so . . . content."

"Okay, I'll bite. Who was she looking at?"

"That's the thing. I don't know; his head had been cut off, but I could tell from the build and the belt buckle that it was definitely a guy."

"Are you sure?"

"Relatively. If it was a girl, she was awfully tall and must have had a cowboy fetish."

"Was she wearing cowboy boots?"

I laughed. "No. She, or he, had on this gigantic silver belt buckle like people in rodeos win when they don't get killed by the bulls."

He shifted awkwardly on the couch and put his hands in his lap.

"Are you okay?" I asked. "Ants in your pants?"

"Sure, sure, I'm fine." But he kept squirming.

My eyes went to his hands and what they were covering. His face went white.

I scrambled to my feet. "Actually, the belt buckle looked like yours." I ran to the back of the couch, putting a barrier between us. "It was you." All at once everything made sense. "You were the secret boyfriend."

"What? Me? No. I barely knew her." But he sounded like a bad actor, high pitched and nervous.

"That's why she never told me. Because she knew I was in love with you. It was you."

He stood up, and I backed away. "Cady, come on. Why do you look like you're about to jump out of your skin? Sit down, and let's talk about this."

"Not until you admit you were her secret boyfriend."

He cast his eyes downward. "I was," he mumbled. "It was me."

"So you've known. All these years, you've known that I loved you in high school. You and Savannah must have gotten a good laugh over the porky, ugly twin pining over you."

"You're not ugly, and we never laughed," Brady said. His voice sounded like a wound, wide open and bleeding. "Savannah adored you; she thought the sun rose and set on you." He came around the couch, hands out, palms up, but I backed away into the kitchen. "She always said how smart you were, how together you were, how she had this"—he tried to find the words—"this emptiness that—"

"I don't want to hear this," I said. "I don't think I can." I heard a strange ringing in my ears, like someone had set off a firecracker right near me. I had the urge to run out the front door, to catapult myself out of this reality, because it was all starting to come together. Brady only wanted to be near me because of Savannah. "You'd been there before," I said. He had his head down, eyes on the floor. "To that ice cream place on the shore that she loved so much. That's why you took me there." He didn't deny it. "And you'd been to the old barn. You knew Bliss."

"Cady."

"She introduced you to her horse."

"Yes." He sounded resigned.

And I saw now that of course Savannah had loved him. Brady was sexy, but he was kind too, and that was what Savannah did: she brought kind people into her midst and made them love her, and then they did things like drive her to ice cream places two hours away and make friends with a horse who hated people. She would have loved how quiet Brady was, how he went to his car during lunch to listen to music and wasn't wrapped up in sports and keg parties.

"And all this time, I thought that maybe the chubby sister had a chance," I said. My cell phone rang, but I didn't answer it.

"Please, Cady, it's not like that. I've been trying to find a way to tell you since that first day at the prison, but then you asked me to help you, and we started spending all this time together. And I really, really enjoyed it. I loved being with you, and I didn't want to ruin that by telling you I had a past with your sister."

The house phone rang six times before the answering machine picked up, Greg's voice echoing, telling callers to leave a message. I heard Patrick talking.

"Cady," he was saying. "Something's happened with the case. Call me immediately."

Brady was quiet while we listened. When Patrick quit talking, I said, "Brady, I need you to leave."

"We didn't laugh at you," he said again. "She never told you about me because she knew how you felt about me and didn't want to hurt your feelings. She didn't want you to think she was taking me away from you."

"Okay," I said, but I wasn't sure I believed it. "Just go." I came around the counter. "I have to call Patrick back." I grabbed for the phone, but my hands were shaking, and I dropped it. "Thanks for telling me the truth." I could hear the bitterness in my voice, and I hated it. I'd been so happy when I found out Savannah had loved someone. Why couldn't I be thankful? I reached down and picked up the phone, waiting for him to leave. Why was I still so jealous of my sister? "Go," I said. I knew I was being horrible. Savannah had loved him. He had loved Savannah. He probably knew things about her that I never did, but all she'd had and all I didn't was coming back to me in a rush, and I couldn't stand looking at him.

Brady raised his hand in what seemed like a final wave. And then I watched him open the door and walk through it. While I was dialing Patrick's number, I heard the motorcycle roar off.

"I need to talk to you about something," Patrick said as soon as he answered. "And I don't want you to say no right away."

Jesus. Why did everyone need to tell me something today? Had he secretly been in love with my sister too?

I felt spent, wrecked inside, and I said, "Okay."

"I want to bring in a psychic. Her name is Charlotte Reid, and she's the real deal. I would have talked to you about her sooner, but she—"

"Retired ten years ago," I finished for him. "I know who she is." She was a twin whose brother had killed himself. I'd read an interview with her after his death. She said Michael was also psychic and ended his life because he didn't know how to process the unspeakable things he knew.

"Believe me," he said. "I've worked with plenty of psychics, most of whom are brought in by the families of victims desperate for answers. And the majority of them are crackpots. Charlotte is different. She has a gift."

"It's not a gift." I went to the front door and opened it. Brady was gone.

"Call it what you want, but she's for real."

"That's not what I'm saying." I closed the door and felt sick. "I don't think what she can do is a gift. It must be terribly painful to know and feel the things that she does."

"That's why she quit. She wanted to shut it off; she said it disturbed her whole life. It was like a staticky radio station that got left on, and she could never get away from the noise."

"I know." I had a flash of Michael, a man I'd never met, hanging in his bedroom closet. "What brought her back?"

He sighed into the phone. "Savannah."

I was still thinking about Brady. "Can we see her now, before dinner?"

"Yes," he said. "I'll come pick you up."

I started to hang up, but I heard Patrick's voice. "Cady?" he asked. "Charlotte said she needs two things from you to make this work."

I was so drained I didn't think I could write my name at that moment, never mind come up with trinkets for a psychic.

"She needs a picture of Savannah, and she needs you to completely clear your mind of anything but your sister."

"But Brady . . ." I started to say, but then I stopped. "Okay. I'll see you in a few minutes."

CHAPTER
46

Charlotte Reid had been beautiful. I saw it as soon as we walked in the door and caught sight of her wedding picture on the mantel. Cheekbones to die for. Perfect glossy hair, long lashes, and a luscious mouth. Now she was an old woman, and every line on her face seemed to tell a story I was dying to hear. Her eyes were still a captivating denim color, and she was slight, sprite-like. She wore lengths of turquoise around her throat and an amber bracelet wound around one arm and rings on every finger. Neither Patrick nor I could take our eyes off her.

"Come in, dear." She held my elbow and smiled at Patrick over her shoulder. "I made some tea with honey. You've been through some trying times these past days." Jesus. What had my dead sister told her?

Charlotte sat us down on a velvet love seat, and she settled on a chaise longue with dark wood and gold tacks. It wasn't until she tilted her head slightly to the side that I realized she looked like Savannah might have looked at seventy.

"I feel like I know you," she said, reaching over and patting my knee. A man came in; I could tell by the color of his eyes and the shape of his mouth that he was Charlotte's son. He set down a pot of tea and a plate of cookies on the coffee table between us. Then he bowed slightly and moved away.

"Don't you?" I asked. Patrick reached out and took a cookie. "Isn't that your secret superpower?" God, this was awkward. "I mean . . ." But I shut my mouth.

She laughed, letting me off the hook. "It is my superpower, but it's not so secret." My knees were touching Patrick's, but there was no room for me to move over. And I liked feeling him close to me. Her house was pretty, very comfortable, and filled with leather club chairs, bright rugs, gold-framed portraits, and hanging marionette puppets. With chipping paint and exquisite detail, they must have been antiques. But even in all that comfortable beauty, I felt nervous. I knew this about Charlotte: she used to be called in on the highest-profile cases, kidnappings and missing children of the extremely wealthy. When Michael hanged himself, she'd stopped working, though she stayed in Princeton and was now somewhat of a recluse. I'd written to her, tried to find her number; I'd done it under the guise of research, but as a psychic, she must have known why I really wanted to see her. "Have some tea, and take a moment to relax, dear. This can be a lot to process all at once."

"Actually, I believe in psychic connections," I said. "Savannah and I knew things about each other that we shouldn't have."

"You were identical?"

"Yes." I passed over one of the last pictures taken of Savannah. It was a beautiful photo from Halloween; she'd been dressed like Little Red Riding Hood with a sassy faux lace-up bodice, a hood, and a flared petticoat that made boys nervous and men stare. She'd been standing on the porch holding on to the railing, with one leg up, a patent leather red shoe on her foot. "Get in the picture," my dad had said. But I'd been dressed like a chubby Dorothy, not nearly as cute, and I couldn't be persuaded.

"You shared the same cells, the same DNA." Charlotte was studying the picture. "For all intents and purposes, scientifically speaking, you were essentially the same person. Of course, those cells divided, and you each developed your own souls, your own minds." Her compassion reminded me of Patrick that first day at the school. He'd never questioned how I knew Savannah was in the Wolfe Mansion. "And she comes to you, doesn't she?"

"In dreams."

She took a sharp breath in. "She leads you to your books?"

"Has she been talking to you?"

"Yes, my dear." Charlotte studied the picture. "She is quite persistent, and she loves you very much." She smiled at me, and I thought perhaps it was the kindest smile I'd ever received. "Now that you're here, I'm hoping she will come back. If she chooses not to come to us today, perhaps you can return with something that belonged to her. Maybe something she wore on her last day."

Panic gripped me from the inside out. The facilitator of the grief group my parents went to for a little while suggested they give Savannah's wardrobe to Goodwill. "My parents gave her clothes away. The few things I kept are long gone." I grabbed at my neck. "Oh God. She's not going to come back again, is she?" I tried to think of what was in all those boxes at the storage unit.

"Cady." Charlotte touched my knee. "Breathe. It's okay. We'll sit here and see what happens." She chewed on her lip for a moment. "Do you have anything left of hers? A stuffed animal? A book?"

I couldn't give her the diaries. "She collected Tweety Bird figurines. I still have them, but they lived on a high shelf in our bedroom." When I'd finally taken them down, they were covered in dust—hadn't been touched in years. I pulled on my hair, hard. I couldn't believe that I had erased my sister and hadn't even been aware I'd done it.

Charlotte leveled her gaze at me. "You did not betray Savannah. If there is one thing she took with her, it was how much you love her."

I'd been hearing that line from shrinks and counselors for more than half my life. "Please don't patronize me. You don't know that."

She raised one eyebrow. "Don't I?"

"Oh God. I guess you would know, wouldn't you?" Suddenly, I was exhausted. "Thank you for saying that."

She leaned forward. "Let's meditate for a moment and wait."

"How will I know if she's here? Will I be able to see her?"

"Probably not," she said sweetly. "It's different for everyone. For me, I get visuals, like screenshots. Sometimes I get a firm directional about what she wants you to do; sometimes other spirits come because the channel is open, and they leverage it." She put her hands on her knees. "We'll have to see what happens. But most of all, you should remember they don't communicate like us; it isn't always direct. We have to accept what they can do now that they are home."

"Home?"

Charlotte's blue eyes somehow seemed surprised. "Yes. She's home. We are all trying to get there; she found a path a little earlier than the rest of us."

And what an odd portal she took to bring her *home*, I wanted to say, but I didn't. Patrick busied himself opening his leather notebook, and I was so relieved he was there.

"Now." Charlotte sat up straighter. Her voice was soft and smooth, almost melodic. "Do you know if she believed in the afterlife?" Somewhere in the house, a phone rang, and I wondered if she knew who it was. "It's okay if you don't know," she said.

"As a matter of fact, I *do* know." One of the things Savannah and I disagreed on was religion—or, more accurately, faith. It was as if she was born knowing there was a master plan, a greater force at work. And she seemed to accept it. I, on the other hand, hadn't been able to make myself believe that there was life after death or anything but eternity in a hole. "Not only did she believe in it," I told Charlotte, "she thought it would be like one big party. It was almost unsettling how comfortable she was with the thought of dying." I felt an ice pick stab of guilt. "I mean, not that Savannah didn't love life; she did. She didn't want to die; she just believed that every next thing was going to be fun, whatever it was."

"Good," Charlotte said.

"Why is that good?"

But she continued with her eyes closed, the eyeballs darting back and forth as if in a dream, as though she hadn't heard me. Patrick squeezed my hand. Charlotte said suddenly, "She's here."

"What? Where?"

"Shh." Charlotte put her finger to her lips. "She's talking."

Without warning, I felt myself begin to perspire, and then I started to cry. I put my hand over my mouth, worrying that Charlotte wouldn't be able to hear Savannah over my blubbering, but I couldn't quiet myself.

Patrick put his arm around me. "It's okay," he whispered, reaching for the tissues on the table. I leaned into him.

Charlotte was quiet for several minutes, her eyes closed, while I tried not to blow my nose too loudly. "I can't see her," she told me. "All I see is an overwhelmingly bright light."

"Is it green?" I asked, feeling suddenly, inexplicably happy.

"Do you see it too?"

"No, but green was Savannah's favorite color." I scanned the room, even though I knew I wouldn't see what Charlotte was seeing. "She's here." I felt her distinctly, smelled her cherry lip gloss, her honey shampoo.

"Yes," Charlotte said. "She's talking to me in pictures. I can't hear what she's saying now, but she's giving me still shots, like a slide show."

"What's she showing you?" *The abandoned house? The man who did it . . .*

"I'm seeing you," she said.

"Me? Why?"

"Because you, Cady, you have the missing piece."

"But——" I felt so frustrated I wanted to throw the teapot across the room, dump the chaise longue with Charlotte in it. "What piece? I don't know what you're talking about."

"The necklace."

"The necklace?" And then I remembered the necklace I never took off except when I went to the prison to see Larry Cauchek, and I felt around my collar for it and pulled it out from under my shirt.

Charlotte's eyes were only half-mast when she opened them. She blinked. "Yes, this necklace," she murmured. "Its twin." And then she closed her eyes again. "The necklace will lead you to your answers." She opened her pretty eyes and touched the amber bracelet on her wrist. Her voice got very stern and forceful, like she was scolding me. "She is only showing you this because you have lived too long in her shadow, my dear." She looked intently at me, her silver hair framing her face like those auras on angels at church. "There are no villains here. Do you understand this?" She fingered the necklace.

"No villains?" I glanced at Patrick. "Excuse me, but what the hell is that supposed to mean? I'm pretty sure murderers are villains." Charlotte blinked at me, and I saw that I had offended her. "I'm sorry," I started, but she put up a hand and closed her eyes, and I realized Savannah was communicating again.

When she opened her eyes, she sighed. "Well," she said in an entirely different voice, a voice people use when they are wrapping things up. "She says you must not be ready. She wants you to let go of her so you can be happy and write the only book that matters to you."

Shit. Did Savannah know about the letters I'd been writing to her since she died? Every year or so, I'd bring them to Deanna and ask about publishing them.

Charlotte stood up. "I am so very sorry I couldn't help you, my dear, but often it is the dead who are more ready to help than the living. You have your belief structures so firmly embedded it's like trying to loosen cement." She began to move toward the door.

"Wait," I said. "I'm ready. I swear, I'm ready."

"Yes," Charlotte said wearily, turning to me. "You are ready." She studied me, and then Patrick, and then me again. "But first you need to understand that Savannah didn't experience the world like everyone else. She needed more to be able to feel things that the rest of us took for granted. Nothing is ever as it seems."

CHAPTER
47

We drove in silence. Patrick squeezed my leg, and I put my hand over his.

"How you doing?" he asked.

It was dusk, and the streets seemed bathed in topaz, which made me feel so sad. I could barely sit up without wanting to double over. "I don't understand any of this. Am I wrong here, or was Charlotte saying I'm supposed to forgive the man who killed my sister?"

"That's what I got out of it, but no one would ever expect you to do that. It's too much." He took his hand off my leg to turn down the radio and then slipped it under my fingers again. "Where to?"

"Not home," I told him. "I don't want to go home."

"Okay. Should we just drive?"

When I told him yes, he turned down the next side street and then onto a windy back road. "What's going on in that smart head of yours?" he asked.

"Couldn't Savannah have given me a name?" I watched the little capes and a town park pass by. He was quiet, driving with one hand on the steering wheel. "She used to make me do her dirty work," I said suddenly. "She was always making me tell our parents lies about where she was, making me do her homework, screening her calls. Maybe she was prettier, all the upperclassmen girls and guys loved her, maybe people were drawn to her in a way they weren't to me, but I was smarter, and she always made me pay for it. And now she's . . . she's dead, and she shows up at a fucking psychic's house." I was crying now, wiping at my face furiously. "In her stupid green light— of course it's green; green is Savannah's favorite color—and whatever Savannah wants, Savannah gets. She shows up and gets everyone all rattled and happy she's there, and then she can't even tell me a name. I'm supposed to fucking figure this out. How dare she, when she can see everything. How dare she keep up this endless fucking scavenger hunt." I wiped my nose with my sleeve. "I've given up my whole life for her, and this is what I get?" We were stopped at a red light, and Patrick was staring straight ahead. "I'm sorry," I said, wiping at my eyes. "I know I sound like a brat."

"You know what you sound like?" Patrick asked, inching the car forward.

"What?" I was sure my eyes were bright red, and I must have looked like a wreck, but when he turned to me, his face was so open, so totally accepting, it made me want to start crying all over again. "You sound like a human being," he said. "A really hardworking, sweet, frustrated human being."

I bit my lip. "I'm exhausted," I told him, and I almost told him about Brady, about how all this time I'd had a crush on Brady and that he'd been at my house an hour ago to tell me he and Savannah had some amazing love affair, and that's when it hit me. We were sitting at the first light on Main, near the high school, and I thought of Charlotte's voice: "Nothing is ever as it seems."

"You know what? I'm not feeling well. Would you mind taking me home?"

He put his hand against my cheek. "You're a little warm. Why don't I call the deli downtown and order some soup for us?"

"I think I'm just exhausted. I need to go home and sleep."

"Are you sure?"

"Yes, I'm so tired." I leaned against the passenger door and closed my eyes, hoping I sounded convincing.

We drove in silence for a few minutes until Patrick pulled in my driveway. "I'll text you in a little while to make sure you're okay," he said.

"Sounds good." I yawned, a big, fake gesture for effect. "And thanks again for taking me to Charlotte's. I think I understand what Savannah was trying to say."

CHAPTER
48

There were things that came back to me in times of crisis, startling images that seemed so banal at the time, but now, while I was watching the whole world close in, I finally understood. As I fumbled for my phone, trying to dial Brady's number, I saw all the pieces that I had not recognized before, but most of all it was the picture in the yearbook, the way Savannah was looking at someone off camera. And now that I knew that someone was Brady Irons, it all made sense.

"I'm sorry I overreacted," I said when he picked up. "I need to see you. Can I come over?" But I was already getting in my car, and I didn't really hear what he'd said.

The only time I'd been in Brady's house was when Colette was having her episode—decompensating, I think Chandler had called it. I knocked once and turned the knob.

"Brady?" I called. "Are you here?" I let myself in the front door, and the house seemed different now, somehow peaceful. I walked to the kitchen and stood at the window overlooking the garden of daisies that, I realized now, must have been for Savannah. "Brady?"

He came from down the hall, his eyes rimmed in red. "I'm so sorry about earlier," he said.

I pulled him into a fierce hug. "No, I'm sorry. Ever since I read Savannah's diary, I've been feeling happy in a way that hasn't happened in a long time. Knowing she loved someone brought me a certain kind of peace I didn't think I'd ever have. And finding out it was you should have made me even happier. I don't know why I freaked out."

We stood, inches apart. Face-to-face, mouth-to-mouth. I couldn't draw my eyes away from his. A current ran between us, connecting, clarifying.

"You know," he said. It wasn't a question.

"Yes." I felt a sob rising in my throat. "Where's the necklace?"

He raised his hand, but I wasn't afraid. Before I could step back or speak, he touched my face. "I've been wanting to confess since we met again at the prison. I can't tell you how many times I've thought about turning myself in."

It was hard to breathe, knowing what I did. We silently walked to a cloth couch in the living room and sat. I noticed he was holding a small, velvet box. "Tell me you didn't mean it," I said. "Tell me you loved her and it was some kind of horrible accident."

He opened his mouth to speak, but something between a cry and a noise a wounded animal would make came out. "Oh God, I am so sorry. So, so sorry. I never meant to hurt her. I didn't want to do it, but she insisted. She always wanted to try new things; she was in such a rush to grow up. After that singer from INXS died and someone told her he may have done it to himself, trying to get off, that's all she talked about." He was crying now, and I was having a hard time understanding him. "I loved her so much. I swear to God I never would have hurt her."

Everything hit me at once, and I grabbed for my neck. Hearing the killer's voice and seeing his hand holding Savannah's necklace, but not being able to identify him. Savannah coming to me in dreams, but never giving me clear clues. She wasn't helping me to catch her killer like I'd thought all these years. She was trying to make me forgive myself and understand that her death wasn't what it looked like. *Nothing is ever as it seems.* Both Larry Cauchek and Charlotte Reid had spoken those exact words. I understood now, watching Brady almost convulse he was crying so hard, that Savannah's death was a pure thing.

Without speaking, he handed me the box. I knew what was in it. I didn't want to open it. I was afraid that if I did, it would be the end of this journey that my sister had been leading me on for half my life. "I can't," I said, feeling a tightness in my chest that was making it hard to breathe. "I don't want it. You keep it."

"No." He opened my fingers and placed the box in my palm. "I kept it all these years with the intent of mailing it back to you. But when I saw you at the pen and we became friends, I knew that one day . . . one day I'd have to give it to you in person." He opened the small black box and removed Savannah's necklace. A piece of her hair was caught in the clasp. It was as though I were seeing something from a time capsule, and when I picked it up, I felt fifteen again. I could hear my sister's laugh, the warmth of her hand on my arm when she whispered a secret to me.

Brady looked so sad, so terribly, awfully, horribly heartbroken, that I didn't expect him to be able to talk, and yet, he did. He started talking and for a long time, he didn't stop.

They used to go to the Wolfe Mansion to be alone. They'd make love on the old queen mattress in the third floor widow's tower, Savannah pretending to be his princess bride, the sun shining in.

"You could see the whole town from that room. It was our secret place," he told me, explaining that lots of kids went there to party on the weekends, but he and Savannah used it after school or late at night in the middle of the week. It was their secret. He'd dragged the mattress up there at Savannah's request, when they first started dating. She had been so persistent, and I knew this was true of Savannah, impossible to say no to. He recounted how it went, the chocolate-covered strawberries they ate, INXS on the boom box. Savannah liked to pretend she was much older, that they were married. Brady blushed as if telling me something far too personal and private to ever be said aloud. He spoke so quietly, I had to strain to hear him. "She wanted me to squeeze her throat. I'd been saying no for months, that she was crazy and it was dangerous. And you know what she did? She laughed at me. She told me to grow up and live a little." I could see the disdain on Savannah's face, the disappointment in her voice when she didn't get something she wanted. "I swear I didn't want to. I had a bad feeling about it, but I did it for Savannah. I would have done anything for her."

"It's okay." I spoke softly, soothingly. "None of us could say no to her. She had this magnetic force that pulled the rest of the world into her orbit. Of course you did what she wanted. We all did." I thought of all the times I'd done her laundry so she could go out or signed her into study hall so she could sneak out back to smoke. I took a shaking breath. I had to know how it happened. But I wasn't sure I could stand to hear the words spoken aloud. "Keep going," I urged. "Tell me the rest."

"She was so fucking beautiful, and I never meant to hurt her. I tried to do it very gently, but she put her hands on the outside of my hands and told me to squeeze harder. She said it felt like she was high on cocaine, like the orgasm might never end."

"I understand," I said, and I did. "You squeezed a little too hard. You didn't know what you were doing."

"No!" The panic on his face was raw. "After that one time, she said that was the only way she wanted to do it. She said it was like flying without wings. But it scared the shit out of me. I kept thinking that if I did it wrong she could get really hurt. So I refused to do it again."

"I don't understand. If you wouldn't choke her, how'd she die?"

"She was so pissed that she threatened to break up with me if I didn't do it again, but I refused. I told her having her alive and mad was better than the alternative. She didn't speak to me for three days, but then she pulled me outside in between classes and told me she had a new plan. She said she'd talked to you and you were going to cover for her with your parents. I was working that day, delivering pizzas, but the afternoons were always so slow that no one would miss me if I was gone for a while. So we'd planned to meet at the Wolfe Mansion." He wiped tears out of his eyes and I felt like I was watching the saddest movie ever made. "I was so happy because I thought she'd forgotten about the whole choking thing. But when I got to the third floor, she explained that she'd researched it and she could make it so she could choke herself and I wouldn't have to do anything."

"What?" This sounded too crazy. Even for Savannah. "So she had made like a torture device or a dog collar or something?"

Brady covered his face with his hands for a moment and didn't speak. Finally, he picked up his head and continued. "I didn't know what it was or even if she had it with her. I don't know, Cady. It was like I just snapped. All of a sudden, I realized that there was something wrong with your sister. She'd told me about the other boys she'd been with and the older girls she smoked pot with and the drugs she'd tried. She talked about it in a way that made me think she was trying to be sophisticated. But that day, I knew it was so much more than that. And I couldn't handle it. I couldn't fucking handle it, so I left."

"What do you mean so much more? I don't understand what you're saying."

"God, even now, I can't explain it. It wasn't about experimenting and pushing the limits. It was like she was daring the universe to make something go wrong. Like each time she did something stupid and walked away from it, she felt like she'd won."

That was so Savannah. Every time she climbed out her window and met Chapman Sharp or Dylan Freeman and didn't get caught, she thought it made her powerful, invincible. "I understand," I said quietly. I reached for Brady's hand and held it. We sat quietly for a moment, feeling each other's warmth before I spoke again. "Tell me the rest."

"I yelled at her that she'd gone too far and I didn't want to be around her anymore." He'd kept his eyes down while he was talking, but now he was staring at me. "The last thing I ever said to Savannah was that she was crazy and we were done."

At that moment, I had a pang so severe in my chest I thought I was having a heart attack, but then I realized I was feeling what Savannah had when Brady yelled at her.

"I stormed out of the house and headed down that rocky slope to my car. I went back to work, but it was slow, so my boss told me I could leave. I clocked out and started to go home. But I was worried about Savannah and felt terrible about yelling at her, so I went back. But by the time I got there—"

"She was already dead."

"Yes," he said. "She had brought the contraption with her. I swear to God I didn't know she was planning on using it that day. I thought she just wanted to talk. It was like a dog collar attached to a leash tied to the bar where you put hangers in the closet." He stopped speaking and shuddered, as if reliving the memory. "I tried to save her. She must have struggled with the collar and made it tighter instead of looser. I got her out of it as fast as I could, but she wasn't breathing. I'd left my cell phone in my car, and I couldn't find hers."

"I had it. She asked me to take her backpack home, and it had her phone in it."

But he kept talking as if he hadn't heard me. "I tried CPR, but she was already gone. And I don't know, I had this crazy thought that it'd be better if it looked like she hadn't done it to herself. So I took the collar and everything with me and ran to my car to call 911."

"You left her there?" I could feel my throat closing. I gripped the necklace harder, digging my nails into the palm of my hand.

"I didn't. I wasn't going to. By the time I got to my car, I could see cops in the woods coming toward the mansion. I thought they could save her." He was trying to wipe his face of all the tears, the snot, but he couldn't. "And then it was too late. I didn't think anyone would believe what really happened."

"But you had an alibi. You were at work. All these years, you let us think that someone had murdered Savannah. The cops never considered anything but homicide, because there was nothing left at the scene. And you knew. You knew all along that it was an accident and she did it to herself."

"I know. I'm so sorry. So, so sorry." He sounded pitiful. "I felt responsible. If I had stayed there, she'd still be alive, so I thought it was my fault. It *was* my fault. I guess I panicked and never told the police or anyone, because I thought that they'd think I was responsible because I could have stopped her."

"Did the police interview you?" I remembered Patrick coming to the house months after it had happened and telling us the cops had interviewed almost everyone at Kingswood.

"Yes, but I told them I was working, and they checked out my alibi with my boss. I guess the time line proved I was at work while—"

"My sister was accidentally strangling herself."

He dropped his head. "Yes."

"What about your fingerprints? They must have found them in the Wolfe Mansion."

"They found everyone's prints in that house. Remember how many kids used to go there to party? The whole thing was a cluster."

I held Savannah's necklace in my hand. "You took a necklace off a dead girl. Why?"

"I didn't. That was the strangest part. When I got there, before we fought, she took it off and gave it to me."

My skin went cold. "I don't believe you. The only time we ever took those necklaces off was to change out the chains."

He put his hands to his heart. "I know. I'd asked her about the pendant once. And she told me it meant you two would always be connected, like you had superpowers. I should have known then"—his voice was broken—"that she was going to do something terrible. But I didn't understand. So I put it in my pocket and thought I'd give it back to her later. But then we had that awful fight and I left and . . ." But he didn't finish.

He collapsed into my arms, and there was nothing left to do but hold him. We cried together until the sun went down and it became almost too dark to see.

"I'm ready," he finally said.

I sat up, wiping my eyes. "For what?"

"For my punishment. To take responsibility for what I did."

All my life, I'd waited for this moment. I told Gabby and Greg and most of all myself that I wouldn't be okay until the man who murdered my sister went to prison for the rest of his life. But here I was sitting a foot away from Brady Irons, and all I wanted to do was protect him. "No," I said. "You didn't hurt her. Savannah did that to herself. Besides, what about Colette? She needs you."

"Colette's parents flew over from France and took her home. She wasn't getting better here, and they thought she needed to be with her family. I tried." He got up, turned on a standing lamp, and then sat next to me again. "I tried to take care of her for five years, but her parents were right to take her home. She's where she needs to be now."

"So you're going to throw away the rest of your life because of something that wasn't your fault?"

He held both my hands in his. "My going to jail won't bring Savannah back, but it's my fault she's gone. If I hadn't walked out on her, I could have stopped her. I deserve to go to prison for that."

"That's bullshit," I said, my voice too loud. "You've already given up your life."

"What do you mean?" He brought my hand to his mouth and kissed my fingers.

"Look at what you've done the last sixteen years. You left town after high school and drifted around the country. You told me once that your dad never forgave you for not joining the army, but you didn't tell me why you didn't go." In all the times that Brady and I had told each other about our lives, I'd never realized that everything he'd done since Savannah's death was with the intent of punishing himself. "And when you came back, you chose to work in a maximum-security prison, spending your days with murderers, rapists, people who have no hope, nothing to live for."

"It was the right thing to do," he said quietly. "It was the only thing. I belonged in prison, and if I was too much of a coward to turn myself in, then at least I could live that life through my inmates."

"That's the thing"—my voice was thick with pleading—"you don't belong there. You didn't do anything wrong. Savannah made the mistake, not you."

"It doesn't matter. I should have gone to the police when it first happened."

"True," I said sadly. "But what matters is that you gave Savannah something that none of the rest of us could."

"What's that?" I could hear my sister's voice so clearly at that moment. How she used to tell me she was bigger than our small town, that she never belonged here. I used to beg her to be happy, I was so afraid she'd leave me, leave our family. I couldn't make her see that everyone loved her. That she was the light that illuminated our paths.

"You made her want to stay. We were twins. Identical. And from the moment I was old enough to understand, I knew that I'd never be enough for her. She was so much more than the rest of us. But you quieted whatever made her so restless. I could see the difference in her those last months. I never knew why she seemed so . . ." I couldn't think of the word. "Settled."

He got up and went into another room that I couldn't see and then came back with a box of tissues. "Thank you for saying that, but it's time."

Suddenly, I couldn't breathe. "For what?"

"I have to turn myself in."

I jumped up. "No! You can't."

"I have to be held accountable."

"You've been accountable every day that you've volunteered at the shelter and tutored inmates and did the best you could for Colette. What's the world going to gain by locking you up?" A few hours before, I'd been in Charlotte Reid's living room, and now I was trying to talk the man who held the secret of my sister's death out of turning himself in. "Go," I said to Brady. He cocked his head at me. "Colette is with her family. Savannah finally made me hear what she's been trying to tell me all these years. And I'm okay. Really. I am."

"You don't look okay." He nodded to my hands. I hadn't realized I was shaking.

"Pack up your house, and get out of here." But even as I was saying it, I realized there was almost nothing downstairs. The few decorations I remembered from when we came to help with Colette—an antique mirror at the base of the stairs and an old painting of a ramshackle house—were gone. "I understand if you can't stay here, but you're not helping anyone by going to jail for a crime you didn't commit."

"What about Patrick?"

"What about him?" I'd forgotten that he thought I was home sick.

"He's a good man and a great cop. If I leave town, he's going to put two and two together."

I hadn't thought about that. "Maybe I can convince him that reopening Savannah's case is too hard on my family and we want him to let it go."

He eyed me as if trying to decide if my plan was brilliant or ludicrous. "Is that really how you want to start off with him?"

"Start what with him?"

He grinned, a small glimpse of the man I'd come to know the last four months. "Your relationship." My eyes widened. "You can't tell me you haven't noticed the way he looks at you. And I haven't even seen you together that much."

Maybe Patrick was the reason why I didn't feel anything for Brady when we'd kissed. "Shit. I don't know. But I do know that I can't let you go down for Savannah's death. You didn't have anything to do with it."

"But I did it." His voice was desperate.

"No, you didn't. You loved a girl who probably didn't know how to love herself until you came along. You loved her so much you vowed to do anything she wanted. And when she took it too far, you said no. You had no way of knowing what was going to happen once you walked out that door."

But Brady was shaking his head. "I don't want to run. I'm tired of pretending."

"Go," I said again. "Savannah wouldn't want you in prison." I swallowed. "She loved you."

"Will you hate me if I leave?"

"I'll hate you if you don't."

Without saying a word, he came to me, held my face in his hands, and kissed me on the lips. "Thank you, Cady." And then he was gone.

I stood in Brady's empty house until a strip of moonlight filtered in through the blinds. I didn't know what to do. I had no one to tell. Gabby would have kept my secret, but I couldn't burden her with that knowledge.

With nothing else to do, I finally pulled open the front door, walked past the garden of daisies, and got in my car. I tried to start it, but my hands were still shaking, and I couldn't get the key in the ignition. My phone rang in my purse, but I didn't answer it. When it rang again, I pulled it out and saw Patrick's name flash on the screen. I knew if I ignored it, he'd keep calling. Or come find me. I pressed the green ANSWER button, but couldn't get any words out.

"We got him," Patrick said.

A million scenarios flashed through my head. Brady had gotten pulled over for speeding and confessed. He'd had a confrontation with the cop who patrolled the Whole Foods shopping center.

"Brady Irons walked right into the station and handed me a manifesto of his confession."

Brady'd been planning to confess all along. He must have written his statement before I'd gotten to his house.

"He didn't do it," I said. "I don't know what he told you, but he didn't do it. She choked herself. She was trying to do some fucked-up sex act, and she fucking strangled herself. You can't arrest him." I was so hysterical I could barely get the words out. "Don't you see, Patrick? He didn't do it."

CHAPTER
49

"Cady?" Greg asked after he'd called my name three times from the foyer and I hadn't answered. The refrigerator door was open, and I'd left the oven on. I still hadn't changed out of my clothes from the day before. He sat on the couch with me. "Are you all right?" But I couldn't answer him. "Did something happen?" Eventually, he gave up trying to get me to talk and wrapped his arms around my shoulders, hugging me in a way he hadn't in years. He put a blanket over me and called Gabby. I hadn't seen her since I'd walked in on her and David, so she had no idea what was going on, but she told David that Greg had found me almost catatonic, and David had called Patrick, who came right over. When Patrick got to our house, he and Greg disappeared into my office for a long time. When they finally came out, Greg came to me on the couch and squatted in front of me. "I'm going to leave you and Patrick to talk this through," he said. "He's much better suited for this job."

"You're a shrink," I'd wanted to say, but I couldn't get the words out. "This is what you do." And then he was gone, leaving me when I needed him most, when I needed him to wade through this quicksand with me trying to understand how something I'd been waiting for half my life now felt so wrong.

Once Greg was gone, Patrick coaxed me into taking a shower while he made me something to eat. When I came downstairs, my hair wet, in a pink T-shirt and gray sweats, he had scrambled eggs, half a cantaloupe, and a glass of orange juice on the counter waiting for me. I brought the plate to the couch and set it down on the coffee table but didn't eat. Instead, I lay down and pulled the crocheted blanket that had been Savannah's over my legs.

"This is what you've always wanted," Patrick said in a soothing tone I imagined he used when he showed up on people's doorsteps in the middle of the night. "For this to be over."

I sat up, dizzy with hunger and exhaustion. "That's just it." I half laughed. "The only person responsible for Savannah's death was Savannah. I wasted so much time, so much of my life trying to avenge my sister. No wonder she never gave me more clues in those dreams I used to have." It occurred to me then that I hadn't dreamed about her in weeks. "She wanted me to keep up this vigil for her, forever be the sun that I revolved around." Patrick put his hand on my back but didn't speak. "Promise," I said plainly, "you'll keep Brady out of jail. You can't arrest him, Patrick. He didn't do anything wrong."

"The DA wants to talk to the ME again. She said if the time line matches up and the coroner can confirm that the injuries could have been self-inflicted, then they will officially rule Savannah's death an accident."

I threw my arms around Patrick's neck. "Oh, thank God." I hugged him hard, but he stiffened with my touch. I pulled back. "What?" I asked. "What's wrong?"

"They still have to charge him with failure to report a death."

"Will he go to jail for that?"

Patrick dropped his eyes. "It's a misdemeanor in the fourth degree. There's no jail time. Just a fine." He stabbed the eggs with a fork and brought them to my lips as if I were a baby he was trying to feed. I took the fork from him and put it back on the plate. "It's okay, Cady; it's over."

"It'll never be over."

"You finally know what really happened to Savannah. Doesn't that change everything?"

"Did you know I tried to kill myself because of her?"

"What?" He grabbed my hands as if I might do it again right then. "God, Cady, no."

"It was about a year after she died, and I didn't want to live anymore hating my life, hating who I was without her, knowing I'd never see her again, that her case would never be solved, that some lunatic was trotting around with his wife and kids with my sister's death in the lines on his face and in the tone of his voice. Breathing was too much effort. Opening my eyes in the morning without my sister was too painful. It literally hurt to push myself through the motions of eating and talking and smiling like my fucking life was okay with me."

In the quiet of a house I hated, I told Patrick what happened. He knew that I'd begun cutting myself after Savannah's murder, but he didn't know that when I was seventeen and it didn't ease the pain anymore, I'd begun researching, which was my custom; it was what I did best. I'd learned that slitting my wrists wasn't guaranteed, even if I made the cuts vertical and got in a hot bath to encourage circulation. And too many people survived swallowing pills. I didn't want to shoot myself; I was vain enough to want to look good, as good as I could in my size-twelve funeral dress in an open casket. And I hadn't wanted my parents to have to clean up too much. Cutting had become a friend to me. It'd comforted me, taken care of me. It took away the constant sting of my life the way a glass of wine soothed frazzled nerves. It was fitting that it serve me one last time. One Saturday night, I found out from a boy in South Dakota who called himself Leviathan that the carotid was the answer. Deep into the night, with only my laptop on for light, he wrote me that if I got the carotid just right, it wouldn't take more than a few minutes, and then the coroner would be able to stitch me up like new.

I decided to do it on a Friday. I hated Fridays, the weekend looming ahead like a big building with nothing in it. My parents were gone most Fridays, prepping the restaurant for the weekend, so I went into their medicine cabinet and took one of my father's straight razors. He was so old-fashioned.

All day during school, I thought about what I would write in my suicide note. I owed my parents that much. I couldn't have them blaming themselves for the rest of their lives. But over and over, during European history and chemistry, I could only come up with one word. *Savannah*. And then I knew. I didn't need a note. No one would wonder if I'd had a secret breakup with a boy or had failed a class. They'd all know: it was too hard to live without my sister.

The most important thing was not to give myself away. I didn't want someone catching on, calling the cops or having my parents get worried and stay home from the restaurant. I just wanted it done. The void of Savannah couldn't be filled, but it could be dismissed, annihilated. When I got off the bus, I called my mom at work to let her know I was home and doing homework. I laid out my schoolbooks on the kitchen table and went to my room.

But my mother had come back, because the pipes had frozen at the restaurant, and my father had told her to get a hairdryer so he could warm them slowly without them bursting. It had been one of the coldest winters on record in New Jersey. I was unconscious when she found me, but because my head was turned to the side, she didn't immediately see the cut. Later that night in the hospital, I overheard her talking to Dr. Bassett. She said when she put her ear to my chest to feel for a heartbeat, she smelled a metallic, tangy odor. Blood. And then she was on the phone with a 911 operator, who was telling her to use a pillowcase to put pressure on the wound. In the quiet of my hospital room, my mother told the doctor that when the paramedics got there, the look that crossed between them told her I was already dead. She begged them to save me, telling them that my twin had been murdered and she couldn't go through it again. As I was slipping away, so close to Savannah that I could smell her honey shampoo, two young-faced, well-meaning men ruined my life by saving it.

It was music that made my mother check on me. I hadn't turned on my radio; that's what gave me away. I had always said I couldn't live without music. And no matter what, I had the radio on or a CD going when I was in my room or doing homework. My high-honor grades had proven time and again that I concentrated better with background noise. But that Friday afternoon, I couldn't decide what song I wanted to be my last—something upbeat like Sugar Ray's "Every Morning" or something melancholy like Candlebox's "Far Behind." I decided to go without. When my mom came home for the hairdryer and didn't hear any music coming from my room, some divine motherly instinct told her to get upstairs and check on me.

"So there you have it," I said when I was done.

Patrick kissed my forehead. "Thank God your mother came home," he said.

But it occurred to me then for the first time that it wasn't my mother. "I'm sure it was Savannah. She sent my mother back. She saved me."

He squeezed my hand. "Savannah loved you."

"I know. She couldn't save herself. But she saved me." We didn't speak for a long while until finally I said, "I remember so clearly the moments before my mother found me. I was with Savannah. I could smell her perfume, and the space I was in was so bright. I remember thinking she was the sun pulling me to her."

Patrick had tears in his eyes. He pulled me to his chest and whispered into my hair, "Savannah may be a star in the sky now, but you're the sun, Cady. You're the sun."

EPILOGUE

I left Greg right after I'd found out about Brady. He'd gone away for three weeks and come home to a woman neither he nor I recognized. There was no drama, no hurt words; it was as if we were roommates whose lease was up and it was time for us to move on. Gabby gave up her apartment and moved in with my brother at the same time I was cleaning out my house. My parents had flown up and had helped me move. I'd called them after Brady had gone to the police. I couldn't talk because I was crying so hard, begging them to forgive me, but they'd said there was nothing to forgive. I just did what any girl who had loved her sister would have done.

David and Gabby offered me their guest room, but they were still in the early stages of their relationship, and I told them the truth when I said that I didn't think I could stand to be around that much happiness. After we split, Greg called to tell me he was seeing Annika. He didn't want me to hear it from anyone else. Although I'd suspected it for a long time, I had thought I'd be bothered by the news. That I wasn't confirmed what I already knew: I was happier without him. And in a strange way, I was happy for them. He deserved someone who would love him more than I did.

Having given the house to Greg and not wanting to live with David and Gabby, I moved in with Chandler and Odion, took the guest room across the hall from Mads's room and let her paint my toenails a different shade of pink every day.

The DA charged Brady with failure to report a death, an unclassified misdemeanor whose only penalty was a thousand-dollar fine. Despite Brady turning himself in and telling the police he was responsible for Savannah's death, there was no evidence that he knew that she had autoerotic asphyxiation devices or had knowledge that she was going to use them.

Patrick got me into the courtroom when Brady was charged. He told me it was no big deal and, after writing a check, Brady would be done with the proceedings in less than ten minutes, but something told me I had to be there. I had to see Brady. During that final court appearance, after Brady learned he was finally officially free, I approached him, touching him, pressing my lips to his face, thanking him for loving my sister, and whispering that no one blamed him. He stood silently embracing me, holding me so hard I couldn't breathe. When he kissed me so gently on the lips I thought maybe I'd imagined it, I knew I'd never see him again.

After it was over, Gabby and David drove me to Chandler's, but we stopped by the post office so I could get my mail. There was one letter in the box, and I knew before I turned the key that it was from Brady. It was dated a few days before. Having a second chance, he told me, meant he couldn't waste it. The rest of his life had to mean something. He ended the letter simply by saying he was moving someplace where he could make a difference. That could have been anywhere—Harlem, rural West Virginia, or even right here in New Jersey.

As I stepped out of the post office, I could see Gabby and David parked in a loading zone waiting for me, but I sat on the steps and brought the letter to my chest. I hadn't known it until that moment, but Savannah coming back to me in dreams, leading me here, to this place, had finally set me free. Brady's guilt stopped him from coming forward sixteen years before, and it prevented us from knowing what really happened. But now, thanks to the dreams that led me to the prison, to Brady, and eventually to the truth, I was finally free. I was free of the hold my sister had had on me not only when she was alive but in the years since she'd been gone. I was free of the unhappiness of my life. And I was free to find someone to love. I reached in my pocket, pulled out my phone, and dialed a number. While I waited for Patrick to answer, I noticed the leaves were turning brilliant colors, the sky was a vivid magenta, and the evening felt optimistic as if everything were brand new again.

ACKNOWLEDGMENTS

If not for Lisa Gallagher, I'd still be wondering what I am going to be when I grow up. Lisa, not only are you a fantastic agent and friend but you're also a cheerleader, a picker-upper-and-duster-off-er, and the one who calms me when I'm about to freak and who makes me giggle when I feel like crying. Every day I am thankful for you.

Suzanne Kingsbury, you are the most fabulous development editor ever and an even better friend. You shaped *Nowhere Girl* from a big, gelatinous mess into a pretty, pretty piece of art. You always go way above and beyond, and I'd be lost if not for you. I hope I never have to write a book without you.

Thinking I'd written a never-to-be-guessed whodunit, I gave a draft of *Nowhere Girl* to my BFF, Sasha Sanford. She called me about forty pages into it and shouted that she'd figured out who had offed poor Savannah. Unfortunately, she was right. Because of Sasha, I asked a friend from college, John McGrath, a criminal defense attorney, to give me some ideas on how to kill someone and get away with it. It was not how I'd thought our first conversation in twenty years would go, but it was enlightening and entertaining just the same. Thank you to Sasha and John for helping me create such a fun ending. Well, it was fun for me, probably not so much for Savannah.

I am fortunate to be publishing my second book with the venerable

St. Martin's Press and Thomas Dunne Books team. Publishers Tom Dunne of Thomas Dunne Books and Sally Richardson of St. Martin's Press are the best. Laurie Chittenden is a fantastic editor, and I'm grateful to work with her. The entire team helped birth this book that started out as a thought when I heard a song in my car. You all have worked tirelessly to bring *Nowhere Girl* to life. Thanks to Pete Wolverton, Brant Janeway, Emily Walters, Ervin Serrano, Angela Craft, Lisa Senz, and my publicist, Katie Bassel. Huge thanks to associate editor Melanie Fried for being on top of everything. You make my job easy.

My good friend and brilliant doctor Patrick Doherty once again was instrumental in helping me get all the medical stuff correct. Pat, I'm in awe of your knowledge, and, even more so, your patience. Thank you for your friendship and time spent answering questions. May I forever write books that involve medicine, so you can never get rid of me. As always, Pat is wicked awesome. Any medical mistakes are all mine.

Police officer Dave Chasteen is not only dedicated to protecting the public but is also a much cherished friend. Another lifetime ago, Dave and I worked together and had way too much fun. Many years after I left corporate life, Dave still had time to answer endless questions about DNA, crime scene procedures, and police protocol. I hope I kill off more characters in future books so I get to talk with Dave about the best way to do it. Dave, I adore you. Any mistakes about blood, cops, and trace evidence are on me.

Nowhere Girl was not the first title I chose for this book. Nor was it the second, third, or fourth. But it is the right one. I spent angst-filled weeks trying to come up with something perfect. Lucky for me, I am surrounded by many amazing people who were instrumental in helping me. Suzanne Kingsbury; Lisa Gallagher; Laurie Chittenden; my husband, Kurt Strecker; my kids, Cooper and Ainsley; Sasha Sanford; Erika Celentano; Carolyn Crehan; Erin Dayton; Sarah Cody Rector; Sarah Wadle; Dave Dyson; and John Peterson, I am grateful for your help. I would be drooling in a corner without you. And thanks to David "Short Legs" Loughborough for your help.

A huge and belated shout-out to my Drew University poetry professor, Bob Ready. Without your encouragement in college and in the years after, I'm not sure that I would be a novelist.

My family made this book happen. My mother, Nancy Moroso, has spent a lifetime supporting me in whatever I wanted to do. My grandmother, Ruth

Boyd, always asks how my books are coming. My step-dad, Nick Nichols, takes great care of my mom and grandmother so I don't have to worry about them. And my in-laws, Marie and Lou Strecker, love me like I'm their own and make me feel like a rock star.

If not for the love, patience, and encouragement of my husband, Kurt, and my kids, Cooper and Ainsley, I have no doubt that I would not be a novelist. The writing process is often overwhelming and never easy. But Kurt, Coop, and Ainsley keep me going by making me believe in myself. In the time that it took to write *Nowhere Girl*, Kurt was always ready with a glass of wine for each of us and an endless supply of words I couldn't think of and answers to which sentence or phrase sounded best. To my three favorite people, I love you madly.

Right up there with my family are my fans. A thank-you to everyone who has written letters and e-mails and come to book signings to show your support. You are the reason I do this. Peace and love.